HAWKSMOOR

HAWKSMOOR

by

PETER ACKROYD

HAMISH HAMILTON

LONDON

First published in Great Britain 1985
by Hamish Hamilton Ltd
Garden House, 57–59 Long Acre, London WC2E 9JZ
Second impression November 1985
Third impression November 1985
Fourth impression December 1985
Fifth impression January 1986

British Library Cataloguing in Publication Data

Ackroyd, Peter, *1949–*
    Hawksmoor.
    I. Title
    823'.914[F]   PR6051.C64
    ISBN 0-241-11664-3

Typeset by Rowland Phototypesetting Ltd, Bury St Edmunds, Suffolk
Printed and bound in Great Britain
by Richard Clay (The Chaucer Press) Ltd, Bungay, Suffolk

For Giles Gordon

Thus in 1711, the ninth year of the reign of Queen Anne, an Act of Parliament was passed to erect seven new Parish Churches in the Cities of London and Westminster, which commission was delivered to Her Majesty's Office of Works in Scotland Yard. And the time came when Nicholas Dyer, architect, began to construct a model of the first church. His colleagues would have employed a skilled joiner to complete such a task, but Dyer preferred to work with his own hands, carving square windows in miniature and cutting steps out of the clean deal: each element could be removed or taken to pieces, so that those of an enquiring temper were able to peer into the model and see the placing of its constituent parts. Dyer took his scale from the plans he had already drawn up and, as always, he used a small knife with a piece of frayed rope wrapped around its ivory handle. For three weeks he laboured over this wooden prototype and, as by stages he fitted the spire upon the tower, we may imagine the church itself rising in Spitalfields. But there were six other churches to be built also, and once again the architect took his short brass rule, his pair of compasses, and the thick paper which he used for his draughts. Dyer worked swiftly with only his assistant, Walter Pyne, for company while, on the other side of the great city, the masons shouted to each other as they hewed out of rough stone the vision of the architect. This is the vision we still see and yet now, for a moment, there is only his heavy breathing as he bends over his papers and the noise of the fire which suddenly flares up and throws deep shadows across the room.

Part One

1

AND SO let us beginne; and, as the Fabrick takes its Shape in front of you, alwaies keep the Structure intirely in Mind as you inscribe it. First, you must measure out or cast the Area in as exact a Manner as can be, and then you must draw the Plot and make the Scale. I have imparted to you the Principles of Terrour and Magnificence, for these you must represent in the due placing of Parts and Ornaments as well as in the Proportion of the several Orders: you see, Walter, how I take my Pen? And here, on another Sheet, calculate the positions and influences of the Celestiall Bodies and the Heavenly Orbs, so that you are not at a Loss on which Dayes to begin or to leave off your Labours. The Designe of the Worke, together with every several Partition and Opening, is to be drawne by straight-edge and compass: as the Worke varies in rising, you must show how its Lines necessarily beare upon one another, like the Web which the Spider spins in a Closet; but, Walter, do this in black lead and not in inke – I do not trust your Pen so far as yet.

At this Walter Pyne hangs down his Head in a sullen Manner, as if he was like to have been Whipp'd at the Cart's Tail, and I could not refrain my self from bursting out in Laughter. Walter was apt to be of a Morose and Sullen cast of Mind, and so to Cheer him I lean'd forward across the Table and gave him Inke readily—see, *says I*, what I will risk to keep you Merry? And now you are not so vex'd please continue: draw the erect elevation of this Structure in face or front, then the same object elevated upon the same draught and centre in all its optical Flexures. This you must distinguish from the Profile, which is signifyed by edging Stroaks and Contours without any of the solid finishing: thus a book begins with a frontispiece, then its Dedication, and then its Preface or Advertisement. And now we come to the Heart of our Designe: the art of Shaddowes you must know well, Walter, and you must be instructed how to Cast them with due Care. It is only the Darknesse that can give trew Forme to our Work and trew Perspective to our Fabrick, for there is no Light without Darknesse and no Substance without Shaddowe (and I turn this Thought over in

[5]

my Mind: what Life is there which is not a Portmanteau of Shaddowes and Chimeras?). I build in the Day to bring News of the Night and of Sorrowe, *I continued*, and then I broke off for Walter's sake: No more of this now, *I said*, it is by the by. But you'll oblige me, Walter, to draw the Front pritty exact, this being for the Engraver to work from. And work trewe to my Design: that which is to last one thousand years is not to be praecipitated.

I had a violent Head-ach and, altho' there was only a small fire in the Closet, I was feeling unnaturall hot and walk'd out into Scotland-Yard; I knew that others imployed in the Office might stare at me, for I am an Object of Ridicule to them, and so I hasten'd my Steps to the Wood yards next the Wharfe where, since the Work men were at their Dinner, I might walk silent and unseen. This being the middle of Winter, and a strong Wind blown up, the River was pretty high for this spot and the Water was at times like to start a second Deluge while, on the Side opposite, the Feilds were quite darken'd as if in a Mist. And then of a sudden I could hear snatches of Song and confus'd Conversation; I whipp'd about, for in no wise could I ascertain where these Sounds came from, until I comforted my self with the Thought that it was the Wherry from Richmond which even then came into my View. So my Perceptions followed one another, and yet all this while my Thoughts were running on my seven Churches and were thus in quite another Time: like a Voyager I am confin'd in my Cabbin while yet dreaming of my Destination. And then, as I stand looking upon the River and the Feilds, I Blot them out with my Hand and see only the Lines upon my Palm.

I walk'd back to the Office, thinking to find Walter engag'd upon the Generall Plan and Upright, but I saw him lolling upon his Stool by the Chimney-Corner, gazing into the Fire as if he saw Strange Visions in the Coles and looking as melancholly as a Female Wretch does upon a Smith-Feild Pile. I trod softly to the Table and saw there one Draught half-made in inke and black lead. Well this is good for Nothing you impudent Rogue, *said I*, come here and see. And Walter in confusion rose from the Fire rubbing his Eyes, and would as like have rubb'd out his Face if he could. Look here Master Pyne, *I continu'd*, I do not like the jetting out of the Pillars after I instructed you to shew Pilasters there: and also here the Portal is near three feet out. Are you so wooden-headed that I must teach you Feet and Inches? Walter thrust his Hands into his Breeches and mutter'd so that I could not hear him. And are you in such a Brown Study, *I told him*, that you cannot answer me?

I was sitting on my Stool, *says he*, and thinking on a Subject.

You will have Stools, Sir, when I beat them from your Arse. *Then I went on*: And in your Thought did you bring off any Conclusions?

[6]

I was thinking on Sir Christopher, and I was considering our new Church of Spittle-Fields.

And what does a green-head say of these Matters? (*I do not give a Fart for Sir Chris*. says I secretly to my self)

Master, *says Walter*, We have built near a Pitte and there are so vast a Number of Corses that the Pews will allwaies be Rotten and Damp. This is the first Matter. The second Matter is this: that Sir Chris. thoroughly forbids all Burrials under the Church or even within the Church-yard itself, as advancing the Rottennesse of the Structure and unwholesome and injurious for those who worship there. Then he scratch'd his Face and look'd down at his dusty Shooes.

This is a weak little Thing to take up your contemplations, Walter, *I replied*. But he gaz'd up at me and would not be brought off, so after a Pause *I continu'd*: I know Sir Chris. is flat against Burrialls, that he is all for Light and Easinesse and will sink in Dismay if ever Mortality or Darknesse shall touch his Edifices. It is not reasonable, he will say, it is not natural. But, Walter, I have instructed you in many things and principally in this – I am not a slave of Geometricall Beauty, I must build what is most Sollemn and Awefull. Then I changed my Tack: from what Purse are we building these Churches, Walter?

From the Imposicion on Coles.

And are the Coles not the blackest Element, which with their Smoak hide the Sunne?

Certainly they feed the Fires of this City, *says he*.

And where is the Light and Easinesse there? Since we take our Revenues from the Under-world, what does it Signifie if we also Build upon the Dead?

There was a Noise in the adjoining Chamber (it is two Rooms struck into one, and thus has more of an Eccho), a Noise like to someone's quick Steps and I broke off my Discourse as Sir Chris. walk'd in, accouter'd as the Boys that run with the Gazette – Hat under Arm, and Breathless, and yet despite his Age not so corpulent neither. Walter rose up in a fright and spilt the Inke upon his Draught (which was no great Loss), but Sir Chris. did not perceive anything of this and stepp'd up to me wheezing like an old Goat. Master Dyer, *says he*, the Commission are expecting your Report on the New Churches: if it be not done already get it done now, since they are in great Hast –

– Hast is for Fools, I murmur'd beneath my Breath.

And your Church in the Spittle-Fields, is it near complete?

It needs only the Lead on the Portico.

Well make hast to buy it now, since Lead is under 9L a tun but in a fair way to go up by next month. And then Sir Chris. stood biting his under-lip like an Infant without his Toy or a Wretch at the Foot of the

Gallows. And the other Churches, *he asks after a Pause*, are they well advanc'd?

I have fixed on their Situacon, *I replied*, and three already are being Laid.

I must have exact Plans of the Buildings as they stand at present, *says he*, and you must press the Joyner to build severall Moddells –

– The Modells are of my own devising, Sir Christopher.

What you will, Master Dyer, what you will. And he waved at my Draughts with inexpressible Weariness before he departed, leaving the Mustiness of his Wig behind him. When I was young and vigorous, and first in his Service, I composed some verses on Sir Chris.:

> The Globe's thy Studye; for thy restless Mind
> In a less limit cannot be confin'd.
> Thy Portrait I admire: thy very lookes
> Shew *Wren* is read in Farts as well as Books.
> He that shall scan this Face may judge by it,
> Thou hast an Head peece that is throng'd with Shit.

But this was in another Time. Now I call'd out to Walter who linger'd in the Paymaster's Closet until Sir Chris. be gone. Did I tell you, *says I* when he returned to me, of the story of Nestor? And Walter shook his Head. Nestor, *I continu'd*, was the inventor of Mechanick Power, which is now so cryed up, and once he designed an Edifice of Gracefull Form but which was so finely contriv'd that it could bear only its own Weight. And Walter nodded sagely at this. It fell down, Master Pyne, with no other Pressure than the setting of a *Wren* on top of it. And he lets out a Laugh, which stops as short as it was begun like the Bark of a Dogge.

Walter is of a reserv'd Disposition and speaks little, but this is of no matter since it is a Temper like to my own. And be pleased to take a Scetch of his Figure as follows: He wears an old Coat with odd Buttons and a Pair of Trowsers patched in Leather so that he is all of a pickle. His awkward Garb and his odd Trim (as they call it in the Office) make him an Object of Humour: Master Dyer's Gentleman, they call him. But this is a fitting Title since thus can I mould him as the Baker moulds the Dough before he pops it in the Oven: I have turn'd him into a proper Scholar, and steer'd him safe among the Books which lie in his way. I acquainted him with certain Prints of the Aegyptian Obelisks, and advised him to studdy them well and copy them; I instructed him in my own Scriptures – in Aylet Sammes his *Britannia Antiqua Illustrata*, in Mr Baxter's Book *Concerning the Certainty of the World of Spirits*, in Mr Cotton Mather his *Relations of the Wonders of the Invisible World* and many other such, for this is fit Reading for one who wishes to become a thoro' Master. The Length of my necessary Instructions is too great to compleat here but there were four things I taught Walter to consider: 1) That it was Cain who built the first City, 2) That there is a true Science in the World called *Scientia Umbrarum* which, as to the publick teaching of it, has been suppressed but which the proper Artificer must comprehend, 3) That Architecture aims at Eternity and must contain the Eternal Powers: not only our Altars and Sacrifices, but the Forms of our Temples, must be mysticall, 4) That the miseries of the present Life, and the Barbarities of Mankind, the fatall disadvantages we are all under and the Hazard we run of being eternally Undone, lead the True Architect not to Harmony or to Rationall Beauty but to quite another Game. Why, do we not believe the very Infants to be the Heirs of Hell and Children of the Devil as soon as they are disclos'd to the World? I declare that I build my Churches firmly on this Dunghil Earth and with a full Conception of Degenerated Nature. I have only room to add: there is a mad-drunken Catch, Hey ho! The Devil is dead! If that be true, I have been in the wrong Suit all my Life.

But to return to the Thread of this History. Sir Chris. presses hard at our Heels, *says I* to Walter, and we must make an Account to the Commission: I will dictate it to you now and you must fair-write it later. And I clear my Throat, savoring the Blood in my Mouth. To the Honble. The Commission for Building Seven New Churches in the Cities of London and Westminster. Dated: 13 January 1712, from the Office of Works, Scotland Yard. Sirs, in obedience to your orders, I most humbly submit my Account, having been instructed by Sir Xtofer Wren, Surveyor to Her Majesty's Works, to have such Churches quite in my Charge. The weather being mighty favourable, there has been great forwardness in carrying on the New Church in Spittle-Fields. The masonry of the West End is now intirely compleated and the Portico is to be covered with Lead presently. The Plaistering is pretty forward, and withinne a month I shall send instructions for the Gallery and Inside furnishing. The Tower is advancing and has been carried up about Fifteen foot higher since my last account of it. (And my own tumbling Thought upon this Topick goes as follows: *I will have one Bell only since too much Ringing disturbs the Spirits*.) Of the other Churches it has been given into my Commission to build: the New Church at Limehouse is advanc'd as high as necessary for the season and it will be for the advantage of that Work to stop for the Present. This figure shewes half the outside of the Building – you will inclose it, Walter, will you not? – designed after a plain manner to be performed most with Ashler. I have added thin Pilasters to the walls, which are easily performed in rendering upon Brick-worke. I have given the ancient forme of Roofe which the experience of all Ages hath found the surest, noe other is to be trusted without doubling the thicknesse of the walles. When the Mason has sent me his Draughts, I will give you a carefull estimate of the charge, and returne you again the originall Designes, for in the handes of the workemen they will soon be soe defaced that they will not be able from them to pursew the Work to a Conclusion. This for the Church at Limehouse. The foundation of the Wapping New Church is carryed up as high as the Ground and ready to receive such sort of fabrick as I inclose draughts and Plans for. This for the Church at Wapping. We desire the honorable Board will be pleased to direct the covering of these respective Fabricks, and that the Ground therein to be walled in with Brick in order to hinder the Rabble and idle Mobb from getting in and finding ways to do continual Mischief. And then add this, Walter: In obedience to your Orders I have survey'd four other Parrishes mencioned and Sites for Churches; and which said Parrishes and Sites are humbly offered as followeth, *viz* And here, Walter, make precise the Situacions of St Mary Woolnoth, the New Churches in Blooms-bury and Greenwich, and the Church of Little St Hugh in Black Step Lane.

That stinking Alley close by the Moor-Fields?

Write it down as Black Step Lane. And then end thus: All which is most humbly submitted by your most humble Servant to command. Signed, Nicholas Dyer, Assistant Surveyour at Her Majesty's Office of Works, Scotland Yard.

And when you have made the fair-coppy, Walter, locke up the inke you whimzey-head. I laid my Hand on his Neck then, which made him to Quake and look asquint at me. No Musick-House nor Dancing for you tonight, *says I* in jest; and added this Thought to my self: no, nor likely to be if you tread in my Footsteps. It was now pritty near eight of the clock, and a Mist so obscured the Moon that the Yard itself was bathed in Red and I felt unquiet while gazing out at it; and in truth I had so many Apprehensions of Mind that they would as like have dragg'd me down to the Earth. But I took my Kersey-coat which hung upon a Pin in the entry, and call'd out to Walter, Be swift with that letter for, as the Preacher says, our Beings in this World are so uncertaine. And he gave his barking Laugh.

I had no sooner walked into Whitehall than I hollad for a Coach; it was of the Antique kind with Tin Sashes not Glass, pinked like the bottom of a Cullender that the Air might pass through the Holes: I placed my Eyes against them to see the Town as I passed within it and it was then broken into Peeces, with a Dog howling here and a Child running there. But the Lights and Ratling were pleasant to me, so that I fancied my self a Tyrant of my own Land. My Churches will indure, I reflected as I was born onward, and what the Coles build the Ashes will not burie. I have liv'd long enough for others, like the Dog in the Wheel, and it is now the Season to begin for myself: I cannot change that Thing call'd Time, but I can alter its Posture and, as Boys do turn a looking-glass against the Sunne, so I will dazzle you all. And thus my Thoughts rattled on like the Coach in which they were carryed, and that Coach was my poor Flesh.

The Crush of the Carriages was so great when we were got up into Fenchurch-Street that I was forc'd to step out at Billiter Lane and mobb it on foot along Leaden-Hall-Street; at last I managed to shoot myself thro' a Vacancy between two Coaches and cross'd the Street that went up into Grace-Church-Street. I walk'd into Lime Street, for I knew my path now and passed thro' many ways and turnings until I was got into Moor-Fields; then just past the Apothecary whose sign is the Ram I found the narrow lane, as dark as a Burying vault, which stank of stale sprats, Piss and Sir-Reverence. And there was the Door with the Mark upon it, and I knocked softly. It was time to even the Account, and then they shall see what fine Things I will do.

For when I trace back the years I have liv'd, gathering them up in my Memory, I see what a chequer'd Work of Nature my Life has been. If I were now to inscribe my own History with its unparalleled Sufferings and surprizing Adventures (as the Booksellers might indite it), I know that the great Part of the World would not believe the Passages there related, by reason of the Strangeness of them, but I cannot help their Unbelief: and if the Reader considers them to be but dark Conceits, then let him bethink himself that Humane life is quite out of the Light and that we are all Creatures of Darknesse.

I came crying into the World in the Year 1654. My Father was a Baker of Sea-Bisket and was born a Citizen of London, his Father being one before him, and my Mother was of honest Parents. I was born in Black-Eagle-Street in the Parish of Stepney, close by Monmouth Street and adjoining Brick Lane, in a wooden house which was tottering to the last degree and would have been pull'd down but for the vast Quantity of wooden dwellings on either side. There are those like me seiz'd with Feaver upon that day when they first came into the World, and I have good reason to Sweat on each fifth day of December for my first Entrance upon the Stage was attended with all the Symptoms of Death, as if I had been sensible of my future Works. My Mother gave me birth (or *hatch'd her Egg*, as they say), all bloody and Pissburnt in the hour before Dawn: I could see the grey Bars of Light rolling towards me, and I could heare the winde which gives signal of the end of Night. In the corner of the narrow mean Chamber, my Father stood with bow'd head since his Dame seemed about to leave this World presently, having endur'd many painful Hours during my Birth. The sunne rose up before the House: I could see it burning, and the shape

[11]

of my Father crossing and crossing againe in front of it so that he seemed a meer Shaddowe. Truly this was a vale of Tears I had come upon, and thus was I like Adam who on hearing the voice of God in the Garden wept in a state of Primal Terrour. Had Nature design'd me to take up only some insignificant and obscure Corner of the Universe this would be but a meer prattling Relation but those who see my Work will wish to be acquainted with my first Appearance in the World: it is a matter of Certainty that, by a narrow Observation of the Temper and Constitution of the Child, we will see in very Embrio those Qualities which afterwards make it remarkable in all Eyes.

My Mother recover'd very soon, and raised me as a sprightly Infant who could turn as nimbly as a dry leaf in a whirle-wind; and yet even then I was possess'd by strange Fancies: altho' other Boys would hunt for butter-flyes and bumble-bees, or whip their Tops in the Dust, I was full of Fears and Bugbears. Where now in the Spittle-Fields my Church rises, there would I weep for no Reason I could name. But I pass over my Infantile years in silence, and go on to that Stage where I was put to learn: I attended the charity school in St Catherine's near the Tower, but all the Advance I made under Sarah Wire, John Ducket, Richard Bowly and a whole Catalogue of Teachers was only to know the Rudiments of my Mother Tongue. These were merry Days and yet not so Innocent neither: among my School-fellows I would play a Game like Blind-man-buffe with its *You are tyed now and I must turn you about Thrice*, and it was known to us Boys that we might call the Devil if we said the Lord's Prayer backwards; but I never did it myself then. There were many other unaccountable Notions among us: that a Kiss stole a minute off our lives, and that we must spit upon a dead Creature and sing

> Go you back from whence you came
> And do not choose to ask my Name.

When the Light began to be Dusky after School, some bold Sparks would creep into the Church-yard and, as they said, catch the Shaddowes of dead Men (and these no simple Phantasies to me now). But such Sport was not for me, and in the most part I kept my own Company: my studdyes were of a more solitary kind, and I laid out my little Money for books. One of my School-fellows, Elias Biscow, lent me *Doctor Faustus* which pleased me, especially when he travelled in the Air, seeing all the World, but I was much troubled when the Devil came to fetch him and the consideration of that horrible End did so much to haunt me that I often dreamed of it. All the time I had from School, on Thursdays in the Afternoon and Saturday, I spent in reading on such things: the next I met with was *Fryar Bacon*, and then I read *Montelion, Knight of the Oracle* and *Ornatus*; borrowing the Book of one Person, when I had read it myself I lent it to another who lent me one of their owne so that, altho' sometimes at School I wanted Pens, Inke, Paper and other Necessaries, I never wanted Books.

When I was not at my Reading, I was often walking about. I had a thousand Threadbare topicks to excuse my absence from School, for I had gotten a haunt of Rambling and could not leave it: at first light I would slip on my Breeches over my Nakednesse, wash me and comb me, and then creep out into the Air. My Church now rises above a populous Conjunction of Alleys, Courts and Passages, Places full of poor People, but in those Years before the Fire the Lanes by Spittle-Fields were dirty and unfrequented: that part now called Spittle-Fields Market, or the Flesh-Market, was a Field of Grass with the Cows feeding on it. And there where my Church is, where three roads meet, *viz* Mermaid Alley, Tabernacle Alley and Balls Alley, was open ground until the Plague turned it into a vast Mound of Corrupcion. Brick Lane, which is now a long well-paved Street, was a deep dirty Road, frequented by Carts fetching Bricks that way into White-chappel from Brick-kilns in the Fields (and had the Name on that account). Here I rambled as a Boy, and yet also was often walking abroad into that great and monstrous Pile of London: and as I felt the City under my Feet I had a habit of rowling Phrases around my Head, such as *Prophesie Now, Devowring Fire, Violent Hands*, which I would then inscribe in my Alphabeticall Pocket-Book along with any other odd Fancies of my own. Thus would I wander, but as like as not I would take my self to a little Plot of Ground close by Angell Alley and along the New Key. Here I used to sit against a peece of Ancient Stone and set my Mind thinking on past Ages and on Futurity. There was before me a stone Pedestal on which was fix'd an old rusty Horizontal Dial, with the Gnomon broke short off, and it was with an inexpress-ible Peacefulnesse that I gazed upon this Instrument of Time: I remember it as well as if it were Yesterday, and not already burried beneath the Weight of Years. (And now I consider: have I been living in a Dreame?) But of this I may speake again in another Place, and I shall return in the mean time to my History for which I will, like a State Historian, give you the Causes as well as the Matter of Facts. I never had any faculty in telling of a Story, and one such as mine is will be contemned by others as a meer Winter Tale rather than that they should be brought to be afraid of another World and subjected to common Terrours which they despised before; for thus, to cut short a long Preamble, I have come to the most grievous story of the Plague.

I am perswaded that most Wretches let the World go wag: all is well, Jack has Joan, the Man has his Mare again, *as they say*, and they walk as

[13]

it were above the Precipeece with no Conception of the vast Gulph and frightful Abyss of Darknesse beneath them; but it is quite another Case with me. The Mind in Infancy, like the Body in Embrio, receives impressions that cannot be removed and it was as a meer Boy that I was placed in the Extremity of the Human State: even now, a Crowd of Thoughts whirl thro' the Thorowfare of my Memory for it was in that fateful year of the Plague that the mildewed Curtain of the World was pulled aside, as if it were before a Painting, and I saw the true Face of the Great and Dreadfull God.

It was in my Eleventh year that my Mother attracted the noisome Distemper; first she had small knobs of flesh as broad as a little silver Peny, which were the Tokens of the Contagion, and secondly the Swellings upon her Body. The Chirugeon came to observe the Marks of the Sicknesse, and then stood slightly apart; *Well what must I do, what will be the End of this?* entreats my Father of him, and the Chirugeon pressed mightily to have her remov'd to the Pest-House adjoining the Moor-Fields, for as he said the Symptoms admitted of no Hope. But my Father would in no wise be perswaded: *Tye her to the Bed then*, says the Chirugeon and he gave my Father some bottles filled with Cordial Waters and with Elixir of Minerals; *You are all in the same Ship*, says he, *and must Sink or Swim together*. My Mother then called out to me *Nick! Nick!* but my Father would not let me go to her; soon she stank mightily and was delirious in her sick Dress. And indeed she became an Object of Loathing to me in her fallen state: there was no help for it but to Dye in her case, and I cared not how soon that might be. My Father wished me to flee into the Fields before the House was shut and marked, but my resolution was not for going: where should I go to, and how could I shift for my self in this fearful World? My Father was yet alive, and I might remain safe from the Contagion: considering these matters, even as the Thing stank on her Bed, I was of a sudden possess'd of an extream chearfulness of Spirits so that I might have sung a catch around my Mother's carcasse (you see what a Life mine was to be).

As I did not want my Liberty yet, but it might be for the future, I hid my self when the House was shut up by a Constable and *Lord Have Mercy On Us* set close over the Cross. A Watchman was plac'd by the Door and, tho' so many Houses in Black-Eagle-Street had been Visited that he would scarce have known who dwelled in them, I had no Desire to be seen, in case it became urgent to me to make my Escape. Then my own Father began to sweat mightily, and a strange smell came off him in the way Flesh smells when put upon the Fire; he laid himself down upon the Floor of the Chamber where his Dame was but, tho' he called out to me, I would not go to him. From the Doorway I stared full in his Face and he stared back at me, and for an Instant our

[14]

Thoughts revolved around each other: you are undone, *says I*, and with my Pulse beating high I left him.

I gather'd some Provisions of Beer, Bread and Cheese and, to avoid my Father's sight, I took my self to a little confin'd Closet above the Chamber where they both now lay in their Extremity: it was like to a Garret, with a window all cobwebbed over, and here I waited until they went to their Long Home. Now in the glass of Recollection I can see every thing: the shaddowes moving across the Window and across my Face; the clock telling the Hour until it fell silent like the World itself; the Noises of my Father beneath me; the little Murmurings in the House adjoining. I sweated a little but had no Tokens of the Sicknesse and, like a man in a Dungeon, I had visions of many spacious Waies, cool Fountains, shady Walks, refreshing Gardens and places of Recreation; but then my Thoughts would switch suddenly and I would be affrighted by Figures of Death who seemed to come in my own Shape and cast fearful Looks around them; then I awoke and all was quiet. No more moans now, *thought I*, they are dead and cold: then of a sudden my Fears ebbed away and I felt at Peace; like the Cat in the Fable, I smil'd and smil'd.

The House was now so silent that the Watch, calling and hearing no Noise withinne, summon'd the Dead-Cart and at the sound of his Voice I started up from my Reveries. There was a Hazard in being found with the Dead, and then (as it were) Imprison'd, and so I looked about me for a means of Escape. Although I was three storeys High, there were great Sheds before the Window (this was in back of the House, adjoining Monmouth Street) and as quick as Lightning I let my self down by means of them to the Ground: I had taken no Thought for Provisions, and had not even Straw to lie upon. Now I stood in the Dirt and Silence, and there were no Lights save those which had been placed by the Corses for the Dead-Carts. And there too as I turned up Black-Eagle-Street, I saw by the flickering Lanthorn my own Parents lying where the Watch had placed them, their Faces all shiny and begrimed: I was as like to have cried out in Fright until I recalled to myself that I was alive and these dead Things could in no manner harm me; and, making myself pritty invisible (for indeed there was little to be seen on so Dark a Night), I waited for the Cart to do its dismal Traffick.

The two Creatures were placed onto a bundle of Carcasses, all ragged and swollen like a Nest of Wormes, and the Bell-Man and two Linkes took the Cart down Black-Eagle-Street, past Corbets Court and through Brownes Lane: I follow'd close on their Heels, and could hear them making merry with their *Lord Have Mercy On Us, No Man Will* and their *Wo To Thee My Honeys*; they were Drunken to the highest degree, and were like to have Pitched the Corses into the Doorways so

[15]

wayward was their track. But then they came out into the Spittle-Fields and, as I was running besides them now in my Wonder or Delirium (I know not what), of a sudden I saw a vast Pitte almost at my very Feet; I stopp'd short, star'd withinne it, and then as I totter'd upon the Brink had a sudden Desire to cast myself down. But at this moment the Cart came to the edge of the Pitte, it was turned round with much Merriment, and the Bodies were discharg'd into the Darknesse. I cou'd not Weep then but I can Build now, and in that place of Memory will I fashion a Labyrinth where the Dead can once more give Voice.

All that Night I wandred in the open Fields, sometimes giving vent to my Passions in loud singing and sometimes sunk into the most frightful Reflections: for in what a Box was I? I was at a great loss what to do, since I had been turned adrift to the wide World. I had not aim'd to return to my own House and indeed it proved impossible to do so: I soon discover'd that it had been pull'd down with several others by it, so noxious was the Air withinne; thus I was forc'd to go Abroad, and take up my old Rambling Humour once more. But I was now more cautious than of old: it was said (and I recall my Parents saying) that before the Pestilence there were seen publickly Daemons in Humane shape, which struck those they met, and those struck were presently seiz'd with the Disease; even those who saw such Apparitions (call'd Hollow Men) grew much alter'd. This was the Common report, at any rate: I believe now those Hollow Men to be a Recreation of all the Exhalations and Vapours of humane Blood that rose from the City like a general Groan. And it is not to be Wonder'd at that the Streets were mighty Desolate; there were in every place Bodies on the ground, from which came such a Scent that I ran to catch the Wind in my Nostrils, and even those who liv'd were so many walking Corses breathing Death and looking upon one another fearfully. *And still alive?* or *And not dead yet?* were their constant Enquiries of one another, tho' there were some who walked in such a Stupor that they cared not where they were going, and others who made Monkey noises into the Air. There were Children, also, whose Plaints could move even the Dying to Pity and their Verse echoes still in the Recesses and Corners of the Town:

Hush! Hush! Hush! Hush!
We are all tumbled down.

Thus was I taught by many Signes that Humane life was of no certain course: we are governed by One who like a Boy wags his Finger in the inmost part of the Spider's web and breaks it down without a Thought.

[16]

It would tire the Reader should I dwell on my various Adventures as a Street-Boy, wherefore at present I shall say no more of them. I return in the mean time to my Reflections arising from these Incidents, and to my Considerations on the weaknesse and folly of Humane life. After the Plague abated, the Mobb were happy againe with their Masquerades, Rush-burying, Morrice-dances, Whitson-ales, Fortune-telling, Legerdemain, Lotteries, Midnight-revels and lewd Ballads; but I was of a different Mould. I had looked about me and penetrated what had occurred, not let it pass like a sick man's Dreame or a Scene without a Plot. I saw that the intire World was one vast Bill of Mortality, and that Daemons might walk through the Streets even as Men (on point of Death, many of them) debauch themselves: I saw the Flies on this Dunghil Earth, and then considered who their Lord might be.

But now the Work of Time unravells and the Night has gone and I am returned to the Office where Walter Pyne is standing at the Side of me, tapping his Shooe upon the Floor. How long have I sat here in my Trance of Memory?

I have been thinking on the Dead, *said I* in haste, and at that Walter turned his Face from me and seemingly searched after his Rule; he does not like to hear me talk of such Matters, and so when he sat himself down I switched my Theme: It is as dusty here as the top of a Slut's cupboard, *I cried*, look at my Finger!

It cannot be helped, *says he*, for when the Dust is cleared away it returns again directly.

I was disposed to be Merry with him now: Is Dust immortal then, *I ask'd him*, so that we may see it blowing through the Centuries? But as Walter gave no Answer I jested with him further to break his Melancholy humour: What is Dust, Master Pyne?

And he reflected a little: It is particles of Matter, no doubt.

Then we are all Dust indeed, are we not?

And in a feigned Voice he murmured, For Dust thou art and shalt to Dust return. Then he made a Sour face, but only to laugh the more.

I went up to him and placed my Hands upon his Shoulders, which made him tremble a little. Hold still, *I said*, I have good News.

What News is this?

I now agree with you, *I replied*. I will place the Sepulture a little way off from the Spittle-Fields Church. And for your sake, Walter, not on the advice of Sir Chris, but for your Sake only. And I have a Secret to impart to you (at this he inclin'd his head): we will build it for the most part under the Ground.

I have Dream'd of this, *said he*. He spoke no more and kept his Back to me as he went about his Labours, tho' pritty soon I heard his low Whistle as he bent over his Sheets.

[17]

We must make Haste, *I call'd* taking Pen and Inke, for the Church must be compleat withinne the Year.

And the yeares turn so fast, adds Walter, and now he is vanish'd and I am gone back to the time of the Distemper when I went abroad among so many walking Carcasses sweating Poison. At first I seemed to be toss'd up and down by spightful Accidents of Fortune, and made the May-game of Chance, until one night I found the Thread in my Labyrinth of Difficulties. It was the last week of July, about Nine in the Night, and I was walking by the Hatters-shop near the Three Tun Tavern in Redcross-street. It was a Moonshiny night but the Moon, being got behind the Houses, shined only a slant and sent a little stream of light out of one of the small Lanes quite cross the Street. I paus'd to give a Glance to this Light when out of the Lane walked a tall and pritty lean Man dressed in a Velvet jacket, a Band and a black Cloack; with him stepped out two Women with white Linnen Hand-kerchiefs wrapped around the lower part of their Faces (so to protect their Nostrils from the Scents of the Plague). The Man had a swift pace, and his Companions troubled themselves to keep up to him, and then to my unutterable Astonishment he pointed at me (in my tattered Coat and ragged Shooes): There is the Hand as plain as can be, *says he*, do you see it plainly above his Head? He was elevated to a strange Degree and call'd over to me, Boy! Boy! Come here to me! Come here to me! And then one of the women with him said, Do not go near him, for how do you know but he may have the Plague? To which he answered: Do not be afraid of him. And at that I came close to them.

What art thou? *says he*.

I am a poor Boy.

Why, have you no Sir-name?

And then strangely I bethought my self of my Schoolboy reading: Faustus, *says I*.

I dare say, *he replies*, that the Devil cannot catch you; and at that the two Women laugh'd heartily. Then he gave me a Coin: there is Sixpence for you, *he says*, if you will come with us. For consider these times, little Faustus, it is a great deal of Money and we mean you no Hurt.

I hugged it as close as a School-boy does a Birds-nest, but I was not easily to be perswaded: might these not be reeking Apparitions, the Spirits of the Pestilence, or might they not be Carriers of the Conta-gion? But then the words of the Woman came back into my Head – *Do not go near him* – and I surmised that these were Humane and incorrupted Creatures. I will go with you, *says I*, for the space of a little way if you will give me good Reason. And I perceived there was an Alteration in the Man's Countenance as *he said*, I will save you

[18]

from Ruin, little Faustus, if you come with me and that will be a Surety.

And so I began to walk with them, and we were got quite up into Fenchurch-street when the Wind blew mightily so that the Tiles of the very Roofs fell down upon the Ground. The Ways were now so dark that I was as bewilder'd as a Pilgrim in the Desert, but at last we came by a narrow Lane (which is to say, Black Step Lane): here I was led thro' a long obscure Entry where I groped my way like a Subterranean Labourer in the Caverns of a Cole-pit; there was no Link nor Watchman's lanthorn but my Companions moved on at a swift Pace until the Man came to a little wooden door where he knocked thrice and whisper'd *Mirabilis* (which was, as I learn'd, his proper Name). On entering this Dwelling I looked about me and saw that it was a mean paper Building, the walls old and ruinous, the Rooms miserable and straite with but dim burning Candles in them. Here were Men and Women, not less than Thirty in Number; and not the meanest sort of people neither but, as we say, in the middling degree of Life. They look'd on me strangely at first but Mirabilis led me by the Hand saying, He had the Sign over his Head, He is the Corn thrashed out of the Chaff, and such like Phrases. I was now in a state of great Perplexity but, seeing that this Assembly smiled mightily upon me and embraced me, I became somewhat easier in my Thoughts. Mirabilis set me down upon a little Stool, then brought me a wooden Dish with a grey liquor in it and bid me drink it off as a Cordial; I swallow'd it without examination and then fell into an extream Sweat so that my Heart beat high. Mirabilis then ask'd me who I desired to see. I said I wanted to see no one so much as my Mother before she Stank (my confus'd Words showing that the Liquor was working withinne me). Then he took up a Looking-glass that was in the Room, and setting it down again bid me look in it – which I did, and there saw the exact Image of my Mother in that Habit which she used to wear, and working at her Needle. This was an Astonishment indeed and my Hair would have lifted off my Hat, if it had been on.

I put down the Glass and my very Thoughts seemed suspended: I had no Power to turn my Gaze but to the Face of Mirabilis who was now speaking to the Assembly and discoursing of Flames, Ruines, Desolations, the rain like a hotte Winde, the Sun as red as Blood, the very dead burnt in their Graves (thus did he Prophesie the Burning of the City). This Company was not like the Meeters with their *Yea, I do say* and their *Let me entreat* and their *Hear ye this* but, as it seemed to me in my befuddled State, they laugh'd and jested with one another. Then they anointed their Foreheads and Hand-wrists with I know not what and seem'd about to Depart. I rose up to go but Mirabilis laid his Hand upon my Arm: Do you sit still, *says he*, and I'll come to you again. At which I was a little frightened to be left alone, and he perceived it: Don't be afraid, little Faustus, *he continues*, there shall Nothing hurt you nor speak to you and, if you hear any Noise, don't you stir but sit still here. So he took up one of the Candles and they went into another Room by a little Door like a Closet-Door, and when he shut the Door after him I perceiv'd a little Window of one broad Square of Glass only that looked into the Room which they were gone into. I wanted to peep but I durst not stir for my Life and then, fatigued and exhausted by the surprizing Turns of this Night, I fell into a sound Sleep; before I did so, I seemed to hear screeching, much like that of a Catte.

And thus began my strange Destiny. I rested with Mirabilis seven dayes, and if any Reader should inquire why I did so I will answer: Firstly, I was a meer poor Boy and had seen my Mother in his Glass; Secondly, the teachings of Mirabilis are trew ones, as I shall explain further hereafter; Thirdly, the most wonderful thing in the Plague Year was that his intire Assembly had been preserv'd from Contagion by his Practises and his Prophesyings; Fourth, I was curious about all these Matters and Hunger and Thirst are not Appetites more vehement or more hard. Now what I know I would be glad to unknow again, but my Memory will not let me be untaught.

I shall Particularize now – like a Drunken Man, there were Occasions when Mirabilis reeled and danced about several times in a Circle, fell at last in an Extasy upon the Ground and lay for a short time as one Dead; meanwhile the Assembly took great Care that no Gnat, Fly or other Animal touch him; then he started up on a Sudden and related to them things concerning their trew Situation. Sometimes he fell upon the Ground and was whispering there unintelligibly to some thing that was neither seen nor heard. And then he would turn and say, Give me some Drink, quickly any thing to drink. On several Occasions he turned with his Face towards the wall intensely and greedily poring thereon, and beckning thereunto, as if he converst with some thing: he so sweated thro' his Cloaths that it stood like a Dew upon them, and then when he arose from his Extasie he desir'd a Pipe of Tobacco. And in the hour before Dusk he whisper'd to me that those whom he chose (as I had been chosen) must be washed and consecrated by the Sacrifice, and that in our Eucharist the Bread must be mingled with the Blood of an Infant. But these things are not to be committed to Paper, but to be delivered by Word of Mouth, which I may do when at last I see you.

I shall say only at this point that I, the Builder of Churches, am no Puritan nor Caveller, nor Reformed, nor Catholick, nor Jew, but of that older Faith which sets them dancing in Black Step Lane. And this is the Creed which Mirabilis school'd in me: He who made the World is also author of Death, nor can we but by doing Evil avoid the rage of

[20]

evil Spirits. Out of the imperfections of this Creator are procreated divers Evils: as Darknesse from his Feare, shaddowes from his Ignorance, and out of his Teares come forth the Waters of this World. Adam after his Fall was never restor'd to Mercy, and all men are Damned. Sin is a Substance and not a Quality, and it is communicated from parents to children: men's Souls are corporeal and have their being by Propagation or Traduction, and Life itself is an inveterate Mortal Contagion. We baptize in the name of the Father unknown, for he is truly an unknown God; Christ was the Serpent who deceiv'd Eve, and in the form of a Serpent entered the Virgin's womb; he feigned to die and rise again, but it was the Devil who truly was crucified. We further teach that the Virgin Mary, after Christ's birth, did marry once and that Cain was the Author of much goodnesse to Mankind. With the Stoicks we believe that we sin necessarily or co-actively, and with Astrologers that all Humane events depend upon the Starres. And thus we pray: What is Sorrow? The Nourishment of the World. What is Man? An unchangeable Evil. What is the Body? The Web of Ignorance, the foundation of all Mischief, the bond of Corrupcion, the dark Coverture, the living Death, the Sepulture carried about with us. What is Time? The Deliverance of Man. These are the ancient Teachings and I will not Trouble my self with a multiplicity of Commentators upon this place, since it is now in my Churches that I will bring them once more into the Memory of this and future Ages. For when I became acquainted with Mirabilis and his Assembly I was uncovering the trew Musick of Time which, like the rowling of a Drum, can be heard from far off by those whose Ears are prickt.

But to go forward a little: that Sathan is the God of this World and fit to be worshipp'd I will offer certaine proof and, first, the Soveraignty of his Worship. The inhabitants of Hispaniola worship goblins, they of Calcutta worship the statues of the Devil, Moloch was the god of the Ammonites, the Carthaginians worshipped their Deity under the name of Saturn and it is the Straw Man of our Druides. The chief God of the Syrians was Baal-Zebub or Beel-Zebub, the Lord of Flies: his other Name is Baal-Phegor, the Gaping or Naked Lord, and his Temple is call'd the Beth-Peor. He is call'd Baal Saman among the Phoenicians, by which is meant the Sunne. Among the Assyrians he is call'd Adrammalech, and also he is called Jesus, the brother of Judas. Even on these British islands Baal Saman was worshipp'd after the manner of the Phoenicians, and this Tradition was carried on by the Druides who committed no Thing to writing but their way of delivering the Mistery was by the secret Cabbala. They sacrificed Boys since it was their Opinion that Humane life, either in desperate sicknesse or in danger of Warre, could not be secured unless a vyrgyn Boy suffered in stead. And this further: *demon* from *daimon*, which is us'd

[21]

promiscuously with *theos* as the word for Deity; the Persians call the Devill *Div*, somewhat close to *Divus* or *Deus*; also, *ex sacramenti* is expounded in Tertullian as *exacramentum* or *excrement*. And thus we have a Verse:

Pluto, Jehova, Satan, Dagon, Love,
Moloch, the Virgin, Thetis, Devil, Jove,
Pan, Jahweh, Vulcan, he with th'awfull Rod,
Jesus, the wondrous Straw Man, all one God.

Walter looks up and saies, Did you hear a person singing?

I hear no Thing but your own Noises, Walter, which are no Musick.

But there was something, *said he* after a Pause, tho' no doubt it was a workman.

Work on yourself, *I replied*, and use your Ears not so much as your Eyes: our Time is being all broken into Fragments with your Whimsies. And at this he goes a little Red.

Now I hear him scratching a Coppy of my Draught, and as I leave the Sphere of Memory I hear the Noises of the World in which I am like to Drown: a Door creaks upon its Hinge, a Crow calls, a Voice is raised and I am no thing againe, for it is a hard Toil to withstand those other sounds of Time which rise and fall like the Beating of a Heart and bear us onward to our Grave.

But let us drop this Matter and look into the Beginning and far End of Things: these Druides held their yearly Sessions in London, close by the Place now call'd Black Step Lane, and their own sacred Misteries were passed on to certain of the Christians. Joseph of Arimathea, a Magician who had embalmed the Body of their Christ, was sent into Britain and was much honoured by the Druides; he it was who founded the first Church of the Christians in Glastonbury where St Patrick, the first Abbot, was entomb'd beneath a stone Pyramidde: for these Christians got a Footing so soon in Britain because of the Power of the Druids who were so eminent and because of the History of Magick. Thus under where the Cathedral Church of Bath now stands there was a Temple erected to Moloch, or the Straw Man; Astarte's Temple stood where Paul's is now, and the Britains held it in great Veneration; and where the Abbey of Westminster now stands there was erected the Temple of Anubis. And in time my own Churches will rise to join them, and Darknesse will call out for more Darknesse. In this Rationall and mechanicall Age there are those who call Daemons mere Bugs or Chimeras and if such People will believe in Mr Hobbes, the Greshamites and other such gee-gaws, who can help it? They must not be contradicted, and they are resolved not to be perswaded; I address myself to Mysteries infinitely more Sacred and, in Confederacy with the Guardian Spirits of the Earth, I place Stone upon Stone in Spittle-Fields, in Limehouse and in Wapping.

So I must take every Part in order: I had it in my Thought to give you this Preface to my Church in Spittle-Fields, for it is a long way which has no Destination, and in this instance it leads us to the Sepulture or Labyrinth which I will build beside that sovereign Church. I have by me the Relation of Kott's Hole (or House under Ground, as it is call'd), newly discovered in a peece of Ground within Two Miles of Cirencester commonly known by the Name of Colton's Field. Two Labourers were digging a Gravell-pit at the foot of a Hill (which they had now sunk four yards deep) when they observ'd the Ground on that side next the Hill to be loose, and presently discovered an Entrance into the Belly of the Hill, which appearing very strange to them, and rather the work of Art than Nature, they got a Lanthorn and ventured in. There they entred a most dreadfull Passage, not above a yard in breadth and foure feet in height, and as Hot as a Stove. It had a Grave-like Smell and was half-full of Rubbidge; there were also here Tablets upon the Wall, which they no sooner touch'd to feel their Substance but they crumbled into Dust: from thence they saw a Passage into a square Room, which when they entered they saw athwart the Roome, at the upper end, the Sceleton of a Boy or small Man; in terrour the Labourers hastily quitted this dark Apartment, which they had no sooner done and reached the upper Air when the Hill sunk down again.

And it came into my Mind on reading this Account that this was the Site of the Mysteries, as Mirabilis had once related them to me: here the Boy who is to be Sacrificed is confin'd to the Chamber beneath the Earth and a large Stone rolled across its Face; here he sits in Darknesse for seven dayes and seven nights, by which time he is presum'd to have been led past the Gates of Death, and then on the eighth Day his Corse is led out of the Cave with much rejoycing: that Chamber is known itself as a Holy Place, which is inshrined to the Lord of Death. Thus when I spoke to Walter of our new Sepulture, or Enclosure, my Thoughts were burryed far beneath: my own House under Ground will be dark indeed, and a true Labyrinth for those who may be placed there. It will not be so empty as Kott's Hole neither: there are no Grave-stones nor Vaults there but it is beside the Pitte, now quite overlaid and forgotten, where my Parents had been discharg'd and so many Hundred (I should say Thousand) Corses also. It is a vast Mound of Death and Nastinesse, and my Church will take great Profit from it: this Mirabilis once describ'd to me, *viz* a Corn when it dies and rots in the Ground, it springs again and lives, so, *said he*, when there are many Persons dead, only being buryed and laid in the Earth, there is an Assembling of Powers. If I put my Ear to the Ground I hear them

[23]

lie promiscuously one with another, and their small Voices echo in my Church: they are my Pillars and my Foundation.

Walter, *I cried*, leave off your Dozing and take up your Penne; Time is pressing upon us, and so write to the Commission thus. Sirs, I beg leave to acquaint the Board that the Church Yard of Spittle-Fields as originally drawn on the Survey will be so very small that Burrials will grow extreamly inconvenient. It were necessary for me to take up the Legg of the Steeple, and the Foote of the Collumns in the Body of the Church, to make more Roome but that I have design'd a Sepulture remov'd from the Fabrick of the Church (as Sir Xtofer himself desires). I have us'd the manner of building the Sepulture as it was in the Fourth Century, in the purest time of Christianity, as you may see from the Draught inclosed. And then upon the Ground I have form'd a white Pyramidde, in the manner of the Glastonbury Church but littel and framed of rough stone without the Lime, this also in the manner of the Early Christians. All which is humbly submitted and, Walter, write it quick while the Heat is upon us.

Thus do I veil my Intention with Cant, like a cozening Rogue, and use this temporary Scaffold of Words to counterfeit my Purpose. As for the Chamber it self: it will be sollid only in those parts that beare weight, and will be so contrived within-side to form a very intricate Labyrinth. I have placed Cavities in the thicknesse of the Walls where I will put these Signes – *Nergal*, that is Light of the Grave, *Ashima*, that is Fault, *Nibhas*, that is Vision, and *Tartak*, that is Chained. These true Beliefs and Mysteries are not be inscribed in easy Figures since the Mobb, being in Ignorance, will teare them down in their Feare. But if Violence does not happen, and it remaines burried from vulgar Eyes, this Labyrinth will endure 1000 yeares.

*

And now hear, as my Work rose from the Burriall Ground, how the Dead do call out to the Living: it is the Custom in our Nation to have the Mason's son lay the heighest and last stone on the top of the Tower its Lanthorn. This Boy, Thomas, the son of Mr Hill, was a sprightly Spark in his tenth or eleventh year and perfectly well made: his Face was fair and varnished over by a blooming, and the Hair of his Head was thick and reclin'd far below his Shoulders. He was in great good Humour on the Morning of his Ascent and saw it as a merry Enterprize, climbing out upon the wooden Scaffold and nimbly advancing his Steps to the Tower. The Labourers and the Mason, his Father, look'd up at him and call'd out *How do you Tom?* and *One step further!* and such like Observations, while I stood silent by my small Pyrammide just lately made. But there was a sudden Gust of Wind and the Boy, now close to the Lanthorn, seemed to lose Heart as the Clowds

[24]

scudded above his Head. He gazed steadily at me for an Instant and I cryed, *Go on! Go on!*; and at this Moment, just as he was coming up to the spiry Turret, the timbers of the Scaffold, being insecurely plac'd or rotten, cracked asunder and the Boy missed his Footing and fell from the Tower. He did not cry out but his Face seem'd to carry an Expression of Surprize: Curved lines are more beautiful than Straight, I thought to my self, as he fell away from the main Fabrick and was like to have dropped ripe at my own Feet.

The Mason his Father calling for Help rushed in the direction of the Pyramidde, where now Thomas lay, and the Work men followed amaz'd. But he had expir'd at once. There was a contusion in his Head which I could not forebear from Noticing as I bent over the Body: the Blood ran out of his Mouth as out of a Bowl, and came pouring upon the Ground. All those around stood stiff like a Figure, motionless and speechless, and I could hardly refrain from smiling at the Sight; but I hid my self with a woeful Countenance and advanc'd up to the Father who was ready to sink down with Grief (indeed the Death of his Son work'd hard upon his Bowels, and dragg'd him by degrees after him to the Grave). A littel Crowd of People was looking on with their *What is the Matter?* and *Is he quite dead?* and *Poor creature*, but I waved them away. Then I held fast to Mr Hill, and stayed silent to help Compose him: He has fled out of his Prison, *said I* at last, but he looked on me strangely and I stopp'd my self. The Mason was now quite stupid with Sorrow; he was alwaies a sullen and dogged Fellow but in his Grief he sett upon God and Heaven at a very foull rate, which pleased me mightily. I kept my Silence but this Reflection was rowling about my Mind as I gazed at the little Corse: He is pretty in Death because he did not feare it. Then the Father made to unbuckle his son's shooes, for I know not what Purpose, but I led him away and spoke to him gently. At any rate, *I said*, give him leave to be buried where he fell and according to Custom: to which in his Agony he assented. Then he began to spew soundly.

And so all this was given to my Purpose: there is a certain ridiculous Maxim that *The Church loves not Blood* but this is nothing to the Case for the Eucharist must be mingled with Blood. Thus had I found the Sacrifice desir'd in the Spittle-Fields, and not at my own Hands: I had killed two Birds, as they say, and as I coached it from White-chappell I rejoyced exceedingly. I am in the Pitte, but I have gone so deep that I can see the brightness of the Starres at Noon.

2

AT NOON they were approaching the church in Spitalfields. Their guide had stopped in front of its steps and was calling out, 'Come on! Come on!'. Then she turned to face them, her left eyelid fluttering nervously as she spoke: 'You have to use your imagination on a building like this. Do you see the decay? It should be lovely and clean, like the top.' She pointed vaguely at the steeple, before bending down to brush some dirt or dust off the edge of her white raincoat. 'What was that falling there?', one of the group asked, shielding his eyes with his right hand so that he might look more clearly at the sky around the church tower, but his voice was lost in the traffic noise which had only momentarily subsided: the roar of the lorries as they were driven out of the market in front of the church, and the sound of the drills blasting into the surface of the Commercial Road a little further off, shook the whole area so that it seemed to quiver beneath their feet.

The guide rubbed her fingers with a paper handkerchief before beckoning the group onwards; they hurried from the vicinity of the noise into the apparent chaos of streets and alleys beside the church, hardly noticing the people who stared at them incuriously. Then they stumbled into each other on the narrow pavement as their guide came suddenly to a halt and, in the relative quiet of this place, adopted a more intimate tone: 'Are there any Germans here?' and she went on without pausing for a reply, 'It was the great German poet, Heine, who said that London defies the imagination and breaks the heart'. She looked down at her notes, and a murmur of voices could be heard from the houses closest to them. 'And yet there are other poets who have said of London that it contains something grand and everlasting.' She glanced at her watch, and now the group could hear the other sounds of the street: the murmured voices were mixed with words from radio or television, and at the same time various kinds of music seemed to fill the street before ascending into the air above the roofs and chimneys. One song, in particular, could be heard coming from several shops and homes: it soared above the others before it, too, disappeared over the city.

[26]

'If we take our stand here and look south,' – and she turned her back on them – 'we will see where the Great Plague spread.' Some children nearby were calling out to each other, so she raised her voice. 'It's difficult to imagine, I suppose, but the disease carried off more than 7000 people in this neighbourhood alone, as well as 116 sextons and gravediggers.' She had remembered her lines, and knew that it was at this point they would laugh. 'And down there,' she continued, cutting them off, 'were the first houses.' They peered in the direction to which she was pointing and at first could see only the outline of a large office building, the cloudy surface of its mirror-glass reflecting the tower of Spitalfields church. The road was wet from a recent shower of rain and it reflected the light which at midday radiated from the neon shop-signs and from the interiors of offices and homes. The buildings themselves were variously coloured – in grey, light blue, orange and dark green – and there were slogans or drawings daubed upon some of them.

She could hear a train in the distance. 'And where we are standing now would have been open fields, where the dead and the dying came.' And as they looked at the site of the plague fields, they saw only the images on the advertising hoardings which surrounded them: a modern city photographed at night with the words HAVE ANOTHER BEFORE YOU GO glowing in the dark sky above it, an historical scene in washed-out sepia so that it resembled an illustration from an old volume of prints, and the enlarged face of a man smiling (although the building opposite this poster cast a deep shadow, which cut off the right side of the face). 'It has always been a very poor district,' she was saying when a group of four children, whose cries and whistles had already been heard, marched between them. They ignored the strangers and, looking straight ahead, chanted:

> What are you looking for in the hole?
> A stone!
> What will you do with the stone?
> Sharpen a knife!
> What will you do with the knife?
> Cut off your head!

They marched on and then turned round to stare as the guide took her party forward, her enthusiasm now diminished as she tried to recall more facts about this neighbourhood: and if I can't remember any, she thought, I'll just have to invent them.

And the streets around the Spitalfields church were soon filled with the children who had come tumbling and laughing out of school, shouting out nonsense words to each other until a general cry of 'Join in the ring! Join in the ring!' was taken up. And the question became 'Who's it?' until the answer was given, 'You're it!' and a small boy was pushed into the centre of the ring, an old sock wound around his eyes, and he was spun three times on the spot. He kept very still and counted under his breath as the children danced around him and called out, 'Dead man arise! Dead man arise!'. Then quickly and unexpectedly he lunged forward with his arms held out in front of him, and the others ran away screaming with excitement and fear. Some of those in flight ran towards the church, but none of them would have dared to enter its grounds.

Where now the boy, Thomas, half-crouched behind the small pyramid which had been erected at the same time as the church itself, was watching them. The late afternoon sun threw his shadow upon the rough discoloured stone, as he traced its hollows and striations with his finger – afraid to look directly at the children, and yet not wanting to miss any of their movements. Thomas could feel the pyramid quiver as the lorries turned roaring into the Commercial Road, sending clouds of dust into the air as they did so: he had once noticed with astonishment how above an open fire the air itself quivered, and now he always associated that movement with heat. The pyramid was too hot, even if he himself could not feel it. He jumped back from it and started to run towards the church; and, as he approached its stone wall, the noises of the external world were diminished as if they were being muffled by the fabric of the building itself.

The church changed its shape as he came closer to it. From a distance it was still the grand edifice which rose up among the congerie of roads and alleys around Brick Lane and the Market; it was the massive bulk which seemed to block off the ends of certain streets; it was the tower and spire which could be seen for more than two miles, and those who noticed it would point and say to their companions, 'There is Spitalfields, and Whitechapel beside it!' But as Thomas approached it now it ceased to be one large building and became a number of separate places – some warm, some cold or damp, and some in perpetual shadow. He knew every aspect of its exterior, each decaying buttress and each mossy corner, since it was here that on most days he came to sit.

There were times when Thomas would climb the fifteen steps and walk into the church itself. He would kneel in front of a small side-altar, with his hands shielding his eyes as if in prayer, and imagine the building of his own church: he constructed in turn the porch, the nave, the altar, the tower but then always he lost his way in a fantastic sequence of rooms and stairs and chapels until he was obliged to begin again. These journeys into the interior of the church were rare, however, since he could not be sure that he would remain

[28]

alone: the sound of footsteps at the back of the church, echoing in the half-light, made him tremble with fear. On one occasion he had been roused from his reverie by voices chanting in unison, 'Take thy plague away from me; I am even consumed by the means of Thy heavy hand and I am falling, falling . . .', and he had left the church quickly, not daring to glance at those who had so unexpectedly joined him. Yet outside he was once again alone and at peace.

From the south wall of the church he could see an area which, although perhaps designed as a cemetery by the architect, was now merely a patch of ground with some trees, faded grass and, beside them, the pyramid. From the east wall there was nothing to be seen except a gravel path which led to the entrance of an old tunnel. The place was now boarded up and, although the large grey stones of its entry suggested that it had been built at an early date (and might even be contemporaneous with the church itself), it had been used as an air-raid 'shelter' during the last war and since that time had like the church itself decayed. Stories had accumulated around this 'house under ground', as the local children called it: it was said that the tunnel led to a maze of passages which burrowed miles into the earth, and the children told each other stories about the ghosts and corpses which were still to be found somewhere within it. But Thomas, although he believed such things, always felt himself to be safe when he was crouched against the stone of the church itself – as he was now, after he had run from the pyramid and the sight of the playing children. And it was here that he tried to escape the memory of that day's events.

He attended the local school, St Katherine's: on charcoal grey mornings he would sit at his desk and savour the sweet classroom smell of chalk and disinfectant, just as he enjoyed the distinctive odour of ink and of his own books. In History class (which was known to the children as the 'Mystery' lesson), for example, he liked to write down names or dates and watch the ink flow across the spacious white paper of his exercise book. But when the bell rang he would walk out into the asphalt schoolyard uncertain and alone; among all the shriek-ing and shouting, he would move surreptitiously from one group to another, or he would pretend to find something of interest by the walls and railings away from the other children. But, if he could, he would always listen when they talked – so it was he learned that, if you say the Lord's Prayer backwards, you can raise the Devil; he learned, also, that if you see a dead animal you must spit on it and repeat, 'Fever, fever, stay away, don't come inside my bed today'. He heard that a kiss takes a minute off your life, and that a black beetle crawling across your shoe means that one of your friends is about to die. All these things he stored up in his memory, for it seemed to him

[29]

to be knowledge that he must possess in order to be like the others; they had somehow acquired it naturally, but he had to find it and then cherish it.

For he was still eager to be with them and even to talk to them, and he did not mind showing that eagerness: on this particular afternoon five planes had passed in formation in the sky above the children, and they had pointed to them and chanted, 'It's a war! It's a war!'. And Thomas, too, joined in the excitement: he experienced no fear but in a curious sense he felt protected as he jumped up and down, waving at the planes as they disappeared into the distance and still shouting with the others. But then one boy came up to him and, with a smile, pinioned Thomas's arm behind his back, levering it upwards until he was forced to cry out in pain. And the boy whispered to him exultantly, 'Are you going to be burnt or buried? Answer me! Are you going to be burnt or buried?' And eventually Thomas muttered 'Buried!' and lowered his head.

'Say it louder!'

And he screamed out 'Buried!' before his tormentor would release him. The others had been alerted to the scene of Thomas's humiliation and now began to crowd around him, singing:

> Thomas Hill is no good,
> Chop him up for firewood.
> When he's dead, boil his head,
> Make it into ginger bread.

He knew that he should not cry, but he stood in the centre of the schoolyard with the tears running down his face; and when they saw the tears the children shouted 'Dry up and blow away!' as his sobs were drowned by the roar of the planes once more flying overhead.

Now he was crouched against the wall of the church, in such a position that he was effectively hidden from the street. He gazed at the grass and trees which bordered this place and, as a leaf fell from one of the branches and drifted slowly to the ground, the vision of the afternoon's pain and humiliation disappeared. The pigeons made elaborate formations around and in front of Thomas, wings upon wings until their shapes were indistinct, and the rustling also comforted him. He turned his face to the sun, and the clouds made a patchwork of shadows upon his body: he looked up at them and they seemed to be disappearing inside the church. And then he was climbing towards them, climbing the tower until the clouds hid him, climbing the tower as a voice called out, *Go on! Go on!*

A wind started up, carrying the odours which suggest the end of summer, and as Thomas awoke he saw the sunlight leave the grass like an eye suddenly closed. He stood up and as he walked away from the church the noises of the world returned; it was colder now and when he entered the street he began running, slightly clumsily as if he were aware of his own body as he ran. And there were some who glanced at him and thought Poor boy! as he hurried towards his home in Eagle Street, which is off Brick Lane.

He was not the only visitor to the church that day. Two boys were standing at a place where three roads meet (Mermaid Alley, Tabernacle Close and Balls Street), saying nothing but digging with their fingers into the mortar of an old wall which was already crumbling. One of them looked at the side of the church, rising up at the end of Tabernacle Close, and then punched his companion on the shoulder: 'Do you want to go down the old tunnel?

'Do you?'
'Do *you*?'
'*Do* you?'
'*Do you*?'

And they continued this ritual incantation until they were beside the locked gates of the churchyard from where they could see the entrance of the tunnel, boarded up with planks which were already rotten and half-covered with foliage which was spreading over the curved roof. The two boys squeezed through the railings of the gates and then, hanging on to each other, walked towards the abandoned tunnel which had been the source and inspiration for so many local stories. They knelt down at the entrance and knocked upon the planks as if they were banging on someone's front door; both of them then began pulling at the wood, gingerly at first but soon with more eagerness and ferocity: one piece came free, and then another, until there was space enough to enter. They sat down upon the ground and gazed at each other: 'Are you going first?'

'Are you?'
'Are *you*?'
'*Are* you?'

Until one of them said, 'You're bigger. You go first'. This was unanswerable: they spat on their hands and touched their thumbs together before the older boy lowered himself through the entry they had made and the other followed.

They stood up in the dark portal, and clutched each other in the manner of those who are in danger of falling. The first boy then tentatively began going down the steps, reaching out for his companion's hand as he did so, and as they descended the sound of their rapid breathing was quite audible in a place which was otherwise silent. When they reached the bottom they paused until their eyes became accustomed to the darkness: a tunnel seemed to appear in

[31]

front of them, although it was of incalculable length, and there were words or drawings on the stones above their heads. The older boy moved a little way into the passage, flattening his right palm against the side although the wall itself was damp and cold, and after six or seven steps he came to a room on the right. They peered in, hesitating while the deeper darkness swirled around them, and slowly there emerged in one corner the outline of a bundle of rags. The older boy started to make his way into this small room when he thought he saw the rags heave and move: something might have been turning in its sleep and he screamed, stepping backward in his fright and knocking the smaller boy to the ground. Was there now a noise coming from within the room, or was it an echo of his scream? But both of them had already scrambled back to the stairs, and were escaping through the aperture they had made. They fell out of the tunnel and then stood up in the shadow of the church, looking in each others' faces for signs of the fear which both of them felt, before running down the gravel path towards the gates and the streets beyond. 'I fell over,' the younger one said when they were once more part of their own world, 'I hurt my knee. Look!' He sat down by the side of the road, and was sick in the gutter. 'You can put some iodine on that,' his friend told him before turning away in the expectation that the other would follow. And the darkness grew like a tree.

*

Thomas was now lying on his bed and, at the time when the two boys were escaping from the tunnel, he was making shadows against the wall with his hands: 'Here is the church,' he whispered to himself, 'And here is the steeple. Open the doors and where are the people?' Then he tired of this game, and turned the page of his book.

He and his mother lived in the upper two storeys of the old house in Eagle Street (beneath them was a dress-making establishment owned by an Indian family). His father, a baker, had died six years before: Thomas remembered a man sitting at the kitchen table, taking up a knife to carve some meat and then falling sideways with a smile upon his face, and his mother with a hand over her mouth. Now he heard the front door opening and then his mother climbing the stairs: 'Thomas!' she called, 'Are you in, Tommy?'. There was a slight quaver in her voice the second time, as if the fact that he did not reply at once meant that in some way he had been harmed. The death of her husband had rendered her timorous; the ground was now made of the thinnest glass through which she could see the abysses beneath her, and she had communicated this fearfulness to her son who always preferred to remain in his small attic room.

During these long summer evenings he would lie on his bed and read, sometimes concealing himself beneath a light cotton sheet which lent the pages an even and gentle glow. As his mother was climbing the stairs, he was reading an historical romance for children entitled *Dr Faustus and Queen Elizabeth*. He had just finished the chapter where the Virgin Queen had sent for the Doctor after she had been informed of his magical powers: for she had been told by a wise man that, if she could unriddle the mystery of Stonehenge, she would bear a child. And so Faustus had sailed to England, only just escaping death as a dark whirlwind threatened to overwhelm his frail bark. And now they were walking together towards the great stones: 'Faith,' exclaimed the Queen with a rueful smile, 'I wish I knew their dark mysteries.' 'Forsooth do not disturb yourself, your majesty,' Faustus replied in an imposing manner, 'I verily do believe that I can unriddle them.' 'Well deuce take you if you cannot,' she replied haughtily. And Thomas had read on quickly, hoping to reach the passage where the Devil takes Faustus into the air and shows him the kingdoms of the world. He had another book beside him, entitled *Some English Martyrs*; he had found it lying discarded at the back of the church, and the first of the stories he had read was of Little St Hugh: that he was 'a child of ten years, the son of a widow. One Koppin, a heathen, enticed him to a ritual house under ground where he was tortured and scourged and finally strangled. Then his body was left there unknown for seven days and seven nights. Immediately Hugh's body was recovered from the pit a blind woman was restored to sight by touching it and invoking the martyr; other miracles followed'. Thomas often gazed at the pictures of the martyrs in this book, with their flesh being carved out by laughing men; their bodies were always thin and yellow but their bowels were very red, and underneath each illustration there was a phrase in Gothic lettering: Prophesy Now, Violent Hands, Devouring Fire, and so on.

His mother had stopped calling his name and was now climbing the second set of stairs to his room; for some reason he did not wish her to see him lying sprawled upon the bed, and so he jumped off it and sat on a chair beside the window. 'How's my Tommy?' she said hurrying towards him and then kissing him on the forehead; he flinched, turning his face away from her, and then pretended to watch something in the street outside in order to account for this gesture.

'What are you thinking about, Tommy?'

'Nothing.'

And then, after a pause, she added, 'It's so cold in this room isn't it?'

But he hardly noticed the cold and, after she had gone downstairs in order to prepare the evening meal, he sat very still in his chair and let the shadows pass across his face. He could hear faint voices from the adjoining houses, and then the chiming of a clock; and he heard, also, the rattle of plates and cups in other kitchens as his mother called for him to come down.

He descended slowly, counting out the stairs so loudly that he might have been hurling abuse; he was shouting out different words as he entered the kitchen, but then stopped abruptly when he saw that his mother was engaged in her unequal battle against the world – a world which, on this evening, adopted the dimensions of the wooden chairs which fell down at her feet, the gas rings of the oven which refused to light, and the kettle that burned her fingers; although growing within this little space there was also, as he knew, his mother's fury at the house and neighbourhood in which she felt herself to be trapped. She had just dropped a packet of butter upon the floor and was running her fingers along the table as she stared at it, when she caught sight of her son standing in the doorway: 'It's all right,' she explained, 'Mummy's just tired'. Thomas bent down to pick up the butter and looked at her shoes and ankles as he did so. 'Look at the dust in here,' she was saying, 'Just look at it!' The sudden anger in her voice disturbed him but, as he stood up from the floor, he asked her in a dispassionate voice, 'Where does dust come from?'

'Oh I don't know, Tommy, from the ground probably.' And as she said this she looked round with increased distaste at the narrow kitchen, before realising that her son was gazing at her and biting his lip in distress. 'I don't know where it comes from, but I do know where it's going to,' and she blew the dust from the table into the air. And both of them laughed before turning their attention to their food: they might have been in competition, for they ate ferociously and did not even glance at each other as quickly and silently they finished their meal. And then Thomas took the empty plates, and carried them in silence to the sink where he began running water over them. His mother gave a little burp, which she did not try to conceal, before asking him what he had done today.

'Nothing.'

'You must have done something, Tommy. What happened at school?'

'I told you, I done nothing.' He never chose to mention the church, since he preferred his mother to believe that he disliked the area as much as she did. At that moment the single bell chimed seven o'clock.

'It's that church again, isn't it?' He kept his back to her and did not reply. 'I told you time and again.' He let the water flow over his fingers. 'I don't like you going there, what with that tunnel and all. It could cave in and then where would you be?' For her the church represented all that was dark and immutably dirty about the area, and she resented the fascination which it obviously held for her son. 'Are you listening to me, young man?'

And then, turning round to look at her, he said, 'I think there's something inside that pyramid. It felt hot today.'

'I'll make you feel hot if you go near it again.' But she regretted the severity of her tone when she saw her son's anxious face. 'It's not good for you to spend so much time on your own, Tommy.' She lit a cigarette and blew the smoke towards the ceiling. 'I wish you was more friendly with the other boys.' He wanted to leave her now and go back to his room, but her dejected expression kept him back. 'I had friends at your age, Tommy.'

'I know. I saw the pictures.' He remembered the photograph of his mother as a young girl, her arm around a friend: both of them had been dressed in white, and it seemed to Thomas to be a painting of a time infinitely remote, a time before he had been thought of.

'Well then.' And a note of anxiety entered her voice again. 'Isn't there someone you want to play with?'

'I don't know. I'll have to think about it.' He examined the table, trying to puzzle out the secret of dust.

'You think too much Tommy, it's not good for you.' Then she smiled at him. 'Do you want to play a game?' She put out her cigarette with a quick movement and took him in her lap, rocking him backward and forward as she chanted a song which Thomas also knew by heart:

> How many miles to Babylon?
> Three score miles and ten.
> Can I get there by candle light?
> Yes, and back again.

And she rocked him faster and faster until he felt dizzy and begged her to stop: he was sure that she would pull his arms out of their sockets, or that he would crash to the floor and be killed. But just as the game had reached its height she let him down gently and, with a sudden and unexpected sigh, rose up to switch on the electric light. And all at once Thomas saw how dark it had become outside: 'I think I'll go up now'. She was looking out of the window at the empty street below: 'Goodnight,' she murmured, 'Sleep tight'. And then she turned round and embraced her son so tightly that he had to struggle to get free while outside, as the amber street lights were illuminated, the local children were playing at catching each other's shadows.

Thomas could not sleep that night, and he was filled with a growing sense of panic as the solitary bell of the Spitalfields church chimed the half-hour and the hour. Once again he contemplated the events in the schoolyard, and in the darkness he imagined other scenes of suffering and humiliation: how the same boys might lie in wait for him, how

[35]

when he passed they would fall upon him and kick him, and how he would not resist until he lay dead at their feet. He whispered their names – John Biscow, Peter Duckett, Philip Wire – as if they were deities to be propitiated. Then he climbed from his bed and leaned out of the open window; from here he could see the silhouette of the church roof, and above it seven or eight stars. In his mind's eye he tried to draw a line between each star, to see what complete figure it might make, but as he did so he felt a pressure on his cheek as if an insect were crawling across it: he glanced down into Monmouth Street, beyond the shed where the coals were kept, and saw what seemed to be a figure in a dark coat looking up at him.

*

It was winter now, and in the late days of October the children of Spitalfields made figures out of old clothes or newspapers and prepared them for the burning. But Thomas spent these evenings in his room, where he was constructing out of plywood and cardboard a model of a house. He used a small penknife to cut windows in its sides, and with his wooden ruler he laid out the plan of the rooms: indeed, so great was his enthusiasm that the little building already resembled a labyrinth. And as he walked to the churchyard in the early afternoon he was considering whether it was necessary to construct a basement: would the model be complete without it, or would it not? He came to the south wall and sat down in the dust, settling against the corner of the buttress in order to reflect upon these matters.

Until he became aware of movement in front of him: he looked up in alarm and pressed himself closer against the great church when he noticed a man and woman walking beneath the trees, which shook in the rising wind. They stopped; the man drank from a bottle before they both settled down upon the earth and lay beside each other. Thomas glared with contempt as they kissed but, when the man put his hand upon her skirt, he grew more watchful. He got up slowly from beside the buttress in order to lie on the ground closer to them, and by the time he had done so the man had taken the woman's breast from her fawn jacket and begun to feel it. Thomas caught his breath, and started rocking himself on the ground in the same rhythm as the man's hand which now worked up and down; he felt a large stone digging in his stomach as he lay sprawled upon the earth but he was hardly aware of the discomfort as the man put his mouth to the woman's breast and kept it there. Thomas's throat was dry and he swallowed several times to try and control his rising excitement; it seemed as if his limbs were growing, like those of a giant, and he was sure that at any moment something would burst from him – he might

[36]

be sick, or he might cry out, and in his alarm he rose to his feet. The man saw his shape against the stone and, grabbing the bottle which was lying by the woman's side, hurled it at Thomas who looked wildly around as it swung in an arc towards him. Then he ran to the back wall of the church, passing the entrance to the abandoned tunnel before he collided with a man who must have been standing there. Without looking up, the boy ran on.

Pleading tiredness he went to bed early that night and, as he lay in his dark room, he could hear the sounds of rockets and flares issuing from the neighbouring streets. He believed that he did not miss such things, but he lay face downward on his bed and put the pillow over his head so that he could not hear them. And once more he watched as the man and woman walked beneath the trees and as they kissed, and now he was taking her breast into his mouth. He rocked upon his narrow bed, his body growing and growing, and he spread out his hands in horror as the ache turned into a stream which he entered and which at the same time left him like blood coming from a wound. When eventually he came to rest, he stared dully at the wall. He did not want to move in case the blood poured from him and soaked the bed, and so he lay quite still in the darkness wondering if he was about to die: just then a rocket rose and exploded in the sky outside his window and, in its instantaneous white light, the plywood model cast an intense shadow on the floor. He started up from his bed in alarm, and then stared down at himself.

When he walked through the streets of Spitalfields on the following morning, the people whom he passed seemed to glance at him in curiosity or amazement, and he was sure that what he had done, or felt, had left some mark upon him. It would have been natural for him now to visit the church and sit beneath its walls, but he could not go back to the spot where he had seen the authors of his woes. He passed its entry two or three times, but then hurried back to Eagle Street with gathering excitement: and his mouth became dry when he entered his own room in order to fling himself down upon the bed. He lay quietly for a moment, listening to his heart beating, and then started tossing up and down with a fierce rhythm.

And then later he went downstairs to stoke up the fire, as his mother had asked him. He turned it around with his poker so that the new coals tumbled into the centre and, as they stirred and shifted in the heat, Thomas peered at them and imagined there the passages and caverns of hell where those who burn are the same colour as the flame. Here was the church of Spitalfields glowing, red hot, and then in his exhaustion he fell asleep. It was his mother's voice which roused him, and in the first few seconds after waking he felt lost.

A succession of bright days did not lift Thomas's spirits; the bright-

[37]

ness disturbed him, and instinctively he sought the shadows which the winter sunlight casts. He felt at peace only in the hour before dawn, when the darkness seemed to give way slowly to a mist, and it was at this hour that he would wake and sit by his window. He had also taken to wandering: sometimes he walked through the streets of London, repeating words or phrases under his breath, and he had found an old square by the Thames in which a sun-dial had been erected. At weekends or in the early evenings he would sit here, contemplating the change which had come over his life and, in his extremity, thinking of the past and of the future.

Then one cold morning he woke and heard the screeching of a cat, although it might have been a human cry; he rose from his bed slowly and went to the window, but he could see nothing. He dressed quickly, combed his hair, and then walked quietly past his mother's bedroom: it was Saturday and she had what she called a 'lie in'. There was a time when he would have crawled into her bed and, as she slept, watched the dust stirring in the shafts of sunlight which entered her room, but now he crept down the stairs. He opened the door and crossed the threshold; as he went out into Eagle Street, the sound of his shoes on the frosted pavement echoed against the houses. Then he passed Monmouth Street and walked beside the church. He could see someone walking in front of him and, although it was not unusual in an area such as this for people to rise and go to their work early, Thomas slowed his pace so that he would not come too close. But as they both turned into Commercial Road the figure ahead, who was wearing some kind of dark top-coat or overcoat, seemed to slow down also – although he gave no sign that he was aware of the ten-year-old boy behind him.

Thomas stopped suddenly and pretended to look into the window of a record shop, although the bright posters and the glossy photographs shining in the neon light now seemed to him as strange as any objects brought up by a diver from the floor of the ocean. He kept himself unnaturally still as he stared at this display, but when after a minute he turned and walked on the other seemed as close as before. Thomas went forward slowly, measuring pace by pace; he might have been engaged in that game where the feet must not touch the cracks in the pavement (or else, children say, you will break your mother's back), except that he never moved his eyes from the black coat of the figure in front of him.

The sun was rising above the houses of Spitalfields, a dull red circle like a reptile's eye, and although the man seemed still to be walking forward he was at the same time coming nearer: Thomas could see quite clearly his white hair, which curled over the collar of his black coat. And then the head turned slowly, and now the face smiles.

Thomas cried aloud, and ran diagonally across the street away from what he had just seen; he was running back in the direction from which he had come, towards the church again, and as he ran he could hear the sound of footsteps chasing him (although, in truth, it might have been the echo of his own running steps). He turned the corner of Commercial Road and then, not looking back, he ran down Tabernacle Close at the end of which were the gates of the churchyard. He knew that he would be able to squeeze his body through the railings in a way that no adult could: as yet the figure in Commercial Road might not have turned the corner, and he might get into the church itself unobserved. As he pushed his way through the gates, he saw the entrance to the tunnel and saw, also, that the planks which had been removed from its front had not yet been replaced. It was to this he ran, as to a place of refuge. He bent down, awkward and breathless, and scrambled through the damp entry: once more he thought he heard movement behind him, and in his panic he sprang forward before his eyes had become accustomed to the darkness. He did not know that there were stairs in front of him and he fell, twisting his leg beneath him as he tumbled down; the light from the opening of the tunnel, which he half-glimpsed as he lay sprawled at the bottom of the steps, then disappeared.

It was the odour of the passage which woke him, since it had crept into his mouth and formed a pool there. He was still lying where he had fallen, one leg tucked beneath his body; the floor of the passage was cold, and he could feel that coldness ascending into him. He seemed to have entered a world of profound silence but, as he raised his head to listen more acutely, straining every sense so that he might better understand his position, he could hear faint murmurs of wind or low voices which might have come from the streets outside or even from the tunnel itself. He tried to rise but fell back upon the ground when the pain returned to his leg: he dared not touch it but stared at it helplessly before leaning back against the damp wall and closing his eyes. Without thought he repeated some words which a boy had once chalked on the blackboard between lessons: 'A lump of coal is better than nothing. Nothing is better than God. Therefore a lump of coal is better than God'. And then he traced his own name with his finger on the cracked and broken floor. He had heard the children's stories about 'the house under ground' but at this moment he felt no particular fear – he had been living in the dark world of his own anxieties, and no infliction of reality could seem more terrible than that.

Now in the dim attenuated light he saw the outlines of the passage ahead of him, and some letters inscribed on the curved roof above him. He turned his head, although it hurt him to do so, but the entrance through which he had come seemed to have disappeared and he was no longer sure exactly where he was. He tried to move forward: he had heard many times, from the adults as well as the children of the neighbourhood, that there was one tunnel in this labyrinth which led straight into the church, and it was in this direction that he must surely try to go. He crawled back into the centre of the passage, and raised himself on his arms: using his elbows for grip, he pulled his body after them while all the time he kept his head up so that he might see what was in front of him. He was moving forward slowly when he thought he heard a sound, a scraping sound, at the end of the passage from which he had just come: he turned his head in terror, but there seemed to be nothing there. Thomas now felt hot despite the coldness of the air; he could sense the sweat running down his forehead and along the side of his nose, and he licked it off with his tongue as it swelled in drops upon his upper lip. The pain in his leg seemed to fluctuate with the beating of his heart so he counted the sequence out loud and then, at the sound of his own voice, he began to cry. He was crawling past small rooms or chambers just outside the range of his ordinary vision and yet he tried to move softly, so as not to disturb those who might dwell in this place. In his agony he forgot that he was still going forward, although his mouth was open and he was gulping for air.

Then a change came over him: the pain in his leg disappeared, and he could feel the sweat drying upon his face. He stopped, shifting himself so that he was once more propped against the cold wall, and then in a clear, calm voice he began to sing a verse which he had learnt many years before:

> Build it up with bricks and mortar,
> Bricks and mortar, bricks and mortar,
> Build it up with bricks and mortar,
> My fair lady.
>
> Bricks and mortar will not stay,
> Will not stay, will not stay,
> Bricks and mortar will not stay,
> My fair lady.

He sang this three times, and his voice echoed down the passages and rooms before fading away in the recesses of stone. He looked at his hands, which had become filthy from his exertions, and he spat on them before trying to wipe them clean on his trousers. Then, when he had forgotten about his hands, he examined the passage with great care, looking all around him with that interested expression children assume when they think that they are being watched. He ran his hand along the wall at each side of him, and just above his head, feeling the

[40]

cracks and patches which had formed there: he clenched his fist and knocked upon the wall, which gave back a muffled sound as if it might contain hollow spaces within itself. Then Thomas gave a great sigh, bowed his head, and fell asleep. He was walking out of the passage; now he was through the upper door and ahead of him was a white tower; now he was standing upon the tower and was poised to dive into the lake. But he was afraid, and his fear became a person. 'Why have you come here?' she said. He turned his back upon her and, as he looked down at the dust upon his shoes, cried, 'I am a child of the earth!' And then he was falling.

When her son had not returned by tea-time, Mrs Hill grew worried. She went up to his room several times, and on each occasion its emptiness disturbed her more: she picked up a book which had been left on a chair, and noticed how carefully her son had inscribed his name on the title page; then she peered down at the model which he had been constructing – her face immediately above the miniature labyrinth. At last she left the room again, closing the door quietly behind her. She went downstairs slowly and sat in front of the fire, rocking herself to and fro as she imagined all of the harm he might have suffered: she could see him enticed into a car by a stranger, she could see him knocked down by a lorry in the road, she could see him falling into the Thames and being carried away by the tide. It was her instinctive belief, however, that if she dwelled upon such scenes in sufficient detail she could prevent them from occurring: anxiety was, for her, a form of prayer. And then she spoke his name aloud, as if she were able to conjure him into existence.

But when she heard the bell of Spitalfields church strike seven, she took her coat and prepared herself to walk to the police station: the nightmare she had always feared had now descended on her. She came out into the street, carelessly dropping her coat at the threshold, but then she turned suddenly and went into the shop beneath her flat: 'Tommy's missing, have you seen him?' she asked the slight, rather nervous Indian girl who was standing behind the counter, 'The little boy, my son?' And the girl shook her head, her eyes wide at the sight of this distraught English woman who had never entered the shop before. 'No boy here,' she said, 'I'm very sorry.' Then Mrs Hill ran into Eagle Street, and the first person she passed was a neighbour: 'Tommy's gone missing!' she shouted, 'My Tommy's gone!' She moved on quickly, the woman following her in sympathy and also in curiosity. 'Mrs Hill's son has gone!' she called out in turn to a young girl who was standing in a doorway, 'Vanished!' And the girl, taking a quick look behind her into the house, went out to her as other women joined the procession following Mrs Hill down Brick Lane: 'It's this place,' she called out to them, 'I've always hated this place!' She was

[41]

half-fainting now, and two of her neighbours caught up with her and helped her to walk. She turned round once only, to look wildly at the tower of the church, but it was already quite dark as the small group of women approached the police station.

When Thomas woke he could no longer move forward: his leg was fixed beneath him and seemed now to have stiffened his entire body, for the slightest motion caused him pain. He stared at the wall ahead of him, and noticed that the darkness was deeper where the stone had crumbled and that the passage now smelt of damp cardboard – like the model which he had been building with the hands which now were so cold and white. He did not want to talk out loud, because his mother had always told him that it was the first sign of madness, but he wanted to make sure that he was still alive. With great pain and deliberation he took out of his left hand pocket a piece of chewing gum, now rolled into a dry ball, and a bus ticket. He read out the words upon it: 'London Transport 21549. This ticket is available from stage no. indicated above and must be shown on demand. Not transferable'. And he knew that, if the numbers on the ticket added up to 21, he would be lucky all month; but he did not seem able to count them at the moment. 'My name is Thomas Hill,' he said, 'and I live at 6 Eagle Lane Spitalfields.' And he put his head upon his knees and wept.

He was in his house again, and his father was leading him downstairs. 'Have you got your ticket?' he was whispering to his son, 'You need your ticket. You have a long way to go.' 'I thought you were dead, Dad.' 'No one is really Dad,' his father was saying when Thomas woke, to find that the pain in his leg had gone and that he no longer felt like crying. The piece of hard gum was still clenched in his hand but, when he placed it in his mouth, the juices of his stomach made him retch. 'Don't mind the smell of the sick,' his father was saying, 'Get into bed now. You're up very late.' The passage was brightly lit and along its sides there were people lying or sitting. They were singing something in unison, although Thomas could only hear the last words which became the refrain:

> If all things were eternal
> And nothing their end bringing,
> If this should be, then how could we
> Here make an end of singing?

They were smiling at him and he walked towards them, arms outstretched, so that they might keep him warm. But he was falling from the tower as someone cried, *Go on! Go on!* and then the shadow came. And when he looked up he saw the face above him.

3

THE FACE above me then became a Voice: *It is a dark morning, Master, and after a fine moonshiny night it is terrible rainy.* And I woke thinking, O God what will become of me? Open the curtains at the Beds feet, Nat (*said I*, smelling my stinking Breath upon the Sheets) and give me Air; then light a Candle quickly, I dream'd of a dark Place last night.

And shall I shut the door, Master, if I open the Window? He takes off my Cap and lays me back upon the Beds head, all the while talking: There is a little Mouse warming itself within the Fender, *says he*, and I have fed it some Milk.

This Boy would feel sorry even for the Stones I break: Damn it, Nat, kill it! *I told him* and he was stopp'd short in his puling Discourse.

I am of your Opinion, *says he*, after a Pause.

Nat Eliot is my Servant, a poor bewilder'd boy whom I keep out of Pitie. He has had the Smallpox, which left him meek, and now he is afraid of every Child and Dog that looks at him. He blushes in Company, or grows Pale and out of Countenance if any one should notice him: so this for me, who must live in a Corner, is a proper Creature. When he first came to me he was afflicted with such a prodigious Stammering that he was seldom able to pronounce one single Word or Syllable without great Agitation and strange Motions in the Face, Mouth and Tongue. But I us'd my Art, and strok'd his Face and cured him: now, when he sits alone with me, he cannot give off gabbering. So on this morning, when I am all over sensible of Pain, he shaved my Head and, since he had me at a stand, talked a mish-mash of Extravagances. You did not eat any thing last night, Master, *says he*, I know it from your Breath that you have not: my Mouse has eaten more than you (and then, remembering my words upon the Mouse, he paus'd). And have you, *he goes on*, forgot what your Mother taught you:

> Beef at Noon,
> Eggs at Night,
> Smile at the Moon
> For the Body is Right.

[43]

And I will give you another Verse, *says I*:

> I've ate Eel-pie, Mother, make my Bed soon
> For I'm sick at heart and shall Die before Noon.

Nat muses a while on this merry Song and then continues in his rushing Fashion: We must all eat, Master, and when you were lock'd in your chamber last night, I know not why and I do not ask, I had two penny worth of Beef and one penny worth of Pudding at the Boiling Cooks over the street yonder. That was the money I had laid by, so you see I am not such a child neither: and when the Cook pressed me to taste another Dish I pushed him off with some Words, Don't you come with that upon me, I told him –

– Nat, *I said*, leave off your idle twittle-twattle. You are magoty-headed.

You are in the right, *he replies*, you are in the right. And he withdraws from me a little with downcast looks.

I have not bin out of my Bed these two weeks, since I was seiz'd on the Street with such a fit of the Gout that I could neither stand nor goe; with the help of a Chair-man I returned to my Lodgings and have lain since in my own Sweat like a Drab. Thus: I have a ganglio form swelling below my left Knee, which will soon become an encystid Tumor as usual in such cases. Also I have a black Spot on the joint of the great Toe of my left foot: the Spot is as broad as a Six-pence and black as a Hat. I know there is no Remedy, for it is the way my Humour is inclin'd: a rich state of Blood loaded with salts, sulphurs and spirituous Particles must at length kindle up a certain fiery Phosphorous which Nature exterminates in a fitt of the Gout. But it is like the gnawing of a Dogge and an actual Flame at the same time, and a man cannot without Horrour think upon this Fire got into his Veins and preying upon his Carcasse.

I call'd last week for a certain Rogers, an apothecary at the corner of Chancery-Lane and Fleetstreet, but when he walked into my Chamber I saw he was a Monkey for, if the language was learned, he who spoke it was Ignorant. Prepare for your Master, *says he* solemnly to Nat, four oyster shells red hot in Cyder: and Nat gaz'd at him in Perplexity as if he had been asked to tell the Stars through the Holes in his Hat. Then, says the Monkey-Doctor sitting at my Bedside, we must put Blisters of cantharides upon the Neck and Feet. And Nat scratch'd himself like a Wherry-man. Raw vapours are imbib'd, *he continues*, thro' the Pores and assimilate some Humour to themselves, so we must throw morbific matter upon the Extremities and this to relieve the Whole by punishing a Part. And I smil'd as Nat sat down in a Tremble.

After I had took his Physic, I made water freely and had a good Stool every day: both were foetid, the water full of clowds and very high-smelling. The Monkey also instructed me to eat sprouts, brocoli, spinage, parsley, turneps, parsneps, selery, lettice, cowcumbers and the like: this being done, I felt relief for three Dayes but I was only crawling out of the Shambles for a while and on the fourth day I could not rise from my Bed because of my Affliction. So now I lye by Day and toss or rave by Night, since the ratling and perpetual Hum of the Town deny me rest: just as Madness and Phrensy are the vapours which rise from the lower Faculties, so the Chaos of the Streets reaches up even to the very Closet here and I am whirl'd about by cries of *Knives to Grind* and *Here are your Mouse-Traps*. I was last night about to enter the Shaddowe of Rest when a Watch-man, half-drunken, thumps at the Door with his *Past Three-a-clock* and his *Rainy Wet Morning*. And when at length I slipp'd into Sleep I had no sooner forgot my present Distemper than I was plunged into a worse: I dream'd my self to be lying in a small place under ground, like unto a Grave, and my Body was all broken while others sung. And there was a Face that did so terrifie me that I had like to have expired in my Dream. Well, I will say no more.

Since I am too Ill to move out of Door I have written to Walter Pyne, inclosing my Instructions for the Churches which are to be dispatch'd with Haste, *viz* Sir Chris. will be with you next week by Tuesday or Wensday, so pray gett all our Accounts in good order and see that Sir Chris. findes noe Confusion through the whole Affair. You must also, Walter, coppy over the great plan of our second Church, in *Lime-house*, and deliver it presently to the Commission: do this on the scale of 10 ft in one inche, and put it in Inke so far as you are certain of it. And write thus at the foote of the Draughte: the Depth from East to West, or from A to C, is 113½ Feet; the Length from North to South, or from E to F, is 154 Feet. Let me hear from you, Walter, when you have done this and I shall wait for your answer with Impatience. And praye minde that the Plummer performes his gutters well. And so fair well for now.

The rest I omit, for many a bitter Pill can be swallowed under a golden Cover: I make no Mencion that in each of my Churches I put a Signe so that he who sees the Fabrick may see also the Shaddowe of the Reality of which it is the Pattern or Figure. Thus, in the church of *Lime-house*, the nineteen Pillars in the Aisles will represent the Names of Baal-Berith, the seven Pillars of the Chappell will signify the Chapters of his Covenant. All those who wish to know more of this may take up *Clavis Salomonis*, Niceron's *Thaumaturgus Opticus* where he speaks of Line and Distance, Cornelius Agrippa his *De occultia philosophia* and Giordano Bruno his *De magia* and *De vinculis in genere* where he speaks of Hieroglyphs and the Raising of the Devilles.

You see there, Nat (for he has come slinking into my Chamber as I write to Walter), you see the great Iron chest by the window with three Locks to it: take this Key and open it. What is in there Master, *says he*, that must be lockd up and Bolted? His Eyes revolved around the Room, and I shoot out a laugh like a Pudding in a Bag: if you could but imagine the various Postures his causeless Fears place him in, you would be a great sharer with me in that Laughter. It is only the Paper to wrap up this Letter, *I told him*, and you must go with it now to my Office. And make haste: it is close by, you Rogue, and I will expect you back again presently.

My Lodgings are in the house of Mrs Best (a Taylor's Widow) in Bear Lane, off Leicester-Fields; it is an old decay'd House, much like its Owner, and for ten shillings a week I have the two upper storeys: a closet, a dining room, and a bed chamber. Nat has his bed below, for I wish no one to be near me when I sleep. The Mistress of the House is a clownish woman, a Relict daubed thicker with Paint than her Sceleton is with Flesh so that she appears very much like a Mossoleum. All her business is with Sisars and Toothpicks, Tweezers, Essences, Pomatum, Paints, Paists and Washes; she has so many Patches upon her Face that she may soon be Pressed to Death like the inhabitants of Newgate. On the first day of my present Sicknesse, she was brought into my Chamber by Nat who knew not what to do for me.

Ah Mr Dyer, *says she*, I see you suffer mightily from the Gout as it was with my husband of dear Remembrance: you do not know the perpetual Watchings, the numberless Toils, the frequent Risings in the Night which Mr Best brought me to. Then she busied herself about my Bedside and gave me, as she said, her best advice: what lies in me, *she whispered*, will be at your Service. She rose to go, but turned like a dry leaf in a wind before reaching the Door: I could not forebear taking notice, *she said*, that you are enamoured of the old Books and does this mean that you have the Poets for Recreation? (I lay back in Pain, which she took for assent.) May I, *she continu'd* in a very familiar Manner, show you the Product of my Idle hours? And with that she went down to her Parlour and brought up with her again several Epitaphs and Elegies of her own composing. Do you wish to hear, Nat Eliot? she ask'd my Boy, feigning to be Coy with me, and as he gaped up at her she spoke thus:

> O Blessed letters; that combine in one
> All ages past; and make one live with all!
> Make us confer with those who now are gone,
> And the dead living unto counsel call!

[46]

There is a want of Sense in that line, *she mutters* before continuing quickly:

> By you th'unborn shall have communion
> Of what we feel, and what does us befall.

Do you like? *said she* fetching a deep Sigh as Nat wept like a Tapster without good liquor. You say true, *he murmured*, you say true and the Relict gave a little satisfied Grin. I was like to have hurled back at her:

> Twas not the Muse but her strong beer that stung
> Her mouth being stopt, the Words came through the Bung.

But I held my peece: I am not yet an ancient Tenent, and can not be merry with her in my Fashion.

It is good Fortune, *Nat said* after she had departed, to have such Company: for what do we know that the Poets may not teach us, and this Mistress can spout well in Rhyme. And why is it, *he went on*, that Rhyme touches my Memory?

Let it touch nothing, *I told him*, or you will be a poor Boy indeed.

But Nat had already gone off in a Dream: Where were you, Master, *he asks*, before I was born and thought of?

I was here and there, *I answered* gazing out of the Window.

But where were you in this City?

I have had so many Dwellings, Nat, that I know these Streets as well as a strowling Beggar: I was born in this Nest of Death and Contagion and now, as they say, I have learned to feather it. When first I was with Sir Chris. I found lodgings in Phenix Street off Hogg Lane, close by St Giles and Tottenham Fields, and then in later times I was lodged at the corner of Queen Street and Thames Street, next to the Blew Posts in Cheapside. (It is still there, *said Nat* stirring up from his Seat, I have passed it!) In the time before the Fire, Nat, most of the buildings in London were made of timber and plaister, and stones were so cheap that a man might have a cart-load of them for six-pence or seven-pence; but now, like the Aegyptians, we are all for Stone. (And Nat broke in, I am for Stone!) The common sort of People gawp at the prodigious Rate of Building and exclaim to each other *London is now another City* or *that House was not there Yesterday* or *the Situacion of the Streets is quite Chang'd* (I contemn them when they say such things! *Nat adds*). But this Capital City of the World of Affliction is still the Capitol of Darknesse, or the Dungeon of Man's Desires: still in the Centre are no proper Streets nor Houses but a Wilderness of dirty rotten Sheds, allways tumbling or takeing Fire, with winding crooked passages, lakes of Mire and rills of stinking Mud, as befits the smokey grove of

[47]

Moloch. (I have heard of that Gentleman, *says Nat* all a quiver). It is true that in what we call the Out-parts there are numberless ranges of new Buildings: in my old Black-Eagle Street, Nat, tenements have been rais'd and where my Mother and Father stared without understanding at their Destroyer (Death! *he cryed*) new-built Chambers swarm with life. But what a Chaos and Confusion is there: meer fields of Grass give way to crooked Passages and quiet Lanes to smoking Factors, and these new Houses, commonly built by the London workmen, are often burning and frequently tumbling down (I saw one, *says he*, I saw one tumbling!). Thus London grows more Monstrous, Straggling and out of all Shape: in this Hive of Noise and Ignorance, Nat, we are tyed to the World as to a sensible Carcasse and as we cross the stinking Body we call out *What News?* or *What's a clock?*. And thus do I pass my Days a stranger to mankind. I'll not be a Stander-by, but you will not see me pass among them in the World. (You will disquiet your self, Master, *says Nat* coming towards me). And what a World is it, of Tricking and Bartering, Buying and Selling, Borrowing and Lending, Paying and Receiving; when I walk among the Piss and Sir-reverence of the Streets I hear, *Money makes the old Wife trot, Money makes the Mare to go* (and Nat adds, *What Words won't do, Gold will*). What is their God but shineing Dirt and to sing its Devotions come the Westminster-Hall-whores, the Charing-cross whores, the Whitehall whores, the Channel-row whores, the Strand whores, the Fleet Street whores, the Temple-bar whores; and they are followed in the same Catch by the Riband weavers, the Silver-lace makers, the Upholsterers, the Cabinet-makers, Watermen, Carmen, Porters, Plaisterers, Lightemen, Footmen, Shopkeepers, Journey-men . . . and my Voice grew faint through the Curtain of my Pain.

Thus did I speak to Nat on the first Day of my Sicknesse and, thinking now on those work men that I mencioned, I see them as they pass by me in the thorow-fare of my Memory: Richard Vining, Jonathan Penny, Geoffrey Strode, Walter Meyrick, John Duke, Thomas Style, Jo Cragg. I speak these Names into the Air and the Tears run down my Face, for I know not what Reason. And now my Thoughts are all suspended and like a Pilgrim moving into the Glare of the Sun I am lost in the wastes of Time.

*

I was in the middle of this earnest Business when Nat comes in, returned from delivering my Letter to Walter, with his *Will you drink a Dish of Tea with your Bread and Butter or will you have a Glass of Ale?* He put me in such Confusion that I would have dismist him with a kick in the Arse, and yet the Particles of Memory gather around me and I am my self again.

And so I may return from this Digression to the Narrative of my trew History: I ought in method to have informed the Reader a few pages ago of my Life as a Street-Boy after my strange converse with Mirabilis, and so I shall go back a little here to where I left off. *I will save you from Ruin, little Faustus* he had said to me, and I have already imparted to you my Reasons for staying with his Assembly in Black Step Lane; for being a Boy pennyless and friendless as I then was, the Key to his Door burned a Hole in my Breeches (as they say) until I imployed it. For altho' my Rambling mood was not yet extinguish'd, it was still my Pleasure to studdye with Mirabilis when I so desired it: he did not press me to stay, nor did he so much as Hint at it, and when the Assembly arrived at Dusk I hasten'd into the Streets and made my self a child of Hazard. There was a Band of little Vagabonds who met by moon-light in the Moorfields, and for a time I wandred with them; most of them had been left as Orphans in the Plague and, out of the sight of Constable or Watch, would call out to Passers-by *Lord Bless you give us a Penny* or *Bestow a half penny on us*: I still hear their Voices in my Head when I walk abroad in a Croud, and some times I am seiz'd with Trembling to think I may be still one of them.

For I was then much like a Glass-Bottle-House Boy, dealing always in the Street dirt: I slept in the days before Winter in Bulk-heads and Shop-doors where I was known (I cou'd not sleep in the House of Mirabilis, where the Noises affrighted me) and in the Winter, when the Plague had abated and the Streets were lighted again, I got into Ash-holes and was the very Figure of a Beggar boy, despicable and miserable to the last degree. Those in their snug Bed-chambers may call the Fears of Night meer Bugbears, but their Minds have not pierced into the Horror of the World which others, who are adrift upon it, know. So those who looked upon me in those past Evil Days shook their Heads and cryed *Poor boy!* or *Tis a Pity!*, but they offred me no Help and let me go: I did not make a Noise then but I laid up all these things in my Heart so that I was as well read in Men as in Books. Truly, said Mirabilis gazing at my Raggs, you are Ship-wracked upon the Isle of Man but do not be downcast; read these Bookes, studdye them well and learn from me, and these Christian Gentlemen who turn their Faces from you will then be Dust under your Feet: when they are consum'd in Flame, the Lords of the Earth will do you no Harm. And thus was I comforted, even though my Portion did seem to be presently one of Confinement and a Gaol.

In this manner I lived from the months August until December when, the Plague almost ceas'd, my Aunt, the sister of my Mother, returned from the town of Watford where she had travelled to escape the Distemper. She began to make enquiries about me in the neighbourhood of Spittle-Fields and, since I was now in the way of strowling abroad in the Streets where I had played as a Child, she soon became acquainted with my sad Condition and thereupon I was had into her House in Coleman-Street. I was now near Fourteen-year-old and she was at a Loss what to do with me for, though she carried fair weather in her Countenance, she was a perfect bundle of Contradictions and would no sooner hit upon a Course than tack herself round and choose another. Nick, *says she* to me, Fetch me that Book and yet let it alone too: but let me see it however, and yet 'tis no great matter either. Her Head was just like a squirrel's Cage, and her Mind was the Squirrel that whirled it round: that I should be bound Apprentice was her first Consideration, but she wearied her self over the question whether it be to a Book-seller, or Toy-man, or Coach-maker. I kept my Peace in this, understanding from Mirabilis that my Fate was already determined, but my Silence only kept this whirligig a spinning: And then again, *says she*, we might go back to the Country, tho' perhaps it is not wise if there is no good Company there, and yet I am all for Quietness.

Her Reflections were soon at a stand, however, for I was only with my Aunt for two month when London was put in to the Oven and the Fire burnt it. It would tire the Reader should I dwell on the *Lamentable Judgment* or *God's Terrible Voyce* (as they call'd it) but I have layed by in Memory how, when the Sun looked red like Blood as it peeped through the Smoke, the People cryed aloud to Heaven, raked in the dung of their rotten Hearts and voiced abroad their inward Filthinesse. As the Houses tumbled upon the Streets with a great roaring Noise, they cryed out *We are undone! We are great Sinners!* and the like: and yet as soon as the Danger was passed, they came back with their

> Hey ho the Devil is Dead!
> Eat, drink, and go merry to Bed!

Thus the Sick confesse to their Contagion only when they are like to Die of it, even tho' they carry their Death with them every where. I saw one Gentlewoman who was burned into a very Emblemme of Mortality: her face, legs and feet were quite consumed to Ashes, the trunk of her Body was much burnt, but her Heart, her filthy Heart, was hanging like a Cole in the midst of it.

My Aunt was in the last stages of Uncertainty. We shall certainly be burnt, *says she* but she could not determine to remove her self and her goods to the open Fields. She ran into the Street and then came back againe: It is a hotte wind, Nick, *she cries*, does it blow this way? I think it does, *she continues* without waiting for my Answer, but perhaps in a little while it might Abate: the Noise is frightful, and yet do I hear it lessen? Hang out your cloathes, *I told her*, and the winde will dry them. For I had no fear of the Flames: they were not for me, as Mirabilis had prophesied, and the Fire came to a Stop at the lower end of Coleman-Street. At which my Aunt rejoyced exceedingly, and complimented herself upon her Resolution.

Little of the City remayned save part of Bread and Bishop-gate Street, all Leadenhall Street, and some of the adjacent Lanes about Algate and Cretchett Fryers. With the old Houses of Timber gone, new Foundations could be layed – and it was for this Reason that I soon came to Stand upon my own Legs. For I conceeved a great Fancy to become a Mason, which occurred to me in the following Fashion: I returned after the Fire to the House of Mirabilis in Black Step Lane (which had been saved from the Flames) and, meeting there my good Master, asked his Counsel now that the City had been laid waste. You will build, *he replied*, and turn this Paper-work house (by which he meant the Meeting-place) into a Monument: let Stone be your God and you will find God in the Stone. Then he pickt up his dark Coat, and in the dusk of the Evening departed away whither I never saw him afterwards.

But to make short this part of my Discourse: my Aunt having no Objection, and the Trade much in need of fresh Hands after the Fire, I was put out as a Mason's Apprentice to one Richard Creed. He was recommended as a Master capable of instructing me, and indeed he was a sober and honest Man. My Aunt could in no wise advance any Money for me, and therefore it was agreed that I should be taken as an Apprentice without Money on condition that I should serve for a while in his House in Ave Mary Lane, near Ludgate Street and by St Pauls Church: my Master promising to teach me the Art and Mysteries of his Trade, the which Promise was fulfill'd. And so fourteen years of my Life were run when I took my present Course, and yet such is the power of Memory that I am to this day troubled, and my Dreams filled with concern, often times imagining that I am still bound to my said Master, and that my Time will never be out. And it is true yet of Time, tho' in quite another sense.

Mr Creed was a pritty learned man and, for the two years which I served in his House as a Factotum so much as a Prentice, he very readily allowed me to use the Library in his private Closet. Here I read Vitruvius his *De Architectura* but newly translated, and I was mov'd exceedingly when I saw in its Ninth Book the pyrammide of stone with the little Cell at its top, and this Inscription at the bottome of the Page: O pigmy Man, how transient compared to Stone! And in Master Freart his *Paralell of Architecture*, in a translation of Mr Evelyn, I saw the engraveing of a very antient Sepulture, with Pyrammides beyond, buried in a wild and uncultivated Place: that Figure so impress'd it self upon my Mind that I have been in a manner walking towards it all my Life. Then I peered into Wendel Dietterlin his *Architectura*, and there were unveiled to me the several Orders: of the Tuscan, which is now mine own, I was then mov'd by its Strangeness and Awefulness; the obscured Shapes, the Shaddowes and the massie Openings so inchanted my Spirit that when looking on them I imagined my self to be lock'd in some dark and Enclosed space. The heavinesse of Stone did so oppress me that I was close to Extinction, and I fancied that I could see in the Engraver's lines the sides of Demons, crumbled Walls, and half-humane Creatures rising from the Dust. There was some thing that waited for me there, already in Ruines.

Thus did I learn of Architecture and, appriz'd that workmen could advance to the degree of Architect in these times, I coveted that office for my self: to become the *Structorum Princeps*, as Mr Evelyn has it, the ingenious Artificer who must be learned in Astrologie and Arithmetick, Musick no less than Geometry, Philosophy as well as Opticks, History no less than Law, was my set Purpose. But you cannot build out of Books, unless it be Castles in the Air, and I decided to step into the World for further Information: I listen'd to the Discourse of the work men in my Master's yard (next St Pauls on which he was then imployed) and held them in Conversation concerning matters of Practice; I also sought occasions to visit the brick-burnings in Whitechappell and here I learned of the earth which lies beneath London: these and like Matters I laid up in my Head, for there was no knowing to what Use they might come.

My Master, as I said, was set to work upon St Pauls after the Fire but the first time that ever I saw Sir Chris. Wren was in my Seventeenth year when I was working in the Yard. Sir Chris. walked in and, tho' even then he was a person of the last Importance, being both Surveyor-General and principall Architect for rebuilding the whole City, I did not know his Face. He had come into the Yard to inquire after the new Stone which had been promis'd but, my Master being absent for a Moment, Sir Chris. talked in a familiar manner to the Clerke who accompanied him. He pointed to some stone saying, This is not in good condition, it is mere Ragg: do you see how the Demand has debased the Materialls?

That is a softer Stone, *says I*, and is about to be placed in Shelter: but it is no Ragg for, look, there are no flint beds nor clay holes near the face.

Then he gave me one of his sharp Looks: where is the Reigate stone, *he asks* (for it was this which he had order'd).

I do not know why you wish for Reigate, *I replied* (thinking him a simple Citizen), for tho' you may be able to cut through it like Wood it

[52]

takes in Water: good Stone ought to defend itself by gathering a Crust. The better Stone, *I went on*, is out of Oxfordshire, down the river from the Quarries about Burford. But if you will wait for my Master –

– No need of a Master with such an Apprentice, *says Sir Chris.* smiling at his Clerk. Then turning to me quickly he ask'd, Can you name Stones? and glanced at my Hands to see what rough Usage they had had in this Trade.

Willingly I expressed to him what I had already learned by Rote: Free-stone, *says I*, and also Brick, Ragg, Flint, Marchasite, Pibble, Slate, Tile, Whetstone, Touch-stone, Pumice, Emry, Alabaster –

– Hold! *he exclaimed*, There is more Method in you than in Vitruvius.

I take my Method, *I replied*, from Master Dietterling.

I don't remember the Book was translated into English that you mention, *says he* taking a Step backward.

No, *I answer'd* a little abashed, but I have looked upon the Pictures.

At this time my Master was come back into the Yard and Sir Chris. (whom I still did not know) said easily to him, Well, Dick Creed, here is a Boy who will teach you some new Tricks. And my Master assured him that I was but a simple Prentice. Well, *says Sir Chris. again*, Master Palladio was a stone mason and he was called lapicida long before he was ever known as architetto. And then he turned to me and tweaked me by the Chin: And what of Roofs, young architetto?

As to Roofs, *I replied*, good Oak is certainly the best and next to Oak good yellow Deal.

Sir Chris laughed, and then paced around the Yard before coming to rest with us again. Can he read and write, Dick? *he asks* pointing at me. And my Master says, Like a Scholar. So Nature and Art combine in One, *he cries* and his clerk smil'd for it was an Allusion.

In a word, Sir Chris. was much taken with me, and earnestly entreated my Master that I should be released into his Charge; to this my Master readily agreed, as a token of his respect for Sir Chris. (and no doubt with the expectation of being repaid in some other Coin). And thus it was that I became Sir Chris. his Gentleman, and after that his Clerke, until in later time I became Clerke of the Works and now as I am, Assistant Surveyour. And yet it was no easy Road, for at once I was whirl'd into a Multitude of Business: Read and approve these Calculations for me, Sir Chris. would say, and when he knew I was master of one Art he would lead me to another; by degrees I was so advanc't in my employment that many of the Despatches concerned my Business, *viz.* Mr Surveyour is also desir'd to send Mr Dyer to Visit the Quarrys in Kent and bring an account of the Rate of Materialls; Mr Dyer also to inquire into the Prices of brick, wainscott, timber and other Materialls; Mr Dyer to prepare a Draught of the Hospitall in perspective by direction of Mr Surveyour; Mr Dyer to put the work of the Sewers immediately in Hand; Mr Dyer to hasten the finishing of the plate of the Ground Plan.

You may see from this Catalogue that I ingraved Draughts for new intended Buildings and coppyed Designes on Paper, which tasks I performed with the utmost Diffidence since I had not been train'd up in that Direction. But when I left them with trembling Hands upon his writing Table, in expectation of hard Words, he merely glanced at them and then wrote, I doe approve of this Designe: Chris. Wren Kt. He used to do his own exact Measure at the beginning, but he was at last overcome by the Multitude and Weight of his own Thoughts: I saw how he cooled little by little and grew weary (some times he became drunken after Dusk, and sat in a Stupor until I led him home). And when he had overwhelm'd himself with other Work so that he could do no more in the Office, I devised my own Plann for the City edifices on which he was engaged; I toild for every Line till I sweated and then when I asked him how he liked it, he said very well as far as he looked but that he was so full of Business that he had but little Time to spare. But then he repented of his Briskness, and guided me forward until I became a proper Master.

It was in these early Years that Sir Chris. his Endeavours were all for St Pauls, but lately reduc'd to Ruines: there was scarce a course of Stones laid, over which he did not walk during the great Construction, and I would follow him with a bundle of Planns tucked beneath my Arm. See here, Nick, *he would say*, unless we take care these Compass arches will not press uniformly. He would bite his under-lip at this but then, when any thing pleased him well, he would cry *Hum!* and clap me upon the Shoulder. He would allwaies climb to the uppermost heights of the Scaffolding and when I held my self back (for it is a dreadfull thing to look down Praecipices) he would beckon me onward and laugh; then quite fresh still he would descend to the Ground and jump down into the Foundations, to emerge bespattered all over with Dust like a Postillion.

He was alwaies agreeable with the work men, and minded me to note their Business for my own Instruction. And so I watched the Carpenters setting up Scaffolds, or makeing Sheds and Fences; the Sawyers cutting Timber; the Labourers clearing away Stones and Rubbidge, or wheeling up Baggs of Lime to the Mortar Heaps; the Masons sawing off Stones or working and setting them; the Plumbers laying Pipes. Very soon I was constantly attending the Work without Sir Chris.: I alone was giving directions to the Men, measuring all the Masons' work (my old Master, Mr Creed, used to welcome me with a sally), keeping account of what Stores were delivered to the Storekeeper, taking care that the Carpenters and Labourers who worked by the Day were imployed as directed and kept to their Business. For it was very usual to see ten men in a Corner very busie about two men's work, taking much Care that every one should have due Proportion of the Labour. One wonderful piece of Difficulty, for which the whole Number had to perform, was to drag along a Stone of about Three Hundred Weight in a Carriage in order to be hoisted upon the Moldings of the Cuppola. And yet I dared not speak harshly to them, for if you find never so just a Fault with an English workman he will reply, Sir I do not come hither to be taught my Trade: I have served an Apprenticeship and have wrought before now with Gentlemen who have been satisfied with my Work. And then unless you soothed him, he would cast down his Tools in a Pother. I would instruct Sir Chris. in what had passed, still glowing with Rage and Indignation, and he would say Poh! Poh! all will be well, all will be well.

And all Manner of Things shall be well for now my Gout is abated, and I am return'd to the Office where Walter is saying, Why do you Sigh? I did not Sigh, *I told him*. But then this Thought presents itself to me: do I make Noises that I do not hear, and do I sigh, when I look back on the Years that have passed and which are so much like a Dreame?

For when I was first with Sir Chris. I could not but wonder at the strange Alteration in my Life, from being a meer Itinerant Mendicant of a Boy: it had all fallen out as Mirabilis had prophesied, and I doubted not but that he had in some way determined it. So I did not leave off my Visitings to Black Step Lane, tho' without Mirabilis the Assembly were in a very poor State and it fell to me to decipher his Books: which I did willingly enough, now that I was come (as I suppos'd) to Man's Estate. In the mean time I said nothing of these Matters to Sir Chris. who would have reviled me at a hard Rate and treated me as a meer Merry-Andrew. He liked to destroy Antient things: sad and wretched Stuff, he called it, and he us'd to say that Men are weary of the Reliques of Antiquity. He spoke in their stead of Sensible Knowledge, of the Experimentall Learning and of real Truths: but I took these for nothing but Fopperies. This is our Time, *said he*, and we must lay its Foundacions with our own Hands; but when he used such Words I was seiz'd with this Reflection: and how do we conclude what Time is our own?

As it turned out, Sir Chris. his own Perswasions were hurled against him, when it came to his Notice that he was building St Pauls Church upon an ancient Ruine. For when we open'd the Ground next to the Scite of the North Porticoe, some Stones were found which on further Inspection, after digging down sufficiently and removing what Earth lay in the way, appeared to be the Walls and Pavement of a Temple: close by was found a little Altar, on hearing of which Sir

[55]

Chris. laughed and whisper'd to me, Let us make a Pilgrimage to the Pitte!

On our Arrival he heaved himself into the Foundacions and there Rummaging among a great many old Stones he found an earthern Lamp – a very mean work, *says he*, and throws it back among the Rubbidge. Then the next Morning the Image of a God was dug out of the Ground, being girt about with a Serpent and bearing a Wand in his Hand (the Head and Feet being broken off). It brings to mind, *Sir Chris told me*, an Observation which Erasmus made: that on the day of St Pauls conversion it was the custom in London to bring in procession to the Church a wooden Staff in which was cunningly wrought a Snake or a Serpent; what think you of that, Nick, since you allwaies have your Head stuck in old Books? And I said nothing, for who can speak of the Mazes of the Serpent to those who are not lost in them? But that some may see and understand an Object, others meerly neglecting it, you have an Instance in Mr John Barber who would not stir from his bed at the Black Boy in Pater-Noster-Row: he thought all the superficies of this terrestrial Globe was made of thin and transparent Glass, and that underneath there lay a Multitude of Serpents; he died laughing, at the Ignorance and Folly of those who could not see the true Foundacions of the World. Thus I also dismiss the narrow Conceptions of this Generation of Writers who speak with Sir Chris. of a new Restauration of Learning, and who prattle something too idly on the new Philosophy of Experiment and Demonstration: these are but poor Particles of Dust which will not burie the Serpents.

And so while others were mouthing such fantasticall and perishable Trash, I kept to my studdy of the antient Architects, for the greatness of the Antients is infinitely superior to the Moderns. It was my good Fortune that in Sir Chris. his Library there was a great Jumble of Books which he had taken up and then tossed aside, so it was here that I examined Cambden's *Remains* and Lisle his *Saxon Monuments*, Nicholas Caussin's *De Symbolica Aegyptiorum Sapientia* and the universall Kircher his *Oedipus aegyptiacus* in which he concludes that the Obelisks are the tables of esoterick knowledge. *And as I write this Walter Pyne takes an exact Account, from my Direction, of my Historicall Pillar beside Limehouse Church: you may hear his Pen scratch*. In Kircher, also I discover'd planns of the Pyramiddes, which gave Demonstration of how the Shaddowe is thrown by the Obelisk across the Desart land, *and now Walter drops Inke across his Paper*. Thus the Subjects of my Thought were the miraculous Memphitic pyramides which the Aegyptians erected to the memory of their Gods who were Kings also: the Summities of these artificial Mountains were so high that from them, as from some august and terrible Throne, they seemed to the People to be reigning after their Death. *This Plan is Ruined from the*

Staine, says Walter but I make no Answer to him. Thus in Sir Chris. his Library I reflected upon these stupendious Works, vast and of a manner Colossale, and of the curious Signs cut upon their Stone. I gaz'd upon the Shaddowes of fallen Collumnes until my Spirit itself became a very Ruine and so, as I proceeded further in my Books, it was a surety that I studdied part of my self. *And Walter leaves the Office now, muttering to himself and walking to the River in order to clear his beating Mind and as I watch him I see* my self once more in my youthful Dayes when Sir Chris. found me in his Library: Those who hasten to be wise, Nick, *said he* looking in on me, have some times lost their own Wits. Get thee to a Privy, I whispered to myself as he went away chuckling.

One remarkable Passage concerning our Relations I was like to have forgot: which was our Discourse in the shaddowe of Stone-henge. Sir Chris., who as I said confus'd antique with antick, was not inclined to make so hard a Journey (it being more than eighty-five miles from London) but I perswaded him otherwise with an account of the Stones: some, by report, were of a lightish blew with a glister as if minerall were amongst them, and some of them again were of a greyish colour and were speckled with dark green. He had a Fancy to set such Stones in the Fabrick of St Pauls – since the Quarries of Hasselborough and Chilmark were close to the border of the Salisbury plain, and the great quarry at Aibury not many miles distant, I put it into his Head that we might discover more of the same curious Stones there. I am no great Traveller, having never been above three miles from London before, but I could not be appeas'd until I had seen this bowing place, this High Place of worship. Master Sammes believes it to be Phoenician, Master Camden thinks it belongs to the idol Markolis, and Mr Jones judges the Structure to be a Roman work consecrated to Coelus; but I got its Imagery by Heart (as they say): the true God is to be venerated in obscure and fearful Places, with Horror in their Approaches, and thus did our Ancestors worship the Daemon in the form of great Stones.

On the day of our Journey I waited on Sir Chris. at his House by the Office; *Coming, coming* he calls out to me from above the Stair-head, *I'm only seeking my Ruffles* and I hear his quick Steps echo through the Bed-chamber. Presently he is down like the Wind, out the Door, and into White-hall, settling his Wigg as he goes: then we coach'd it to the Standard in Cornhill, where the Stage for the London to Lands-End Road waited. What Company have we for the Coach? *he asks* of a Servant of the Inn.

Two only, and both Gentlemen, *he replies*.

I am pleased at this, *Sir Chris. says* to us both, but he was not so pleased neither: when he rode in a London coach, one arm would be out of the Coach on one side and the other on the other, but he was

[57]

sore pressed for so much Room on this Journey. He took the place fronting to the Coach-box and clapped his Cloak-bag beneath his Legs: Well, *says he* smiling civilly upon the Company, I hope no one will smoke Tobacco since my Clerk here grows melancholy upon its Vapours. And I dared not deny it, for who knows but it may be true?

We pass'd along Cornhil, Cheapside, St Pauls Church-Yard (where Sir Chris. leaned out of the Coach, looking piercingly), Ludgate Hill, Fleet Street, The Strand, Hay-Market, Pickadilly (where Sir Chris. took out his Linnen and blew a Piece of Jelly from his Nose into it) and then past the Suburbs thro' Knightsbridg, Kensington, Hammersmith, Turnham Green and Hounslow: the Coach-man was driving at full career, as is too usual with them, but Sir Chris. says to me with a look of inexpressible satisfaction, You must acquire, Nick, the right Knack of hunouring the Coach's motion. And then he smiled upon our fellow-Travellers again. At this point, crossing Baker Bridge with the Powder-mills on the right and the Sword-mills on the left, we were jolted almost to Death by a number of large Holes: Don't spill us, *Sir Chris. calls up*, and then he gets out his Pocket-Book for his own Calculations, at which he continu'd until he slept. Thus on thro' Staines and across the Thames by means of a Wooden-bridge to Egham and, after an easie Descent by the New England Inn on the left, we crossed over Bagshot Heath and came to Beugh-wood and Bagshot.

Sir Chris. had now woken from his Doze and was engaged in familiar Conversation with one of the Companions of our journey: he had taken off his Wigg and played with it on his Lap as he talked, plucking at it as if it were a Goose. He loved to act the Schoolmaster with those unskilled in his Arts and, since he did not so much as notice me as he continued with his Discourse, I was able to fall into a Sleep until he woke me with his *Nick! Nick! We are come to a Halt! We are come to a Halt!*

We had arriv'd at Blackwater, a small place where we took Ayre by an Inne and, having need to Shit, I used the House of Office. Here it was agreed that we would Stick for the Night: Sir Chris. was all for going on, but he saw that the Journey had brought on me a small Feaver (since I sweat when I am away from home). Time is pressing, *says he*, but Nature presses on you more. He laughed then, and was inexpressibly merry after with the Travellers at Supper. When we climbed up to our Chamber at last, I very weary, he scanned the *Observations and Rules for Guests* affix'd to the Wall: Remember ye, *says he* intoning the Words as if they were meer Foolishness, that ye are in this world as in an Inne to tarry for a short space and then to be gone hence. At night when you come to your Inne thanke God for your Preservation: next morning pray for a good Journey. We must be on our knees then, Nick, *he goes on*, but I fear more from the Lice in these Beds than from the Roads. Then you must pray to the God of Lice, *I replied*, and hurried down to the Yard to vomit up my Meal.

On the next Day we passed thro' Hartley Row, eventually descending to Basingstoke, and it was when we had reached Church-Oakly that Sir Chris. desired to set up a Magneticall Experiment in the Coach. The other Travellers being willing to observe his Art, they tucked their Shooes up beneath them to give him more Room upon the Floor; he took out the sphericall Compass from his Cloack-bag and produc'd like a Conjuror a peece of Plane Board. The Magnet was half immersed in the Board, till it was like a Globe with the Poles in the Horizon, and he was about to bring on his steel-filings (the others looking on Transfix'd) when of a sudden there was a terrific Quake: going fast over a Bridge close to Whitchurch, the Driver had turned short and two of the Horses were over the Bridge; only the wheel horse hanging dead was able to keep the Coach from going over, as I lay tumbled on the Floor with my Fellows. Sir Chris., trying his Agility to get out of the window, was like to have jumped into the River as I watched but instead he dropp'd into the Dust. I thought it to be a terrible Fall, but he stood up with a good grace and looked puzzled at the Ground: then he seemed to have a need to Make Water and unbutton'd his Breeches in sight of us. One by one we escap'd through the same Window, and then were forced to sit in the Cold till a Team of Horses could be sent from Whitchurch to pull the Coach away from the Bridge; that night we stopp'd at a wretched Inn where we were smirked at by the Hostess. You could not have Prayed last night, *said I*, as the Observations recommended. No, *he replied*, and I have lost my Compass as a Penance for it.

The latter part of our Journey from the entrance of Wiltshire into Salisbury was very rough and abounded with Jolts, the Holes we were obliged to go through being very many and some of them Deep; and so it was with much Relief that we left the Coach at Salisbury and hired two Horses for the road across the Avon to the Plain and Stone-henge. When we came to the edge of this sacred Place, we tethered our Horses to the Posts provided and then, with the Sunne direct above us, walked over the short grass which (continually cropt by the flocks of Sheep) seemed to spring us forward to the great Stones. I stood back a little as Sir Chris. walked on, and I considered the Edifice with steadinesse: there was nothing here to break the Angles of Sight and as I gaz'd I opened my Mouth to cry out but my Cry was silent; I was struck by an exstatic Reverie in which all the surface of this Place seemed to me Stone, and the Sky itself Stone, and I became Stone as I joined the Earth which flew on like a Stone through the Firmament. And thus I stood until the Kaw of a Crow rous'd me: and yet even the

[59]

call of the black Bird was an Occasion for Terrour, since it was not of this Time. I know not how long a Period I had traversed in my Mind, but Sir Chris. was still within my Sight when my Eyes were clear'd of Mist. He was walking steadily towards the massie Structure and I rushed violently to catch him, for I greatly wished to enter the Circle before him. I stopped him with a Cry and then ran on: when Crows kaw more than ordinary, *said I* when I came up to him all out of Breath, we may expect Rain. Pish, *he replied*. He stopped to tye his Shooe, so then I flew ahead of him and first reached the Circle which was the Place of Sacrifice. And I bowed down.

Master Jones says it is erected on the Cubit measure, *says Sir Chris.* coming after me and taking out his Pocket-Book, and do you see, Nick, its beautifull Proportions?

It is a huge and monstrous Work, *I answered* standing straight, and it has been called the Architecture of the Devil.

But he paid no heed to me: They must have used tall trees for Levers, *he continu'd* squinting up at the Stones, or they discover'd the art of ordering Engines for the raising of Weights.

Some said Merlyn was the Father, *I replied*, and raised these Stones by the hidden Mysteries of Magick.

Sir Chris. laughed at this and sat upon the Stone in the inner Circle. There is an old rhyme, Nick, *says he*, which goes thus:

> This Fame saies, Merlyn to perfection brought
> But Fame said more than ever Merlyn wrought.

And he lean'd forward with a Smile.

You are sitting on the Altar Stone, *I said*; and he jumped up quickly like one bitten. Do you see, *I continu'd*, how it is of a harder Stone and designed to resist Fire?

I see no Scorch marks, *he replied*: but then he wandred among the other Stones as I recall'd another merry Verse:

> Will you wake him?
> No, not I,
> For if I do
> He's sure to Cry.

When we were not close about each other I could talk freely again: For these are all places of Sacrifice, *I call'd out*, and these Stones are the Image of God raised in Terrour!

And Sir Chris. replied in a loud Voice: The Mind of Man is naturally subject to Apprehensions!

Upon this I told him that Peter della Valle, in his late Travels to the

Indies, writes that at Ahmedabad there is a famous Temple wherein there is no other Image but a little column of Stone – named Mahadeu which in their language signifies the Great God. And that there are such structures in Africa, being Temples dedicated to Moloch. Even the Egyptian name Obelisk, *I said*, means consecrated Stone.

And he answer'd: Ah Master Dyer, as the Prophets say, the old Men shall dream Dreames and the young Men shall see Visions and you are young still.

The skie was getting wonderful Dark with a strong Winde which swirled around the Edifice: Do you see, *I said*, how the Architraves are so strangely set upon the heads of the Upright stones that they seem to hang in the Air? But the winde took my words away from him as he crouched with his Rule and Crayon. Geometry, *he called out*, is the Key to this Majesty: if the Proportions are right, I calculate that the inner part is an Exagonall Figure raised upon the Bases of four Equilaterall Triangles! I went up to him saying, Some believe they are Men metamorphosised into Stone, but he payed no Heed to me and stood with his Head flung back as *he continu'd*: And you see, Nick, there is an Exactness of Placing them in regard to the Heavens, for they are so arranged as to estimate the positions of the Planets and the fixed Starres. From which I believe they had magneticall compass Boxes.

Then the Rain fell in great Drops, and we sheltered beneath the Lintel of one great Stone as it turned from gray to blew and green with the Moisture. And when I lean'd my Back against that Stone I felt in the Fabrick the Labour and Agonie of those who erected it, the power of Him who enthrall'd them, and the marks of Eternity which had been placed there. I could hear the Cryes and Voices of those long since gone but I shut my Ears to them and, to keep away Phrensy, stared at the Moss which grew over the Stone. Consider this, *I told Sir Chris.*, the Memphitic pyramid has stood about three thousand and two hundred years, which is not as long as this Edifice: but it was twenty years in building, with three hundred and sixty thousand men continually working upon it. How many laboured here, and for how long? And then I went on after a Pause: the Base of the pyramidde is the exact size and shape of Lincolns-Inn-Fields, and I have some times in my Mind's Eye a Pyrammide rising above the stinking Streets of London. The sky had cleared as I spoke, the clowds rowled away, and as the Sun struck the Ground I looked towards Sir Chris. But he seemed altered in Feature: he had heard nothing of my Matter but sat leaning his Head back upon the Stone, pale as a Cloth and disconsolate to a strange Degree. I lay no Stress upon the Thing called a Dream, *he said*, but I just now had a Vision of my Son dead.

It was Evening now, and as the sloping Rays of the Sunne shone on the ground beyond the Stones, we could easily distinguish the sepulchral Tumuli which lie in great Numbers around there; and this Phrase occurred to me as I looked upon them: the Banks where wild Time blows. At the sight of the Shaddowes which Stone-henge now cast upon the short Grass, Sir Chris. cleared up his Countenance: Well you see Nick, *says he*, how these are Shaddowes on a known Elevation to show the equal Hours of the Day. It is easy to frame the Pillars that every Day at such a Time the Shaddowes will seem to return, *he continued*, and I am glad to say that Logarithms is a wholly British art. And out pops his Pocket-Book again as we made our Path towards our Horses which were quietly munching upon the Grass. I shall subjoyn as a Corollary to the foregoing Remarks that Sir Chris. his Son died of a Convulsive Fitt in a foreign Land, the which News we did not receive until several Months after the Events here related.

And now these Scenes return to me again and, tho' here in my Office, I am gone backward through Time and can see the Countenance of Sir Chris. as once it was in the shaddowe of Stone-henge. Truly Time is a vast Denful of Horrour, round about which a Serpent winds and in the winding bites itself by the Tail. Now, now is the Hour, every Hour, every part of an Hour, every Moment, which in its end does begin again and never ceases to end: a beginning continuing, always ending.

I have that Sentence now, *says Walter* turning to face me.

I glanced up, rubbing my Eyes: Then read it back to me, you, you –

– But he interrupts with his Recitation: The great Tower at the West End of the Church at Limehouse is advancing, tho' the Masons have been in want of Portland Stone, which has somewhat hindered its Progress.

That is finely Put, *said I* smiling at him, but go one Inch further with this: There is nothing else in hand save the Clearing of the Earth and Rubbidge from under the Vaults. Your honourable Servant, Nicholas Dyer.

That is All?

That is All.

To explain this Matter, and to wind up Time so that I am returned to my present State: Beside my Church at Limehouse there had antiently been a great Fen or Morass which had been a burying-place of Saxon times, with Graves lined with chalk-stones and beneath them earlier Tombs. Here my work men have found Urns and Ivory Pins once fasten'd to wooden Shrouds, and beside them Ashes and Skulls. This was indeed a massive Necropolis but it has Power still withinne it, for the ancient Dead emit a certain Material Vertue that will come to inhere in the Fabrick of this new Edifice. By day my House of Lime will catch and intangle all those who come near to it; by Night it will be one vast Mound of Shaddowe and Mistinesse, the effect of many Ages before History. And yet I had hot and present Work on hand, for I was in want of the Sacrifice to consecrate this Place: the Observations of Mirabilis upon the Rites, which I explained further back, are pertinent to this Matter; but this onely by the way.

I have built my Church in Hang-Mans-Acre, by Rope-Makers-Field and Vyrgyn-Yard, near which Ground lay a Congregation of Rogues or Vagabonds who lived by the common Sewer which runs into the Thames. This Settlement of Sturdy Beggars or Strowling Men (whose Clothes smell as rankly as Newgate or Tyburn as their Countenances speak of Decay and Sicknesse) was a source of Contentment to me, for these counterfeit Aegyptians (as they are call'd) are Instances of Vengeance and Ill Fortune, the Church being their Theatre where they may become Objects for our Meditation. It is common in speaking to them to give them the title of *Honest Men* for they are indeed the Children of the Gods, and their Catch goes thus:

> Hang Sorrow and cast away Care
> For the Devil is bound to find us!

They are so hardened in this sort of Misery that they seek no other Life: from Beggaring they proceed to Theft, and from Theft to the Gallows. They know all the Arts of their dismal Trade, and tune their Voices to that Pitch which will raise Compassion with their *God bless you Master* and *May Heaven reward you Master; Do you have a half-penny, a farthing, a broken Crust*, they cry, *to bestow upon him that is ready to Perish?* When I was a Street-boy and slept in Holes and Corners I became acquainted with the miserable Shifts of this Life: in our great City there are whole Fraternities of them living together, for even these forlorn Wretches subsist with a sort of Order and Government among themselves. They are indeed as perfect a Corporation as any Company in England – one scowrs one Street (as I observ'd at the time) and another another, none interloping on the Province, or Walk as they call it, that does not belong to them. They are a Society in Miniature, and will nurse up a brood of Beggars from Generation to Generation even until the World's end. And thus their place is by my Church: they are the Pattern of Humane life, for others are but one Step away from their Condition, and they acknowledge that the beginning and end of all Flesh is but Torment and Shaddowe. They are in the Pitte also, where they see the true Face of God which is like unto their own.

I had gone to Limehouse in the afternoon to Survey for my self the south-western corner of the Foundacions which was afflicted by too much Dampnesse; I was musing upon this Matter, taking a Path towards the River, when I came close against the Settlement of

[63]

Beggars which consisted of as many Ragged Regiments as ever I saw mustered together. I walked a little away from them, to get the Stink from my Nostrils, when I encountered by the side of a muddy Ditch a sad and meagre Fellow who kept his Head upon his Breast. When I stood beside him, my shaddowe stretching across his Face, he looked up at me and muttered as if by Rote, Good your Worship cast an Eye of Pity upon a poor decay'd Tradesman. He was reduced to the utmost Extremity, wearing nothing but old Shreds and Patches like a Stall in Rag-Fair.

What was your Trade? *I asked him*.

I was a Printer in Bristol, Master.

And you fell into Debts, and were forced to Break?

Alas, *said he*, the Disease that afflicts me is far different from what you conceeve of it, and is such as you cannot see: my State is one of fearful Guiltinesse from which I can never Break.

I was much taken with his Words, for he had come like a Bird into my Lime-House, and I sat my self down beside him. For a half-penny, *he continued*, I might read you the Book of my Life? And I assented. He was a little man and had a high quavering way of Talk: his Eyes could not look at me and stared every where but in my Face. And as I sat with my Hand beneath my Chin he narrated his History in short, plain Words as if he had been reduced to the State of a meer Child through his Miseries (and this Thought came to me as he spoke: need the Sacrifice be a Child, and not one who has become a Child?).

This was his Wandring Life as he related it to me: He had set up in Trade in Bristol, but pritty soon he became attach'd to Brandy and Strong-water and let his Affairs slide; he remained continually at the Tavern where he was either drunk or ingaged in a quarrell, and left all his Business to his Wife who could not drive the Trade. Thus he became Insolvent and his Creditors, hearing of this, pressed upon him at so hard a Rate that he was in great fear of being taken by the Sergeant to the Kings-Bench: tho' he knew of no Warrant to apprehend him, nevertheless it was put into his Mind to flee (so great are the Bugbears that our own Guiltinesse creates); which course he took, leaving his Wife and Children who, bound to his Estate, were summarily brought into the Hazard. And have you seen them since that Time? *I asked him*. No, *he replied*, I see them only in my Mind's Eye and thus they haunt me.

He was a poor Wretch indeed, and a perfect Figure of that Necessity which puts a man to venture upon all manner of dangerous Actions, suggests strange Imaginations and desperate Resolutions, the product of which is only Disorder, Confusion, Shame and Ruin. As the Great rise by degrees of Greatnesse to the Pitch of Glory, so the Miserable sink to the Depth of their Misery by a continued Series of

Disasters. Yet it cannot be denied but most Men owe not only their Learning to their Plenty, but likewise their Vertue and their Honesty: for how many Thousands are there in the World, in great Reputation for their Sober and Just dealings with Mankind, who if they were put to their Shifts would soon lose their Reputations and turn Rogues and Scoundrels? And yet we punish Poverty as if it were a Crime, and honour Wealth as if it were a Vertue. And so goes on the Circle of Things: Poverty begets Sin and Sin begets Punishment. As the Rhyme has it:

> When once the tottering House begins to shrink,
> Upon it comes all the Weight by strange Instinct.

Thus it was with this sick Monkey before me, waiting to be tied to the Tree. I turned my Face upon him after this Recital of his Woes and whisper'd,

How are you called? I am called Ned.

Well, go on, my Ned. And so, Master, I became this poor Dunghil you see before you.

And why did you come here? I am here I know not how, unless there be some Lodestone in that new Church yonder. In Bath I was brought to the Brink of Eternity; in Salisbury I was consum'd to a meer Sceleton; in Guildford I was given up for a Dead Man. Now I am here in Lime-house, and before this in the unlucky Isle of Dogs.

And how are you? I am mighty weary and sore in my Feet, and could wish the Earth might swallow me, Master.

And where will you go, if it be not under the Earth? Where can I go? If I leave here, I must come back.

Why do you look so Fearfully on me, Ned? I have a Swimming in the Head, Master. Last night I dreamed of riding and eating Cream.

You are very much a Child. I have become so. Well, it is too late to be sorry.

Do you mean there is no Hope? No, not any Hope now. I have no means of continuing.

And will you make an End of it? What End do I have but the Gallows?

Well, if I were in your case I would prefer self-murther to a Hanging.

At this he passionately flew out and said, How can you? But I put my Finger to his Cheek, to still its Motion, and his Storm soon blew over. He was mine, and as I spoke my Eyes were brisk and sparkling.

Better that you choose your own Occasion, and not be the Top whipp'd by Ill Fortune. Well, Master, I understand you and I know what you would have me do.

I speak nothing, but let you speak. And I know nothing, but what I suppose you would have me know. And yet I cannot do it.

[65]

You cannot fear Death for the pain of it, since you have endured more Pain in Life than you shall find in Death. But then what of the World to come, Master?

You are past believing in the Old Wives Tales of Divines and Sermonisers, Ned. Your Body is all of you, and when that's done there's an End of it. And it is the End I have been seeking for this Poor Life. I am no thing now. I am undone.

The Night was coming on, being within half an Hour of Sunset, and the Light began to be dusky as I gave Ned my Knife. It grows Cold, *said he*. You will not be here so long, *I replied*, that it will freeze you. We walked together towards the Church, the work men now being gone to their Homes, and when Ned fell a'crying I bid him keep on: he was so poor a Bundle of Humanity that his Steps were but small and tottering, but at last I brought him to the brink of the Foundacions. Then with his eyes wide and his arms across (one Hand clasping the Knife), he gazed upwards at my half completed Work as the Rays of the Sunne lengthened and the Stone grew dull. Then his gaze was fixt for a considerable time upon the Ground, for he durst not Stir from this life: he was as like to fall into a Melancholly fit, but I have more Mercury in my Temper and I guided his Knife till he fell.

I let slip an *Ay me* as I crouched to see him in the Darkness beneath the Church, then I rose from my Knees in a dung Sweat and burst out Laughing; for indeed there would be no great Miss of him. Yet I walk'd away at once, lest my Case should be discovered to the Watchman, and I hurried across Rope-Makers-Field to the River side; but as I did so I was forced to pass the Congregation of Beggars who were sat beside small Fires to fry their Scraps of Rottenness. They were ill-looking Vermin and even by their flickering Lights I could see their unkempt Hair, swarthy Countenances, and long rusty Beards swaddled up in Raggs: some Heads were covered with Thrum caps, and others thrust into the tops of old Stockings so that, with their Cloaths of diverse colours, they looked like nothing so much as Ancient Britons. I wrapped my Coat around me and hurried on, my nostrils filled with the Scent of their reeking Dung-hills and puddles of Piss.

Some of them seemed elevated strangely, and danced about a pitiful Fire in one corner of the Field: they stompt and roared like those being whipt at Bridewell, but that their Lashes came from strong Liquor and Forgetfulnesse. And as the Winde gusted from the River I heard Snatches of their Song, *viz.*

A Wheel that turns, a Wheel that turned ever,
A Wheel that turns, and will leave turning never.

I must have stood listening in a strange Posture for this Band of
Rogues caught sight of me and let out a loud Bawling and Calling to
one another; and then a confus'd Hurry of Thought and Dizzinesse
came upon me like a Man often meets in a Dreame. I ran towards them
with outstretch'd Arms and cried, Do you remember me? I will never,
never leave thee! I will never, never leave thee!

4

AND AS the cry faded away, the noise of the traffic returned with increased clarity. The group of vagrants were standing in a corner of some derelict ground, where unwanted objects from the city had over the years been deposited: broken bottles and unrecognisable pieces of metal were strewn over a wide area, crab grass and different varieties of tall ragweed partially obscured the shapes of abandoned or burnt-out cars, while rotting mattresses sank into the soil. A hoarding had been erected by the river side: it was of a dark red colour, but from here the images were indistinct and only the words HAVE ANOTHER BEFORE YOU GO were still visible. Now, in the early summer, this forgotten area had the sweet, rank, dizzying odour of decay. The vagrants had started a fire, piling up the old rags and newspapers which they found lying beside them, and were now dancing around it – or, rather, they stumbled backwards and forwards with their fire as the wavering centre. They shouted out words in the air but they were too deeply imbued in alcohol or meths to know either the time or the place in which they found themselves. A light rain fell across their faces as they stared upward from the turning earth.

Some distance away from them, in a corner of the ground closest to the Thames, a solitary tramp was staring at the figure in the dark coat who was now walking away: 'Do you remember me?' the tramp cried out, 'You're the one, aren't you! I've seen you! I've watched you!' The figure paused for a moment before hurrying on; then the tramp's attention shifted and, forgetting all about the man (who had even now reached the river and stood with his back towards the city), he bent over once more and continued digging with his hands into the damp earth. Behind him the outline of the Limehouse church could be seen against the darkening sky; he gazed up at the building, with its massive but now crumbling and discoloured stone, and rubbed his neck with the palm of his right hand. 'It's getting cold,' he said, 'I'm off. I've had enough of this. I'm cold.'

It was about half-an-hour before sunset and, although the other vagrants would stay by the fire until they dropped exhausted on the ground and slept where they fell, he started making his way to a derelict house (early Georgian in appearance) which stood at the corner of Narrow Street and Rope-Maker's-Field. This was an area in which there were many such dwellings, with their windows boarded up and their doors fastened with planks, but this particular place had been used for many years – and, as such, it was recognised and permitted by the police. The theory was that the employment of this one house prevented the vagrants from trying to enter the church or its crypt as a resting place but, in truth, none of them would have ventured into St Anne's.

The tramp had reached Narrow Street when he paused, recalling with sudden ferocity the back of the man who had walked away from him towards the river, although he could not remember when precisely this event had occurred. He turned around quickly and then, seeing nothing, with a slow step he walked into the house. The rain was being blown in as he entered the hallway, and he paused to look down at his cracked and gaping shoes; then he examined the moisture on his hands before rubbing them against the wall. He peered into the ground floor rooms to see if there were any faces he recognised as 'trouble': there were some who picked quarrels with anyone who came near them, and others who screamed or called out in the night. There had even been occasions when, in a place such as this where tramps sheltered, one would get up in the middle of the night, kill another, and then go back to sleep again.

Three of them were already settled in the house: in the far corner of the largest room, a man and woman were lying against an old mattress: both of them seemed old, except that time moves fast for vagrants and they age quickly. In the middle of the room a young man was frying something in a battered saucepan, holding it gingerly above the fire which he had lit on the cracked stone floor. 'This is something, Ned,' he said to the tramp who now entered the room, 'This is really something, Neddo'. Ned glanced into the saucepan and saw food of an olive colour sizzling in its own fat. The smell made him feel uneasy: 'I'm off!' he shouted at the young man, although they were only a few inches apart.

'It's terrible rainy, Ned.'

'I'm not happy here. I'm off!'

But instead of going outside he walked into the next room, which was used as a latrine; he pissed in a corner and then came back, glaring at the young man who was still bent over his fire. The old couple paid no attention to either of them: the woman had a dark brown bottle in one hand, and waved it around as she continued with what seemed to be an interrupted conversation. 'Dust, just look at the dust,' she was saying, 'and you know where it comes from, don't you? Yes, you know.' She turned her head sideways and glanced at her companion, who was bowed down with his head between his knees. Then she started singing in a low voice,

> Shadows of the evening
> Steal across the sky . . .

But her words became confused, and she repeated 'sky' or 'night' several times before relapsing into silence. She stared out of the window's broken panes: 'Now look at those clouds there. I'm sure there's a face in there looking at me.' She handed the bottle to her companion, who held it for a minute without bringing it to his lips. Then she grabbed it from him.

'Thanks for the drink,' he said abashed.

'Are you happy there?'

'I have been happy but I'm not happy now,' and he lay down with his back to her.

Ned had also settled himself into a corner, sighing as he did so. He put his hand into the right hand pocket of his capacious coat, which he wore even in the heat of summer, and took out an envelope; he opened it, and stared at the photograph which was inside. He cannot remember now if he had found it or if it had always been his, and it was so creased that the image upon it was almost unrecognisable; it appeared, however, to be a picture of a child taken in front of a stone wall, with some trees set back upon the right hand. The child had his arms straight down by his sides, with the palms outward, and his head was tilted slightly to the left. The expression upon his face was unclear, but Ned had come to the conclusion that this was a photograph of himself as a small boy.

The bell of Limehouse Church rang as each of them, in this house, drifted into sleep – suddenly once more like children who, exhausted by the day's adventures, fall asleep quickly and carelessly. A solitary visitor, watching them as they slept, might wonder how it was that they had arrived at such a state and might speculate about each stage of their journey towards it: when did he first start muttering to himself, and not realise that he was doing so? When did she first begin to shy away from others and seek the shadows? When did all of them come to understand that whatever hopes they might have had were foolish, and that life was something only to be endured? Those who wander are always objects of suspicion and sometimes even of fear: the four people gathered in this house by the church had passed into a place, one might almost say a time, from which there was no return. The young man who had been bent over the fire had spent his life in a number of institutions – an orphanage, a juvenile home and most recently a prison; the old woman still clutching the brown bottle was an alcoholic who had abandoned her husband and two children many years before; the old man had taken to wandering after the death of his wife in a fire which he believed, at the time, he might have prevented. And what of Ned, who was now muttering in his sleep?

He had once worked as a printer in Bristol, for a small firm which specialised in producing various forms of stationery. He enjoyed his work but his temperament was a diffident one, and he found it difficult to speak to his colleagues: when in the course of the day he had to talk to them, he often stared at his hands or looked down at the floor as he did so. This had also been his position as a child. He had been brought up by elderly parents who seemed so distant from him that he rarely confided in them, and they would stare at him helplessly when he lay sobbing upon his bed; in the schoolyard he had not joined in the games of others but had held himself back, as if fearing injury. So he had been called a 'retiring' boy. Now his work-mates pitied him, although they tried not to show it, and it was generally arranged that he was given jobs which allowed him to work alone. The smell of ink, and the steady rhythm of the press, then induced in him a kind of peace – it was the peace he felt when he arrived early, at a time when he might be the only one to see the morning light as it filtered through the works or to hear the sound of his footsteps echoing through the old stone building. At such moments he was forgetful of himself and thus of others until he heard their voices, raised in argument or in greeting, and he would shrink into himself again. At other times he would stand slightly to one side and try to laugh at their jokes, but when they talked about sex he became uneasy and fell silent for it seemed to him to be a fearful thing. He still remembered how the girls in the schoolyard used to chant,

> Kiss me, kiss me if you can
> I will put you in my pan,
> Kiss me, kiss me as you said
> I will fry you till you're dead

And when he thought of sex, it was as of a process which could tear him limb from limb. He knew from his childhood reading that, if he ran into the forest, there would be a creature lying in wait for him.

Generally after work he left quickly and returned through the streets of Bristol to his room, with its narrow bed and cracked mirror. It was cluttered with his parents' furniture, which to him now smelled of dust and death, and was quite without interest except for a variety of objects which gleamed on the mantelpiece. He was a collector, and at weekends he would search paths or fields for old coins and artefacts: the objects he discovered were not valuable, but he was

[71]

drawn to their status as forgotten and discarded things. He had recently found, for example, an old spherical compass which he had placed at the centre of his collection. He stared at in the evening, imagining those who in another time had used it to find their way.

Thus he lived until his twenty fourth year when, on one evening in March, he agreed to go with his work-mates to the local pub. He had not been able to concentrate on his work all that day: for some reason he had been experiencing a peculiar but unfocussed excitement; his throat was dry, his stomach tightened into cramps, and when he spoke he confused his words. When he arrived in the saloon bar he wanted to drink some beer quickly, very quickly, and for a moment he had an image of his own body as a flame: 'What'll you have? What'll you have?' he called out to the others, who looked at him astonished. But he was filled with good fellowship and, as he waited for his order, he saw a discarded glass with some whisky still in it; surreptitiously, he drank it down before turning to his friends with a broad grin.

The more he drank that evening, the more he talked; he took everything that was said with a terrible seriousness, and interrupted other conversations continually. 'Let me explain,' he was saying, 'Try and see it my way for once.' Certain thoughts and phrases which had occurred to him in the past, but which he had kept to himself, now acquired real significance and he shouted them out in astonishment even as he faintly sensed the incredulity and horror which he would later feel at his own behaviour. But this did not matter if at last he was about to create a vivid impression upon the others: and that need became all the more desperate when he was no longer able to distinguish their faces, and they had become moons which encircled him. And he left his own body in order to howl at them from a distance: 'I shouldn't be here,' he was saying, 'I shouldn't be telling you this. I stole money. I stole it from the firm – you know when she puts the wages in the packets? I stole a lot, and they never found out. Never. You know I was in prison for stealing once?' He looked around as if he were being hunted. 'It's terrible there, in a cell. I shouldn't be here. I'm a professional thief.' He took hold of a glass, but it slipped out of his grasp and shattered as it hit the floor; then he got up from his stool and swung blindly towards the door.

It was early morning when he woke up, fully clothed, on his bed and found himself staring at the ceiling with his arms rigid by his sides. At first he felt quite serene, since he was being borne aloft by the grey light approaching him in neat squares from the window, but then the memory of the previous evening struck him and, staring wildly around, he sprang up from the bed. He gnawed at his right hand as he tried to recall each event in order but he saw only an image of himself as blood red, his face contorted with rage, his body veering from side to side, and his voice magnified as if all the time he had been sitting alone in a darkened room. He concentrated on that darkness and was able to glimpse the faces of the others, but they were stamped with horror or detestation. And then he remembered what he had said about theft, and about prison. He got up and looked into the mirror, noticing for the first time that he had two large hairs growing between his eyebrows. Then he was sick in the small basin. Who was it that had spoken last night?

He was walking around in circles, the smell of the old furniture suddenly very distinct. There was a newspaper in his hand and he started reading it, paying particular attention to the headlines which seemed to be floating towards him so that now a band of black print encircled his forehead. He was curled upon the bed, hugging his knees, when the next horror came upon him: those who heard him last night would now have to report his theft, and his employer would call the police. He saw how the policeman took the telephone call at the station; how his name and address were spoken out loud; how he looked down at the floor as they led him away; how he was in the dock, forced to answer questions about himself, and now he was in a cell and had lost control of his own body. He was staring out of the window at the passing clouds when it occurred to him that he should write to his employer, explaining his drunkenness and confessing that he invented the story of theft; but who would believe him? It was always said that in drink there was truth, and perhaps it was true that he was a convicted thief. He began to sing,

> One fine day in the middle of the night,
> Two dead men got up to fight

and then he knew what was meant by madness.

The terror began now: he heard a noise in the street outside his window, but when he stood up he turned his face to the wall. Everything in his life seemed to have led him towards this morning, and he had been foolish not to see the pattern taking shape ahead of him; he went to his wardrobe and inspected his clothes with interest, as if they belonged to some other person. And it was while he was sitting in his faded armchair, trying to remember how his mother had bent forward to caress him, that he realised he was late for work; but of course he could not go there again. (In fact his colleagues had realised that night how drunk he had become, and paid little or no attention to his conversation: his remarks about theft and prison were thought to be an example of a strange sense of humour which he had never revealed to them before.) At some hour his clock sounded its alarm

[73]

and he stared at it in horror: 'My God!' he said aloud, 'My God! My God!'. And so the first day passed.

On the second day he opened his window and looked about with curiosity; he realised that he had never properly noticed his street before, and he wanted to discover exactly what it was like. But it was like nothing, and he saw faces staring up at him. He shut the window quietly, waiting for his panic to subside. That night he talked in his sleep, finding the words for his bewilderment which he would never hear. And the second day passed. On the third day he found a letter which had been pushed under his door: he made a point of not looking at it but then, in exasperation, he placed it under the mattress of his bed. It occurred to him now to draw the curtains as well, so that no one should suspect he was indoors. Then he heard scuffling noises outside his room and he shrank back in terror: a large dog, or some other animal, was trying to get in. But the noises stopped. On the fourth day he woke up realising that he had been forgotten: he was free of the whole world, and the relief dazed him. He dressed quickly and went out into the street, pausing only to glance up at his own window before entering a pub where an old tramp with matted hair watched him intently. In his distress he picked up a paper, and saw that he was reading an account of a robbery. He stood up quickly, overturning the small table at which he had been sitting, and walked out. Then he returned to his small room and addressed the furniture which smelled now like his parents. And the fourth day passed: that night, he peered into the darkness but could see nothing and it seemed to him that his room, with all its familiar objects, had at last disappeared. The darkness had no beginning and no end; this is like death, he thought just before falling asleep, but the disease affecting me is one I cannot see.

His terror became his companion. When it seemed to diminish, or grow easier to bear, he forced himself to remember the details of what he had said and done so that his fears returned, redoubled. His previous life, which had been without fear, he now dismissed as an illusion since he had come to believe that only in fear could the truth be found. When he woke from sleep without anxiety, he asked himself, What is wrong? What is missing? And then his door opened slowly, and a child put its head around and gazed at him: there are wheels, Ned thought, wheels within wheels. The curtains were now always closed, for the sun horrified him: he was reminded of a film he had seen some time before, and how the brightness of the noonday light had struck the water where a man, in danger of drowning, was struggling for his life.

He now sometimes dressed in the middle of the night, and took off his clothes in the late afternoon; he was no longer aware that he put on

[74]

oddly matched shoes, or that he wore a jacket without a shirt beneath it. One morning he left his room early and, to avoid being seen by the police (who he believed to be watching him), went out by the back entrance of the building. He found a shop several streets away, where he bought a small wristwatch, but on his return he became confused and lost his way. He arrived at his own street only by accident and as he entered his room he said out loud, 'Time flies when you're having fun'. But everything seemed quite different to him now: by approaching his room from another direction, Ned at last realised that it had an independent existence and that it no longer belonged to him. He put the wristwatch carefully on the mantelpiece, and took up the spherical compass. Then he opened the door, and stepped over the threshold.

As soon as he had left the room and walked into the air, he knew that he would never return and for the first time his fears lifted. It was a spring morning, and when he walked into Severndale Park he felt the breeze bringing back memories of a much earlier life, and he was at peace. He sat beneath a tree and looked up at its leaves in amazement – where once he might have gazed at them and sensed there only the confusion of his own thoughts, now each leaf was so clear and distinct that he could see the lightly coloured veins which carried moisture and life. And he looked down at his own hand, which seemed translucent beside the bright grass. His head no longer ached, and as he lay upon the earth he could feel its warmth beneath him.

The afternoon woke him with a shout – two children were playing a little way off, and they seemed to be calling out to him. He stood up eagerly trying to catch their words, which had ended with something like 'All fall down', but when he walked towards them they ran away laughing and shouting,

> Sam, Sam, the dirty man,
> Washed his face in a frying pan!

He felt hot suddenly, and then realised that he had put on his dark overcoat before leaving: just as he was about to remove it, he saw that he was wearing a pyjama jacket beneath it. He walked awkwardly to a wooden bench, and sat there for the rest of the afternoon as those who passed by cast nervous glances at him. Then at dusk he rose up and began walking away from the streets he had known as a child, following the curve of the long road which he knew would take him into the open fields. And this was how his life as a vagrant began.

And how does it feel to go down into the water with your eyes wide open, and your mouth gaping, so that you can see and taste every inch of the descent? At first he went hungry because he did not know how

[75]

to beg and, when food was given to him he could not eat it; but as he moved towards London he was taught the phrases of supplication he might use. In Keynsham, he slept by the roadside until he learned that he must always look for the night's shelter before it became dark. In Bath, he began to notice discarded cigarette ends and the other human refuse which he placed in the capacious pockets of his overcoat. By the time he had reached Salisbury he had been instructed in the arts of other vagrants, and in his shreds and patches had at last come to resemble them as he crept across the short grass to Stonehenge.

It was just after dawn and a weak sun patted him on the head as he approached the stones. Two cars were parked nearby, so Ned was cautious: he knew that the indifference which he encountered in cities could turn to anger or hostility in the open country. In fact he thought he could hear the voices of two men – they were shouting and may have been engaged in an argument of some kind – but when he came closer to the monument he could see no one. In relief he scuffed his muddy shoes in the dew, and as he looked back he could see the trail he had left gleaming in the early light; then he turned his head a second time, and the trail had faded. A crow called somewhere above him, and so frail was he now that a gust of wind blew him towards the circle – when he looked up he saw that he was already beneath the stones, and they seemed about to fall upon his head. He bent over, covering his eyes, and there were voices swirling around him – among them his own father saying, 'I had a vision of my son dead'. He fell against a stone and in his dream he was climbing the steps of a pyramid, from the summit of which he could see the smoking city until he was woken by the rain falling on his face. A slug had crawled over him as he lay upon the ground, leaving a silver thread across his coat. He rose to his feet, clutching at the damp stone as he did so, and then continued his journey under a dark sky.

His body had become a companion which seemed always about to leave him: it had its own pains which moved him to pity, and its own particular movements which he tried hard to follow. He had learned from it how to keep his eyes down on the road, so that he could see no one, and how important it was never to look back – although there were times when memories of an earlier life filled him with grief and he lay face down upon the grass until the sweet rank odour of the earth brought him to his senses. But slowly he forgot where it was he had come from, and what it was he was escaping.

In Hartley Row he could find nowhere to sleep and, as he crossed a bridge to escape from the lights of the town, a car swerved to avoid him: he fell backwards against an iron hand-rail and would have toppled into the river if he had not somehow found his balance. When the dust had cleared he unbuttoned his trousers and, laughing, pissed by the roadside. The adventure exhilarated him and he took the spherical compass out of his pocket and in an impulsive gesture threw it in a wide arc away from him; but he had gone only a few yards along the same road when he retraced his steps to find it. At Church Oakley he contracted a slight fever and, as he lay sweating in an old barn, he could feel the lice swimming in the unaccustomed heat of his own body. At Blackwater he tried to enter a pub but he was refused admission with shouts and curses: a young girl brought out some bread and cheese, but he was so weak that he vomited up the food in the yard. At Egham he was standing on a wooden bridge, staring down at the water, when he heard a voice behind him: 'A travelling man, I see. I like to see a travelling man'. Ned looked up, alarmed, and there standing beside him was an elderly man carrying a small suitcase: 'We are all travellers,' he was saying, 'and God is our guide'. He had his arms outstretched, palms outward, and as he smiled Ned could see the slight protuberance of his false teeth. 'So don't despair, never despair' – and he looked wistfully down at the water – 'Don't do it, my friend'. He knelt down on the road and opened his suitcase, handing Ned a pamphlet which he stuffed into his pocket to use later as the material for a fire. 'You will reach your destination, for God loves you,' and he stood up with a grimace. 'For your sake He might let the sun turn back in its course, and let time itself travel backwards.' He looked down at his trousers, and then brushed the dust off them. 'If He cared to, that is.' Then, as Ned still said nothing, he looked towards the town: 'Any chance of lodgings there, is there?' He walked on without waiting for a reply, as Ned, too, travelled forward through Bagshot and Baker-bridge until he reached the suburbs of the city.

And after a few days he arrived in London, by way of the unlucky Isle of Dogs. He had heard that there was a hostel in Spitalfields and, although he was not clear in which direction he should travel, somehow he guided himself towards it: he had, after all, the old spherical compass still in his pocket. And so he found himself walking down Commercial Road, and perhaps he was also muttering to himself there since a young boy ran away from him in obvious fright. His legs were stiff, and his feet aching: he might have hoped that the earth would swallow him, but the sight of the church ahead of him drew him forward since he had come to understand during his wanderings that churches offered protection for men and women like himself. And yet as soon as he reached the steps of the church, and had sat down upon them, he was once more seized with apathy and with an aversion for any action or decision. With his head down he gazed at the stone beneath his feet as the solitary bell tolled above him: anyone who came upon him unawares might think he had been metamorphosised into stone, so still he seemed.

[77]

But then he heard a rustling somewhere to his left and, looking up, he saw a man and woman lying with each other beneath some trees. A dog had once tried to mount him when he was walking through a field: he had hit it several times with a large stone until eventually it had run away, bloody and yelping. And now he was once again filled with the same rage as he screamed out incomprehensible words to the couple who, on seeing him, sat up and stared without rising to their feet. A plane passed overhead and at once his fury disappeared; he would have resumed his silent contemplation of the cracks and hollows in the stone beneath his feet if someone, alerted by the sudden screaming, had not been walking towards him from the street. The setting sun was in Ned's face, and he could not see clearly, but he assumed it was a policeman and prepared himself for the customary dialogue.

The figure approached him slowly, not altering his pace, and now stood at the bottom of the steps looking up at him; and his shadow covered Ned as he asked his name.

'My name is Ned.'

'And tell me, Ned, where do you come from?'

'I come from Bristol.'

'Bristol? Is that so?'

'So it seems,' Ned said.

'It seems you're a poor man now.'

'Now I am, but then I was in trade.'

'And so how did you come to be here?' the man asked him, reaching out to touch Ned's right cheek with his finger.

'I don't know how I came to be here, to tell you the truth.'

'But do you know how you are?'

'I'm weary, Sir, very weary.'

'So where are you going to now, Ned?'

He had forgotten that he had come to find the hostel: 'I don't know,' he answered, 'Anywhere. One place is as good as another when you're roaming. I might go and then again I might come back.'

'You're like a child, I see.'

'I might have become one, Sir, but I'm nothing really.'

'That's sad, Ned. All that I can say is that's sad.'

'It's sad, to say the least.' And Ned looked up at the darkening sky.

'It's time, isn't it?'

'It's certainly time,' Ned said.

'Time, I mean, for you to be on your way again. This is not the place for you.'

Ned remained silent for a moment: 'And where shall I go to?'

'There are other churches,' he replied. 'This one is not for you. Go towards the river.'

[78]

Ned watched the man, who pointed southward and then walked slowly away. He got up, suddenly cold, but as soon as he moved away from the church his weariness left him and he went back in the direction from which he had come – along Commercial Road, across Whitechapel High Street, and then down towards the Thames and Limehouse, all the time rubbing the spherical compass in his pocket. This was an area haunted by other vagrants, most of them suspicious and solitary, and as he passed them he looked for those signs of degradation which tramps always recognise in each other – he wanted to see how much further he would have to fall now that he, too, had entered the great city.

He stopped at Wapping, by the corner of Swedenborg Court, and saw a church rise up beside the river – was this the place which the figure had pointed to, saying 'there are other churches'? The experiences of the evening had left him wounded and alert, so that now he looked fearfully around; he could hear the sigh of the river upon the mudflats, and the confused murmur of the city behind him; he gazed up at the human faces in the clouds, then he looked down upon the ground and saw the small whirlwinds of dust raised by the breeze which came from the Thames and brought with it also the sound of human voices. All of these things turned around him for ever, and it seemed to Ned that it was no longer he who was watching and hearing them: it was someone other.

He found that he was walking by the back of the Wapping church towards a park which adjoined it; here also protection might be gained and, as he hurried past the blackened stones, he caught sight of a small brick building in a far corner of the park. The place was now clearly abandoned although, as Ned approached it, he could see the letters M SE M OF engraved above the portal (the others had no doubt been obliterated by time). He peered in cautiously and, when he was sure that no other tramp was using it as a shelter, he passed the threshold and sat down against the wall; at once he began to eat some bread and cheese which he had taken from his pocket, looking around ferociously as he did so. Then he began to examine the rubbish which had been left here: most of it was familiar enough, but in one corner he found a discarded book with a white cover. He put out his hand to touch it and for a moment drew back, since the cover seemed to be protected by a sticky wax. Then he picked it up and noticed that over the course of time the pages had curled and clung together although, when he shook them, a photograph fell upon the ground. He gazed at if for a while, making out the features of a child, and then placed it in his pocket before he began painstakingly to separate the pages, smoothing each one down with his hand before he tried to read it. He concentrated on the words and symbols which were written here, but the print was now so smudged and overlaid that much of the book was quite unintelligible: he saw a triangle, and a sign for the sun, but the letters beneath them were unfamiliar. Then Ned looked out, gazing at the church, thinking of nothing.

There was a woman in the doorway, her clothes as patched and torn as Ned's own. She was patting her hair with the palm of her right hand and saying, 'Do you want it? Come and get it if you want it.' She was peering at him and, since he had said nothing in reply, she knelt down on the floor by the entrance.

'I don't want it,' he said, rubbing his eyes, 'I don't want anything.'

'All you men want it. I've had experience of all types of men,' and she laughed, throwing her head back so that Ned could see the wrinkles around her neck.

'I don't want it,' he repeated in a louder voice.

'I've had them all,' and she looked around the abandoned building. 'Most of them in here. It's nice in here, isn't it? Snug.' Ned started twisting a lock of his hair between two fingers so that it became as hard and as taut as wire. 'Let's have a look at it,' she said, craning her head towards him, and he flattened himself against the wall.

'Look at what?'

'You know what I mean. Every man's got one. Wee Willie Winkie.'

'I've got nothing, I've got nothing for you.' And he clutched the book he had been reading.

She crawled towards him and put her hands down on the damp soil as if she were about to dig for something; Ned rose slowly to his feet, his back still against the wall, and he did not take his eyes from her face. 'Come on,' she whispered, 'Give it to me' – and then she made a lunge for his trousers. In panic Ned put out his foot to stop her, but she grabbed it and tried to bring him down to the ground: 'You're a powerful man,' she said, 'but I've got you!' And then with all his strength he crashed the book down upon her head; this seemed to surprise her, for she let go of him and looked upwards, as if the object had fallen from the skies. Then very carefully, and with a measure of dignity, she rose to her feet and stood by the entrance of the shelter, glaring at him. 'What kind of man are you, anyway?' And she wiped her mouth with her arm: 'Look at you, you pathetic object! They don't give you money out of charity, they give it you out of fear.' And he looked at her wide-eyed. 'Do you think they care about you, you daft bugger? They just don't want you coming after them, they don't want to see you in the mirror when they look at their fat faces!'

'I don't know about that,' he said.

'They think you're mad, talking to yourself and all. It wouldn't take them long to go mad if they had you around, oh no it wouldn't.' And then she mimicked a high, quavering voice: 'Pity me, oh pity me, can you spare me something for a cup of tea?' He looked down at himself as she went on, 'Don't hurt me. I've suffered enough. I'm ugly. I'm smelly. Pity me.' And then she gazed at him in triumph. She was about to say something else when she noticed the crumbs of the bread and cheese which Ned had been eating: and, lifting up her skirts, she kicked her legs in the air as she sang,

> When I was a little girl I lived by myself
> And all the bread and cheese I got I laid upon the shelf.

For a moment she too might have pitied him, but then she laughed, dusted down her skirt and left without another word. Ned, still fighting for breath after the struggle, saw that he had ripped the binding of his book and that the pages were now being carried by the wind across the park and towards the church.

It was some evenings later when Ned, preparing his meal in the red brick shelter, heard a confused murmur of voices outside; at once he grew alarmed and crouched in a corner but, after a few moments, he realised that the shouts and calls were not directed against him but were coming from the far side of the little park. He peered out of the entrance and saw a group of children jumping and shrieking in a circle: two or three of them had sticks which they were throwing at something in the middle, as their cries echoed against the walls of the church. Then Ned saw that they were surrounding a cat which was hurling itself in fear against one child and then another in order to break free, only to be caught and hauled back into the centre of the circle; it had scratched and bitten some of them but the sight of their own blood seemed only to have provoked more frenzy in the children who, in their joy and fury, were now smashing their sticks against the lean body of the animal. Their look of rage was terrible to Ned: he remembered it from his own childhood, which at this moment descended upon him again. And he knew that, if they became aware he was watching them, their rage would soon be turned against him: it was not unusual for gangs of children to set upon a tramp and beat him senseless, shouting 'Bogeyman! Bogeyman!' as they kicked or spat at him.

He left the shelter and hurried down the small path which led into Wapping Wall, not daring to look back in case he should draw the children's glances upon him. He walked beside the river up to Limehouse, and the damp wind unsettled him; when he reached Shoulder-of-Mutton Alley he could see an abandoned warehouse ahead of him but, in his haste to reach it, he fell and gashed his leg against a piece of metal which had been left on the waste-ground through which he now trod. He was tired and yet, when eventually he lay down inside the warehouse, he could not sleep. He looked down at himself and, suddenly disgused at what he saw, said out loud, 'You have dug your own grave and now you must lie in it'. He closed his eyes and, leaning his head against the rotten wood, he had a sudden vision of the world – cold, heavy, unendurable like the awkward mass of his own body as at last he slept.

*

And the years have passed before he wakes now, after a night in the same warehouse beside the Thames – although, during the night, he had returned to Bristol and watched himself as a child. The years have passed and he has remained in the city, so that now he has become tired and grey; and when he roamed through its streets, he was bent forward as if searching the dust for lost objects. He knew the city's forgotten areas and the shadows which they cast: the cellars of ruined buildings, the small patches of grass or rough ground which are to be found between two large thoroughfares, the alleys in which Ned sought silence, and even the building sites where he might for one night creep into the foundations out of the rain and wind. Sometimes dogs would follow him: they liked his smell, which was of lost or forgotten things, and when he slept in a corner they licked his face or burrowed their noses into his ragged clothes; he no longer beat them off, as once he had, but accepted their presence as natural. For the dogs' city was very like his own: he was close to it always, following its smells, sometimes pressing his face against its buildings to feel their warmth, sometimes angrily chipping or cutting into its brick and stone surfaces.

There were some places, and streets, where he did not venture since he had learnt that others had claims there greater than his own – not the gangs of meths drinkers who lived in no place and no time, nor the growing number of the young who moved on restlessly across the face of the city, but vagrants like himself who, despite the name which the world has given them, had ceased to wander and now associated themselves with one territory or 'province' rather than another. All of them led solitary lives, hardly moving from their own warren of streets and buildings: it is not known whether they chose the area, or whether the area itself had callen them and taken them in, but they had become the guardian spirits (as it were) of each place. Ned now knew some of their names: Watercress Joe, who haunted the streets by St Mary Woolnoth, Black Sam who lived and slept beside the Commercial Road between Whitechapel and Limehouse, Harry the Goblin who was seen only by Spitalfields and Artillery Lane, Mad Frank who walked continually through the streets of Bloomsbury, Italian Audrey who was always to be found in the dockside area of Wapping (it was she who had visited Ned in his shelter many years before), and 'Alligator' who never moved from Greenwich.

But, like Ned, they inhabited a world which only they could see: he sometimes sat on the same spot for hours at a time, until its contours and shadows were more real to him than the people who passed by. He knew the places where the unhappy came, and there was one street corner at a meeting of three roads where he had seen the figure of despair many times – the man with his feet and arms splayed out in front of him, the woman embracing his neck and weeping. He knew the places which had always been used for sex, and afterwards he could smell it on the stones; and he knew the places which death visited, for the stones carried that mark also. Those who passed in front of him scarcely noticed that he was there, although some might murmur to each other 'Poor man!' or 'Such a pity!' before hurrying forward. And yet there was once a time, as he walked by the side of London Wall, when a man appeared in front of him and smiled.

'Is it still hard for you?' he asked Ned.

'Hard? Now there you're asking.'

'Yes, I am asking. Is it still bad?'

'Well, I'll tell you, it's not so bad.'

'Not so bad?'

'I've known worse, after all this time.'

'What time was it, Ned, that we met before?' And the man moved closer to him so that Ned could see the dark weave of his coat (for he would not look into his face).

'What time is it now, Sir?'

'Now, now *you're* asking.' The man laughed, and Ned looked down at the cracks in the pavement.

'Well,' he said to this half-recognised stranger, 'I'll just be on my way now.'

'Don't be long, Ned, don't be long.'

And Ned walked away without looking back, and without re-membering.

As he had grown older in the city, his condition had become worse: fatigue and listlessness now held him, as slowly all his expectations were lowered like a bird which falls silent when a cloth is placed over its cage. One night he had stood in front of an electrical show-room and had watched the same flickering images upon a row of television sets; the programme, perhaps designed for children, showed some cartoon animals scampering across fields, gardens and ravines; from their terrified expressions it was clear to Ned that they were trying to escape from something, and when he opened his eyes again he saw a wolf blowing the chimney off a small house. Ned pressed his face

[83]

against the glass front, and mouthed the words as the wolf spoke them, 'I'll huff and I'll puff, and I'll blow your house down!' All night these images swirled around his head, growing larger and more vivid until the sleeping figure was engulfed in them, and he woke the next morning bewildered at his own rage. He wandered through the streets crying, 'Get lost! Just bugger off! Get lost!', but his voice was often drowned in the roar of the traffic.

A few days later he began to scrutinise each person who passed him, in case there was one who might know or remember him, or who might even now come to his aid; and when he saw a young woman looking idly into the window of a watch-repairer's, he glimpsed in her face all the warmth and pity which might once have protected him. He followed her as she walked down Leadenhall Street and up Cornhill, Poultry and Cheapside towards St Pauls : he would have called out to her, but as she turned the corner of Ave Maria Lane she joined a crowd watching the demolition of some old houses. The ground shook under Ned's feet as he came after her and instinctively he looked up at the gutted interiors of the houses; their sinks and fireplaces were visible from the street as a great iron ball was swung against an exterior wall. The crowd cheered, and the air was filled with a fine debris which left a sour taste in Ned's mouth. In that instant he lost sight of her: he hurried forward towards St Pauls, calling out for her as the dust belched out of the old houses behind him.

It was after this that he entered what was known as the 'strange time'. Exhaustion and malnutrition had weakened him to such an extent that even the taste of his own saliva made him retch; cold and dampness entered his body so that he shook with a fever which would not abate. He was talking to himself now for most of the day: 'Yes,' he would say, 'Time is getting on. Time is certainly getting on'. And he would rise up from the ground, look around, and then sit down again. He had a curiously weaving and tentative walk, taking several steps backward and then pausing before moving forward again: 'We don't want any rubbish round here,' one policeman had said to him as he stood quite still in the middle of the yard, and Ned had waited, eager to hear more of this, before being pushed violently into the thorough-fare. Where now he heard words which fascinated him, for they seemed to be repeated in a certain pattern: on one day, for example, 'fire' was a word which he heard frequently and then on the next it was 'glass'. He had a recurring vision in which he saw his own shape, watching him from a distance. And then when sometimes he sat, bewildered and alone, he glimpsed shadows and vague images of others who moved and talked strangely – 'like a book,' he had said. And sometimes, also, it seemed as if these shadows recognised or knew Ned for they would walk around and cast their eyes upon him as

[84]

they did so. And he called out to them, 'Pity me. Do you have a farthing or a broken crust?'

When he got up from the wooden floor, he was thirsty, and his throat was sore as if he had cried out the same word over and over again. 'And why should they pity me?' he thought as he walked away from the river. It was a cold, grey morning and Ned could smell the scent of burning rags or rubbish which came from the Tower Hamlets Estate on his right side. He walked into the Commercial Road and, raising his arm above his head so that it cast a slight shadow across his face, he could see Black Sam lying in the doorway of a betting shop: a heavy blanket was draped over his body, concealing his face and chest, but he had no shoes and his naked feet protruded into the street. Ned walked across to him and sat down by his side; there was a half-empty bottle near him, and he reached over to take it. 'Don't touch that,' Black Sam muttered beneath his blanket, 'Don't fucking do it!' Then he removed the blanket, and they looked at each other without animosity. Ned's throat was still sore and he could taste the blood in his mouth as he spoke. 'Can you smell that burning, Sam? Something's burning somewhere.'

'It's the sun. What about that sun?' And Sam reached for the bottle.

'Now,' Ned said, 'Now there's something.'

'It's a cold and dark morning without the sun, Ned, and that's the truth of it.'

'It'll come,' he murmured, 'It'll come.' A column of smoke rose up in front of them, and Ned glanced at it in alarm. 'I'm not going to run,' he said, 'I've done nothing.'

Black Sam was whispering something to himself, and Ned leaned over eagerly to hear it: 'It keeps on turning,' he was saying, 'It keeps on turning'.

Ned noticed a small stream of piss issuing from beneath the blanket and running across the pavement into the gutter. But then he raised his head just in time to see the cloud cover vanish from the earth – although the pillar of acrid smoke lent the sun a blood-red colour. 'I don't know how long I'll be here,' he said to Sam, 'I'll go now and then I'll come back.' And he rose to his feet, steadied himself, and began walking to that patch of derelict land by the river where the vagrants danced around their fires.

The bell of Limehouse Church was ringing when Ned woke up in the old house; the others (the old couple and the young man) were asleep, for it was still night, and so he rose cautiously. He left the room without thought, opened the door and crossed the threshold into the street known as Rope-Maker-Field. It was a clear, calm night and as he looked up at the bright stars he gave a deep sigh. He started walking towards the church itself, but weakness and lack of food now so

[85]

wearied him that he was able to take only small and tottering steps. Then he stopped before the church, crossed his arms over his chest and contemplated the futility of his life. He had come to the flight of steps which led down to the door of the crypt and, as he sensed the coldness which rose from them like a vapour, he heard a whisper which might have been 'I' or 'me'. And then the shadow fell.

5

THE SHADDOWE falls naturally here since the Clowds, tho'
they be nothing but a Mist flying high in the Air, cast their Shade
upon the surface of the Water; learn how to do this in Stone and
look you, Walter, *I added*, how the body of the Water moves. All things
Flow even when they seem to stand still, as in the hands of Clocks and
the shaddowes of Sun-dials. But Walter kept his Hands in his
Breeches and squinted at the Ground; the Office was still within
our Sight, even as we stood by the Thames, and he looked uneasily towards it. I asked him the Matter. Do not trouble your self, *he
replied*.

I will know what is the Matter, *I told him*.

Nothing is the Matter, what should be the matter?

You trouble me now indeed, Walter Pyne.

It is nothing, *said he*, it is a Trifle, it is not worth talking of.

And I replied: Do not put me off with such Stuff as that.

It was Sad work to get the Truth out of him, and he was as like to
have held his Tongue if I had not stood very High upon it and
prevailed with him to Answer. They talk of you in the Office, *he said*
(and I grew Pale), and they tell me that you stuff my Head with
mildew'd Fancies and confus'd Rules (and the Sweat formed on my
Brow), and they say that the Ruines of Antiquity lie too heavily upon
you (I looked out over the River), and they say that I must follow
another Master if I am to rise (I drew Blood from my Mouth but stood
quite still).

My Mind became like a Blank, a paper unwritten: And who are
these who tell you so? *I asked* at last, not looking at him.

They are those who profess themselves to have nothing but friendly
intent towards me.

And then I turned my Eyes upon him and spoke: You are a Fool to
believe any Man your friend, you must trust no Man, nor believe any
one but such as you know will sin against their own Interest to lie or
betray you. I know this to be so, Walter. He withdrew from me a little
at that, but then I laughed out loud at him; these good Friends are
meer Flyes, *I said*, who will feed on Excrement or a Honey-pot equally:

I would rather my Life was hid in Obscurity than that my Actions should be known to them, for the smaller their Value of me the more I am at Liberty. But here I checked my self: should I once begin to speak freely, I should blirt out All and so hang my self. All this while Walter was gazing out at a Wherry in which there was a common man laughing and making antic Postures like an Ape: a merry Fellow, *said I* to break Walter's mood.

No, not so merry, *he answered*.

We walked back towards the Office and as we spoke with each other the Wind blew our Words in our Faces. And once more I asked him: Who are these who speak to you of me?

They are known to you, Sir.

They are known to me as Villains, *I replied* but I did not press Walter further on this Matter. And yet I am not blinde to those who work against me: Mr Lee, the Comptroller's Clerke, as heavy and dull as an old Usurer; Mr Hayes, Measuring Surveyour, as changing and uneasy as a Widow without a Fortune and one who emits his Unquietness like a Contagion; Mr Colthouse, Master Carpenter, a silly, empty, morose Fellow who has as much Conceit, and as little Reason for it, as any Man that I know; Mr Newcomb, Paymaster, who has but a low Genius and yet some of his Remarks would make a Body laugh at his Folly; Mr Vanbrugghe, Artificer, whose Productions are but sad and un-digested Things like a sick man's Dreames. These are all Ginger-bread Fellows, meer Tattlers, and I would as soon eat a Dish of Soup in a Common Ordinary as smile wildly in their Company. But since I keep my Time out of their dispose, therefore they contemn me.

And Walter is saying – it is a foolish Phrensy to care for Praise.

And the best things have the fewer Admirers, *I replied*, because there are more Dunces than able Men. Consider the work of Mr Vanbrugghe, which is much cryed up: when he tried to build the little Church of Ripon, the Cornices were so small that they could not weather the Work or throw off the Rain!

Then the Weight of this Life fell upon me, and I could scarce speak. I went presently out of Scotland Yard into Whitehall: I walked to the Chandlery and then, to still my beating Mind, I entered into the Church-Yard beside the Abbey. I take Delight in stalking along by my self on that dumb silent Ground, for if it be true that Time is a Wound then it is one that the Dead may Heal. And when I rest my Head upon the Graves I hear them speaking each to each: *the grass above us*, they say, *is of a blew colour but why do we still see it and why are we not pluckt out of the earth?* I hear them whispering, the long dead, in Cripplegate, in Farringdon, in Cordwainers Street and in Crutched Fryars: they are pack'd close together like Stones in the Mortar, and I hear them speak of the City that holds them fast. And yet still I burn at Walter's recent

Words as this Thought comes to me: why do the Living still haunt me when I am among the Dead?

In rage at my self I walked from the Church-Yard and went up into Charing Cross: I passed the Mews Yard, through Dirty Lane, and then walked down Castle Street towards my Lodging. When I entered Nat Eliot was cleaning some Plates in the Kitchin: Lord Sir, *says he*, are you back so soon? And up he jumps from his Stool to take off my Boots. There was a Caller, *he goes on* (making a pease-porridge of his Words), who desired me to acquaint you of his being here and that he desired if it might not be Troublesome that he might be admitted to you.

Did he speak so plainly?

But Nat paid no heed to my Jest and continu'd: My Master is not withinne, I told him, and is I know not where. He was very much of an ordinary Man and when he enquired your Business I said I will not be pumpt, I said you mistake your Fellow in me. He had mittins on his Hands, and a Fur-Cap on his Head, Master.

So, so, so, *I said* as I walked up to my Chamber, we will see, we will see.

Nat followed me and, taking up my Cap, stands in front of me: do you know that this Morning I went to buy a new one, *says he* (for my Cap was now fray'd), so when I stand looking outside the Hat-makers by Golden Square, the tradesman's boy comes out to me, Master, and says well he says do you see any thing you like for you look as if your Pockets had but Holes. What's that to you, says I, I have Money to pay for any Thing I like, and I shan't be huffed at for looking: do you know that saying, all that Glisters is not Gold and then I added again to him –

– No more Nat, *I said*, tho' you would slobber your Fingers if you held your Tongue.

And he looked down upon the Ground. I am sorry to have given you so much Trouble, *he replied*. Then he went away; but he crept back later when I called him, and read me to Sleep.

All was revealed on the next Day, when I was by chance walking through Covent-Garden. As I turned out of the Piazza, on the right hand coming out of James-Street, I was jogged in the Elbow and, looking at my Neighbour, saw that it was one of my Assembly from Black Step Lane: I knew him as Joseph, a common man in Cloth-Coat and speckled Breeches. I called for you, *he whispered*, but your Boy denyed me.

I was not in the House, but why did you come for me there? And I gave him a furious Look.

You have not heard the News?

What News? *I asked* shuddering.

He was a Man of uncouth and halting Speech, but I peeced together

[89]

his story as follows, *viz*: Two days before, some Report of our Activities was spread abroad, and thereupon a Riot was raised among the Streets by our Meeting-House, the people becoming very clamorous against it; there were six withinne the House and, on hearing a confus'd Noise approaching them, they first bolted the fore door, and then padlock'd the Back door, which was glazed, and began to fasten the Shutters belonging to it. The Mobb then threw Stones at the Windows, and among them Flint-stones of such a Size and Weight as were enough to have kill'd any Person they hit (which was their Purpose). They likewise stopp'd those passing thro' Black Step Lane, robb'd them of their Hats, tore off their Wiggs, and buffetted them on suspicion that they were Enthusiasticks (their canting Term): Joseph was one of these and escap'd scarcely with his Life. The Mobb had now crowded into both Lanes running each side of the House (a Disease comes out in Pus and runs so), and they forc'd the Doors. There was no help for those inside but to give themselves up to the Mercy of the Mobb, who shewed none but barbarously mangled them, hacking and hewing them until there was no Life left in their Bodies. The House itself was quite destroy'd.

I was so confounded at this Discourse that I could not answer a Word but put my Hand across my Face. Be easy in your mind, Sir, *Joseph continu'd*, for your Part is not discover'd and the Dead cannot speak: the Remainder of us are not known. This soften'd me a little and I took him to The Red Gates, an Ale-house near to the Seven Dials, where we sat from Six till within a Quarter of Ten discoursing on these Events till by degrees I became quite Calm. It is an ill Wind etc., and in this Extremity I was moved to fashion a new Designe which would bring all back into Order and so protect me. For I had previously been at a Loss how to conduct my own hot Business without being discover'd soon enough, since it had occurred to me that the Labourers at Spittle-Fields and Limehouse might have Suspicions against me. Now I pressed the man Joseph into my Service for, as I said to him, our Work could not be hindered by the Rages of the Mobb: just as it was within my Commission to raise more Churches, so it was my fixt Intention to build the sovereign Temple on Black Step Lane.

And what of the Sacrifices we must perform? *said he* smiling upon the Company in the Tavern.

You must do that for me, *I answered*. And then I added: Pliny the Eldest has an Observation that nullum frequentius votum, no Wish more frequent among Men than the Wish for Death. And then: Shall a Man see God and live? And then: You may find all you need among the pick-pocket Boys in the Moor-fields.

Why then, *says he*, here's a Health to my Arse; and he raised his Pot.

This is agreed, *I replied*.

[90]

When I left him it was a very dark Night and yet I stept towards the Hay-market to entertain my self, there mixing with a Crowd about two Ballad-singers who sang a mad Catch in the glare of their Lanthorns:

> For that he was some Fiend from Hell who stole,
> Having for Pride been burnt there to a Cole.
> I could not tell where this foul Thing should be:
> A Succubus it did appear to me.

And then they seemed to turn their Faces to me, tho' they were quite blind, and I walked on into the Night.

*

It was my set Purpose to rid my self of the workmen who were even then imployed about my Church in Wapping; they were wooden-headed Fellows but, as I suspected, they looked on me strangely and whisper'd behind my Back. And so I wrote thus to the Commission: Of the New Church of Wapping, Stepney, call'd St Georges-in-the-East, the Foundacions have been begun without that due Consideration which is requisite, so that unless I take them up again I am out of all Hope that this Designe will succeed; I have no prejudice against the Workmen but that they are Ignorant Fellows. I have admonished them to the utmost of my Power to perform the Workes according to the agreements, but notwithstanding I have observ'd the Mortar not altogether so well beat, and a vast Quantity of Spanish has been mix'd with the Bricks altho' the Workmen pretend that there is no more than what is allowed by the Commissioners. I therefore pray you to give me liberty to bring in my own Workmen to build the said Church at Wapping. I have examined and enquired into their Abilities, and conceeved that they are fit for the Places desired: and have set their Charge as before at 2/– per diem. All of which is humbly submitted, Nich: Dyer.

After this I awaited the Issue, which was not long in coming favourable to me. The work men were dismissed and while the Foundacions were empty Joseph did his Work: the Blood was spilled in its due Time, and became (as it were) the Wave on which my Bark rose. Yet first it was necessarie to conceal the Corse and, with the Reason that the Foundacions were so ill laid that I must needs take them up againe without any Delay, I worked with Joseph in this Manner: I dug a Hole of about 2 Feet wide, in which I placed a little Deal-box containing nine Pounds of Powder and no more; a Cane was fixed to the Box with a Quick-match (as Gunners call it), and reached from the Box to the Ground above; along the Ground was laid a Train of Powder and, after the Hole was carefully closed up again with

[91]

Stones and Mortar, I then lit the Powder and watch'd the effect of the Blow. This little Quantity of Powder lifted up the Rubbidge which had formed the Foundacions; and this it seemed to do somewhat leisurely, lifting visibly the whole Weight about nine Inches which, suddenly jumping down, made a great Heap of Ruines in that Place where now the Corse lay quite buried. He had been a little pretty Boy, about as tall as my Knee and but lately turned upon the Streets to beg. These were my Words to him:

> Boys and Girls come out to play,
> The Moon doth shine as bright as Day.

And these were his last Words to me: Dan never do so no more. Pitie I cannot, for I am not so weak; but it is not to be believed that he who holds the Knife or the Rope is without his own Torment.

My Inke is very bad: it is thick at the bottom, but thin and waterish at the Top, so that I must write according as I dip my Pen. These Memories become meer shortened Phrases, dark at their Beginning but growing faint towards their End and each separated so, one from another, that I am not all of a peece. Here laying beside me is my convex Mirror, which I use for the Art of Perspecktive, and in my Despair I look upon my self; but when I take it up I see that my right Hand seems bigger than my Head and that my Eyes are but glassy Orbs: there are Objects swimming at the Circumference of the Glass and here I glimpse distended a cloaths chest beneath the Window, with the blew damask Curtains blowing above it, a mahogany Buroe beside the Wall and there the Corner of my Bed with its blankets and bolster; there is my Elbow-chair, its Reflection curved beneath my own as I hold the Mirror, and next to it my side-board Table with a brass Tea-Kettle, lamp and stand. As my Visual rays receive from the Convex superficies a curved Light, these real Things become the surface of a Dream: my Eyes meet my Eyes but they are not my Eyes, and I see my Mouth opening as if to make a screaming Sound. Now it has grown Darke, and the Mirror shows only the dusky Light as it is reflected on the left side of my Face. But the voice of Nat is raised in the Kitchen below me, and coming back to my self I place a Candle in my Lanthorn.

And in this small Circle of Light I set down all exactly as it occurred. I must write of extreme Things in the dismal Night, for it was by Ratcliffe Dock that I built in trust to the dark Powers and above the filthy passages of Wapping, with its Lanes and Alleys of small Tenements, my third Church rises. Here all corrupcion and infection has its Centre: in Rope Walk lived Mary Crompton, the bloody Midwife who had six Sceletons of children of several Ages in her

Cellar (these Sceletons are now to be seen at the Ben-Johnson's Head near St Brides Church). The Watch found two other Children also destroyed, lying in a Hand-baskett in the Cellar and looking like the Carcasses of Catts or Doggs, their Flesh eat with Vermin. And this one Mary Crompton averred that she had been moved and seduced by the Divil who appear'd to her in Humane form as she passed by Old Gravill Lane. It was next to this place, in Crab Court, where Abraham Thornton carryed out his Murthers and Tortures: on the Murder of the two young Boys, he said upon Oath that the Divil put him upon it when an Apparition came to him. The Black-Boy Tavern in Red-Maide Lane is also very unfortunate for Homicides, and has seldom been Tenanted. An old woman who last lodged there sat musing by her Fire and happened by Accident to look behind her and saw a dead Corps, to her thinking, lie extended upon the Floor; it was just as a Body should be, excepting that the Foot of one Leg was fix'd on the Ground as it is in a Bed when one lies with one Knee up (as I lie now); she look'd at it a long while, but on a sudden this melancholy Spectacle vanished – it is held by common report that this was the Apparition of a Man murdered, but it is my Belief that it was an ancient Murtherer returning to the Spot of his old Glory.

Here in Angell Rents next the Ratcliffe High-way was Mr Barwick barbarously killed, his Throat being cut, the right side of his Head open'd and his Scull broke: I suppose it was done with a Hammer or some such Weapon. A Tub-woman that carries Ale and Beer to the private Houses thereabouts heard the Victim and his Destroyer call out, and when I walk among these Passages I hear such Voices still: *How can you strike a sick Man, you are a Dead Man, O Christ do not do it, Damn you are you not dead yet* echo by the River. The Murtherer was afterwards hang'd in Chains near the place of his Crime – thus it is call'd Red Cliff, or Ratcliffe, the hanging Dock opposite my Church where the Bodies of the Damned are washed by the Water until they fall to Bits from the effects of Time. Many cry out *Jesus, Maria, Jesus, Maria* as they go to their Deaths but there was one Boy who killed his whole Family in Betts-Street and was taken in Chains to the Dock to be hang'd: when he saw the Gibbet he laugh'd at first, but then he raved and cried for Damnation. The Mobb could hardly forebear tearing him to Pieces, and yet they knew that if they trod upon the same Stones where Malefactors are done to Death, they would suffer a brief Agonie also. Destruction is like a snow-ball rolled down a Hill, for its Bulk encreases by its own swiftness and thus Disorder spreads: when the woman nam'd Maggot was hanged in Chains by here, one hundred were crushed to Death in the Tumult that came to stare upon her. And so when the Cartesians and the New Philosophers speak of their Experiments, saying that they are serviceable to the Quiet and Peace of Man's life, it is a great Lie: there has been no Quiet and there will be no Peace. The streets they walk in are ones in which Children die daily or are hang'd for stealing Sixpence; they wish to lay a solid Ground-work (or so they call it) for their vast Pile of Experiments, but the Ground is filled with Corses, rotten and rotting others.

Be informed, also, that this good and savoury Parish is the home of Hectors, Trapanners, Biters who all go under the general appelation of Rooks. Here are all the Jilts, Cracks, Prostitutes, Night-walkers, Whores, Linnen-lifters, who are like so many Jakes, Privies, Houses of Office, Ordures, Excrements, Easments and piles of Sir-reverence: the whores of Ratcliffe High-way smell of Tarpaulin and stinking Cod from their continuall Traffick with seamen's Breeches. There are other such wretched Objects about these ruined Lanes, all of them lament-able Instances of Vengeance. And it is not strange (as some think) how they will haunt the same Districts and will not leave off their Crimes until they are apprehended, for these Streets are their Theatre. Theft, Whoredom and Homicide peep out of the very Windows of their Souls; Lying, Perjury, Fraud, Impudence and Misery are stamped upon their very Countenances as now they walk within the Shaddowe of my Church.

And in this world of Corrupcion I had as like forgot the House for Buggaronies next to the High-way, where grave Gentlemen dress in Women's cloaths, then patch and paint their Faces. They assume the Language as well as the Shape of Women, *viz* For God's sake, Ladies, what do you mean to use a tender Woman, as I am, with such Barbarity (the Cord is wound around its Neck and its Body suspended by Ropes), I come to make you a civil Visit and here you have prepared Cords and cruel Bands to bind me (the Rods are laid upon its pale Back), I beg of you to use me kindly for you will find me a Woman like your selves (and it comes off with a great Sigh, Nature discharg'd).

This puts me in mind of a Story: there is an Inn on the road between White-chapel and Limehouse, where on one gusty Evening a Gentle-man rode up and ask'd for Lodgings. He took his Supper with some other Travellers, and astonish'd the Company as much by the powers of his Conversation as by the elegance of his Manner. He was an orator, a poet, a painter, a musician, a lawyer, a divine and the magick of his Discourse kept the drowsy Company awake long after their usual Hour. At length, however, wearied Nature could be charmed no more but on observing the Fatigue of the society, the Stranger dis-cover'd manifest signs of Uneasinesse: he therefore gave new force to his Spirits, but the departure of his Guests could not be long delay'd and he was eventually conducted to his Chamber. The remains of the Company retired also, but they had scarce closed their Eyes when the house was alarmed by the most terrible Shrieks that were ever known.

[94]

Frightened at what they heard, several of them rang their Bells and, when the Servants came, they declared that the horrid Sounds proceeded from the stranger's Chamber. Some of the Gentlemen immediately arose, to inquire into the extraordinary Disturbance; and while they were dressing themselves for the purpose, deeper Groans of Despair, and shriller Shrieks of agony, again astonished and terrified them. After knocking some time at the Stranger's door, he answered them as one woken from Sleep, declared he heard no Noise and desired he might not again be disturbed. Upon this they returned to their Chambers and had scarce begun to communicate their Sentiments to each other when their Converse was interrupted by a renewal of yells, screams and shrieks which once more they traced to the Stranger's chamber, the door of which they instantly burst open, and found him upon his Knees on his Bed, in the act of Scourging himself with the most unrelenting Severity, his Body streaming with Blood. On their seizing his Hand to stop the Strokes he begged them, in the most wringing tone of Voice, that as an act of Mercy they would retire for the Disturbance was now over. In the morning some of them went to his Chamber, but he was not there; and, on examining the Bed, they found it to be one Gore of Blood. Upon further Enquiry, the servants said that the Gentleman had come to the Stable booted and spurred, desired his Horse to be immediately saddled, and then rode at full speed towards London. The Reader may wonder how I, who make no mention of my being there, should be able to relate this as of my own Knowledge; but if he pleases to have Patience, he will have intire Satisfaction in that Point.

The Night is now so cold that I must put my Coat upon the Bed to warm me, and I meditate upon what follows as if it were a Dreame: for was it not a Dreame to see Sir Chris. his Hands steeped in Blood up to the Wrist-bones, and then scratching his head until his Wigg was tainted with it? It was his filthy Curiosity to pore in Humane Corses and so to besmear himself that he might trace each Nerve and all the private Kingdom of Veins and Arteries. I remark on it in this Place, after the history of the Gentleman Traveller, so that you may anatomise the Mind of him who looks into that Blood and Corrupcion and not only of him who Whips it from himself and spills it upon a Bed.

Sir Chris. was well known to those impannelled as Coroners to be a Man who understood the Anatomical Administration of the Humane Body, by means of his geometrical and mechanical Speculations, and one who showed such keen Inclination to cut the fresh Corses that he could be call'd upon in the Ministration of their Office. So it was that one day when I was working with him, on the making of Sewers at the West End of a Church, a packet arrived with a Messenger who desir'd an answer instantly – the Letter saying that the Corps of a Woman was even then lying in the Gate-house at Southwark Reach, having been taken from the River, and that if Sir Chris. should bring his Instruments they would be much obliged to him. Well, well, *says he*, another Body: I had been hoping for one. And then he asked the Messenger what was the fatal Stroke?

She drowned herself in the Thames, Sir, or so it seems.

Good, good, *Sir Chris. goes on* hardly hearing this News, but we have little time to prepare ourselves: have you the Stomach for it Nick?

It is not my Stomach, *I replied* and he laugh'd out loud, while the Messenger looked on bemus'd.

Come then, *says he*, we will cross the River and see about this Affair. And so we walked straight to the Wharf at White-hall, where we hired an Oarsman to take us over. And even tho' the River-men set up their usual cacophony of Billingsgate abuse, Sir Chris. was lost in the Anticipation of his Work: Anatomy, *says he* as the Oaths fly about him, is a noble Art – *You shitten skulled son of a Turd that has Spit your Brains in my Face, who was begot in Buggery, born in a House of Office, delivered at the Fundament* – just as, Nick, the Body it self is a perfect peece of Work from the Hand of the Omniscient Architect – *You Brandy-Faced Bawdy Son of a Brimstone Whore.* Sir Chris. listens for a moment to the River-men and then speaks once more: Do you know that I have shown the Geometric Mechanics of Rowing – *Piss up my arse, Buggaronie* – to be a Vectis on a moving or cedent Fulcrum – *Every time you Conjobble with your Mother may she beget a Bellyfull of Crab lice.* And then he smiles upon our Oarsman saying, He is a good Gentleman; and the Oarsman on hearing this shouts out to us: Well, Sirs, can you riddle me a riddle?

Oh yes, *says Sir Chris.*, is it a Rhyme?

And then the man sings:

> Riddle my Riddle, my ree,
> And tell me what my Riddle shall be.
> Long, white and slender,
> Tickles Maids where they are tender
> Lyes where Hair grows,
> And hath long Slit under the Nose.

Why, *cries Sir Chris.*, this is a Bodkin! And the Oarsman, looking sourly upon him, says You are right, Sir. And Sir Chris., lying back and smiling, trails his Finger in the Water until we reached the other Side.

We coach'd it at once to the Gate-house (being only about a Mile from where we landed) and thereupon the Coroner took us into a small Chamber where the naked Body of the Woman was to be seen.

[96]

Sir Chris. rapidly surveyed the Corse: She must have been a fine woman when she was dressed, *he muttered* as he started work upon her with his Surgeon's Tools. The Romans held it unlawfull to look on the Entrails, *says he* as he cuts into the Skin, but now Anataomy is a free and generall Practice. You see here, Nick, (shewing me the Inside of the Corse as he spoke), you see the Valve at the entrance of the gut Colon, and here the Milkie Veins and the Lymphatick Vessels (he looked up, his Hands dangling and bloody, and I heard a Roaring in my Ears); so we have discover'd the art of Transfusion of the Blood from one living Animal to another. It is of use, *he continued*, in Pleurisies, Cancers, Leprosies, Ulcers, Small Pox, Dotage, and all such Distempers.

There was a lady, *I said* when Sir Chris. had paused, who seeing Hoggs and other Creatures cut up and their Bowels taken out, tormented her self with the Thought that she also carried about with her in her own Body such stinking Filth, as she call'd it, inclosed. Upon which she conceeved a sudden Abhorrence, and hated her own Body so that she did not know what Course to take to free her self from Uncleanness.

Meer Phrensy, *Sir Chris. replied*. See here, the Body is still fresh and what is this Corrupcion you mention but the Union and Dissolution of little Bodies or Particles: have you no Sense, Nick? I kept my Peace but I thought to myself: The meerest Rake-hell has a finer Philosophie.

The Coroner now returned into the Room, having gone out for Air, and asked Sir Chris. his Judgment on this poor, poor Girl (as he put it). It was not self-murther, *he replied*, and I am induced to believe that she was knocked down with a Blow on her left Ear, from the large Settlement of Blood there (and he pointed to the Head with his little Hammer): after she was fell'd to the Ground by the Blow it is probable, with the Gripe of a strong Hand, that she was throttled, and this to be understood from the Stagnation on both sides of her Neck under her Ears; and from the Settlement of Blood on her Breast, *he went on*, I am inclined to believe that the person who throttled her rested his Arm on her Breast to gripe the stronger. She is not long Dead, *he continu'd*, for although she was found floating upon the Thames, I find no Water in the Stomach, Intestines, Abdomens, Lungs, or cavity of the Thorax. She did not drown her self for Shame neither, since her Uterus is perfectly free and empty.

I survey'd the woman's Face, flinching as if my own Body had felt the Blows she endured, and then I saw what she had seen: Well Madam, *says her Murtherer*, I was walking here as I generally do, will you not walk with me a little? And I saw the first Blow and suffer'd the first Agonie of her Pain. He has taken a white Cloath from his

[97]

Breeches, looks at it, then throws it upon the Ground and his Hand goes around my Throat: You need not be afraid, *he whispers*, for you will be sure to get what you Want. And now I feel the Torrents of my own Blood surging in my Head.

And so ends your first Anatomy lesson, *says Sir Chris.* to me, but be pleased to wait now till I have washed my self.

Sir Chris. was always strowling abroad to seek out fresh Wonders, so filling his Head that it had become a pure Cabinet of Curiosities. On one Day he comes in after our Work is complete: Shall we see the sixteen-foot Worm brought from a young Gentleman and now lying in a Bottle at the House of Mr Moor, *he asks*, or shall we visit the Demoniack new clapp'd up in Bedlam? I advised him that the Worm was smaller than the Prodigy reported, having my self gone to observe it two days before; and, since there is nothing finer in an idle Hour than to make merry among the Lunaticks, I agreed to take that Course and walk with him that Way. We were admitted thro' the iron Gate of Bedlam and, having given Sixpence, turned in thro' another Barricado into the Gallery of the Men's Apartments where there was such a ratling of Chains and drumming of Doors that it made a body's Head ache. The Noise and Roaring, the Swearing and Clamour, the Stench and Nastinesse, and all the Croud of afflicted Things to be seen there, joyn'd together to make the Place seem a very Emblem of Hell and a kind of Entrance into it.

We walked through with Linnen pressed against our Nostrils, and Sir Chris. gave his bright Glances all around at this assembly of derang'd Creatures. Some of the Mad who peeped through their Wickets were indeed known to him, for he had set them down in his Pocket-book before, and when one magoty-brained Fellow called out *Masters, Masters!* Sir Chris. murmured to me, Do not turn back but go on a little and see the Conclusion to his Cries. For there were others who, on hearing him, went back to hear what he had to say and, when they came close to his Wicket, he provided them all with a plentifull Bowl of Piss which he cast very successfully amongst them, singing out: I never give Victuals but I give Drink and you're welcome, Gentlemen. He is a merry Fellow, *said Sir Chris.* with a laugh. Then as we passed down this Passage we were knocked against certain Women of the Town, who gave us Eye-language, since there were many Corners and Closets in Bedlam where they would stop and wait for Custom: indeed it was known as a sure Market for Lechers and Loiterers, for tho' they came in Single they went out by Pairs. This is a Showing-room for Whores, *I said*.

And what better place for Lust, *Sir Chris. replied*, than among those whose Wits have fled?

The Singing and Ranting now grew so loud that Sir Chris. said no more to me but motioned me towards the Gate which led into the Gallery of the Women's Apartments. Here we discovered some more unhappy Objects, *viz.* a Woman who stood with her Back against the Wall crying *Come John, Come John, Come John* (I believe that to be her Son who is dead, Sir Chris. told me) while another was tearing her Straw in peece-meal, swearing and blaspheming and biting her Grate. There was yet another talking very merrily at her peeping Hole, but when we came near her she was saying Bread was good with Cheese, and Cheese was good with Bread, and Bread and Cheese were good together. Sir Chris. bent down to listen to her and said Quite so, quite so, before the Stink sent us away from her Cell. We went back into the Mens Apartments where there were others raving of Ships that may fly and silvered Creatures upon the Moon: Their Stories seem to have neither Head nor Tayl to them, *Sir Chris. told me*, but there is a Grammar in them if I could but Puzzle it out.

This is a mad Age, *I replied*, and there are many fitter for Bedlam than these here confin'd to a Chain or a dark Room.

A sad Reflection, Nick.

And what little Purpose have we to glory in our Reason, *I continu'd*, when the Brain may so suddenly be disorder'd?

Well that may be, that may be, *said he hurriedly*, but where is our new Demoniack? And he walked up to a Gaoler who he knew by Sight, and begins to converse with him; then he wags his Fingers at me to come forward. The Man is lockt away from the Spectators, *he told me* when I came up to him, but we are at Liberty to see him if we so please. This placed me in some Fear and Confusion, and I must have turned Pale or seemed Uneasy for Sir Chris. clapped me on the Shoulder saying: He cannot hurt you, Nick, he is in Chains; come, we will visit the Man for a Minute only. And so the Gaoler led us up a back stair-case to the private Chambers of Bedlam where those who are not fit for Entertainment are placed in Confinement. The Creature is in here, *the Gaoler told us* in a Sombre voice, but be comfortable, Gentlemen, he is nicely tyed.

When we went forward, and our Eyes grew accustomed to the thin Light, we saw the Man lying upon the Ground. In his Fitts, *said the Gaoler* rolling his Eyes, he has been blown about the Room or born up suddenly from his Chair, and would as like have flown away but the Holders of him hung at his Arms and Legs. At this Sir Chris. smiled but did not show it to the Gaoler. And then, *he continu'd*, he was lain down as if dead upon the Floor as he is now, Sirs, and then without the natural help of Arms or Legs has broken into such wild Curves and Bounces as cannot be described. Sir Chris. looked at the Lunatick but said nothing. And then, *he went on*, there were amazing hideous Sounds to be heard coming from him – sometimes as of Swine, or

Water-mills, or of a Bear, and they mix up into a Peal of Noises. And then –

– Have done, have done, *murmured the Creature* from the Ground, in a low Voice which affrighted me.

You see that his Lips did not move! *exclaimed the Gaoler*.

Have done, I said! And the Demoniack rose from the Floor: Sir Chris. and I stepped back a Pace, at which the Man laughed out loud. Then he paid no more Heed to us: there were Rushes strewed on the Floor to keep his Bones from being broken, and he took them up and handled them as if they had been a Pack of Cards, every way acting the Gamester to the life; then he ordered the Rushes as if they had been Dice, then as if he had been playing at Bowl, with the various Postures of the Bowler.

Sir Chris. looked on silently and at last took out his Pocket-book, at which point the Demoniack spat a Ball of Phlegm at him. Then he began to Speak: The other day I lookt for your Worships Nativity, which lies in the Quadrature of a Magnet, in the Sextile of the Twins that always go in the Shade. Guard yourself from the Horse-flies. And he added: Thus have I puzled all thy Scholarship. At this I laugh'd and the Madman turned to me crying: What more Death still Nick, Nick, Nick, you are my own! At this I was terribly astounded, for he could in no wise have known my name. And in his Madness he called out to me again: Hark ye, you boy! I'll tell you somewhat, one Hawksmoor will this day terribly shake you! Then his Tongue rolled inwards all in a Lump, and his Eye-balls turned backwards, nothing but the White of them being seen. And the Gaoler made Signs for us to leave.

Who is this Hawksmoor, *Sir Chris. asked me* as we left the Mad-House and entered the Fields.

No one, *I answered*, no Man I know. Then leaving him I went quick into a Tavern, and swallow'd pot after pot of Ale till I became drunken.

*

I kept my own list of Wonders as much as did Sir Chris., tho' he would have been more afraid of the truth of my Stories than the Ape is of the Whip. Thus he was like to ridicule in my Hearing the Discourse concerning Mr Greatrack, the Irish stroker: pains strangely flew before his Hands, Dimness was cleared and Deafness cured by his Touch, running Sores were dried up, obstructions and stoppings remov'd and Cancerous Knots in the Breast dissolv'd. And then there was the narrative of the Child, Mary Duncan, who, when she pointed with her Finger at Neck, Head, Hand-wrists, Arms and Toes there did bloody Thorns appear. I kept among these Memorials the story of the woman in Islington who was deliver'd of a Child with the head of a Cat, for while she was Big she was frightened exceedingly by one which had got into her Bed. And when the Duke of Alva ordered three hundred Citizens to be put to Death together at Antwerp, a Lady who saw the Sight was presently afterwards deliver'd of a Child without a Head. So lives the Power of Imagination even in this Rationall Age. There has also been in the News the History of Mr John Mompesson of Tedworth, who has related the moving of Chairs by Spirits invisible, the plucking of Hair and Night-cloaths, the great Heat, the singing in the Chimney, the scratching and the panting. For those who wish the Sight of such Ghosts and Apparitions I say this: it is of no long Duration, continuing for the most part only as you keep your Eyes steady (as I have done); the Timerous see meerly by Glances, therefore, their Eyes always trembling at the first sight of the Object, but the most Assured will fix their Look. There is this also: those who see the Daemon must draw down their Eyes with their Fingers after.

This mundus tenebrosus, this shaddowy world of Mankind, is sunk into Night; there is not a Field without its Spirits, nor a City without its Daemons, and the Lunaticks speak Prophesies while the Wise men fall into the Pitte. We are all in the Dark, one with another. And, as the Inke stains the Paper on which it is spilt and slowly spreads to Blot out the Characters, so the Contagion of darkness and malefaction grows apace until all becomes unrecognizable. Thus it was with the Witches who were tryed by Swimming not long before, since once the Prosecution had commenced no Stop could be put to the raving Women who came forward: the number of Afflicted and Accused began to encrease and, upon Examination, more confess'd themselves guilty of Crimes than were suspected of. And so it went, till the Evil revealed was so great that it threatened to bring all into Confusion.

And yet in the way of that Philosophie much cryed up in London and elsewhere, there are those like Sir Chris. who speak only of what is Rational and what is Demonstrated, of Propriety and Plainness. *Religion Not Mysterious* is their Motto, but if they would wish the Godhead to be Reasonable why was it that when Adam heard that Voice in the Garden he was afraid unto Death? The Mysteries must become easy and familiar, it is said, and it has now reached such a Pitch that there are those who wish to bring their mathematicall Calculations into Morality, *viz.* the Quantity of Publick Good produced by any Agent is a compound Ratio of his Benevolence and Abilities, and such like Excrement. They build Edifices which they call *Systems* by laying their Foundacions in the Air and, when they think they are come to sollid Ground, the Building disappears and the Architects tumble down from the Clowds. Men that are fixed upon *matter, experiment, secondary causes* and the like have forgot there is such a thing in the World which they cannot see nor touch nor measure: it is the Praecipice into which they will surely fall.

[101]

There are those who say further that these are meer Dreames and no true Relations, but I say back to them: look upon my Churches in the Spittle-fields, in Limehouse, and now in the Parish of Wapping Stepney, and do you not wonder why they lead you into a darker World which on Reflection you know to be your own? Every Patch of Ground by them has its Hypochondriack Distemper and Disorder; every Stone of them bears the marks of Scorching by which you may follow the true Path of God. Now, these men of Reason assert that such Signs are but the Stuff of deep Melancholists or cozening Rogues but even in the Bible, that Book of the Dead, there are innumerable Instances: Evil Angels were sent among the Aegyptians, *Psalm 78.49*, God asked Sathan whence he came *Job 1.7*, and Sathan raised the Great Wind *5.19*. Divils entered the Swine, *Luke 8.33* and the Unclean Divil entered the Man, *Luke 5.35*. And of the Demoniack: No Man cou'd bind him, *Mark 5*. And divers other Passages: the Witch of Endor, that Pythoness whom Saul consulted *1. Sam 28* and who brought forth Samuel: an Old Man cometh up, and he is covered with a Mantle. And then as the Witch in *Josephus verse 13* saith: I saw Gods ascending out of the Earth.

But some good Gentlemen of the present Age might ask me, Where is your Proof? And I answer: regard my Churches and the way their Shaddowes fall upon the Ground; look up at them, also, and see if you are not brought into Confusion. And I say further: if every thing for which the Learned are not able to give satisfactory Account shall be condemned as False and Impossible, then the World itself will seem a meer Romance. Let this suffice also: the Existence of Spirits cannot be found by Mathematick demonstrations, but we must rely upon Humane reports unless we will make void and annihilate the Histories of all passed things. But those who dare not say, There is no God!, content themselves by saying that Daemons are but Bugs and Chimaeras. I dispute not with such Persons: when a Man is of short sight he will be so in the midst of Prodigies or Miracles, and will mistake the Candle of his Reason for the Noon-day Sunne. He will see nothing but Extension, Divisibility, Solidity, Mobility: he forgets his frail Mortality, and goes groping in the Dark.

And o God it is Dark still: Certainly you slept very sound, *says Nat*, and I have already done all my little Jobs and the Floor is so clean, Master, there is no Place to Spit and all the while I was by my leathern Bucket you were murmuring Words in your Sleep –

– Nat, *I said*, Nat I thought I had just lit a Candle and laid me down for an Instant.

No, Master, it is already Seven.

And the Night has passed?

It has gone like an Arrow tho' it is but an ill Morning and the Post-Master's Boy, who I contemn, has given us this.

And Nat puts down a little Pacquet which had inscribed upon it: *To Mr Dyer, left at the Post-House in Leester-Fields*. He stands next to me and peers at it, but a strange Trembling seiz'd me: Go on your way, Master Eliot, *I said*, and bring me some Beef and Eggs. When he left the Room I opened the Pacquet and there found a small Paper sent by a Hand unknown to me, which was written in large plain Letters thus: *I have sin yr work in Gods name. I am hear this fortnighet, and you shall hear from me as soon as I com into Whytehill. I ham with all my art your frind and the best frind in the world if I get my service for all is due and my mouth quiet.* As I read this Message which seem'd to Threaten me, my Bowels mov'd and I ran from my Bed to the Stool-pan; I sat there and looked about fearfully, as if the very Walls menac'd me, and I was near Shitting away my Life. Then I heard Nat come up the Stairs and I call'd out to him, I am at Stool: leave the Beef by the Door! Which he quickly did, and walk'd down again to the Kitchin.

This letter was not so cunningly writ that I could not puzzle out its Meaning: by some foul Chance, my Company at Black Step Lane had been discover'd, and with it my own earnest Business beside the Churches. I was now fix'd indeed and in an Instant become once more the Child crouched in an Ash-pit, in too much Agonie of Mind to cry out against the World. I rose from my Pot and laid my self down upon the Bed, as like to call for a Shroud as for a Pair of Breeches. I knew all the Acts were against me: In the 39 of Eliz 4 it was enacted that all Persons using any subtile Craft, or telling Destinies or Fortunes, should be taken and deemed Rogues, Vagabonds, sturdy Beggars, and shall be stripped naked from the Middle upwards and whipp'd till his or her Body be bloody. But that was as Nothing; I could be indicted on the Statute Primo Jacobi cap 12: that to feed, imploy or reward any evil Spirits is a Felony – that I did thus quondam malum Spiritum negotiare. It was further enacted that any Person or Persons using Witchcraft, Sorcery and all their Aiders, Abettors and Counsellors, being convicted and attainted of the same Offences, shall suffer Pain of Death as a Felon without Benefit of Clergy. This did stick in my Mind (as they say), and as I lie upon this Bed I rise up and enter the Stone Room of Newgate and I am stapled fast down to the Floor; now I am re-mov'd to the Bar of the Court of the King's Bench and Sir Chris. is come to bear Witnesse against me; now I am dragg'd to the Carte and I laugh at the Mobbe around me; and now my Hands are being tyed and the Cap is draped over my Face; and as I am dying I am pull'd by the Legs. Thus my Fear crept through the Passages of my Senses: it presented itself in Figures, it adhered to Sounds, introduced Odours and infused it self in Savours. And I said softly to my self, *Oh no, my Sentence is just.*

[103]

But then my sanguine Humour came up again, and I bit my Hand till the Blood came from it: I know my own Strength, *says I*, for it has been tried and, if I foresee Storms, it is fit I should prevent them. Why should I shrink before an ignorant and covetous Rogue? When I find who wrote this, I will utterly destroy him.

And then this became the Thread of my Thoughts which led me through a Labyrinth of Fear: this insipid Letter, *says I*, is ill writ by Designe to lead me out of the right way of my Suspicions. Thus the Fellow writes Whytehill when the meerest Squab knows it is White-hall. And who are those that watch me or speak against me but only those in the Office? And who would know of my Designes but only those who steal into my Closet or question Walter Pyne about my Work? And who has set Walter against me and, as it may be, follow'd me? And yes, yes Indeed there is one who haunts Walter and gives him brave Words – one Yorick Hayes, the Measuring Surveyour, and one who if I were remov'd from the Office flatters himself that he would leap up into my Place. It may be he who writes: I shall Watch him, and Track him, and Crack him like a Crab-louse. The Thought of how I might get him out of the Way fill'd me with a Delight which ran in my Blood and set me walking about my Chamber.

And as I walked I conceeved a Bait of my own to catch this Sprat, this Homunculouse, and I wrote back thus: I understand not your Meaning by your Writing, explain yourself in your next and lett me know. I did not sign my Name but put upon the Cover: *Mr Hayes*. Then I placed the Letter in the Waistband of my Drawers and call'd out for Nat, who came running into me.

You have not touch'd your Beef, *says he*, and you have drank Nothing neither: I say to Mrs Best that I know not what to do with you, and you are like the little Shrinking Man of the Fable who –

– Enough, Nat.

You are in the right, *says he* and Yawns.

And then I went on: Nat, if you see any mean-faced, covetous idle Fellows lingering in this Quarter, and any such who cause you Uneasinesse, watch them and tell me. He looked at me surpriz'd and said nothing further but yawned again. Then, with a little Whistling under my Breath, I dress'd my self. Here was a Bold one indeed, but as I walk'd to the Office, my Feares returned. Each Passer-by who looked on me struck me with a fresh Terrour: I was a perfect Mystery to my self and was affected by so many various Passions that I scarce knew which way I travell'd. I entered Scotland-yard like a Guilty thing and, wheeling about to see that I was unobserv'd, I left my Letter to Mr Hayes in the Passage where the Rogue was assured of Discovering it.

Then, once again in my own Closet and among my own Planns and

Papers, I took Heart and press'd forward with the Negociacions concerning my Work. Quickly I wrote to the Commission thus: The Church of Wapping Stepney moves forward. The Walls are now coming up to a height of fifteen or sixteen feet everywhere; the Mason has had a good Quantity of Portland Stone, although he has not made that Advance with the Work as might be expected. The Frost has pritty much affected some of the Brickwork that was done about the beginning of November: some must be taken out and new laid. But I am content. I am also inclosing Scetches of a very spacious and curious Peece of Painting to be placed at the West End of the Church – being the Figure of Time, with Wings display'd. Under the Feet of Time lyeth the Pourtrait of a Sceleton about 8 Foot in Length, under which is Glory in the form of an Equilateral Triangle within a spacious Circle. This being a most proper Emblemme for a Christian Church, and one that hath been imployed since the early days of Christianity. Your humble servant: Nich. Dyer.

This is the only Picture which will be unveiled to the Commissioners, and my own Work remains conceal'd: for, in the third of my Churches, must also be represented a huge dark Man with red Eyes holding a Sword and clad in a white Garment, a Man holding a golden Sphere and dressed in Red, a Man with a hood of dark Linen over his Head and with his Hands raysed. When my old Mirabilis first acquainted me with such Stuff, I told him they brought into my Memory the Stories I had heard in my Childhood. And why should they not, said he, since it is in Childhood that our Sorrows begin? And how could I now forget the Corse withinne the Foundacions?

There was a Noise in the Passage and I took my self to my Doorway as if by Chance: it was the man Hayes entering, as I had thought, but I dared not glance at the Letter I had left as a Snare for him. We bowed to each other civilly enough, and then I turned as if I had forgot some thing. But I paus'd at my Door and, moving my Head a little, I saw out of the Corner of my Eye the clown Hayes pick up the Letter, open it, read it swiftly, and throw it down without so much as looking at me. You are a dead Man, I thought to myself, so to taunt me.

And then the Serpent speaks: Mr Dyer, says he, I have examin'd the Ground by Wapping Church.

Did you look upon the Dust, as the Preacher tells us?

And he smiled for a Moment at my Jest before continuing: It will be very chargeable and difficult to make a Sewer there, Mr Dyer.

But it must be done, Mr Hayes, there is no other Place.

Then I must wait till the Foundations of all the Pillars are layed, he goes on, so pray do me the Favour to tell me when this is done.

Have you view'd the Designe? I ask'd showing my Teeth to him in a Grin.

[105]

Yes, it is in my Box.

I would be glad to have it againe in my Possession, Mr Hayes, since I have no Coppie.

He saw then that he could not Shake me. He made to enter his own Chamber and, with his back towards me, spoke as it seemed into the Air: This is the third Church is it not, Mr Dyer?

Let alone, puppy, let alone was my Thought as I measured him up for his Shroud. Yes, *I said*, yes, it is the third.

Part Two

6

'IS IT the third?'

'Yes, the third. The boy at Spitalfields, the tramp at Limehouse, and now another boy. The third.'

'And this was at Wapping?'

'Yes.'

Hawksmoor looked out of his window at the streets below, from which no noise reached him; then his eyes grew larger as he looked at the window itself and noticed the patina of dust thrown up by the city; then he altered his gaze once more and concentrated upon his own image as it was reflected in the window – or, rather, the outline of his face like an hallucination above the offices and homes of London. His head ached and he closed his eyes at last, pressing his fingers lightly against his temples before asking, 'And why do they think there's a connection?'

The young man behind him was about to sit on a small office chair but he stood up again awkwardly, brushing his sleeve against an indoor plant which quivered in a stream of air from the ventilation system. 'The connection is, sir, that they were all strangled, all in the same area, and all churches.'

'Well this is a mystery, isn't it? Do you like mysteries, Walter?'

'It's a mystery they're trying to solve.'

And Hawksmoor was impatient to see it for himself. The strip lighting in the corridors emitted a vague hum which pleased him, but when he looked up he could see its exposed cables covered in dust: part of the corridor was in darkness, and so they waited in darkness for a little while before the doors of the lift opened for them. And as he and his assistant drove away from New Scotland Yard, he gestured at the streets outside and murmured, 'It's a jungle out there, Walter.' And Walter laughed, since he knew Hawksmoor's habit of parodying the remarks made by their colleagues. A song was passing through Hawksmoor's head – One for Sorrow, Two for Joy, but what was the third for?

The oddly shaped tower of St George's-in-the-East, which seemed to have burst through the roof rather than simply to rise from it, was visible as they parked by the river; and, as they walked across Ratcliffe Highway towards the church, Hawksmoor bit the inside of his mouth and drew blood: once again, as with every such inquiry, he was faced with the possibility of failure. The church and its precincts were already cordoned off, and a small crowd had gathered in front of the white tape – a crowd composed largely of local people who had come out of curiosity to stare at the scene of the child's death. And there were murmurs of 'here he is!' and 'who's he?' as Hawksmoor passed quickly through them and ducked under the tape before walking around the side of the church to a small park behind. An inspector and some young constables from the local CID were crouched over, looking at the ground beside a partly ruined building which had the words M SE M OF still visible above its entrance; the inspector was dictating observations into a tape-recorder but, as soon as he saw Hawksmoor striding towards him, he switched it off and stood up, grimacing at a pain in his back. Hawksmoor chose not to see it and came very close: 'I am Detective Chief Superintendent Hawksmoor, and this is my assistant Detective Sergeant Payne: your Divisional Superintendent has been in touch with you about my involvement?'

'Yes, he's been in touch, sir.' Hawksmoor, satisfied that everything had been explained, turned round to look at the rear wall of the church and wondered how long it had taken to erect. A group of children were peering through the railings of the park, their faces pale beside the dark iron. 'Some queer found him late last night,' the inspector was saying and then he added, since Hawksmoor did not reply, 'Some queer might have done it.'

'I need a time.'

'About four in the morning, sir.'

'And there is an identification?'

'The father –' and the inspector glanced over at two figures, a man sitting down upon a bench beneath an oak tree with a woman constable standing and looking down at him, one hand upon his shoulder. A siren could be heard somewhere in the distance. Hawksmoor took out a pair of spectacles from his top pocket and examined the man: he knew the face of shock and this one seemed no different, although now the father looked up and caught his gaze. Hawksmoor held his breath until the man looked down upon the ground, and then he turned suddenly to the inspector.

'Where is the body?'

'The body? The body's gone, sir.'

Hawksmoor examined the man's uniform. 'Perhaps you have been told, inspector, that you must never move the body until the investigating officer has arrived?'

'But the father came, sir –'

[110]

'Never move the body!' And then he added, 'Where has it gone?'

'It's gone for examination. It's gone to the pathologist.'

And so the atmosphere of the murder was already destroyed. He walked over to the father, who started to get up from the bench until Hawksmoor waved him down. 'No, no,' he said, 'Don't move. Stay where you are.'

The father smiled apologetically, but his face was so red from grief that it seemed raw and unformed. Hawksmoor imagined himself peeling off the layers of skin and flesh until there was nothing left but the gaping holes of mouth and eyes. 'He was such a friendly boy,' the father was telling him, 'He was always so friendly.' Hawksmoor bowed his head. 'I was asked to bring something of his,' the father was saying, 'Is it for the dogs? I couldn't take any of his clothes, I just couldn't, you know, but I brought you this' – and he held a children's book in front of him. Hawksmoor wanted to touch its bright cover, but already the father was leafing through it and sighing. 'He used to read this book over and over. So many times.' Hawksmoor watched his hand turning the pages, and then by chance saw an engraving of an old man with a stick, while beside him a child scraped a fiddle. Even as he stared at it he remembered other such illustrations from his own books: a picture of a graveyard with a hare reading from one of the tombs, of a cat sitting beside a pile of stones. There had been verses beneath them which seemed to go on for ever, line being added to line in succession, but he could not now recall the words. He took the book from the father's hands and gave it to the policewoman before asking him gently, 'When did you last see your son?'

'Do you mean what time?'

'Yes, can you remember the time?'

And the man frowned with the effort, as if nothing really existed before the fact of this death. He might have been sitting there for ever in the shadow of St George's-in-the-East. 'It must have been about six yesterday evening. Yes it was, because the clock struck.'

'And did he say –'

'Dan. He was Dan.'

'And did Dan say where he was going?'

'He said he was going out. He just opened the door and went out. That was the last time.'

Hawksmoor rose and said, 'We're doing all we can. We'll keep you informed.' And the father stood up beside him in order to shake his hand, in an almost formal gesture. Walter had been watching all this from the middle of the park, and now he cleared his throat as Hawksmoor came up to him saying, 'Well, we might as well go and see it'.

The body of the child was already in place in the examination room

[111]

when they arrived. Labels had been tied around its left ankle and around both of its wrists; the head had been placed in a wooden block, with the nape of the neck resting in the curvature. The pathologist had just finished washing his hands and glanced up at the two men with a smile: Hawksmoor made a point of smiling also, but none of them glanced at the naked corpse which lay only two feet away. 'You don't waste any time,' the pathologist said as he took a tape-recorder out of his pocket.

'Time is not on our side.'

The pathologist, not hearing this, bent over the body and spoke softly into the tape-recorder: 'I am now examining the external surface of the body. The face has become engorged and discoloured blue, the eyes are bulged and showers of tiny petechiae in the eyelids and conjuctivae indicate asphyxia. The tongue is protruding through the teeth. A small amount of blood has trickled from burst vessels in the ears but not in the nose. There is evidence of the emptying of the bladder and back passage. No evidence of sexual assault. I am looking now for fingertip or nail impressions on each side of the neck at around voice-box level –' and then, after a sudden pause, he continued – 'None of these. Several scratches on the neck which could have been made by the victim trying to prise off the attacker's hands. From the injuries I would say that he was strangled as he lay on the ground, with his murderer either kneeling or sitting astride him. The lividity here has formed well. Minor bruises under the scalp and over the spine suggest that he had been pressed on his back during the strangling. There is no impression of a ligature, and there are no bite marks. There are some teeth pressure marks on the reverse of the lips.' And as he talked Hawksmoor gazed at the feet of the corpse, trying to imagine them in the act of running, but the pathologist now switched off his tape and Hawksmoor relaxed.

The mortuary assistant came forward and cut both of the boy's hands off at the wrist, taking them to a separate bench for examination. The pathologist then made a single incision from the throat to the pubic region, cutting in a slight curve to avoid the umbilicus; then he stripped the tissue away from the ribs. The tongue, aorta, oesophagus, heart and lungs were removed in a single operation and placed on a dissecting table beside the gutted corpse. The stomach contents were put in a glass jar. Once again the pathologist switched on his recorder as Hawksmoor suppressed a yawn: 'There is bruising behind the voice box, and a fracture of the hyoid bone, which suggests that the killer had considerable strength –' at this last phrase his voice rose a little and he glanced at Hawksmoor. 'So I would say definitely asphyxia by strangulation.' The pathologist's hands, which he now held over the corpse, were red and dripping: he was about to scratch his head, but stopped in mid-gesture. His assistant was now carefully examining the nails on each finger of the severed hands. Hawksmoor, watching all this, felt a rapid tic in his left eye and turned away so that no one might see it.

'I need to know when,' he said, 'In this case when is more important than how. Do you have a time-table?' For although images of this murder now surrounded him, and the parts of the body had become emblems of pursuit, violence and flight, they were as broken and indistinct as the sounds of a quarrel in a locked room. Only the phases of time could be known clearly: the quickening and deepening of respiration at the first shock of the hands around the throat; livid congestion and laboured respiration as the grip tightens and consciousness becomes confused; infrequent respiration, twitchings, loss of consciousness; terminal vomiting and death. Hawksmoor liked to measure these discrete phases, which he considered as an architect might consider the plan of a building: three to four minutes for unconsciousness, four to five minutes for death.

'And so do you have a time-table?' was his question.

'A time-table is going to be difficult.'

'And how difficult is difficult?'

'You know that temperature rises sharply during asphyxiation?' Hawksmoor nodded and put his hands in his pockets. 'And you know that heat loss is variable?'

'And so?'

'I don't know about the time. Even if I allow for a rise of temperature of six degrees at death, and even if the rate of cooling was only two degrees an hour, his present body heat would mean that he was killed only six hours ago.' Hawksmoor felt the tic returning as he listened to this intently, and he rubbed his eye. 'And yet the extent of the lividity is such that the bruises were made at least twenty-four hours ago – normally they can take two or three days to come out like this.' Hawksmoor said nothing, but stared in the man's face. 'You say the timing is crucial, superintendent, but I have to say that in this case I don't understand the timing at all.' The pathologist at last looked down at his bloody hands, and went towards a metal sink to wash them. 'And there's another thing,' he called out over the sound of running water, 'There are no impressions, no prints. A strangler's fingers pressed into the neck will leave a curved nail impression, but there are only bruises here.'

'I see.' And Hawksmoor watched Walter suddenly leave the room.

'I will have to do more tests, superintendent, but I'm almost sure that there are no prints.'

'Could the murderer have chilled his hands?'

'That's possible, certainly. Or they might just have been very cold.'

[113]

'And if there was a struggle, I suppose the boy might have clutched the fingers to loosen them and then disturbed the prints?' Although this sounded like a question the pathologist did not answer it, and for the first time Hawksmoor stared down at the opened corpse. He knew it was not yet completely cold, and in that moment he felt its heat blasting his face, and as the air crumpled like silk around him it was his own body upon the table.

Walter was sitting with his head bowed forward over his knees when Hawksmoor eventually joined him in the corridor. He put his hand on the young man's shoulder: 'Well, Walter, what do you make of that timing?'

Walter looked up at him in alarm, and Hawksmoor averted his eyes for a moment. 'It's impossible, sir.'

'Nothing is impossible. The impossible does not exist. All we need is a new death, and then we can proceed from the beginning until we reach our end.'

'And what end is that, sir?'

'If I knew the end, I could begin, couldn't I? I can't have one without the other.' And he smiled at Walter's evident perplexity. 'Don't worry, I know what I'm doing. Just give me time. All I need is time.'

'I'm not worried, sir.'

'Good. And since you're so happy you can go and see the father. Tell him what we've found out. But don't tell him too much.'

And Walter sighed: 'Thank you very much. I appreciate the gesture, sir.'

Hawksmoor remembered another phrase which his colleagues used: 'Life is full of grief, Walter, life is full of grief.'

*

He walked back to St George's-in-the-East, which in his mind he had now reduced to a number of surfaces against which the murderer might have leaned in sorrow, desperation or even, perhaps, joy. For this reason it was worth examining the blackened stones in detail, although he realised that the marks upon them had been deposited by many generations of men and women. It was now a matter of received knowledge in the police force that no human being could rest or move in any area without leaving some trace of his or her identity; but if the walls of the Wapping church were to be analysed by emission spectroscopy, how many partial or residual spectra might be detected? And he had an image of a mob screaming to be set free as he guided his steps towards the tower which rose above the houses cluttered around Red Maiden Lane, Crab Court and Rope Walk. To the right of it he heard a confused murmur of voices, and to the left of it he heard the sounds from the river, until at last in front of him he could see, even in the light of the early afternoon, the diffused whiteness of the arc-lights which had been erected around the scene of the small boy's murder. Only two detective constables remained on the site, and their task was to guard it from the sightseers who had come to gaze upon this place and who would otherwise have collected pieces of stone or wood as souvenirs of this death. Hawksmoor stood watching the scene for a few minutes until he was roused by the bell striking the hour: he glanced up at the church (which by some trick of perspective seemed about to fall on him), and then he wandered away from its grounds and walked towards the Thames.

The gloom of the secluded wharves and muddy banks had always attracted him and, when he came to Wapping Reach, he stared down at the shadows of the clouds moving quickly over the surface of the water. But when he removed his glasses and again looked down, it seemed to him that the river itself was perpetually turning and spinning: it was going in no certain direction, and Hawksmoor felt for a moment that he might fall into its darkness. Two men passed on a small boat – one of them was laughing or grimacing, and seemed to be pointing at Hawksmoor, but his voice did not carry over the water; Hawksmoor watched this dumb-show pass until it turned the bend towards Tower Bridge and vanished as suddenly as it had arrived.

It had started to rain and he began walking along the river-bank away from Wapping and towards Limehouse. He turned left down Butcher Row, for he could see now the tower of St Anne's Limehouse ahead of him, and he entered that area of abandoned houses and derelict land which still divides the city from the river. Then he stopped suddenly in confusion: the dampness had released a close, rank smell from the lush vegetation which spread over the stones and sprang up between wires, and he could see a vagrant squatting on the ground with his face turned up to catch the rain. So he turned away from this waste-land and crossed into Shoulder-of-Mutton Alley, and there was silence by the time he came to the front of St Anne's.

Hawksmoor could have produced a survey of the area between the two churches of Wapping and Limehouse, and given at the same time a precise account of the crimes which each quarter harboured. This had been the district of the CID to which he had been attached for some years, before he was assigned to the Murder Squad, and he had come to know it well: he knew where the thieves lived, where the prostitutes gathered, and where the vagrants came. He grew to understand that most criminals tend to remain in the same districts, continuing with their activities until they were arrested, and he sometimes speculated that these same areas had been used with similar intent for centuries past: even murderers, who rapidly became

[115]

Hawksmoor's speciality, rarely moved from the same spot but killed again and again until they were discovered. And sometimes he speculated, also, that they were drawn to those places where murders had occurred before. In his own time in this district, there had been a house in Red Maiden Lane in which three separate murders had been perpetrated over a period of eight years, and the building itself gave such an impression to those who entered it that it had stayed unoccupied since the last killing. In Swedenborg Gardens Robert Haynes had murdered his wife and child, and it was Hawksmoor who was called when the remains were found beneath the floorboards; in Commercial Road there had been the ritual slaying of one Catherine Hayes, and then only last year a certain Thomas Berry had been stabbed and then mutilated in the alley beside St George's-in-the-East. It had been in this district, as Hawksmoor knew, that the Marr murders of 1812 had occurred – the perpetrator being a certain John Williams, who, according to De Quincey whose account Hawksmoor avidly read, 'asserted his own supremacy above all the children of Cain'. He killed four in a house by Ratcliffe Highway – a man, wife, servant and child – by shattering their skulls with a mallet and then gratuitously cutting their throats as they lay dying. Then, twelve days later and in the same quarter, he repeated his acts upon another family. He was transformed, again according to De Quincey, into a 'mighty murderer' and until his execution he remained an object of awe and mystery to those who lived in the shadow of the Wapping church. The mob tried to dismember his body when eventually it was brought in a cart to the place of burial – at the conflux of four roads in front of the church, where he was interred and a stake driven through his heart. And, as far as Hawksmoor knew, he lay there still: it was the spot where he had this morning seen the crowd pressing against the cordon set up by the police. And it did not take any knowledge of the even more celebrated Whitechapel murders, all of them conducted in the streets and alleys around Christ Church, Spitalfields, to understand, as Hawksmoor did, that certain streets or patches of ground provoked a malevolence which generally seemed to be quite without motive. And he knew, also, how many murders go undetected and how many murderers remain unknown.

And yet in the crimes which he had investigated, there was always so strong a sense of fatality that it seemed to Hawksmoor that both murderer and victim were inclined towards their own destruction; it was his job only to hurry the murderer along the course which he had already laid for himself – to become, as it were, his assistant. It was this fatality, also, which gave such resonance to the last words of those about to die and, as Hawksmoor walked on from Limehouse to Spitalfields, he passed rooms and corners where such words had often been spoken: 'There's something wrong in my kitchen', 'Next time you see me you will know me', 'I want to finish a letter', 'You will be happy soon'. He was now crossing Whitechapel High Street, passing that spot where the last man had been hanged in chains: the murderer's words on this occasion had been, as Hawksmoor knew, 'There is no God. I do not believe there is any and, if there is, I hold Him in defiance'. Now he could see the church of Spitalfields ahead of him.

He never neglected the opportunity of studying the pattern of murder, and the instincts of the murderer, in all their various forms: in the eighteenth century, for example, it was quite usual for the noses of the victims to be bitten off during the act of strangling but that custom, as far as Hawksmoor was aware, had completely disappeared. And it was important for him, also, to master his subject so thoroughly that he knew the seasons and the rules of death: stabbings and strangulations were popular in the late eighteenth century, for example, slashed throats and clubbings in the early nineteenth, poison and mutilation in the latter part of the last century. This was one reason why the recent cases of strangling, culminating in the third corpse at Wapping, seemed to him to be quite unusual – to be taking place at the wrong time. He did not speak of such things to his colleagues, however, who would not have understood him.

He walked into the police station, off Brick Lane, where an Incident Room had been established after the body of Thomas Hill had been found in the abandoned tunnel some nine months before. Two or three constables looked up incuriously as he came in, and he made no effort to introduce himself to them; the telephones rang occasionally and one man, smoking furiously, was bent over a typewriter. Hawksmoor watched him for a moment and then sat quietly in the far corner of the room: the open files, the plastic cups lying on the floor, the pieces of official paper pinned casually to a cork board, the discarded newspapers, the telephones ringing again, all of this disorder confused and wearied him. 'Well if you feel up to it,' one young man was saying, 'You could do that. This is true. This is true.' And then his companion answered, 'But it was raining'. Hawksmoor watched them standing together and wondered if there was any connection between the two remarks: he considered the matter carefully as the men moved a few inches backward and forward as they talked, and concluded that there was none. He listened again and he heard the phrases, 'I fell asleep', 'I dreamed' and 'I woke up' – and he repeated to himself the words, 'asleep', 'dreamed' and 'woke' to see if their shape or sound accounted for their position in the sequence which the two men were unfolding. And he saw no reason for them; and he saw no reason for the words he himself used, which came out of him like vomit, which

[117]

carried him forward without rhyme or meaning. And the lives of these others gripped him by the throat and kept him huddled on his seat. Then an older man in uniform came up to him saying, 'We were expecting you, sir.'

Hawksmoor suppressed the instinct to rise from his chair in alarm. 'That's right. That's why I'm here.'

'Yes, I heard you'd been called in, sir.'

Hawksmoor had noticed before how the older police officers seemed to lose their ability to react, as if they could no longer deal with the reality which they encountered every day; and he decided to test this man a little. 'The operation,' he asked, 'is it going according to the book?'

'Yes, to the book. It's coming along nicely, sir.'

'But perhaps there is no book in this case, inspector.'

'Well this is true, sir, this is true.'

'I'm glad you know what is true.' Hawksmoor scratched his cheek as he spoke. He was playing a part: he knew this, and believed it to be his strength. Others did not realise that their parts had been written for them, their movements already marked out like chalk lines upon a stage, their clothes and gestures decided in advance; but he knew such things, and thought it better to have chosen. The uniformed officer seemed not to have heard his last remark, and looked blankly at him. And so Hawksmoor went on, 'I'm worried about the time.'

'The time? You mean the time now –'

'No, the time then, the time of the murder. I have no time.'

'That is a question, sir. I'm aware of that –' He took out a cigarette and put it between his lips, letting it hang there without lighting it. 'Yes,' he said, 'That is a question.'

'And every question has an answer, inspector. Is that true?'

'Yes I suppose you're right there, sir, you're very right there.'

Hawksmoor watched him closely: he wanted him to break down and confess his ignorance, or cry out in bewilderment at the deaths he had seen: anything, so that he might relieve Hawksmoor of his own feelings. But the inspector had now wandered to another desk, starting a desultory conversation with a young constable who shifted from one foot to another as he spoke. Hawksmoor rose and walked out of the room.

A police car drove him through the grey evening until he got out at the corner of Grape Street, near the Seven Dials. He rented a small flat here in an old house beside the Red Gates, a pub which he now passed while lost in his own thoughts; and as he mounted the stairs he considered the steps in the tower of the Wapping Church. He had almost reached his own door when he heard a voice beneath him calling out, 'Cooee! Cooee! It's only me, Mr Hawksmoor! Have you got a minute?' He paused and looked down at his neighbour as she stood in the open doorway, the light from her small hall casting her shadow upon the landing. 'Is it you Mr Hawksmoor? I'm that blind without my glasses.' And he saw her looking at him greedily. 'There's been a gentleman calling for you.' She fingered the edge of her cardigan which barely concealed the outline of her plump breasts. 'I don't know how he got through that front door. Don't you think it's shocking, Mr Hawksmoor –'

'That's right, Mrs West. That's quite all right.' He gripped the dusty banister with his right hand. 'Did he say what he wanted?'

'I didn't think it was my place to enquire, Mr Hawksmoor. I said I'm only Mr Hawksmoor's neighbour I'm not his housekeeper and knowing him he wouldn't thank me if I was!' Hawksmoor wondered how well she did know him and, as she laughed, he watched the dark mound of her tongue. And as she laughed she stared at him also; she saw a tall man wearing a dark coat, despite the summer heat, slightly balding but with a moustache darker than was usual in a man of his age. 'Then he said would you be back? I said I couldn't tell, you don't keep such regular hours. And then he said neither did he.'

Hawksmoor climbed the last stairs. 'I'll see to it, Mrs West. Thank you.'

She took a step out onto the landing in order to watch him before he climbed out of sight. 'That's all right. I'm always here. I'm not going anywhere, not with my legs, Mr Hawksmoor.'

He opened his door, just enough for him to slide through so that, even if she had craned her neck, she would not be able to see the interior of his flat. 'Thank you,' he called out before closing the door, 'Good night. Thank you.'

He entered the main room and stood by the window, looking out at the building opposite; he could see shapes there, but then he realised that they were reflections of the house in which he now stood – and he did not know if he was looking out or looking in. The smell of cooking ascended from Mrs West's kitchen, and as he thought of her bent over her plate he could hear vague sounds of shouting and laughter from the Red Gates. And for a moment everything was real: this was how life had always been.

He turned round with a start, thinking he had seen a sudden movement in a corner of the room. There was a convex mirror propped there (it was of the type generally used in shops to deter thieves), and he lifted it up to see if anything had crawled behind it; but there was nothing. He carried the mirror into the centre of the room, and the dust from its edges came off on his fingers; then he held it up against the light of the window and, although he tried to gaze calmly at the reflection, his calmness was broken by the sight of his

[119]

face staring distended out of the frame with the world itself curved around it. And he could see the same person he had always been – the character which does not age but which remains cautious and watchful, and which stares out with the same intensity. He tried to smile at himself, but the smile would not last. So he remained still until his face became an object like the others swimming in the circle of his gaze – an armchair, a grey carpet, a lamp upon a dark wooden table, a transistor radio placed upon its side, and the bare white walls around all of these things. He put down the mirror. Then he raised his arms above his head and clenched his palms, for it was time to make his visit.

He was about to leave the flat as quietly as he had arrived but then on a sudden instinct he slammed the door and, as he went out into the early evening, he enjoyed the sound which the heels of his shoes made on the pavement. As he walked down St Giles Street he could see two street musicians ahead of him, one of whom was singing a melancholy pop-song while the other begged for money. Hawksmoor recognised the refrain, although he could not remember where he had heard it:

> I will climb up, climb up, even if I
> Come tumbling down, tumbling down.

And when the singer gazed at him he felt uneasy; he could find no coins in his pocket, and stared helplessly as the other gambolled around him with open palms. It was only when he had gone a few yards further that he realised that the singer had been blind.

It had grown cold by the time he reached the home where his father was kept; he believed that he was late but, as he hastened down the gravel drive, he felt the old agony return at the sound of plates rattling within the building and the bark of a dog somewhere in the yard behind the large brick house. 'He's waiting for you,' the nurse said with a smile which lasted only as long as she looked at him, 'He's missed you, he really has.' They walked together down a corridor where the smell of old age lingered and then gusted suddenly as a door slammed in the distance. Some of those who passed Hawksmoor glared at him, while others came up to him, all the time talking and then fingering his jacket – perhaps they thought they knew him well, and were continuing with a conversation which had only recently been broken off. One old woman stood in a night-dress, her back against the wall, and repeated 'Come John, come John, come John' into the air in front of her, until she was taken gently by the arm and led away still muttering. This was a quiet place, although Hawksmoor knew that it was only the drugs which kept most of them from screaming.

'Oh it's you,' his father murmured when Hawksmoor approached him; then he stared down at his hands, groping at them as if they belonged to someone else.

And Hawksmoor thought: this is how I will see you always, bent down and looking at your own body. 'I've just come to see how you are, Dad,' he said loudly.

'Well please yourself. You've always pleased yourself.'

'And how are you keeping?'

'I keep myself to myself.' And he glared at his son. 'I'm all right.' And there was another pause before he added, 'There's life in the old dog yet'.

'Are you eating well?'

'I couldn't tell you about that. How do I know?' He sat very still on the edge of his narrow bed when a nurse passed with a trolley.

'You look healthy enough.'

'Oh yes. Well, I haven't got worms.' And then suddenly his hands trembled uncontrollably. 'Nick,' he said, 'Nick, is there still more to come? What happened to that letter? Did they find you out?'

Hawksmoor looked at him astonished. 'What letter, Dad? Is this a letter you wrote?' He had a sudden image of the mail being burnt in the basement of this place.

'No, not me. Walter wrote it. You know the one.' And then the old man gazed out of the window. His hands had stopped trembling but he made shapes in the air with them, all the time murmuring under his breath. Hawksmoor leaned forward to hear and, as he came closer to his father, he smelt once again his flesh and his sweat.

And he could still remember the days, many years before, when after his mother's death he could smell the drink on his father's breath as he lay sodden and snoring in his armchair. Once Hawksmoor had opened the door of the toilet, and he was sitting in front of him with his shrivelled cock in his hand. 'Don't you knock,' he said, 'before coming in?' And after that Hawksmoor always felt ill when he ate the food his father prepared. But there came a time when his disgust seemed to cleanse him, and he grew to enjoy the silence of the house and the purity of his hatred. And slowly, too, he learned to hold himself back from all others: he despised their laughter and their talk about sex, and yet he was still fascinated by such things, like the popular songs which unnerved him but which sometimes so over-whelmed him that he eventually woke from them as from a trance.

On his thirteenth birthday he had seen a film in which the central character was a painter who, unable to sell his work, grew cold and hungry as he went from one unsuccessful interview to the next; eventually he had become a vagrant, sleeping in the streets of the city where once he had walked in hope. Hawksmoor left the cinema in a

[121]

mood of profound, terrified apprehension and, from that time, he was filled with a sense of time passing and with the fear that he might be left discarded on its banks. The fear had not left him, although now he could no longer remember from where it came: he looked back on his earlier life without curiosity, since it seemed to lack intrinsic interest, and when he looked forward he saw the same steady attainment of goals without any joy in their attainment. For him, the state of happiness was simply the state of not suffering and, if he cared for anything, it was for oblivion.

He was leaning forward to listen to his father, but he heard only the words, 'Here comes a candle!', before the old man looked up at him and, with a smile like that of a child, spat in his face. Hawksmoor recoiled, and looked at him in horror before wiping his cheek with the sleeve of his raincoat: 'I'm late!' he shouted, 'I'm going!' And there was a general wailing and commotion in the ward as he departed.

*

Mrs West heard the ringing and looked down into Grape Street: 'Is it you again?'

'Is he not back yet?'

'He's come and he's gone. He's always rushing around.'

She was bored with her own company on this summer evening.

'You can come up and wait for a minute,' she said, more quietly now, 'He may not be long.'

'I'll just come up for a minute then. I can't stay.' And Walter Payne ascended the stairs.

Mrs West was waiting for him at her door, having hastily replaced her cardigan over her blouse which, even so, gaped open at one or two points. 'You just missed him. Didn't you hear him slam that door. It's shocking.' She was discomposed enough to lean against Walter as she bent down over a teapot and a plate of biscuits. 'What do you fancy? Go on, have a brandy snap. Be a devil.' And then she added as Walter sat down with a sigh, 'I suppose it's important is it?'

'I work with him –'

She interrupted. 'Oh, *him*. Don't ask me anything about him. I can't give you any information there. My hands are tied.' And her hands came out before her, one placed on top of the other as if they were bound together at the wrist. Walter looked down in alarm, while at the same time Mrs West noticed the brown spots on her wrinkled and faded skin. 'I can't fathom *him*,' she said, almost to herself, before glancing curiously at the plate of brandy snaps and then grabbing another one. Walter would have liked to pursue this subject, but she carried on talking as she ate. 'But these old houses, you see, you never know what you're hearing. Sometimes I wonder what it was like

[122]

before my time, but you never know . . .' And her voice trailed off just before she stuffed another biscuit into her mouth. 'And I didn't catch your name.'

'It's Walter.'

'Well then, Walter, tell me a bit more about yourself.'

'Well, like I told you, I work with him upstairs.' And both of them now looked up at the ceiling, as if Hawksmoor might even then have his ear to the floor. 'Previously I was with computers.'

Mrs West settled herself comfortably in her chair. 'Now that's a subject I *don't* understand. Like my thermostat.'

'It's simple. You feed in the information and out comes the answer.' Walter never tired of this subject, although his eagerness seemed to exhaust Mrs West. 'You know, you could put the whole of London in the charge of one computer and the crime would go right down. The computer would know where it was going to happen!'

'Well that's news to me, Walter. And how does this computer know what to do?'

'It's got a memory bank.'

'A memory bank. Now that's the first time I've heard about any-thing like that.' She shifted in her seat. 'What kind of memory?'

'The memory of everything.'

'And what does this memory do?'

'It makes the world a safer place.'

'Pull the other one!' she said as she lifted her skirt slightly and kicked her leg in the air. Her curiosity now sated, she moved over to the television and switched it on; and in companionable silence they both settled down to watch the cartoons which had appeared on the screen. Mrs West shrieked with laughter at the antics of a wolf and the little creatures it was pursuing; even Walter found himself amused by the inhabitants of this harmless world. But when the cartoon was over she gazed out of the window.

Walter rose to leave: 'It doesn't look as if he's coming back, does it?'

Mrs West shook her head. 'No he's out again for the night if I know him.' And Walter wondered what she meant. 'You can come again,' she said as he left the flat. Then she went to her window and watched him as he walked away, her hands drumming against her sides.

And it was not long after that Hawksmoor returned. When he opened the door of his flat, the full weariness of the evening hit him: he longed for sleep, since there was something screaming within him which needed to be laid to rest. The lights of Grape Street were reflected in his dark room, and he had only just entered it when he shrank back in alarm: something was sitting, or crouching, in the corner. He turned on the light quickly, and saw that it was only a jacket he must have flung there. 'My second skin,' was the phrase which occurred to him, and he repeated it softly to himself as he prepared for sleep. Then he dreamed, as others do, although he had learned how to forget his dreams.

*

The next morning he was sitting in his office, his back to the light, when Walter came in whistling. 'Don't you knock,' he asked, 'before you walk in?'

Walter paused until he saw that he was smiling. 'I called at your flat last night, sir, to tell you the news.' For some reason Hawksmoor blushed but, since he said nothing, Walter continued – although more hesitantly than before. 'It's as we expected, sir.' He laid some papers down on Hawksmoor's desk. 'The only blood and tissue groups were from the victim. Nothing at all off the other one, the assailant.'

'And did the other one leave no prints or marks?'

'As I said, nothing at all.'

'Doesn't that strike you as odd?'

'It's unusual, sir.'

'Good thinking, Walter.' Hawksmoor put on his glasses and pretended to examine the papers which Walter had brought to him. 'I want you to type out a report for me,' he said at last, 'and I want you to address it to the Assistant Commissioner. Put in all the usual details – date and time of discovery, list of responsible officers, you know what I mean.' He leaned back and took off his glasses: 'And now, Walter, I will give you the facts as I understand them'.

And these were the facts, as far as anybody understood them at this time. On the evening of November 17 in the previous year, the body of a boy later to be identified as Thomas Hill, who had been missing from his home in Eagle Street for seven days, was discovered in one of the passages of the abandoned tunnel by Christ Church, Spitalfields: he had been strangled, apparently by hand since there were no ligature marks around the neck; and several ribs were broken which, with internal bruising, suggested that he had fallen from a height of at least thirty feet. Despite the most exhaustive examination, however, no trace of his murderer had yet been found – certainly no print marks, and no particles of the killer's clothes, were discovered anywhere in the vicinity. A thorough search of the grounds and of the tunnel had revealed nothing but a bus-ticket, and some pages torn from one of the many religious pamphlets on sale in the church itself: no significance could be attached to any of these items. House-to-house enquiries had been equally unsuccessful and, although certain suspects had been closely questioned, no real evidence of guilt was forthcoming. Then on May 30 of this year a vagrant known as 'Ned', but whose real name

[124]

was Edward Robinson, was found by the door of the crypt beneath St Anne's Limehouse; it was assumed at first that in a drunken stupor he had fallen down the steep flight of steps which lead to the crypt, but forensic examination revealed that he had been strangled – again no trace of the murderer was found upon the tramp or in the surrounding grounds. The only possible clue to the killer's identity was a photograph, very badly creased and damaged but apparently that of a small child, which had been found in a pocket of the vagrant's overcoat. There was no reason to connect this killing with the murder of Thomas Hill six months previously, and in fact it might have been safe to assume that Edward Robinson had been a victim of one of the innumerable and often violent quarrels which break out between those inhabitants of the area known to the police as 'transients'. Exhaustive questioning, however, had revealed no evidence of a fight or quarrel. The absence of prints or saliva upon the dead man had once more baffled the forensic scientist, and it was he who eventually surmised that there was a 'comparability factor' between the two cases. And then on August 12 of this year the body of a small boy, Dan Dee, was discovered in the ground behind St George's-in-the-East, Wapping. It transpired that the victim had left his house in Old Gravel Lane around six the previous evening in order to join his friends in a game of football beside the Tower Hamlets Estate; when he had not returned by eleven, his anxious parents contacted the police but it was not until the following morning that a constable had found the child's corpse lying beside an abandoned shelter in the grounds of the church. He had been strangled, apparently by manual means, but again no prints were found on the neck or body. House-to-house enquiries, a thorough search of the grounds, and exhaustive forensic tests had revealed nothing: an unhappy fact which Hawksmoor now added to the end of his report.

He could not help smiling as he recounted the details of these murders, and by the time he had finished he felt quite calm. 'So you see, Walter,' he said in a lower tone now, 'We live in the shadow of great events'. And then he added: 'If only we knew what they were.'

'He must be a madman, sir, mustn't he?'

Hawksmoor looked down at his hands, placed flat upon the desk: 'Don't assume that.'

'But I can assume he's dirt!'

'But the dirt needs the cleaner and the cleaner needs the dirt.' He drummed the fingers of his right hand on the desk. 'And tell me, Walter, tell me what else you think.'

'You mean, what do I think is the story?'

'We have to assume there is a story, otherwise we won't find him, will we?' His hand was still once more.

[125]

'It's difficult to know where to begin, sir.'

'Yes, the beginning is the tricky part. But perhaps there is no beginning, perhaps we can't look that far back.' He got up from his desk and went over to the window, from where he could see a thin pillar of smoke rising into the clouds. 'I never know where anything comes from, Walter.'

'Comes from, sir?'

'Where you come from, where I come from, where all this comes from.' And he gestured at the offices and homes beneath him. He was about to say something else but he stopped, embarrassed; and in any case he was coming to the limits of his understanding. He was not sure if all the movements and changes in the world were part of some coherent development, like the weaving of a quilt which remains one fabric despite its variegated pattern. Or was it a more delicate operation than this – like the enlarging surface of a balloon in the sense that, although each part increased at the same rate of growth as every other part, the entire object grew more fragile as it expanded? And if one element was suddenly to vanish, would the others disappear also – imploding upon each other helplessly as if time itself were unravelling amid a confusion of sights, calls, shrieks and phrases of music which grew smaller and smaller? He thought of a train disappearing into the distance, until eventually only the smoke and the smell of its engine remained.

He turned from the window, and smiled at Walter: 'I'm sorry, I'm just tired'. There was a noise in the corridor outside, and abruptly he walked back to his desk. 'I want new men brought in,' he said, 'add that to the report. The others are getting nowhere, and I don't like their methods –' he could see once again the chaos in the Incident Room, and the detective with the cigarette hanging from his mouth – 'And next time, Walter, next time tell them nothing is to be moved, nothing at all!'

Walter rose to go, but Hawksmoor put up his hand to detain him. 'Murderers don't disappear. Murders aren't unsolveable. Imagine the chaos if that happened. Who would feel the need to restrain himself then?' And for a moment Hawksmoor saw his job as that of rubbing away the grease and detritus which obscured the real picture of the world, in the way that a blackened church must be cleaned before the true texture of its stone can be seen.

Walter was impatient to be gone. 'And so what do we do next?'

'We do nothing. Think of it like a story: even if the beginning has not been understood, we have to go on reading it. Just to see what happens next.'

'So it seems that we've lost him, sir.'

'I don't mind losing him for the moment. He'll do it again. They always do it again. Trust me on that.'

'But we have to stop him before then, don't we?'

'All in good time, Walter, all in good time.' Walter glanced at him curiously, and he hesitated. 'Of course I want to stop him. But I may not have to *find* him – he may find me.' And then he paused. 'What time is it now?'

7

WHAT A Clock is it, dear Mr Dyer? I have let my Watch run down.

It is almost six o'clock, *I replied* as I took off my dark Kersey-coat and placed it upon a Pin by the doorway. Mrs Best gasps at this and, looking down on me from the Stair-head as I entered the street Door, puts a Hand up to her Breast. And this Thought ran around in my Head for a Moment: you damn'd confounded pocky Whore.

The time goes so swiftly, *says she*, I wish I were able to Recover it a little and that, Mr Dyer, in more ways than One.

Time cannot be restored, Mrs Best, unless it be in the Imagination.

Ah the Poets, the Poets, Mr Dyer. Then she looks on me again and says sighingly: I would have no need for the Memory of Things past if that which were Present were more agreeable. She put her hand upon the Rail as she spoke and then cried out: more Dust, and I cleaned here only yesterday!

It was my Desire to make my self pleasing to her at this Point, for in the wide World who was there to trust besides? Are you Sick, *I asked* her.

I am I know not how, *she replies* as she comes down the Stairs to me, but I sicken for want of Company: I must entertain my self with my little Dogge and Catte; I am a poor Widow, as you see, Mr Dyer, and in this antient House there are so many Noises to Disturb me. Then she laugh'd giving me a little Push, and I smelt the Liquor upon her Breath.

Well Mrs Best, they say these old Houses have as many ghostly Tenents as a Mossoleum, so you will not starve from want of chit-chat.

It is not Words but Deeds I require, *she replied*, and you know, Mr Dyer, I do not have a bit of Nun's flesh about me.

At this I stepped back from her and was at a Loss what to say, but even then Nat Eliot came from my Closet and I called up to him, Nat you Rogue, come down to the Kitchin and employ your self about my Supper. And Mrs Best said to him also: tell Mr Dyer about the Gentleman, Nat.

Which Gentleman, *I asked*.

He left no Name is that not right, Nat?

And no message neither, *added Nat*.

And this Image was drawn in my Mind: Mr Hayes, the maggot-headed Rogue and no good Surveyour and writer of Letters that threaten me, had come to the Door of my Lodgings when he knows that I am not withinne, so that he might Disturb me and Confound me and Perplex me. I have watched him these last Seven days, since I left my own Note to him. And I beleeve that he follows me where he may.

Mrs Best was talking above my Thoughts, and I could hear her latest Noises like the tolling of a Bell: Nothing, *says she*, is to be heard of but Disputes about Elections do I say right Mr Dyer? (You are right, *adds Nat* furiously) I saw Mrs Wanley in the street – she has the House by the Corner (I know that House! *cries Nat*) – and her Conversation was a little Surprizing to me, for this Politicking is a Fever even the Women seem to catch (What can be done about it? *asks Nat* confounded at the News). Well, *she continu'd* laughing at Nat who had sat himself down upon the bottom Stair, a little Opera may drive away that Sicknesse, am I not right again, Mr Dyer? And then she sang out:

> Tho' the Years sail away on a Wherry,
> Be merry, my friends, be merry.
> And tho' Time may spill from the Cup,
> Drink it up, my friends, drink it up.

I will eat now, *says I* putting on a cheerful Air to fitt her Catch, for if I go to Bed hungry I will rise in the Night.

Oh, *says she*, be sure to wear your Night-gown and I will be obliged to you.

Nat enters the Kitchin and I climb the Stairs of Eternity to my Chamber, expecting a Moment when one small Thrust shall plunge me into the Pitte. Mr Hayes, Mr Hayes, what do you know and what can I do? I am so far from finding an End to my Work as never to be able to hope for any End: when I enter'd my Closet, I went to Stool at once and the vast Outpouring caused me Torment.

And then, on the next Day, another Stroke fell upon me. I knew how to guard my Thoughts in the Office, and even with Walter Payne I was more private than before tho' I knew not how this affected him. The villain Hayes still watch'd me and on this morning he happened to be examining some Draughts in my Chamber as I worked there with Walter. Do I understand this right, *says he*, that in the new church of St Mary Woolnoth you wish the wooden Cornice to be continu'd round, the Ceiling plain without pannells, and the steps in the Cupola to be of Portland stone?

[129]

That is how I have fashion'd it, Mr Hayes.

And there is to be no Pinnacle?

There is no Necessity for a Pinnacle: those express'd in the first Designes were much too Slender.

Well, well, *says he*, you are the Architect. And then he goes on: does Sir Chris. know of this, and of the long Delay?

I gave him a Report on the Pinnacle long before this, *I replied* keeping down my Bile, and as for the Delay Sir Chris. knows that the death of the Mason stopp'd our Work. He knows also, *I continu'd*, that I will complete my Church withinne the Time granted to me even tho' the originall Building was in so bad a Condition. (To give this Fact another Turn: the death of his son, Thomas, by falling from the Tower of the Spittle-Fields Church, work'd strangely upon the Mason, Mr Hill. He died suddenly in his Chamber for, when taken with an apoplectical Fitt, he fell upon his Hearth where the Coles lay lighted, and his Back and Side were so grievously Burnt that there was no Hope for him.)

Well Mr Dyer, *says* the Serpent Hayes once more, it is all within your Hands to make or to mar. And with this he left my Chamber, smiling upon Walter.

The Smile enraged me and I could no more restrain my self: It is the work of Providence, *I said* to Walter, that most Men are not able to foretel their own Fate, for there was one in this Room who must surely die.

We all must Die, *murmur'd Walter* looking strangely upon me.

Yes, *I replied*, but it is hard to say who is Sick and who is Well.

I left the Office at Six and when the Rogue Hayes parted from me in the Passage I returned his Bow but coldly. It was a misty Evening, but it was not so obscure that the little Hawks-eyed creature could not follow me: so I walked with all speed up Whitehall and turned into the Strand, and for all this space I could hear the sound of Heels following me. I looked back once but the Villain hid himself from me: well, well, *says I to my self*, I will lead you a Dance for one day you must learn how to lead Apes in Hell. I quicken'd my Pace towards the Seven Dials and did not trouble to turn my Head, for I knew that he would not wish to lose me; but yet when I came to St Giles I crossed over with all Speed and the Run of the Coaches must have kept him on the other Side. Then I hasten'd thro' Grape Court and turned into the Red Gates at the half-paved Entry there. Here I let the Mist leave me as I stood by the Door: I walk'd in bravely enough but, when I saw the Letter by the Counter, I was close to sinking down upon the Floor. It was address'd, *To Mr Dyer to be left for him at the Red Gates by Grape Court: With Care*. But who could prophesy where I was to be, and who could calculate upon my Arrival on this Day? I open'd the Letter with trembling Hands and read what could not be indur'd: *This his to lett you know that you shul be spoken about, so betid you flee the Office by Monda next or you may expect the worse as suer as ever you was born.*

This filled me with horrible Apprehensions and I stagger'd to a Corner where I might groan over them; the Tap-boy ask'd me what I wished but I made no Answer until he came by me and touched me on the Arm, at which I shivered terribly. Do you call Sir, *said he* laughing, and I demanded a Pint of strong Ale. And as I drank these were my Reflections: I knew this Hayes, this Dog, by the Excrement he sent to me. I could smell him out, for he left his Ordure every where. And it was not so strange, neither, that he had placed his Letter here for had he not hounded me hither? Then I rejoyced, for tho' he might conceeve himself to be the Pursuer in truth it was I who follow'd him; we were fix'd in the same Center and, tho' moving contrary Ways at first, we were sure to encounter somewhere or other upon the Circumference. Thus he could no more escape me than a convicted Thief escapes the Gallows. If the Wind be in the right Corner, he will have Flam for Flam. And then I considered this: the Villain gives me Hints and Whispers but how much has he truly learned of my Work? Has he knowledge of Mirabilis or of the man Joseph? There was no Question but that he could not know of the Sacrifices, for the Blood was spill'd in Darknesse and Secresy, but it was a Topick unsettled with me if he had ever followed me to Black Step Lane before it was ransacked by the idle Mobb.

The Noise and the Vapours of the Ale-house now began to affect me, and my Thoughts were soon so confus'd and all in a Heap that under the Weight of them my poor Mind sank back. For I thought I heard a Door closing, and the sound of Steps crossing the Threshold; and there seemed to come the Voice of a Woman calling, Is it you againe? Like an eccho came the Reply, Is he not yet back? There was then such a Roaring in my Ears that I woke as if from a Trance and looked about me in Astonishment. But I check'd my self: and so, *said I*, do you waste your Time by becoming a Mirror for outward Things? Your Work is too pressing for you to sit by an Ale-house stove, so be gone and contemplate Mr Hayes his Fate in your Chamber. The Tavern was quiet now, and the Customers sat nodding against each other like the stinking Snuff of a Candle when it is just going out in an over-heated Socket. Who is that worshipful Lump of Clay, that Thing which lolls by the Stove in an Elbow-chair? That Thing is me, and as I rise I reel but keep my Step. Thus I wandred across St Giles and then beyond, but I was not so Drunken that I did not keep my Wits from being scattered: when I reach'd my Lodgings I took a Sweat and went to Bed, very hot and my Pulse high. I did not sleep so well after, but had some confus'd Doses.

[131]

I woke next Day with a light Head that allow'd strange Fancies in: I would as like have staid all day in my Gown and be denied to everybody, but then a fresh Idea gave me the Resolution to get up with a good heart. I dress'd my self and took my best Periwigg from its little Box before Nat came in to rouse me: Well sir, *I said* to him when he enter'd (and he made an aukward Stop when he heard me address him thus), I have just had a Thought I will not exchange for fifty Guineas.

He was urgent with me to discover it but I would not, and soon enough his wandering Mind was set upon another Course. Mrs Best, *says he*, sent message last Night if you would play a little Quadrille but you had not returned and I could not answer for you, I waited and waited till I grew quite Tired and then it was about the Middle of the Night when I heard a Noise –

– Peace, Nat, *I replied*, you will disturb me this Morning with your Chatter for I have another Fish to Fry. And then I hugg'd my self closely.

It was with great Exultation that I walk'd into the Office and, having greeted Walter who was staring out of the Window as pale as if he had seen his own Spectre, I entered the Closet of Mr Hayes. I saw him thinking, *O God here he comes! here he comes!* but I approach'd him with all the Civility imaginable and ask'd him if he might grant me a Favour. He gave me a Bow and entreated me to proceed, saying that he would give me as much Favour as he could. Then I discours'd with him thus: that the Mason, before his own Fatality and in Grief at his Son's death, had not paid much heed to the Outwalls of St Mary Woolnoth facing Lombard Street, and that these Walls were in consequence wanting not less than seven or eight Foot in Height. When they were completed, then the Scaffolding might after that be intirely struck and taken away: no more Delay and, *I added*, since you have worked in strict Partnership with the Mason I would be very much obliged if you would inspect his Work and see what is necessary to finish it. The Villain told me that if it lay in his Power he would give me Satisfaction in this regard, for he too had been sensible of the Delay; then I thank'd him again, and he thank'd me for coming so modestly to him. And thus I drew him by Smiles into Perdition. Are you still affected by the Vertigo? *I asked*. I have a little Trouble, *he replied* to my great Delight.

He was as good as a dead Man, a Jack-pudding to be eaten, and as I returned to my own Closet I made my Guts to shake with Laughter like a trodden Quagmire. Walter was perplex'd by my sudden Mirth and asked me, how it was? And I replied, it was very well.

Here is something to encrease your Laughter, *says he* presently, there is a letter here from the Vicar of Mary Woolnoth.

From Priddon?

The same. He trusts that you will inform him when you have fixed a time for removing the Heathen Rubbidge – or so he puts it in his canonical Speech.

The Man is a Fool, *I said*, to talk of Rubbidge; I would sooner put him in the Cart when I hear the Clapper of the Rubbidge-men.

For in truth the Parson Priddon is a peece of hypocritical Holinesse who wears an old-fashioned Coat and has his Stockings hanging about his Legs; and yet his Face is red and plump, and his Eyes sparkling. He speaks of God from his Pulpit but knows no more of It than the May-fly knows of the Water above which it buzzes or the Mobb know of the Sunne when they feel its Heat upon their sweaty Faces. No Churchman has so well observ'd the Act of Uniformity, for in King Charles the Second's time who was more eager than him for putting the Penal Laws in execution; in King James's who a greater Stickler for abolishing them; in King William's who more violent for sending home the Dutch Blew-Guards in the English service; and now in Queen Anne's who more complaisant to our Dutch allies? Walter has left my Closet to make Water but on coming in again *he says*: And will you remove that Poor stuff, as Priddon calls it?

To go back a little: the church of St Mary Woolnoth, having been grievously damaged in the Fatal year 1666 and its Sides, Roof and Part of the Ends damnified by the Fire, it was admitted within the authority of the Commission as a fit Church for restoring. It was mostly built of Stone, Square and Boulder yet what was destroy'd, as the Front to Lombard Street, I have re-erected in Free-stone. But first it had been necessary for me to inspect and secure the Foundacions, and it was while the work men were digging by the Side of the Church that they found severall human Bones in the Gravell. They kept on in their Digging in order to uncover the Bodies that were burried there but, as they were thus imployed, part of an antient Chappell fell in upon them. To cut the Matter short, they had found here a primitive Church, with a semi-circular Presbyterium or Chancel which came near to the Form of a Cross; and the Foundations were not of Rubbidge but of Kentish rubble-stone, artfully worked and consolidated with exceeding hard Mortar in the Roman manner. Inscriptions were then uncover'd to DEO MOGONTI CAD and DEO MOUNO CAD: they pleased me exceedingly when I viewed them, for the tradition reported by Mr Cambden is that the god Magon, or Idol of the Sunne, made good this quarter of the City.

Parson Priddon, who watched my Labourers from the safety of his House next the Church, hastened into the Street when I arriv'd to inspect the Ruines. Then he peer'd uneasily into the Pitte where the Chapel had been found, saying, Pray, sir, by your leave I will look upon this idle Stuff. I advis'd him to wear a Jack-cap of Leather to keep him from the Hurt of falling Brick or Timber, and at this he takes a Step away: what a happy Occasion it was, *says he*, when the Supreme Being brought Peace and Tranquillity to our Minds and saved us from such Idolatry! But he stopp'd short in his canting Discourse when a work man carried to me another Stone on which, after I had scraped off the Incrustation, I found the inscription DUJ.

What is that, *asked the Parson*, is it some new Absurdity?

It is not the particular name of a God, *I replied*, but in the British tongue DU means Dark, and it may be that here was a Patch where Nocturnal sacrifices were once perform'd.

At this he drew himself up a little saying, I cannot assent to spiritual Raptures; all this Darknesse is past, Mr Dyer, and it has been revealed to us that we have a Rationall God. We walked a little away from the Pitte, for the Dust was falling upon our Cloathes, and I held my peace. Then he goes on: What is this DU but the Language of Infants, Mr Dyer? I told him that I agreed with him upon that, but he had already struck into his Theme as if he were mounting the Pulpit as he spoke: What is this DU when we see how God guides the whole of his Creation in the wonted course of Cause and Effect which we may prove, Mr Dyer, by considering the unaffected Simplicity of Nature. And at this point the venerable Priddon raised his Arm around him, tho' I could see only the courts and alleys of Cheap-side. I grant you, *he said* hastily, that the Streets are but a poor Prologue to my Theme but look you Heavenwards (and he raysed his Voice as he looked up at the Sky) and you will be filled with a pleasing Astonishment if you could see with the aid of a Telescope so many Worlds hanging above one another, moving peacefully and quietly round their Axles and yet shewing such an amazing Pomp and Solemnity. If we consult our Reason as well as our Interest, Mr Dyer, we will pity the poor Heathens and regret their coming hither.

But in the walls of Pardon Church-Yard before the Fire, *I replied*, to the North of St Pauls –

I did not know it.

– In that Church-yard was artificially and richly painted the Dance of Macabre or Dance of Death. Is that not like this DU?

It was most unadvisedly done, sir, *replied the good Parson*, and, once dwelt upon, it will provoke Melancholly. Besides, all our Ceremonies can be as well explained by plain Reason.

But what of Miracles?

Ah Miracles, *he said* taking my Arm as we walked towards Grace-church Street, Miracles are but divine Experiments.

But was not Christ risen from the Dead?

This is the very truth, Mr Dyer, but I will insinuate to you another

[134]

Truth which will explain how all these Controversies may be decided. It is known that Christ was burried three Days and three Nights, is it not? I replied very willingly that it was. And yet the Scriptures say, *he went on*, that he was buried on Friday night and rose again before day on Sunday.

That is so.

And so, Mr Dyer, how do you propose to unriddle this Enigma?

It is a Puzzle indeed, sir.

Then he gave a little Laugh and continued: Well, we are in need only of an Astronomer, for a Day and two Nights in the Hemisphere of Judaea is in the contrary Hemisphere two Days and a Night: that makes up the Summ imploy'd in the Scriptures. For as you know, *he went on* merrily, Christ suffered for the whole World.

He gave me a look of Infinite wisdom as we walked forward, but then he stopped of a sudden and raised one Finger to his Ear. Listen, *says he*, I hear the Faith spouting from the Lips of Children, yea, from the Mouths of Babes. And as we turn'd the corner into Clements Lane, three or four Children came towards us singing:

> When I did come to the old church stile,
> There did I rest for a little while;
> When I did come to the old church yard,
> There the bells so loud I heard;
> When I did come to the old church door,
> There I stopped me to rest a little more.

This Rhyme carried so many things into my Memory that I was like to break into Weeping, but I kept my Countenance and smiled upon them. Parson Priddon had at this Instant seen a little Girl who was like to a Bawd in Embrio: in his merry Humour, he stroaked her upon the Head and told her to be good and to mind her Book; whereupon the Creature very barbarously took hold of that nameless Part of him and almost squeez'd and crush'd those Vitals to Death before running off with the others. Murther, murther, *Priddon calls out*, and I could not forebear from laughing out loud, at which he looked sideways at me; but after a little while he had recover'd himself and said in a more grave Style, I must eat now. Monday is a day of Game and I cannot be without my Meat! I must eat!

So he returned at once to his House where I willingly accompanied him, having other Business to do about the Church; and no sooner had we passed thro' the Entry than he was calling into the Kitchin for a couple of Geese roasted by one of the clock at the farthest. Then, when the cry of *Sir, Dinner's upon the Table!* came, he was up from his Chair in a moment and soon beseiging his Goose with heaps of Cabbage,

Carrots and Turneps. After he had digested his Meat and given two great Belches, he grew more composed and expressed to me in an utterly fatigued Fashion that the little Child would be a Theme for his next Sermon: for even in her Infancy had she not demonstrated that we are but imperfect and confus'd Coppies of the universall Pattern? A Woman is a deep Ditch, *said he*, her House inclines to Death and her Paths unto the Devil.

That Girl will go upon the Town pritty soon, *I added*.

Well, sir, that is the Fate of these Females bred up in the Streets; it is the Mobb way of usage, for no doubt in Imagination they have already committed many hot Rapes upon her. I have never been married myself, *says he* going off into a Trance. And then he recalled his Topick: It is a fact, sir, *he went on* while taking another glass of French wine, that the Mobb is now everywhere in tumult, with such hideous Yelling and Howling that I can scarce hear my self speak in my own House. Do you notice how I have put dubble Iron-bars to the Windows – and he waved a little Goose-bone at them – for they have been attacking Dwellings in the neighbourhood and the Watch do nothing but scratch their Arses.

The wine was heating my own Blood as *I replied*: Who then can talk of the Good of Mankind and the publicke Benefit when there is nothing but Rage and Folly on the Streets? Here the Parson belched again. Men are not rational Creatures, *I continu'd*, they are sunk into Flesh, blinded by Passion, besotted by Folly and hardened by Vice.

Will you take some Pudding, Mr Dyer?

They are like Insects who, having their Birth in Excrement, from thence borrow their Colour and their Smell.

Parson Priddon was blowing upon his Dish of Broth as I spoke. Yes it is a filthy Crowd, *says he*, and so we must thank God for civil Government; for although the Grave will equal all Men, and it may be that niceties of Birth and Quality will not be observed hereafter, it is necessary for the Order and Oeconomy of the Universe that there should be differences of Breeding and Dignity. Will you send me that Tooth-pick case by you?

And I put down my Knife to speak: The Mobb will bait Cripples as well as Bears, and they will turn a wild Bull loose upon the Streets for Sport. When the Hangman leaves the Wretch kicking in the Air at Tyburn, the women and children fight to pull him down by the Legs. Then they take a peece of his Cloathes, kiss it, and spit upon it.

Ah, these are sad Times. Will you pass me that Tooth-pick case, Mr Dyer?

And yet we must be Merry, *I went on* changing my Mood, for they are the Glass of our Age in which we may all see ourselves.

Well, well, Mr Dyer, everything is in Motion and we may all be chang'd by and by. He was like to have discoursed next on the quiddities of Time but, since I was straitened in that Commodity, I presently took my leave of him as he reached for the Tooth-pick case.

And now Walter hands me the Letter from Priddon: I can scarce read it, *I said*, since I broke my Spectacles when I dropped them on the Ground by St Mary Woolnoth. But you may do this business for me, Walter, by writing to the good Parson that he need not fear the Contagion of these Heathen altars: tell him that we are building as fine a peece of Christianity as he is like to see in London. Walter took up his Pen and waited, for he knew there was more to come. And did you inform the Mason's assistant, *I added*, that my Tablet must be made of hard Stone and set rough upon the Stroake?

It is all done, *said he* with a Sigh.

And when the Tablet is finished, Walter, make it plain that no one is to come near it: I wish to have care of it and be my own Carver. It will be my Inscription. Walter turned to the Window in order to hide his Face from me, tho' I knew what Thoughts were swarming through his Head. He fears that he will become an Object of Scorn and Suspicion for conducting my Orders and seeming too close with me. Why be so Dismal? *I asked him*.

I? I am not Dismal.

I see it even in your Posture, Walter, but there is no need for this Gloominesse. Then *I added*: They do not sing my Praise now but they will never, never forget my Work.

At this point he turned round of a Sudden: Oh *I* quite forgot, *says he*, Sir Christopher sent word that he must see your Ground-platts and your Uprights without delay: he visits the Commission tomorrow and must be thoroughly familiar with them.

Who tells you this?

Master Hayes informed me, *he replied* reddening a little.

And where may Sir Christopher be?

He has gone to Crane Court to read a Lecture there. Shall I inform Mr Hayes to have the Plans taken there? Then he stopp'd short when he saw my Visage. Or shall I carry them myself?

No, *I replied*, I will go with them in a Moment since I have other business with Sir Chris. But I could not refrain from adding: Mr Hayes is not to be spoken of, and have I not told you to trust nobody except yourself?

So it was in some Discomposure of Mind that I coach'd it to Crane Court where the Greshamites, or Fellows of the Royal Society, or Virtuosi, or Mountebanks, or Dogs, dissect the Mites in Cheese and discourse upon Atomes: they are such Quacks as you would desire to Piss upon, and I would rather stay in my Closet than indure one of their Assemblies where they tittle-tattle on their Observations and

Thoughts, their Guesses and Opinions, their Probabilities and Conceptions, their Generations and Corruptions, their Increasings and Lessenings, their Instruments and Quantities. And yet it was of Necessity that I waited on Sir Chris. : if I showed him the Draughts, he would approve them instantly, but if I neglected to make them known to him he would at some later time examine them with great Intensity and discover all manner of seeming Faults.

Is Sir Christopher Wren withinne? *I ask'd* of a mean-faced Porter when I arrived at the Door.

He is with Gentlemen of the highest Importance, *says he*, and you can on no account be admitted to him. And then he added with a haughty Look: some foreigners are present.

I have Papers of the highest Importance, *I replied*, and with a severe Countenance (from biting my Lip) I brush'd by him.

There was a great number of People in the Hall, some of whom were known to me by Sight, and I walk'd to the Stairhead so that they might not take Notice of me: for look, they would say, here is Master Dyer, a mean Architect, and no fit Man for our Discourse. I could hear Sir Chris. his Voice and it put me in so sudden a Fear that I could not go near him but walked up into the Repository and Library (which is three Rooms struck into one). I sat here upon a Stool and, to calm my self, surveyed the Books around me: *A Discourse on the Air Register* lean'd against *Hypothesis on Earthquakes* which was near to toppling upon *A Discourse on Fire and Flames*. And I could have laughed out loud at these Reasoners engaged in their wise Disputes. I took down from its Shelf Dr Burnet's *New System of the World*, and saw that some skilful Philosopher had written upon the Frontispiece, IN CONFUTATION OF MOSES; you could as easily set a Mouse-Trap Maker against an Ingineer.

The Repository smelt of Damp and Cole-dust but when I rose quickly to take a sudden Cramp from my right Leg, I knocked my Head against some living Thing above me; I might have scream'd out but, glancing up in Terror, I saw it was a strange Bird petrified and suspended upon a Wire. You have found one of our Rarities, a Voice in a Corner said to me and, squinting into the Gloom, I saw an odd-shaped and melancholy-visaged old man pointing to the Bird upon the Wire. It is a white-fronted Goose from Aegypt, *says he*, and now beleeved quite Lost from the World. And yet, *he adds* coming towards me, you know the Poet's words:

> Nothing is lost when once it is Designed,
> It is Eternal work when perfect of its Kind.

Quite eternal, *says he* stroking the Bird's drooping Wing with his

Finger, quite, quite eternal: tho', *he added* quickly, it is also of great Use for our Aerial Mechanicks. I touch'd the Wing of the Bird also, for I could think of nothing to say. You see around you, *he goes on*, the Relics of many of Nature's kingdoms: in this Bottle you may view a Serpent found in the Entrails of a living Man and there, in that Box yonder, Insects which breed in Man's teeth and flesh; in the wooden Chest beside it, you will see all manner of Mosses and Mushrooms and in there, on that Shelf, certain Vegetable Bodies petrified. There in that Corner, *he continues* wheeling around, is a Monkey from the Indies which is as tall as a Man, and in this Cabinet here some marine Gems from the Islands of Barbados: the Mysteries of Nature will soon be Mysteries no more; and he snuffled a little as he spoke. But I forget myself, *he adds*, have you seen the Abortive put up in Pickle which is but newly come? No? Then you must view this Homunculus. At which point he leads me by the Arm to a glass Jar set upon a Table in which the Thing was suspended. We dissect tomorrow, *says he*, all being well; I am interested for myself in its Mathematicall Ratios.

And then I thought: this Embrio has no Eyes and yet it seems to look upon me. But I spoke out loud to cover my Confusion: What are these Instruments, sir?

You see here, sir, *he replied*, the Tools of our Profession; here is a Hygroscope which is a practical Invention to show the Moisture or the Dryness of the Air; and at this he gives a little Cough. Then as he entered the main part of his Discourse on Selenoscopes, Muscovy Glasses, Philosophical Scales, Circumferentors, Hydrostaticall Ballances, and the rest, my Mind wandred into the following Reflections: such vain Scrutinyes and Fruitless Labours are theirs, for they fondly beleeve that they can search out the Beginnings and Depths of Things. But Nature will not be so discover'd; it is better to essay to unwind the labyrinthine Thread than hope to puzzle out the Pattern of the World.

And you are acquainted with the Science of Opticks? *he asks* putting his Face close up to mine.

Do I see Visions, sir? This Answer pull'd him up short and he made no Reply, for those who are not engaged in what is call'd Practical or Useful Learning are now dismissed as meer Verbalists and students of Umbratick Things. But if Usefulnesse be their Rule, I do not know that a Baker or a skilful Horse-leech may not contest with them. I do indeed have some Observations of my own, *I now replied* as he was about to take his leave of me, which in due Course I shall publish.

Oh sir, *says he* pricking up his Ears, and what may these be?

They will be my Observations, *I told him*, on Toasting Cheese By A Candle Without Burning Fingers. And the old man looked at me astonished as I left the Repository and stepped quietly down the Stairs.

[139]

Sir Chris. had not yet begun his Discourse to the Assembly, but as I entred the back of the Room he was showing an Experiment with the Air-Pump: a sprightly black Cat was placed in the glass Chamber and in a few Moments, upon Sir Chris. exhausting the Air, it fell into Convulsions and would have expir'd but that the Air was again admitted. He did not Bow to the Assembly who gave him great Applause at this, but brought some peeces of Paper from his Pocket as the Cat, meanwhile, ran screeching through my Legs and out of the Door.

The Company buzzed like Flies above Ordure but, when it had settled itself again, Sir Chris. thus began: Mr Bacon, Mr Boyle and Mr Lock moved the first Springs of this illustrious Society, which is call'd the Royal Society. They are reason enough why we should be gathered here, for it is by their Example that we have learned that the Experimentall Philosophy is an Instrument for Mankind's domination of Darknesse and Superstition (and I crie out inwardly as he speaks: *but look behind you*), and that through the Sciences of Mechanicks, Opticks, Hydrostaticks, Pneumaticks as well as Chymistry, Anatomy and the Mathematicall Arts we have begun to understand the works of Nature (*but not your own corrupcion*). This has not been the work of one enlightened Generation only: in the Air, the more accurate history of Winds and Meteors has been achiev'd by the Lord Bacon, Des Cartes, Mr Boyle and others. In the earth, new lands by Columbus, Magellan and the rest of the Discoverers, and the whole Subterranean world has been described by the universally learned Kircher (*listen to a few sighes from Hell*). The history of Plants has been much improv'd by Bauhinus and Gerhard, beside the late account of English vegetables published by Dr Merret, another excellent Virtuoso of this Society (*another giddy son of a Whore*). Natural History has found a rich Heap of Materialls in the particulars of the Venae Lacteae, the Vasa Lymphatica, the several new Passages and Glandules, the origination of the Nerves and the Circulation of the Blood (*he that is filthy, let him be filthy still*). We proceed by Rationall Experiment and the Observation of Cause and Effect: the Ancients pierced meerly in the Bark and Outside of Matter, but the only things that can stick into the Mind of Man are built upon impregnable Foundations of Geometry and Arithmetick: the rest is indigested Heaps and Labyrinths (*this is a plain lie*). Thus there are many secret Truths which the Ancients have passed over for us to uncover: we have seen the spots of the Sunne, and its conversion about its own Axis; we have seen the laterall Guardians of Saturn and Jupiter, the various Phases of Mars, the Horns of Venus and Mercury (*and does not your Heart stop at the Immensity of the Void that surrounds them?*) And at last, Gentlemen, Astronomy has taken to herself another Assistant, Magneticks, so that true Science has at last discover'd the Secrets of the Attracted Sea and the Magnetical Direction of the Earth (*oh the horror of Waves and the Night*). Terrors only confound weaker Minds but such Bugbears were produced by Speculation, and chiefly prevailed in Time past when the old way of Learning flourished (*how can you speak of Time past who does not understand the meaning of Time?*) Men began to be frighted from their Cradles, which Fright continu'd to their Graves. But from that period in which the real Philosophy appeared there has scarce been any Whisper remaining of such Horrours (*and yet for most Men Existence is still no better than a Curse*) and every Man is unshaken by those Tales at which his Ancestours trembled: the course of Things goes quietly along in its own true Channel of Cause and Effect. For this we are beholden to Experiments; for although the New Science has not yet completed the Discovery of the True world it has already vanquished those wilde inhabitants of False worlds. And this brings me to the second great work of this Royal Society (*the Company shift hither and thither on their Chairs: they long to be gone, and their Bollocks are itching for Whores*), which is to judge and resolve upon Matters of Fact – whether Camphire comes from Trees, do Horns take root and Grow, can Wood be turned to Stone, do Pebbles grow in Water, what is the nature of petrifying Springs, and such like Questions do concern us (*these are meer winter Tales for schoolboys*). We take an exact view of the Repetition of the whole Course of the Experiment, observe all the chances and regularities of Proceeding, and thus maintain a critical and reiterated Scrutinie of those Things which are the plain Objects of our Eyes (*I, Nicholas Dyer, will give them Things to look upon*). This is a learned and inquisitive Age, Gentlemen, a prying and laborious Age, an Age of Industry: it will be as a Beacon for the Generations to come, who will examine our Works and say, It was then that the World began anew. I thank you.

As alwaies, Sir Chris. remained as still as a Statue as they clapp'd him, but he received with every possible mark of Friendlinesse those who came to him after the Company had departed their several Ways. I held myself in Readiness at the back of the Room, but he seemed to pay no mind to me while I stood there; then, much trembling, I approached him with the Draughts ready in my Hand. Ah Nick, *says he*, Nick, I cannot be concerned with these now: but come this way, and see something for your Amusement. I was at a Loss for Words (having gone to much Trouble to transport the Upright Planns) but I followed him in company with a very few others into a further Room. This is a curious Peece of Art, *says he*, as we enter'd, which I did not make Mencion of in my Discourse; and he pointed to a Landskip which hung before a Curtain. It is moved by clockwork as you shall see, *he continues*, and thus is it called the Moving Picture. Then he clapp'd his Hands and we watched: indeed it looked as an ordinary

Picture but then the Ships moved and sailed upon the Sea till out of Sight; a Coach came out of the Town, the motion of the Horses and Wheels being very distinct, and a Gentleman in the Coach seemed to salute the Company. I stood up and said in a loud voice to Sir Chris.: I have seen this before but I do not know in what Place. And in front of the astonished'd Eyes of the Company I left the Room, walking out into Crane Court where I breathed but uneasily. Then I went directly to my Lodgings, and fell into a profound Sleep.

It was Nat who woke me at the Close of Day. As please you sir, *says he* putting his Head around the Door, there is a Gentleman below who wishes to speak with you.

I jumped up from my Bed with the Thought that this was the serpent Hayes come to my House to force me to confesse all. I desired him to walk up, in as loud a Voice as I dared, while I swiftly dried the Sweat from my Brow with a peece of Linnen cloth. Yet I came to my Senses pretty fast for I knew that Step upon the Stairs very well; it was not so fast now but still full of Purpose, and in comes Sir Chris. bowing: I came to see how you do, Nick, *he says*, since you left us so suddenly. And he gave me a cautious Look before smiling at me. I feared you were Sick, *he continued*, or grew faint from want of Air since the College sometimes stinks of Spirit and Chymick Operations.

I stood uneasily in front of him: I was not sick, sir, but I had other Business and so went on my way.

I was vexed with myself for not studdying your Draughts of St Mary Woolnoth, *Sir Chris. went on* smiling and speaking softly as if indeed I were a Sick man, are they with you now by any Chance?

I have them here, *I replied* and took from my Buroe the Uprights and the Ground Platts.

Is this new drawing Paper? *he asked* as he snatch'd them from me, It has a coarser Surface.

It is my customary Paper, *I answer'd* but he paid no Heed.

He scrutinised the Draughts but quickly: the little Turret marked A is a noble piece of Work, *says he*, and I presume the Cornices are of Stucco?

Yes, that is my Purpose.

Good, good. And the Steps? I see no Steps.

They are not marked, but there are Eight: they have a fourteen inch tread and a five inch rise.

That is good, that is resolved upon. Your Draughts are well made, Nick, and this work will stand tryal in a Hurricano, I have no Doubt. And then he goes on after a Pause: certainly we would have had an old and rotten Church if it had not been for the Fire. He had Time on his Hands, as they say, and now he settled himself into my Elbow-

Chair: I have long been of the Opinion, *says he*, that the Fire was a vast Blessing and the Plague likewise; it gave us Occasion to understand the Secrets of Nature which otherwise might have overwhelm'd us. (I busied my self with the right Order of the Draughts, and said nothing.) With what Firmness of Mind, *Sir Chris. went on*, did the People see their City devoured, and I can still remember how after the Plague and the Fire the Chearfulnesse soon returned to them: Forgetfulnesse is the great Mystery of Time.

I remember, *I said* as I took a Chair opposite to him, how the Mobb applauded the Flames. I remember how they sang and danced by the Corses during the Contagion: that was not Chearfulnesse but Phrenzy. And I remember, also, the Rage and the Dying –

– These were the Accidents of Fortune, Nick, from which we have learned so much in this Generation.

It was said, sir, that the Plague and the Fire were no Accidents but Substance, that they were the Signes of the Beast withinne. And Sir Chris. laughed at this.

At which point Nat put his Face in: Do you call, sirs? Would you care for a Dish of Tea or some Wine?

Some Tea, some Tea, *cried Sir Chris.* for the Fire gives me a terrible Thirst. But no, no, *he continued* when Nat had left the Room, you cannot assign the Causes of Plague or Fire to Sin. It was the negligence of Men that provoked those Disasters and for Negligence there is a Cure; only Terrour is the Hindrance.

Terrour, *I said* softly, is the lodestone of our Art. But he was too busied about his own Thoughts to hear me.

We can learn, Nick, to control Fire. Since it is the Dissolution of heated Sulphureous Bodies, we need satiated Air and then it will be quite Extinguish'd. But this is for Futurity. As for the Contagion, I made a Diary at that time of Wind, Weather and other Conditions of the Air such as Heat, Cold and Weight: all these together give a true account of Epidemical diseases.

You may tell that, *I answered*, to those dying of the Distemper: they will be greatly comforted. Then Nat came in with the Tea as *I continued*: There were those, sir, who were made fearful by the two great Comets which appeared in the end of 1664 and in the beginning of 1665.

I remember them, *says he* taking the Dish of Tea without a word to my Boy, what of it?

And it was said that they gave off a great hollow Sound which signified Disasters to come.

This is meer Schoolboy prattle, Nick. We can already prophesy the place of Comets among the fixed Starres, we need only Line, Distance, Motion and Inclination to the Ecliptick.

I was pleased to think my Face was in Shaddowe as *I continued*: But

[143]

what of those who say 1666 contained the Number of the Beast, and so boded some ominous and direful Matter?

It is one of the greatest Curses visited upon Mankind, *he told me*, that they shall fear where no Fear is: this astrological and superstitious Humour disarms men's Hearts, it breaks their Courage, it makes them help to bring such Calamities on themselves. Then he stopped short and looked at me, but my Measure was not yet fill'd up so I begg'd him to go on, go on. And *he continued*: First, they fancy that such ill Accidents must come to pass, and so they render themselves fit Subjects to be wrought upon; it is a Disgrace to the Reason and Honour of Mankind that every fantasticall Humourist can presume to interpret the Skies (here he grew Hot and put down his Dish) and to expound the Time and Seasons and Fates of Empires, assigning the Causes of Plagues and Fires to the Sins of Men or the Judgements of God. This weakens the Constancy of Humane Actions, and affects Men with Fears, Doubts, Irresolutions and Terrours.

I was afraid of your Moving Picture, *I said* without thought, and that was why I left.

It was only Clock-work, Nick.

But what of the vast Machine of the World, in which Men move by Rote but in which nothing is free from Danger?

Nature yields to the Froward and the Bold.

It does not yield, it devours: You cannot master or manage Nature.

But, Nick, our Age can at least take up the Rubbidge and lay the Foundacions: that is why we must study the principles of Nature, for they are our best Draught.

No, sir, you must study the Humours and Natures of Men: they are corrupt, and therefore your best Guides to understand Corrupcion. The things of the Earth must be understood by the sentient Faculties, not by the Understanding.

There was a Silence between us now until Sir Chris. says, Is your Boy in the Kitchin? I am mighty Hungry.

He can go to the Boiling cooks, *I replied*, and choose us some Meat.

That is the Answer, Nick, to all of our Problems.

He shifted in his Seat, and I smelt a Fart as I called Nat to us and gave him his Charge. And Nat bows low to Sir Chris. saying, And what kind of Meat can I get you, sir, may it be beef, mutton, veal, pork or lamb?

Mutton, and I will be obliged.

And will you have it fat or lean?

Fat.

Much done or little done?

Much done.

Very good, sir, and will you have a little Salt and Mustard upon the side with your Roll, to make a proper Feast?

Begone Nat, *I murmur'd*, before this Gentleman anatomises you. And with a look of Horrour Nat rushed out of the Room. He is a poor Boy, *I said*, and you must Excuse him.

He once had the Small-pox did he not, Nick?

That is so.

Sir Chris leaned back, satisfied: I could tell it by his Face. And there is a Residue of a Stammer there, if I heard him aright?

He was once confounded by it, but I cured him.

By what means, sir?

By magick art, sir.

You must discourse on that Topick, *says he* laughing, at the Society: if you can be perswaded to stay long enough.

After a little while Nat brought in the Meats and was as like to have stood in a corner and watched us eating if I had not waved him away. To go back a Bit, *continued Sir Chris.* after he had finished his Portion, Of all nations we were most us'd to order our Affairs by Omens and Praedictions, until we reached this Enlightened Age: for it is now the fittest season for Experiments to arise, to teach us the New Science which springs from Observation and Demonstration and Reason and Method, to shake off the Shaddowes and to scatter the Mists which fill the Minds of Men with a vain Consternation. And then he gave his Eloquence a Stop.

It had started to Rain so fast that I got up from my Chair to close the Shutters, which made my Chamber exceeding dark. But I saw no need for a Candle as I composed my self and gave Sir Chris. this Reply: You say that it is time to shake off the Mist, but Mankind walks in a Mist; that Reason which you cry up as the Glory of this Age is a Proteus and Cameleon that changes its Shape almost in every Man: there is no Folly that may not have a thousand Reasons produc'd to advance it into the Class of Wisdom. Reason itself is a Mist. At this point Sir Chris. held up his Hand, palm forward, but *I continued*: These Philosophers or Experimenters who are so bold as to trust in their Reason or their Invention or their Discoveries are like Cats that try to hide their Excrement in the Coles, for in the dust of their Elaboratories they conceel the true state of Nature. I may give you an Instance: they cannot conceeve how the Foetus is form'd in the Womb so that the Fancy of the Mother can wound the Embrio, and yet it is so –

– These are but Fables, Nick. Sir Chris. then called for a Light and at once Nat brought in a Candle to place it in the Lanthorn; but in his Haste he dropp'd the Taper and the Room was filled with Smoak. I do not Rely upon such Stories, *Sir Chris. went on*, but upon my own

[145]

Observation, to test if such-and-such be true: I put my Faith in Experience.

You speak of Experience, *I replied*, and hold it to be consistent with Reason? At this he nods sagely. But may it not be that Experience is inconsistent with Reason: the Gulphe in which Truth lies is bottomless and it will wash over whatever is thrown into it.

He shakes his head as the Candle falters and then flares up: This is but a windy Conceit of Knowledge, Nick, a Maze of Words in which you will lose your self.

As he spoke, Nat was crouch'd upon the Floor, gazing at us wide-eyed. I know this is an Age of Systems, *said I* at last, but there is no System to be made of those Truths which we learn by Faith and Terrour: you may make your Planns to explain the effects of the Lodestone, the Ebbing and the Flowing of the Sea, or the Motion of the Planets, but you cannot lead to any Cause that satisfies the Truths of those who have looked into the Abyss or seen Sacred Visions. Or of those, *I added* falteringly, who say that Daemons stir up Raptures and Exstasies in Men. I watched the Shaddowe of Nat upon the Wall, and saw how he trembled.

There are no Spirits, *says Sir Chris softly*, rising and going to my Window to view the Street beneath.

I looked at him searchingly but his Face was hidden from me. But what of that Demoniack, *I cried*, locked up in Bedlam, who spoke so truly to me and who said – and here I was about to Blirt out all, so I checked myself. Then the Room suddenly fell quiet as the Rain stopped. But indeed, *I continued* recovering myself, I am only a builder of Churches.

Sir Chris. now gave a glance down at Nat bent in the Corner and I saw them observing each other in the Gloom before he spoke: Ah, Nick, what dark or melancholy Passions can overshadow the Man whose Senses are always so full of so many various Productions as yours are?

You need not humour me, *I said*, rising and then sitting down again.

You live too solitary, Nick.

I am no more solitary in my Closet than you are in your Elaboratory: my strange and extravagant Passions, as you call them, are no different from the Hypotheses you build in the Air when you describe that Imaginary world of Attommes and Particles which is all of your own Making. Your World and your Universe are but Philosophicall Romances: how can you call me Phrensied?

Your Mind has a Distemper, *he replied*, which I may cure: I am aware of the Composition of the Blood, and so I can better understand the difference between Phrensies and Inspirations.

Then I saw the shaddowe of Nat his head slowly turn to me. Yes, *I said*, yes, and what of your Microscopical Glasses for what do we see with their Aid but frightful Shapes and Figures? When the Breath is condens'd on a Glass does not the Microscope show us Snakes and Dragons withinne it? There is no Mathematicall Beauty or Geometrical Order here – nothing but Mortality and Contagion on this Ordure Earth.

Sir Christopher walked over to face me, before placing his Hands upon my Shoulders: This is a meer Rabble of Words, Nick, which you must place in Order for your own good Health. There is no Truth so abstruse nor so far elevated that Man's Reason may not reach it: what you understand, you may control. Keep hold of this Truth, Nick, and all will be well.

I was quieter now: And when Reason bids us goodnight, sir, what then?

Why should you ask me such a Question?

I grew angry with him once more: your Zeal, *I said*, is more for Experiments than for the Truth, thus you will turn Experriments into a Truth of your own devising.

This does not signifie two-pence, Nick.

But, *I went on* looking at Nat again, while you pursew your Rationall Philosophy the general Practice of the World shows that we are in a state of Rapine – like people on a full Career on the Ice, all slide directly into the same Hole they saw their Companions sink into just before them. And I heard Nat laugh at this.

That does not justifie the Folly of it, *Sir Chris. replied*.

There is a Hell, sir, there are Gods and Daemons and Prodigies: your Reason is but a Toy, your Fortitude downright Madnesse against such Terrours.

He looked at me steadily enough for one who has been Destroy'd: You have many unseasonable Passions, *says he*, and I could wish you a better Mien. But the years we have been acquainted cannot be obliterated by the Expression of your Melancholy temperament.

I admit, *I replied* softly, I am of a Melancholick humour but it has been aggravated by many Hardships of which you know nothing.

I know now, Nick. Just after this the Clock struck Ten, and he went to the Window to see if the Rain had entirely ceased. He stared out at the Moon above the Houses: I have stayed late enough, *says he* after a Moment, it has been a dreadfully Stormy Day, has it not, but now it has cleared for a fine Night. Then he shook me by the Hand in a most familiar Manner, as Nat rose from the Corner and showed him to the Stairs.

I sat upon my Bed and looked down at the Floor. When I heard the Door being closed behind Sir Christopher I called out, Nat! Nat!, and as he came running back into my Chamber I lowered my Voice

[147]

and whispered to him, Nat, I have said too much, Nat, I have said all.

He came up close to me and put his Head upon my Shoulder: it is no matter, *says he*, for he is a good Gentleman and will never harm you.

And yet as he spoke I repeated to myself: What must I do? What must I do? But then I bethought myself of Vitruvius his phrase, *O pigmy Man, how transient compared to Stone* and remembered that this sad Humour of mine would soon be changed, as each Humour makes way for another and cannot even be recollected once it has passed. When my Name is no more than Dust, and my Passions which now heat this small Room are cooled for ever, when even this Age itself is for succeeding Generations nothing but a Dreem, my Churches will live on, darker and more solid than the approaching Night.

And Nat was saying to me: Your story of the poor Creatures sliding thro' the Ice made me to Laugh, Master, and it put me in Mind of a Song I learnt I know not how when I was a little Child, and I will sing it now to cheer you if I can. And at that he suddenly placed himself before the Window and began:

> Three Children sliding thereabout,
> Upon some Ice too thin,
> That so at last it did fall out
> That they did all fall in.

> Yee Parents all that Children have
> And yee that have none yet,
> Preserve your Children from the Grave,
> Teach them at Home to sit.

I do not recall how it ends, Master, *says Nat* at a Loss. But then, as he stood before me, at last I wept.

*

To go on with my Story: my Sorrow being parted from me (and no Harm coming from Sir Chris., as it turned out), I was perfectly Easy of Manner with the Serpent Hayes until the Time had come for my Purpose. And then at about Six of the Clock in the Evening, three weeks after the Events just related, I approach'd him in his Closet and in the politest possible Manner asked if he might take a Glass with me? He said that he had much Businesse to compleet, but when I gave him to understand that the church of St Mary Woolnoth needed his Attention, he readily assented: now, thought I, go you like a Bear to the Stake. I took the Villain first to Hipolyto's in Bridge-street, near the Theatre Royal, where we crack'd the first Bottle of French claret;

Hayes was of a greedy and covetous Disposition, and grew thirsty as he drank the Wine I paid for. Then we walk'd on to the Cock and Pye in Drury Lane, where a second and third Bottle succeeded on the Table; then we took a turn to the Deville Tavern opposite Katherine Street, and all the while I watched his Glass attentively. Then we coach'd it to Black-Marys-Hole by St Paul Churchyard (for he was now too drunken to walk). This was such a Place that the Walls were adorned with many unsavoury Finger-dabs, and marks sketched by unskilful Hands with candle-flame and charcole. The Floor was broken like an old Stable, the Windows were mended with Brown-paper and the Corners were full of Dust and Cobwebs. Over the Mantle on a little Shelf were half a dozen long bottles of Rosa Solis with an Advertisement for the speedy Cure of a violent Gonorrhea. There was a handful of Fire in a rusty Grate and a large earthern Chamber Pot in the chimney-corner: the Mixture of Scents that met us when we first entred were those of Tobacco, Piss, dirty Shirts and uncleanly Carcasses, but Hayes was so drunken that he did not so much as regard it. I like it here, *says he* entering through the Door with a staggering Gait, and yet I do not remember choosing it.

I led him to a Table and, when the Boy approach'd us, call'd for Brandy. Tell me, *says Hayes*, how Licquour makes Men see things Dubble: for see this here (and he pick'd up a Pipe) this is Dubble to me now. What Mistery is this?

You must wear the plant called Fuga Demonum, *I told him*, to prevent the seeing of Visions.

What? *says he* squinting at me. And then he goes on: But there are many, many different things in this World, are there not Master? For whereas I might say, I would eat more Cheese if I had it, a Northern man would speak it thus (and here he opened his Mouth to one side like a Fish) Ay sud eat mare cheese gyn ay had et, and a Western man thus (and here he lowered his Head down into his Neck) Chud eat more cheese an chad it. His Eyes were brisk and sparkling: more Brandy, I thought to myself, before the Spirit sinks utterly. But there must be rules, Mr Dyer, *he was saying*, do you agree with me there? There must be rules, sir. Then he sank back in his Chair, and his Eyes lost their brightnesse.

I have had Letters, *said I* to make Tryal of him in his Infirmity.

I have had Letters, too.

But these ones threaten me, *I replied*.

They threaten you? And he gave me a blank Look: the Rogue is cunning even in his Cups, was my Thought. Now he had fixed his Wigg to the Chair and reached but to Spew, while still I smiled upon him; then he looked around himself as if suddenly waking and, seeing

[149]

some Sots pissing against the Wall, he went to join them. But he was not able to Walk, only to Reel, so he took out his Gear and pissed under the Table where we sat. I poured his Glass: No, no, no more, *says he*, no more, I have a Pain in my Stomach. He got up again and, staring straight ahead, went towards the Door; I walked with him and asked him which way he was travelling. To my Lodgings, *he replied*. I suppose you go along Lombard Street? He assented to this, and *I said*: then I will help you.

The Night was far advanc'd, and the Clock struck Eleven as we entered the Street; I wanted no Coachman to see us, so I took him by the Arm and led him thro' Alleys to the Church. He had so got his Load, as they say, that he came along with me quite willingly and was even ready to sing out loud as we cross'd the dark and empty Lanes. Do you know this one, do you? *he asks*:

> Wood and clay will wash away,
> Wash away, wash away,
> Wood and clay will wash away –

– I have forgot the rest, *he adds* as he links his Arm in mine. Then on reaching Lombard Street he looked up at me: Where are we going, Nick?

We are going Home, *says I* and pointed out to him the Church of St Mary Woolnoth with the Scaffolding upon it.

This is no Home, Nick, at least not for a Live Man.

He makes to Laugh out loud, but I put my Hand over his Mouth: Quiet, I said, the Watchman may hear us!

To which he replied: There is no Watchman, the Watchman has gone from this Site, why did you not know this when you wrote expressly? And then he goes on: Let me climb up the Scaffolding, let me climb up and see the Moon.

No, no, *I replied* softly, let us visit the new Work. And so we crept, both of us Laughing, to the Place where the Pipes were being laid. He bent over to look at this Work, tho' he could see but little, and then I stroked him and put my Hands around his Neck. I owe you a Pass, *I whispered*, and now you shall have it. He made no Crie, and yet it is possible that I myself uttered one: I do not know. I read once of an Englishman in Paris who rose in his Sleep, unlock'd the Door, took his Sword and went down towards the river Seine where, having met with a Boy, he kill'd him and returned still asleep to his Bed: so it was with me, for when I came to my self Hayes was lying beneath the Pipes and wooden Planks had been put over his Corse. Then I trembled at what I had done, and looked up at the new Stone of the Church to stare away my Feare. Thus I remained under the Shaddowe of the

Walls for a good while, until I grew sensible of the Cold, and then I walked with swift Pace back into Lombard Street.

I was just got into Grace-Church-street when I pass'd a Constable, who asked me if I needed a Link on so dark a Night? I told him that I knew my Way very well and needed no Light nor Watchman, while all the while I was as like to have made a Stool-pan of my Breeches. Your Servant, sir, *says he* at last, and a safe Night to you. I looked fearfully behind me until he had gone into Great Eastcheap and then, being acquainted with these Streets, I put a good Distance between us. At Cripple-gate I whipt into a Coach and made him drive away as if the Divill were behind me; but it was not until I sank back in the Vehicle that I found I still had the dead Man's linnen Kerchief grasp'd in my Hand: I dropt it out of the Flap of the Coach which opens just behind the Coachman. In this manner I travelled as far as Drury Lane, where I took myself next into an Ale-house but, what with the Running and the dreadful Apprehensions, I was almost as wet with Sweat as if I had been plunged into the Thames. I lean'd against the rotten Wall of the Tavern but, as soon as I had recovered my Breath, I was seized with an unusual Merriment: I call'd for Strong-water and made my self Drunken as soon as may be.

I knew not what Time it was when a Mask came to my Table and brightened upon me at a strange Rate: Captain, *says she*, my dearest Captain, will you take a Turn with me? And then she fluttered me in the Face with her Fan and languish'd upon me, taking my own Glass to her Lips.

You have no Shame in doing this? I ask'd her as she settled down beside me.

Never fear, my Captain, those things like Shame are meer Bugbears for Children, *she replied*. I drive my Trade like an Honest woman, and I am as sound as a Eunuch which is the main Point. Kiss me, Captain, and I will show you.

But do you not fear God?

She mov'd back a little from me: Fuh, *says she*, I hate all that Stuff.

Then I took her Wrist and whisper'd to her: Have you any Rods?

She gave me Eye-contact and smiled then: You are a flogging Cully, I see, Captain. Well, well, I am an old Partner in that Game. So after some more merry Discourse the Harlot took me with her to the Dog Tavern where she kept her Room: come in, *says she* after I mounted the Stairs behind her and was a little Fatigued, come in and be at your Ease while I clean myself. And then in my Sight she washed her Bubbies and sweetened her Arm-pits. With her Cloaths off, she smelt as frowzily as an old Goat but I turned my Face to the Wall and did not so much as move a Finger as she went to work on me. You are new to this Game, *says she*, for I see that the Body is still fresh.

8

THE SKIN was being stripped from Hawksmoor's back and he was trapped, shuddering, in this dream until he screamed and the scream became a telephone ringing beside him. He froze in a jack-knife position; then he picked up the receiver and heard the message: 'Boy found dumped by church. Body still fresh. Car coming'. And for a moment he did not know in what house, or what place, or what year, he had woken. But he tasted the foulness of his mouth as he stumbled from the bed.

Now, in the warm car, he considered the duties he would have to perform; as he passed St George's, Bloomsbury, he speculated about the photographs he would require – both to mark the position of the body, with the individual folds and creases of its clothing, and to record any materials clutched in the hands or fluids trickling from the mouth; as he travelled down High Holborn and across Holborn Viaduct, past the statue of Sir Christopher Wren, the police radio emitted three bursts of unintelligible sound which seemed for a moment to illuminate his driver's face; as the car moved along Newgate Street, he considered the scale of the projection and detail drawings he would need but, as he stared at the back of his driver, small phrases from the dream returned to him and he shifted uneasily in his seat; as he was driven down Angel Street, the glass of an office-block glowed just before the morning sun was obscured by a cloud, and he could see other buildings reflected in its surface; and as he entered St Martin's-le-Grand he remembered certain words but not the tune which accompanied them: Set a man to watch all night, watch all night, watch all night . . .

And now, as the car moved into Cheapside and then Poultry, its siren echoing through the streets of the city, Hawksmoor was able to concentrate upon the objects for which he would soon be searching – fibres, hair, ash, burnt paper and perhaps even a weapon (although he knew that no weapon would in fact be found). On an occasion such as this, he liked to consider himself as a scientist, or even as a scholar, since it was from close observation and rational deduction that he came to a proper understanding of each case; he prided himself on his

[152]

acquaintance with chemistry, anatomy and even mathematics since it was these disciplines which helped him to resolve situations at which others trembled. For he knew that even during extreme events the laws of cause and effect still operated; he could fathom the mind of a murderer, for example, from a close study of the footprints which he left behind – not, it would seem, by any act of sympathy but rather from the principles of reason and of method. Given that the normal male tread is twenty eight inches, Hawksmoor had calculated that a hurried step was some thirty six inches, and a running gait some forty inches. On these objective grounds, he was able to deduce panic, flight, horror or shame; and by understanding them, he could control them. All of these matters occupied his attention, as he drove towards St Mary Woolnoth, so that he might conceal from himself his rising excitement at the thought of viewing the body and for the first time entering the crime.

But when he came to the corner of Lombard Street and King William Street, he saw at once that a policeman was holding up a white sheet while a photographer was preparing his camera. 'Don't!' he shouted as he quickly left the car, 'Don't do anything yet! Just move out of the light!' and he gestured them away from the steps of St Mary Woolnoth. He did not glance at the body, however, but stopped on the pavement in front of the iron gates and looked up at the church: he saw a curved window, with pieces of glass as thick and dark as pebbles, and then above it three smaller square windows which gleamed in the autumn light. The bricks around them were cracked and discoloured, as if they had been licked by flame, and as Hawksmoor's gaze crept upward six broken pillars were transformed into two thick towers which seemed to him like the prongs of a fork which impaled the church to the earth. Only now did he look at the corpse of the dead boy which lay along the fourth of eight steps and, as he opened the gates and approached it, certain complicated thoughts disturbed his calm. Even though there was a slight dawn rain, he took off his dark coat and placed it on top of some polythene sheets which had already been laid down.

The boy looked as if he had opened his eyes wide in mock terror, perhaps trying to frighten some other children during a party game, but at the same time his mouth was gaping open in what might have been a yawn. The eyes were still bright, before the muscles relaxed into the dull and fixed stare of eternal repose, and the gaze of the child disconcerted Hawksmoor. He called for a roll of adhesive tape used in collecting evidence; bending over the corpse, he placed a piece of the tape against the neck: he could smell the body as he leaned towards it, and through the tape his fingers could touch it. Yet as he felt the neck he was compelled to look away and he stared up towards a stone tablet

[153]

on which was inscribed, 'Founded In the Saxon Age and Last Rebuilt by Nicholas Dyer, 1714'. The passage of time had partly erased the letters, and in any case Hawksmoor made no effort to understand them. He got up quickly: his sweat might look like rain, he thought, as he handed the adhesive tape to the police officer. 'There is nothing on the neck,' he told him. Then he climbed up the last four steps and entered the silent church; it was in darkness still, and he realised that the windows only reflected the light, like a mirror. Glancing behind to make sure that no one could see him, he approached the baptismal font in a corner, cupped his hands in its stale water, and rubbed them over his face.

The young officer came up to him as he left the church and murmured, 'She found him. She stayed here until she saw a copper' – he was nodding towards a red-headed woman who was sitting on an old stone just within the gates. Hawksmoor apparently paid no attention to her, and looked up at the side of the church facing King William Street: 'What is this scaffolding here for?'

'It's for the excavations, sir. They're excavating here.'

Hawksmoor said nothing. Then he turned back to face the officer: 'Have you made a note of the weather conditions?'

'It's raining, sir.'

'I know it's raining. But I want the precise temperature. I want to see how the body cools.' He looked up at the sky and the rain fell down upon him, over his cheeks and across his open eyes as he stared upwards.

The area had already been cordoned off at his instructions; large canvas screens had been placed around the gates and sides of the church to conceal the police operation from the gaze of those people who would inevitably congregate at the spot where a murder had been committed. Now that Hawksmoor was satisfied that he had staked out the right territory, with the body at its centre, he took charge of the operation in all of its aspects. More adhesive tape was used on the trousers, socks, sweater and shirt of the victim; soil was taken from his shoes, together with control specimens of the earth close at hand, and the shoes were then placed in a polythene bag. The body was now stripped under the arc-lights, so that it acquired a bright pallor, and each item of clothing put in a separate bag which Hawksmoor insisted on labelling himself and then handing to the exhibits officer. Nail-scrapings were taken, before the hands were bagged and then sealed with tape. At the same time, the ground was being searched for fibres, footprints or smears: anything of even remote interest to the investigating team was given a serial number, registered in a master-log, and then deposited in a padded transit box. Throughout these activities Hawksmoor, still without his overcoat despite the steady light rain, kept up a low whispering; it would have appeared to anyone who knew nothing of police procedure that this man had gone entirely mad, and was talking to himself within two feet of a corpse, but in fact Hawksmoor was reciting his own observations into a small tape-recorder.

His last comment was, 'Nothing else here', when the pathologist arrived; he was a small, corpulent man who nevertheless conveyed a certain air of stateliness as he slowly climbed the steps of St Mary Woolnoth. He nodded to Hawksmoor and then, murmuring 'Yes, I see the body', he knelt down beside the corpse and opened a small brown bag. For a moment he paused, his fingers quivering.

'I'm sorry to get you up so early,' Hawksmoor was saying but he had already taken out his knife and with one rapid movement had cut through the abdomen; he now placed a thermometer beside the liver of the dead child and then leaned back to survey his handiwork. Then, whistling almost imperceptibly, he stood up in order to talk to Hawksmoor.

'You hardly need me to tell you, do you, superintendent?'

'I do, sir, thank you very much. Eventually I need you to tell me the time.'

'Ah well, time waits for no man.' He stepped back and looked at the broken pillars. 'It's a fine church, isn't it, superintendent? They don't build them like that any more . . .' His voice trailed off as his attention was once more drawn to the body.

'I don't know who "they" are, Sir.' But he was already down on his knees, blinking as the arc-lights were suddenly turned off. They were somehow embarrassed in each other's company and, as the pathologist waited to take a second reading of the temperature, Hawksmoor walked behind the canvas screens and across the street to Poultry. From the corner there, he could see the front of the church entire: he had passed it before but he had never looked at it, and now it seemed startlingly incongruous in its setting despite the fact that other buildings so pressed in upon it that it was almost concealed. He imagined that very few who passed its walls realised that they were the walls of a church and as a result the building, massive through it was, had managed to disappear from sight. And even for him it was only now, after this death, that it emerged with the clarity and definition which it must have possessed for those who looked upon it when it was first built. Hawksmoor had often noticed how, in the moments when he first came upon a corpse, all the objects around it wavered for an instant and became unreal – the trees which rose above a body hidden in woodland, the movement of the river which had washed a body onto its banks, the cars or hedges in a suburban street where a murderer had left a victim, all of these things seemed at such times to be suddenly drained of meaning like an hallucination. But this church had grown larger and more distinct in the face of death.

He walked back to the steps and the pathologist took him aside for a few moments; then he called the other officers over to him. 'The situation now is this,' he explained quietly as the sun rose above the buildings, 'That the body can be moved up to the mortuary where the professor will be carrying out the post-mortem. What we want to know now, of course, is what we have learned here which might be of interest to the professor.' He looked across at the corpse as one label was attached to each wrist and ankle. It was placed in a polythene bag which was sealed at both ends and then, wrapped within an opaque transit sheet, it was carried to a stretcher before being taken to a police van parked at the corner of Lombard Street. Some women cried out in grief or alarm as the stretcher was taken through the small crowd which had assembled; and when a young girl tried to touch the side of the plastic sheet, her arm was knocked roughly away by one of the policemen carrying it. Hawksmoor saw all this and smiled, before turning round to face the red-headed woman who had discovered the body.

He watched her now with some interest as she sat by the railings of the old church and, thinking herself unobserved among all this activity, took out a small pocket mirror from her handbag; she was patting her hair into shape, turning slightly to one side and then to the other as she did so. Then she stood up, and he noticed that the damp stone had left a large stain on the back of her dress. Hawksmoor was interested in her because he always studied the reactions of those who came across the corpses of the violently slain – although most of them simply ran from the sight, as if to protect themselves from the agony and corruption which a murdered body represents. It was his belief that even the finder of that body can become an accomplice in its fate and, by completing the process which leads to its dicovery, can also suffer guilt. But this woman had stayed. He walked over to the officer who had been interviewing her: 'Did you get what you could out of her?'

'I got what I could, but it wasn't much. She doesn't have a clue, sir.'

'And I don't have a clue. What about time?'

'She only recalls time insomuch as it was raining, sir.'

Hawksmoor looked at the woman again; now that he was closer to her he noticed a certain slackness around her mouth, and the expression of puzzled intensity as she stared at the twin towers of the church. And he understood why she had not fled, but had stayed watching over the body of the murdered boy until someone else had come. 'She doesn't know the time of day, sir,' the officer added as Hawksmoor walked towards the woman.

He approached her slowly, so as not to alarm her. 'There now,' he said when he came to her, 'It was raining when you found him?'

'Raining? It was raining and it wasn't raining.' She stared into his face, and he flinched.

'And what was the time?' he asked her softly.

'Time? There was no time, not like that.'

'I see.'

And then she laughed, as if they had been sharing some enormous joke. 'I see you,' she said and gave him a push with her hand.

'Did you see him?'

'He had red hair like me'.

'Yes, you have nice red hair. I like your hair very much. And did he speak to you?'

'He don't say much, not him. I don't know what he said.'

For one instant Hawksmoor wondered if she was talking about the boy. 'And what did he do?'

'He seemed to be moving, do you know what I mean? And then he wasn't moving. What do they call this church?'

He had forgotten and in panic he swung round to look at it; when he turned back she was peering into her handbag. 'Well, Mary,' he said, 'We'll be meeting again soon, I hope?' At this she started crying, and in his embarrassment he walked away from her into Cheapside.

Generally he knew by instinct the likely length of an investigation, but on this occasion he did not: as he fought to get his breath he suddenly saw himself as others must see him, and he was struck by the impossibility of his task. The event of the boy's death was not simple because it was not unique and if he traced it backwards, running the time slowly in the opposite direction (but did it have a direction?), it became no clearer. The chain of causality might extend as far back as the boy's birth, in a particular place and on a particular date, or even further into the darkness beyond that. And what of the murderer, for what sequence of events had drawn him to wander by this old church? All these events were random and yet connected, part of a pattern so large that it remained inexplicable. He might, then, have to invent a past from the evidence available – and, in that case, would not the future also be an invention? It was as if he were staring at one of those puzzle drawings in which foreground and background create entirely different images: you could not look at such a thing for long.

He retraced his steps to the church where, to his annoyance, he found that Walter had been watching him. The red-headed woman was being led away and he spoke loudly so that she might hear. 'What time do you call this, then?'

'I don't know the time, sir. I was told to collect you.' Walter seemed

[157]

very pale in the early morning light. 'I was told you were going to the Incident Room.'

'Thank you for telling me.' And as they drove to Spitalfields Walter turned the radio to the conventional police wavelength, but Hawksmoor leaned forward and shifted the dial. 'Too many stories,' he said.

'Is it the same man, sir?'

'It's the same MO.' Hawksmoor emphasised the last two letters, and Walter laughed. 'But I don't want to talk about it yet. Give me time.'

The music of a popular song now came from the radio as Hawksmoor gazed out of the window; and he saw a door closing, a boy dropping a coin in the street, a woman turning her head, a man calling. For a moment he wondered why such things were occurring now: could it be that the world sprang up around him only as he invented it second by second and that, like a dream, it faded into the darkness from which it had come as soon as he moved forward? But then he understood that these things were real: they would never cease to occur and they would always be the same, as familiar and as ever-renewed as the tears which he had just seen on the woman's face.

Walter was now preoccupied with another subject: 'Do you believe in ghosts, sir?' he was saying as Hawksmoor stared gloomily out of the window.

'Ghosts?'

'Yes, you know, ghosts, spirits.' After a pause he continued. 'I only ask because of those old churches. They're so, well, old.'

'There are no ghosts, Walter.' He leaned forward to turn off the song on the radio and then he added, with a sigh, 'We live in a rational society'.

Walter glanced at him: 'You sound a bit frail, sir, if you don't mind my saying'.

Hawksmoor was surprised, since he did not realise that he sounded like anything. 'I'm just tired,' he said.

By the time they had reached the Incident Room at Spitalfields, from where all the enquiries on these murders were still being so-ordinated, the telephones were ringing constantly and a number of uniformed and plain clothes officers were moving about the room, calling and joking to one another. Their presence unnerved Hawksmoor; he wanted nothing to happen until he understood the reasons for its happening, and he knew that he would quickly have to dominate this investigation before it ran out of control. A video unit was being placed in a corner of the room, and Hawksmoor stood in front of it in order to speak. 'Ladies and gentlemen,' he said very loudly. Their noises ceased and as they looked towards him he felt quite calm. 'Ladies and gentlemen, you will be working in three shifts, with an incident officer in charge of each shift. And there will be a conference each day –' He paused for an instant as the lights flickered. 'It has often been said that the more unusual the murder the easier it is to solve, but this is a theory I don't believe. Nothing is easy, nothing is simple, and you should think of your investigations as a complicated experiment: look at what remains constant and look at what changes, ask the right questions and don't be afraid of wrong answers, and above all rely on observation and rely on experience. Only legitimate deductions can give any direction to our enquiry.' A policewoman was now testing the video equipment which was being installed and, as Hawksmoor spoke, pictures from the various scenes of the murders – Spitalfields, Limehouse, Wapping and now Lombard Street – were appearing on the screen behind him so that momentarily he was in silhouette against the images of the churches. 'You see,' he was saying, 'The propensity for murder exists in almost everyone, and you can tell a great deal about the killer from the kind of death he inflicts: an eager person will kill in a hurried manner, a tentative person will do it more slowly. A doctor will use drugs, a workman a wrench or shovel, and you must ask yourselves in this case: what kind of man murders quickly and with his bare hands? And you must remember, too, the sequence of actions which follows the murder: most killers are stunned by their action. They sweat; sometimes they become very hungry or thirsty; many of them lose control of their bowels at the moment of death, just as their victims do. Our murderer has done none of these things: he has left no sweat, no shit, no prints. But one thing remains the same. Murderers will try and recall the sequence of events: they will remember exactly what they did just before and just after –' And at this point Hawksmoor always assisted them, since he liked to be entrusted with the secrets of those who had opened the door and crossed the threshold. He spoke gently and even hesitantly to them, so that they knew he was not judging them. He did not want them to falter in their testimony but to walk slowly towards him; then he might embrace them, in the knowledge they both now shared, and in embracing them despatch them to their fate. And when, after all the signs of fear and guilt, they confessed, he felt envious of them. He envied them the fact that they could leave him joyfully. '– But they can never remember the actual moment of killing. The murderer always forgets that, and that is why he will always leave a clue. And that, ladies and gentlemen, is what we are looking for. Some people say that the crime which cannot be solved has yet to be invented. But who knows? Perhaps this will be the first. Thank you.' And he stood very still as the incident officer for that morning arranged the men and women into various teams. A cat, adopted as a mascot, was accidentally kicked during these activities and ran screeching out of the room, brushing against Hawksmoor's right leg as he walked over to Walter who was now staring at the keys of a computer.

Walter sensed him at his shoulder: 'I don't know how you managed without them, sir,' he said without turning around, 'In the past, I mean.' After a noise which was as faint and yet to Hawksmoor as disquieting as a human pulse, certain letters and digits moved across the small screen. Walter now looked up at him in his eagerness: 'Do you see how it's all been organised? It's all so simple!'

'I seem to have heard that somewhere before,' Hawksmoor replied as he bent forward to look at the names and addresses of those convicted or suspected of similar crimes; and of those who had used a similar *modus operandi* – manual strangulation, with the murderer sitting or kneeling on the body of the victim.

'But it's much more efficient, sir. Think of all the agony it saves us!' He now entered a different command, although his hands barely seemed to move across the keyboard. And yet despite his excitement it seemed to Walter that the computer itself only partly reflected the order and lucidity to which he aspired – that the composition of these little green digits, glowing slightly even in the morning light, barely hinted at the infinite calculability of the world outside. And how bright that world now seemed to him, as a face formed in an 'identikit' composition, flickering upon the screen with green shading in place of shadow so that it resembled a child's drawing. 'Ah,' Hawksmoor said, 'the green man did it.'

And when he grew bored with all this information, he decided that it was time to return to St Mary Woolnoth and resume the investigation there. It was almost midday when they reached it, and the autumn sun had changed the structure of the church so that once more it seemed quite strange to him. He and Walter were walking around to the side facing King William Street, when for the first time he noticed that there was a gap between the back of the church and the next building – an open patch of ground, part of which was covered with transparent sheeting. Hawksmoor looked down at the exposed soil and then drew back. 'I suppose,' he said, 'these are the excavations?'

'It looks like a rubbish tip to me.' Walter surveyed the deep furrows, the small pits with planks laid across them, the yellow clay, the pieces of brick and stone apparently thrown haphazardly to the edges of the site.

'Yes, but where did it come from? You know, Walter, from dust to dust . . .'

And his voice trailed off when he realised that they were being watched. A woman, wearing rubber boots and a bright red sweater, was standing in the far corner of the excavations. 'Hello love!' Walter shouted to her, 'We're police officers. What are you up to?' His voice had no echo as it passed over the freshly dug earth.

'Come on down and see!' she called back. 'But there's nothing here! Nothing's been touched overnight!' In confirmation of this, she kicked a piece of plastic sheeting which remained firmly in place. 'Come on, I'll show you!'

Hawksmoor seemed to hesitate, but at this moment a group of children turned the corner into King William Street and he suddenly descended into the site by means of a metal ladder. Tentatively he crossed around the edge of the open pits, smelling the dankness of the earth as he did so. It was quieter here beneath the level of the pavement, and he lowered his voice when he reached the archaeologist: 'What have you found here?'

'Oh, flint blocks, some bits of masonry. That's a foundation trench there, you see.' As she talked she was scraping the skin off the palm of her hand. 'But what have *you* found?'

Hawksmoor chose to ignore the question. 'And how far down have you reached?' he asked her, peering into a dark pit at his feet.

'Well it's all very complicated, but at this point we've got down to the sixth century. It really is a treasure trove. As far as I'm concerned we could keep on digging for ever'. And as Hawksmoor looked down at what he thought was freshly opened earth, he saw his own image staring back up at him from the plastic sheeting.

'Do you mean this is the sixth century here?' he asked, pointing at his reflection.

'Yes, that's right. But it's not very surprising, you know. There's always been a church here. Always. And there's a lot more to find.' She was certain of this because she saw time as a rock face, which in her dreams she sometimes descended.

Hawksmoor knelt down by the side of the pit; as he took a piece of earth and rubbed it between his fingers, he imagined himself tumbling through the centuries to become dust or clay. 'Isn't it dangerous,' he said at last, 'To dig so close to the church?'

'Dangerous?'

'Well, might it fall?'

'On us? No, that won't happen, not now.'

Walter, who had been examining the wooden supports which held up the church, had joined them: 'Not now?' he asked her.

'Well, we did find a skeleton recently. Not something you would be interested in, of course.'

But Walter was interested. 'Where did you find it?'

'It was there, next to the church, where the pipes are being laid.

They were pretty new, too.' Hawksmoor glanced in the direction to which she pointed, and he could see soil which was the colour of rust. He looked away.

'And how new is new?' Walter was asking her.

'Two or three hundred years, but we haven't completed our tests yet. It may have been a workman who was killed when the church was rebuilt.'

'Well,' said Hawksmoor. 'It's a theory, and a theory can do no harm.' Then he suggested to Walter that they might leave, since time was pressing, and they ascended into the street where once more they heard the noises of traffic. He looked up at an office-building on the other side, and saw the people moving around in small lighted rooms.

And it was while Walter lingered with the policemen who were still methodically searching the immediate area of the murder that Hawksmoor noticed the tramp kneeling by the corner of Pope's Head Alley, opposite the north wall of St Mary Woolnoth. He seemed at first to be praying to the church but then Hawksmoor realised that, although the pavement was still damp after the morning rain, he was finishing a sketch in white chalk. He crossed the road slowly and stood by the side of the kneeling man: for a moment he looked with horror at his hair, which was thickly matted into slabs like tobacco. The tramp had drawn the figure of a man who had put a circular object up to his right eye and was peering through it as if it were a spy glass, although it might equally have been a piece of plastic or a communion wafer. He paid no attention to Hawksmoor, but then he looked up and they stared at each other; Hawksmoor was about to say something when Walter called out and beckoned him towards their car. 'We ought to go back,' he was saying when Hawksmoor came up to him. 'They've found someone. Someone's confessed.'

Hawksmoor drew his hand three times across his face. 'Oh no,' he muttered, 'Oh no. Not yet.'

The young man sat, with bowed head, in a small waiting room; as soon as Hawksmoor saw his hands, small with the nails bitten down to the flesh, he knew that this was not the one. 'My name is Hawksmoor,' he said, 'and I am involved with this enquiry. Can you go in?' He opened the door to the interview room. 'In you go. Sit down over there. How do you do? Have they treated you well, Mr Wilson?' There was a muttered reply which Hawksmoor did not care to hear: the man sat down on a small wooden chair and started rocking slightly, as if he were trying to comfort himself. At this point Hawksmoor did not want to go on; he did not want to enter this chamber of tortures and look around within it. 'I'm going to interview you,' he said very quietly, 'with regard to the murder of Matthew Hayes, whose body was found at the church of St Mary Woolnoth at about 5.30 a.m. on Saturday,

[162]

October 24. The boy was last seen alive on Friday, October 23. You have given yourself up. What do you know about his death?' Walter came in with a note-book, as the two men stared at each other across the table.

'What do you want me to say? I've already told them.'

'Well, tell me. Take your time. We have plenty of time.'

'It doesn't take any time. I killed him.'

'Who did you kill?'

'The boy. Don't ask me why.' And once more he bowed his head; but he looked up at Hawksmoor in the silence which followed, as if pleading with him to make him go on, to make him say more. He was hunched forward, rubbing his hands against his knees, and in that instant Hawksmoor saw the man's thoughts as a swarm of small flies trapped in a bare room, swerving to one side and then another in an effort to break free.

'Well I am asking you why,' he said gently, 'I have to know why, Brian.'

He did not register the fact that Hawksmoor knew his name. 'What else can I do, if that's the way it is? I can't help it. That's the way it is.'

Hawksmoor examined him: he saw that his fingers, now clenched, were stained with nicotine; he saw that his clothes were too small; he saw the carotid artery pulsing on the side of his neck, and he restrained an impulse to touch it. Then without a trace of eagerness he enquired, 'And how do you go about killing, when you get the chance?'

'I just get hold of them and I do it. They need to be killed.'

'They need to be killed? That's a bit strong, isn't it?'

'I don't see why it is. You should know –' And he was about to say something when, for the first time, he noticed that Walter was standing behind him, and he stopped short.

'Go on. Would you like a glass of water, Brian?' With a sudden gesture Hawksmoor motioned Walter out of the room. 'Go on, I'm listening. It's just you and me.'

But the moment had gone. 'Well it's up to you to do something then, isn't it?' The young man concentrated upon a small crack in the floor. 'I can't be held responsible once I've told you.'

'You haven't told me anything I didn't know.'

'Then you know everything.'

He was clearly not the murderer whom Hawksmoor was seeking, but it was generally the innocent who confessed: in the course of many enquiries, Hawksmoor had come across those who accused themselves of crimes which they had not committed and who demanded to be taken away before they could do more harm. He was acquainted with such people and recognised them at once – although they were

[163]

noticeable, perhaps, only for a slight twitch in the eye or the awkward gait with which they moved through the world. And they inhabited small rooms to which Hawksmoor would sometimes be called: rooms with a bed and a chair but nothing besides, rooms where they shut the door and began talking out loud, rooms where they sat all evening and waited for the night, rooms where they experienced blind panic and then rage as they stared at their lives. And sometimes when he saw such people Hawksmoor thought, this is what I will become, I will be like them because I deserve to be like them, and only the smallest accident separates me from them now. He noticed a rapid nervous movement in the young man's cheek, and it reminded him of a coal which dims and then brightens when it is blown upon. 'But you haven't told me anything,' he heard himself saying, 'I want you to tell me what happened.'

'But how can I confess if you won't believe me?'

'But I do believe you. Go on. Go on with it. Don't stop now.'

'I followed him until I was sure I had him alone. It was down by that street, the one in the paper. He knew I was after him but he didn't say much. He just looked at me. Who said he could live? I wouldn't mind being dead if someone could do it like that. Do you know what I'm saying?'

'Yes, I know what you mean. How many have you killed, Brian?'

And the man smiled as Walter entered the room with a glass of water. 'More than you know. Many more. I could do it in my sleep.'

'But what about the churches? Do you know about those?'

'What churches? There are no churches. Not in my sleep.'

Hawksmoor grew angry with him now. 'That doesn't make any sense,' he said, 'That doesn't make any sense at all. Does it make any sense to you?' The man turned towards Walter, his arm outstretched for the glass of water, and as he did so Hawksmoor noticed some livid welts on his neck where he had been mutilating himself. 'You can go now,' he told him.

'You mean you don't want me to stay here with you? You don't want to lock me up?'

'No, Mr Wilson, that won't be necessary.' He could not look into the man's eyes, and so he got up to leave the room; Walter followed him, smiling. 'Send him home,' Hawksmoor said to the constable outside, 'Or charge him with wasting police time. Do what you want with him. He's no use to me.'

He was still angry when he entered the incident room and approached one of the officers: 'Have you got anything for me?'

'We have some sightings, sir.'

'Do you mean we have witnesses?'

'Well, let's put it this way, sir –'

[164]

'Let's not, if you don't mind.'

'I mean, we have statements, which we're checking now.'

'So let me see them now.'

A sheaf of photocopies was given to him, and Hawksmoor looked over each one rapidly: 'It was about midnight when the witness saw a tall man with white hair walking down Lombard Street . . . at three a.m. the witness said she heard an argument, one low voice and one high voice, coming from the direction of the church. One of the men sounded as if he were drunk . . . Then about thirty minutes later he saw a short, plump man walking hurriedly away in the direction of Gracechurch Street . . . She heard a young boy singing in Cheapside at about eleven p.m. . . . He saw a man of average height dressed in a dark coat trying the gates of St Mary Woolnoth . . . then she heard the words, We are going home. The witness did not know the time'. None of these apparent sightings interested Hawksmoor, since it was quite usual for members of the public to come forward with such accounts and to describe unreal figures who took on the adventitious shape already suggested by newspaper accounts. There were even occasions when a number of people would report sightings of the same person, as if a group of hallucinations might create their own object which then seemed to hover for a while in the streets of London. And Hawksmoor knew that if he held a reconstruction of the crime by the church, yet more people would come forward with their own versions of time and event; the actual killing then became blurred and even inconsequential, a flat field against which others painted their own fantasies of murderer and victim.

The officer, hesitating slightly now, came up to him: 'We've got the usual mail, sir. Do you want to look at that as well?' Hawksmoor nodded, gave back the sheaf of witnesses' statements and then leaned over the new bundle of papers. There were more confessions, and letters from people explaining in great detail what they would like to do with the murderer once he had been caught (some of them coincidentally borrowing effects from the murderer's own repertoire). Hawksmoor was accustomed to such messages and even enjoyed reading them; there was, after all, some amusement to be derived from the posturing imaginations of others. But there were other, more impersonal, letters which still enraged him: one correspondent requested more information, for example, and another proffered advice. Did the police know, he now read, that children often murder other children and might it not be a good idea for you to interview the poor boy's schoolfellows? Question them severely, since children were such liars! Another correspondent asked if there had been any mutilation of the body and, if so, what form did it take? He put the paper down and stared at the wall in front of him, biting his thumb nail as he did so. When he looked at the desk again, another letter caught his attention. The phrase DON'T FORGET was printed across its top, suggesting that the lined paper had been torn from a standard memorandum pad. Four crosses had been drawn upon it, three of them in a triangular relation to each other and with the fourth slightly apart, so that the whole device resembled an arrow:

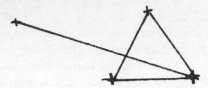

The shape was familiar to Hawksmoor; and suddenly it occurred to him that, if each cross was the conventional sign for a church, then here in outline was the area of the murders – Spitalfields at the apex of the triangle, St George's-in-the-East and St Anne's at the ends of the base line, and St Mary Woolnoth to the west. Underneath had been scrawled, in pencil, 'This is to let you know that I will be spoken about'. And there followed another line, so faint that Hawksmoor could hardly read it, 'O misery, if they will die'. Then he turned the page and he trembled when he saw the sketch of a man kneeling with a white disc placed against his right eye: this had been the drawing which he had seen issuing from the hand of the tramp beside St Mary Woolnoth. Beneath it was printed in capitals, 'THE UNIVERSAL ARCHITECT'. And he wondered at this as, surreptitiously, he placed the letter in his pocket.

'So what do you make of it?' was the question he asked Walter as they sat together later in Hawksmoor's office, contemplating the sign of the arrow which now lay on the desk between them.

'I don't really make anything of it. If the computer –'

'And the tramp?'

Walter was puzzled at this. 'It could be the same man who did the drawing. And that sign might be a tramp sign, No Hope Here, or something. Shall I have it analysed?'

'And one of the tramps was killed. We could make a connection there.' Hawksmoor saw a pattern forming, but its vagueness angered him.

'As far as I can see, sir –'

'As far as *you* can see, Walter, tell me what *do* you see?'

He was taken aback at this: 'I was simply going to say, sir, that we have to be logical about this.'

'Oh yes by all means let's be logical. Tell me this logically, then. How did he know about the churches?'

'The crosses may not be churches.'

Hawksmoor paid no attention to this. 'I never mentioned the churches. Not to anyone outside. Of course they must be churches.'

This last remark was directed again at Walter, who now shifted uneasily under Hawksmoor's gaze as he tried to think of something more positive to add. 'And that tramp *was* there, wasn't he?'

'I know he was there, Walter. That's what worries me.'

*

The evening was misty as Hawksmoor left the office, and a circle of roseate light had formed around the almost full moon. He walked up Whitehall and then turned right into the Strand, noticing at that moment how the exhalation of his breath mingled with the mist. Someone behind him was saying, 'I have said too much!' but when he turned his head he could see only two children coming towards him through the cold evening. And they were singing:

> Then he unto the parson said,
> Shall I be so when I am dead?
> Oh yes, oh yes, the parson said,
> You will be so when you are dead.

But this must have been an illusion, for then he heard 'Penny for the guy! Penny for the guy!'. He peered into the pram which the two children were pushing in front of them, and saw a straw effigy with painted face. 'What are you going to do with that?' he asked as he dropped three small coins into the open hand of one child.

'We're going to burn him.'

'Well wait, don't do it yet. Wait.' He walked on and, as he turned up Katherine Street, he thought he heard the sounds of one particular step following him: he turned around quickly with a sigh, but he could see only the crush of evening travellers with their bodies bent forward. Then he walked a little further and heard the same step again, echoing louder in the mist. 'I'll lead you a dance,' he whispered to himself, and quickened his pace as he turned sharply left into Long Acre, crossed among the heavy traffic coming out of St Martin's Lane, and darted through the small alleys of that vicinity. When he turned once more, he smiled because he could see no one still in pursuit.

In fact Walter had been following him. The behaviour of his superior was beginning to alarm him, not least because he was closely associated with Hawksmoor and would undoubtedly rise or fall with his reputation. There were those in the office who considered Hawksmoor to be 'old fashioned', even to be 'past it'; it had been precisely in order to mitigate those opinions that Walter had tried to interest him

[167]

in computer technology. But the oddity of Hawksmoor's behaviour in recent days – his sudden rages and no less abrupt retreats into silence, his tendency to walk off by himself as if walking away from the case altogether – all this, combined with his apparent inability to make any progress in his investigations of the murders, was a cause of some concern to Walter. It was his belief that Hawksmoor was suffering from personal problems, and that he was probably drinking. Walter was nothing if not enterprising: the only way to satisfy himself about such matters, and eventually to safeguard his own career, was to watch him closely. And Hawksmoor had not, as he believed, eluded his pursuer. He had gone back to his flat in Grape Street, and as he stood in front of the window he remembered part of the song he had just heard. And all the while Walter was gazing up at him, examining with curiosity his pale countenance.

9

I LOOKED DOWN upon the Street, as the Sunne rose above the mean Rents opposite, and yet I saw it not for all my Thoughts revolved upon the late Destruction of Mr Hayes and my hot Bout with the Harlot: a Torrent of Images threatened to o'erwhelm me, when I was rous'd from my Stupor by someone gazing upon me. I whirl'd about, but it was only Nat crept into the Room. You have a pale Look indeed, Master, *says he*.

Leave me, *I whispered*, I am sick and would be solitary for a while.

There is Blood upon your Gown, Master, let me –

Leave me! And in that Instant I bethought myself of the Writings I kept and which could still condemn me in spite of Mr Hayes his Extinction. Nat! Nat! *I called out* as he was about to slink away. Do you know the little Box beneeth the Bed, Nat?

I have seen it this Day and every Day since I entered your Service, which was a great Time ago, and it has never been moved –

Nat, leave off your Ramblings, take this Key and open it. There is a Notebook inside it which I wish you to find. Dig deep withinne the Linnen, Nat: you may tell it by the Bees-wax which covers it. And, when you hear the Car-men calling for the Rubbidge, give it to them. But cover it first with stinking Stuff, so that they care not to look into it. And all this while Nat was rummaging in the Box with *I see it not* and *It is not in this Corner* and *It is missing from this Spot* until he stands up solemnly and declares: It is gone.

Gone?

It is not here, not there, not anywhere. It is Gone.

I put my Face against the Glass, groaning and contemplating this further Turn, till like a Louse I jumped: for tho' my own Back was but patched and peeled, and my Box had vomited up its Secrets I knew not whither, I could not absent my self from the Office on such a Day as this; so, with much Pain, I put on my Cloathes and coach'd it to Scotland Yard. Yet I need not have been in as great a Hurry since Mr Hayes was not miss'd at first; he was constantly attending the Works and giving directions to the Workmen, going from place to place as he thought fit and (he being a Bachelour without Family to raise the

Alarm) those in the Office merely ask'd, Has Mr Hayes left Word, or a Note in his Door, to let us know where he is to be found? It was said, I suppose he has not murdered any Body? And who laugh'd the loudest but myself?

It was after Noon when the Corse was discovered beneeth the Pipes new laid by St Mary Woolnoth, which fact was made known to me in the following Manner: Mr Vannbrugghe, a great cryer up of News, blew into my Closet like a dry Leaf in a Hurricanoe. He pulls off his Hat to me and cries, he is my Humble servant (when the Rogue is thinking all the while, Kiss my Ballocks). I hate, *says he*, to be a Messenger of Ill News. Then he settled himself upon the Arm of a Chair and assumed as solemn an Air as any Parson on a Holyday: Mr Hayes, Sir, is dead, murdered most Foully.

Dead?

Quite dead. Where is Walter?

I kept my Countenance: Mr Hayes dead? If this is so, I have heard nothing of it. And I rose from my Chair in feigned Disbelief.

Well that is strange, *he replied*, since it was Walter who discovered the Body. Where is Walter? I must speak with him.

I sat down at once and answered him trembling: I have not seen him, sir, but I have no doubt I will.

I am so much taken by the Rogue's adventure, do give me leave to question him myself.

How did Hayes die?

He died a servant to your Church, for some Ruffian must have set upon him as he inspected the Foundacions of St Mary Woolnoth.

In Lombard Street?

I believe it is there, Mr Dyer. He looked on me oddly at this, and indeed I scarce knew what I was saying as in my Thoughts I contemplated the sight of Walter gazing down at the Corse of Mr Hayes.

Did you tell me how he died?

He was choaked to Death.

Choaked?

Strangled, like a Bear on a Leash. What Age is this, *he goes on*, when the Churches are not hallowed?

He looked at me then with half a Smile, and it came into my Mind to jest with edge tools (as they say), knowing that from Death springs Laughter: if you have forgot your Age, *I replied*, consult your Glass.

At that he gave a very genteel turn to the Ribbon of his Cravat-string: I see, *says he*, that you leave off the Grimaces of a feigned Sadnesse and, to speak plainly, I did not like the Man myself.

I liked him well enough, *I declared*, and I wished no Harm to come to him. Again I tried to rise from my Chair saying, I must go now to discover the Truth in all this. But there came a sudden Giddinesse into

[170]

my Head: there was a scent of Orange-Flower-water in the Room, I saw Vannbrugghe his little Mouth wag but I heard only confus'd Words as I bowed down and stared at the Dust upon the Floor.

When I returned to my self he was showing his Teeth in a Smile. This Death has taken away your Spirits, *says he*, but it cannot be helped: we all must die although (for he could never resist a Quixoticism) I admit I will never do anything with as little Desire in my Life. I gave him a Glance and at that he slunk away or, as the Rakes term it, he brush'd off, having had the worst of the Lay: just as a Rod is the best argument for the back of a Rogue, so Contempt is the best Usage that ought to be shown to a Fool. *Your Servant, Sir* he calls out as he turns into the Passage. Yes, he loves me as an Ivy does the Oak, and will never leave me till he has hugg'd me to my Ruine.

When I could no longer hear his Step I hasten'd to the little Desk upon which Walter fair-writes, but there was nothing so much there as a Peece of Paper to reveal to me where he had been, and where he was now. His Repository was lock'd against it, but I had watched Walter and knew that he hid his Key beneath a Board where no Nail was: it was removed by me with the utmost Ease and Quietness but, upon opening the Box, I saw only a pile of Bills and Measurements. But then a little Paper dropped down to the Ground, and when I bent to pick it up I saw plainly that Walter had written upon it, *O Misery, Them Shall Dye.* I puzzled over this for a Moment, but there was so much Noise and Whispering around the Office that I could not remain by myself and, in fear of Censure, I walked into the Passage to join the Throng. Mr Lee, Mr Strong, and Mr Vanbrugghe were there engaged in Talk and as I walked toward them they call'd out, Where is Walter? What has become of him? Is he withinne? and such like Questions.

I doubt not but that he is being Examined, *I replied*, and that he will return to us presently. Vanbrugghe did not look upon me as I spoke but waited for me to finish with an indifferent Air, and then began to discourse about Mr Hayes his suddaine Death, who he supposed his Murtherer to be, and other Trifles. My Thoughts were travelling down a different Road: Is it not just, *said I* after a while, that he be Buried where he Fell? And to this the Pack concurred, as a proper Course for one so devoted to the Work of the Office. Then I walk'd out into the Yard to puzzle once more the meaning of Walter's words, for they strangely afflicted me. And how could it be that Walter had made so sudden a Discovery of the Corse? I wheel'd and wheel'd about, not knowing whether to go or to stay, and the Wind would not let me think but blew upon my Face bringing the Scents of the River; so at last I enter'd my Closet and shut the Door, at which Time I had a sudden Vision of Walter running in Fear down Lombard Street.

I wrote his Words upon a Paper – *O Misery, Them Shall Dye* – but I could still find no clew to unravel their Sense. Then after a while it came to me to anagrammatize its Letters and thus I spell'd out in Horrour: *Dyer Has Smote Me Ill*, with the initials *YH* for the name of Yorick Hayes. And I stared astonished at my Labours: for how could it be that the Villain had foretold his own Fate, when he was making merry in his Cups only minutes before his Extinction? And yet if these were Walter's own words, how might it be that he could communicate with the Dead Man unless it be by some Instillation of his Spirit? And when had he composed this troublesome Stuff? All these blinde Feares whirled about me: Walter, Walter, *I said out loud*, do I not talk madly? And at this there was a Knock upon the Door and I bounded up like a Dog afraid of Whipping. But it was only the coxcomb Vanbrugghe once more making his Bow: Mr Hayes, *says he*, was a great Frequenter of Plays and, once we have put him in a Shift and given him over to the Clerk of the Parish, we thought to take ourselves to the Play-House in his Memory. Do you agree, Mr Dyer?

I was about to speak out, but the Callus of this man's Vanity has made him invulnerable and he takes everything you say in good Part. It is agreed, *I replied*.

But to go on with my Theme: a Coroner's Jury had been summoned and met to make an Inquiry how the Party (as they called him) came by his Death, and such Witnesses as could be got besides Walter were examined; but their Testimonies appeared very obscure in the apprehension of most People. Some under examination confirmed that they had seen a lofty man in a dark Coat waiting about Midnight at the end of Pope's Head Alley, while others declared that they had observed a drunken Man by the New Church, and yet others beleeved that they had heard violent Singing in the Dusk of the Evening. All these had but a confus'd sense of Time, and it became clear that there was nothing Certain. So it is that the World makes its own Demons, which then the People see.

Mean-while the villain Hayes was clean'd and shav'd and put into his Shift: he was left to lie in his Coffin for just one Day, with a square peece of Flannel over his Face and Neck to obscure the Signs of his Death, before he was taken thro' Cheapside and Poultry to be buried by the east wall of St Mary Woolnoth. Sir Chris. had conceeved a great Dislike of Funerals and, sighing, he looked upon the Walls new built rather than down into the Grave. Mr Vannbrugghe glanced around at the Company with a melancholy Air but, as we threw sprigs of Rosemary upon the Coffin, he repeated in a jovial Tone the words of the Service: From dust to dust, *says he*, From dust to dust. Then he leaned over to whisper at me behind his Hand: I do not see you at your Devotions, Mr Dyer.

I have faith in the true Religion, *I replied* unthinking.

Well, well, *says he* smiling, Mr Hayes is now our Scholar in these Matters.

Then we returned down Cheapside in the same Order as we came, Walter still being absent and, it was thought, suffering from melanchollic Sicknesse after being surpriz'd by the Discovery of the horrid Corse. Yet all of us (save Sir Chris.) made Merry, taking Heart from that Catch, *and I yet alive!* : at five o'clock of the same Day, we made our way thro' New Inn, crossed Russell Court and steered to the Playhouse. Mr Vannbrugghe, after his Devotions at the Barbers, was all improved by Powder, Washballs and Perfume so that he was as fragrant as a Bermoodoes Breez or any sweet-bag: here is a self-conceited Puppy who was born a Boy and will die before he is a Man. Coming too soon for the Play we took a Turn in the Lobby, which is nothing but a Rendez-vous of all Extravagances, or rather the Shambles where young and old are expos'd to Sale. For among the Saunterers with their Hands in their Pockets come the Ladies from the Stews: all of them patched and painted, where beneath they are Old and Yellow and fit only to turn Stomachs. And then on a sudden Glance I observed the Harlot who had encounter'd me on that fatall Night: at once I turned away from her and busied myself in the reading of Advertisements fix'd to the Pillars.

Well, well, *says she* walking up close to me and talking to some black Devil in a Mask, do you see how the Captain stared at us and gnashed his Teeth as if he could eat us for looking at Him? Captain, *says she* again coming beside me, you turn your Back upon me as you have done before. And she laugh'd as I shuddered and burned. Here now, *she goes on* taking my sweating Hands in her own, these are mighty Hands which could work much Mischief. Before I could speak, the Porter moved among the Company saying, The Play begins when it is exactly six by your Watches, will you please to go in, will you please to go in? Another Day then, Captain, *says she*, or let it be another Night? And she took herself off with a Smile.

After a Pause to find my Breath I walked into the Pit where the others were already sat upon the Benches: they were not the best Seats neither, since the Gentlemen in front of us had so powdered their Perriwigs that they endangered my Eyes as soon as they turned round to stare at the Company. At first I beleeved they stared at me for the most part, since I was sadly discomfited after my Discourse with the Harlot, but my Perturbation soon passed when I saw that there was no Meaning to their Looks, either to Themselves or each other. So it was with an easier Mien that I settled my self down to watch this Assembly with its Amorous Smirks, its A la Mode Grins, its Antick Bows – the World being but a Masquerade, yet one in which the Characters do not know their Parts and must come to the Play-House in order to studdy

[173]

them. Let there be no Stop to Bawdy so that those in the Pit can see themselves; fill the Stage with Villainy, with Swearing and Blaspheming and Open Lewdness. The grossest Touches will be most true.

And now the Curtain was drawn to show a dark Room where some one was playing a Pack of Cards; above him some dozen Clouds were trimm'd with Black, and there was a new Moon something decay'd. And then for a moment I was environ'd by these painted Scenes and lived among them even as I sat in the Pitt: now my Lord All-Pride leads Doll Common away, and the Scene is drawn to show a Chamber of Tortures where he says, Do you like this Ribbon (pointing to a Whip), this Cutt of the Sleeve (pointing to a Knife), this Stocking (pointing to a hanging Rope)? And I was a Child again, watching the bright World. But the Spell broke when at this Juncture some Gallants jumped from the Pitt onto the Stage and behaved as so many Merry-Andrews among the Actors, which reduced all to Confusion. I laugh'd with them also, for I like to make Merry among the Fallen and there is pleasure to be had in the Observation of the Deformity of Things. Thus when the Play resumed after the Disturbance, it was only to excite my Ridicule with its painted Fictions, wicked Hypocrisies and villainous Customs, all depicted with a little pert Jingle of Words and a rambling kind of Mirth to make the Insipidnesse and Sterility pass. There was no pleasure in seeing it, and nothing to burden the Memory after: like a voluntarie before a Lesson it was absolutely forgotten, nothing to be remembered or repeated.

When this Masquerade was complete, the prattler Vanbrugghe led us on to the Grey Bear tavern, where the whimzey-headed and the slender-witted and the shallow-brained come to sip their Brandy and make their Chit-chat on what they have just view'd. And so sir, *he cried* as we waited for the Tapster, how did you like the Play?

I have forgot it, sir.

So soon?

I asked him what he said, for there was such a mish-mash of Conversation around us that I could scarcely understand him – the frequenters of Taverns have Hearts of Curd and Souls of Milk Sop, but they have Mouths like Cannons which stink of Tobacco and their own foul Breath as they cry What News? What's a Clock? Methinks it's Cold to Day! Thus is it a *Hospital For Fools*:

DRAMATIS PERSONAE

John Vanbrugghe: An Architect in Fashion
Nicholas Dyer: A Nothing, a Neighbour
Sir Philip Bareface: A Courtier

[174]

Moneytrap: A Jobber
Various Gentlemen of the Town, Rakes, Bullies and Servants

VANNBRUGGHE. (*Taking up his glass*) I said, sir, forgot so soon?

DYER. (*Sits down*) There was nothing that I recall save that the Sunne was a Round flat shining Disc and the Thunder was a Noise from a Drum or a Pan.

VANNBRUGGHE. (*Aside*) What a Child is this! (*To Dyer*) These are only our Devices, and are like the Paint of our Painted Age.

DYER. But in Meditation the Sunne is a vast and glorious Body, and Thunder is the most forcible and terrible Phaenomenon: it is not to be mocked, for the highest Passion is Terrour. And why was it, too, that this Scribbler mock'd Religion? It is a perilous Case.

VANNBRUGGHE. Amen to that. I pray the Lord. Ha, ha, ha, ha, ha! But let me tell you plainly, sir, this Scribbler was just; Religion is only the quaint Leger-de-main of strong-pated Statesmen who, to over-awe the Capriciousness of the giddy Multitude, did forge the Image of some Punisher of all Humane actions.

DYER. (*Aside*) A small rational Sir Fopling this!

VANNBRUGGHE. Have I told you this Story? When a Widow, hearing in a Sermon of the Crucifixion, came to the Priest after, dropped him a Courtsie and asked him how long ago this sad Accident happened? When he answered, about 15 or 16 hundred Years ago, she began to be comforted and said, Then by the grace of God it may not be true. (*Laughing*).

DYER. (*In a low tone*) Interest is the God of your World, who may be sacrificed to Hypocrisie.

VANNBRUGGHE. (*Aside*) I find he knows me! (*To Dyer*) What was that?

DYER. It was nothing, nothing at all.

There is an uneasy Silence between them

VANNBRUGGHE. And how do your Churches, Mr Dyer?

DYER. (*In alarm*) They do very well, sir.

VANNBRUGGHE. You build in Greenwich next?

DYER. (*Wiping sweat from his brow*) I build first in Bloomsbury, and then in Greenwich.

VANNBRUGGHE. How interesting. (*He pauses*) The Play was well received, was it not?

DYER. The Audience had so humble an Opinion of itself tonight that it thought what pleased the People of Fashion ought also to please it.

VANNBRUGGHE. And yet there was that to please all: the Language was enrich'd with beautiful Conceptions and inimitable Similitudes. (*He stares at Dyer*) Are you not of my Mind in this at least?

DYER. No, I am not of your Mind, for the Dialogue was fitted up with too much Facility. Words must be pluckt from Obscurity and nourished with Care, improved with Art and corrected with Application. Labour and Time are the Instruments in the perfection of all Work. (*Aside*) Including churches.

VANNBRUGGHE. (*Coughs in his glass*) Here is a Speech that would fright me into Nothing! (*To the Boy*) Fill some Brandy, sirrah! (*To Dyer*) But the greatest Art is to speak agreeably about the smallest Things, to spread a general evenness of Humour and a natural decency of Style.

DYER. (*Looking at him scornfully*) So that is why Wits swarm like Egypt's Frogs. If I were a Writer now, I would wish to thicken the water of my Discourse so that it was no longer easy or familiar. I would chuse a huge lushious Style!

VANNBRUGGHE. (*Interrupting*) Ah the music of Erudition, it is unimaginable to weaker Wits.

DYER. (*Ignoring him*) I would imploy outlandish Phrases and fantasticall Terms, thus to restore Terrour, Reverence and Desire like wild Lightning.

VANNBRUGGHE. (*Offended*) I do not wish for meer Words: I wish for Matter.

DYER. And what is matter, according to the Greshamites, but blind Attomes?

VANNBRUGGHE. (*Laughing*) Well let us drop that Matter.

They stand again without speaking, only drinking

VANNBRUGGHE. (*Inclining his head*) See this Man's manner as he walked by me: he has lately been in the powdering Tub of Affliction and it has affected his Step. (*He calls out and smiles at the Man*) Sir Philip, Sir Philip! (*Aside to Dyer*) His sword is tyed as high as the Waist-band of his Breeches, do you see, and it has no more Motion when he walks than a Two-foot Rule stuck into the Apron of a Carpenter. (*To Sir Philip Bareface*) You have been to Court, I hear, what's done?

SIR PHILIP. Extraordinary News, I do assure you.

DYER. (*Aside*) Only when you are hanged, sirrah.

SIR PHILIP. The events in Silesia have caused great Consternation: I never approved of our Affairs there after my Lord Peterborough was called away. It is true my Lord Galway is a brave General and a Man of excellent Parts (*he breaks off to look around cautiously*) but what, then, if Luck is not on his side? (*He whispers now*) Did you read of my Lord in the *Spectator*?

DYER. (*Aside*) I have seen Mr Addison among the Buggerantoes in Vinegar Yard: truly he is a Man of Parts.

SIR PHILIP. (*Still whispering*) I see nothing ahead but endless Broils and

Divisions. But here is Master Moneytrap who will tell us more News. Pray Sir (*addressing him*) what Intelligence from the City?

MONEYTRAP. There are those frighted at the News from Silesia. But I can tell the secret of that: Stocks may fall, but I say buy.

VANNBRUGGHE AND SIR PHILIP. (*In unison*) Buy?

MONEYTRAP. Yes, buy, for they fall only by degrees to rise further. Yesterday South Sea stock was 95 one quarter and Bank was 130!

SIR PHILIP. This is strange News indeed.

CHORUS OF GENTLEMEN AND SERVANTS. What News is this? What News is this? (*And then they sing*)

> Bankrupts, Elopements, Thefts and Lotteries
> Strange News from Petersburg and Flanders,
> Fast Mails from Frankfurt and Saxony
> Bring Chit-chat, Jobbing, Venery and Slanders.

Exeunt Sir Philip and Moneytrap, in conversation. Vannbrugghe and Dyer talk apart.

DYER. (*Having listen'd attentively to the Song*) Was I not saying that Poetry is now sunk and miserably debas'd? It is as low a Thing now as the music of Italian Opera, and not even as Sweet as the Songs we heard in Childhood. For the best Authors, like the greatest Buildings, are the most ancient: this is but a cold Age of the World, filled with a generall Imperfection.

VANNBRUGGHE. No, no, the Fables and Religions of the Ancient World are well nigh consum'd: they have served the Poet and the Architect long enough, and it is now high time to dismiss them. We must copy the present Age, even in our Songs.

DYER. (*Aside*) His Eyes and Countenance show a great Alteration, for this Matter touches him keenly. (*To Vannbrugghe*) If we copy the present Age, as you put it, we will be like those people who judge only by Resemblance and are therefore most delighted with Pictures of their Acquaintance. We will be like the Greshamites who will deal only with that which they *know* or *see* or *touch*: and so your Playwrights catch the Audience as Woodcocks and Widgeons are caught, by a lowd Bell and a greasie Light.

VANNBRUGGHE. (*Aside*) He has a solemn Air, but still he mocks me. (*To Dyer*) Well said, sir, you have brought yourself off cleverly. And so you would lugg down old Aristotle, Scaliger and all their Commentators from the high Shelf, and let the Moths flutter round your Gabardeen, so that you can furnish Prose with Episodes, Narrations, Deliberations, Didacticks, Pathetics, Monologues, Figures, Intervals and Catastrophes?

DYER. (*Aside*) Methinks he strives to shine in his Talk the more to

[177]

Insult my own. (*To Vannbrugghe*) I will say this only: that there is scarcely any Art or Faculty wherein we do not come short of the Ancients.

VANNBRUGGHE. (*Spitting upon the floor*) But the bounds of the Mind are yet unknown: we form our Judgments too much on what has been done without knowing what might be done. Originals must soar into the region of Liberty.

DYER. And then fall down, since they have Wings made only of Wax. Why prostrate your Reason to meer Nature? We live off the Past: it is in our Words and our Syllables. It is reverberant in our Streets and Courts, so that we can scarce walk across the Stones without being reminded of those who walked there before us; the Ages before our own are like an Eclipse which blots out the Clocks and Watches of our present Artificers and, in that Darkness, the Generations jostle one another. It is the dark of Time from which we come and to which we will return.

VANNBRUGGHE. (*Aside*) What is this Stuff about Time? (*To Dyer*) This is well said, but this Age of ours is quite new. The World was never more active or youthful than it is now, and all this Imitation of the past is but the Death's Head of Writing as it is of Architecture. You cannot learn how to build from the Instructions of a Vitruvius or to manage a good Mien from a Tomb-painting: in the same Fashion, that which truly pleases in Writing is always the result of a Man's own Force. It is his proper Wealth, and he draws it out of himself as the Silk-worm spins out of her own Bowel. And speaking of Bowels –

They break off for a Minute as Vannbrugghe repairs to the Jakes; and Dyer listens to the assembled Company who can now be heard.

RAKE. Why are Women like Frogs, sirrah?

HIS COMPANION. Tell me, why *are* Women like Frogs?

RAKE. Because only their lower parts are Man's Meat. Ha, ha, ha, ha!

HIS COMPANION. And I will tell you another. A plain country-man, being called at an Assize in Norfolk to be a Witness about a peece of Land that was in Controversy, the Judge asked him what call you that Water which runs on the south side of the Close? The Fellow answered, My Lord, our Water comes without Calling. Ha, ha, ha!

Dyer scowls and then looks upon two Gentlemen in another Corner, who are inflamed with Liquor and speaking wildly.

FIRST GENTLEMAN. You hear this on Rep?

SECOND GENTLEMAN. Pozz. It was his Phizz and the Mobb saw it: it was in the News. As sure as Eggs are Eggs.

FIRST GENT. Ah but these Eggs give me disconsolate Dreams, and make me melancholy for Days after.

SECOND GENT. And do you know why you do not like Eggs?

FIRST GENT. Why do I not like Eggs, sirrah?

SECOND GENT. Because your Father was so often pelted with them!

DYER. (*To himself*) There is nothing but Corruption withinne, a hollow sounding Box: whatsoever I see, whatsoever I hear, all Things seem to sound Corruption! (*He turns towards Vannbrugghe, who has come back to the Table*) What was I saying?

VANNBRUGGHE. You were extolling the Ancients.

DYER. Yes, so I was. The Ancients wrote of General Passions, which are the same, but you wish only for that which is *lively* or *new* or *surprizing*. But the Ancients knew how Nature is a dark Room, and that is why their Plays will stand when even our Playhouses are crumbled into Dust: for their Tragedy reflects Corruption, and Men are the same now as they have ever been. The World is still mighty sick. Did you hear during the late Plague –

VANNBRUGGHE. (*Laughing*) I had quite forgot that Distemper.

DYER. – Did you hear of the Victim who persewed a young Girl, kissed her and then said, I have given you the Plague! Look here! And then he opened his Shirt to show her the fatall Tokens. There is a Horrour and Loathsomeness there that must affect us all.

VANNBRUGGHE. (*Aside*) But there is a mixture of Delight in the Disgust it gives you. (*To Dyer*) I see, sir, that you are for strolling in Dirty Lanes and among the Cole-pits, like the Irish among their Boggs.

DYER. Yes, for in such Places may the Truth be found.

VANNBRUGGHE. And so the Fumes issuing from a Jakes are for you Incense from an Altar: for they also have allwaies been the same!

DYER. Should I peruse the casual Scratches and inside Daubings made upon the Walls, in order to take my Inspiration from their Novelty?

VANNBRUGGHE. (*Growing impatient*) There is nothing so pedantick as many Quotations, and your reverence for the Ancients is an excuse for meer Plagiarism.

DYER. This is not so. (*He gets up from the Table, walks awkwardly about, and then resumes his Seat*) Even the magnificent Vergil has borrowed almost all his Works: his Eclogues from Theocritus, his Georgicks from Hesiod and Aratus, his Aeneid from Homer. Aristotle himself derived many things from Hippocrates, Pliny from Dioscorides, and we are assur'd that Homer himself built upon some Predecessors. You will have Variety and Novelty, which is nothing but unruly Fancy. It is only from Imitation –

VANNBRUGGHE. (*Laughing*) Plagiarism!

DYER. (*With a grave countenance*) – Only from Imitation that we have Order and Massiveness.

VANNBRUGGHE. (*Sighing*) Words, words, words breeding no thing but more Wordiness which represents no thing in Nature, either, but a meer Confused Idea of Grandeur or Terrour. Pray speak that you

[179]

may be understood, Mr Dyer: Language was design'd for it, they say.

DYER. So you would have me speak Plain, when then my Words would blast you! (*Vannbrugghe raises his Eyebrows at this, and Dyer adopts a lower tone*) Reality is not so plain, sir, and will escape you as the Mist escapes the Squab who puts out a Hand to grasp it.

Enter Pot-boy

BOY. Do you call, sirs, do you call? Coffee or Brandy, Gentlemen? I have a fresh Pot a making.

VANNBRUGGHE. Make it Brandy, for this is thirsty work.

He takes off his wig for a moment to cool himself, and Dyer notices his Hair.

DYER. (*Aside*) It is strangely Black beneeth his Wigg: the clear Water has been used to turn it.

VANNBRUGGHE. (*Staring at him*) And you were saying?

DYER. (*In confusion, lest he was heard*) I have lost my Thred. (*He hesitates*) I am troubled by many Thoughts.

VANNBRUGGHE. Why so? Tell me your Affliction: do you speak of Mr Hayes?

DYER. That Piece of Deformity! (*He checks himself*) No, I speak of Walter who is Sick.

VANNBRUGGHE. You are condemned –

DYER. Condemned? To what? Speak! Quick!

VANNBRUGGHE. – You are condemned to be always fearful. It is your natural Temper.

DYER. (*Hastily*) Well, enough of this. (*Clumsily, to break the silence between them*) And I can press my Theme still further, for Milton copied Spenser –

VANNBRUGGHE. No doubt you were more charmed by Milton's Hell than by his Paradise.

DYER. – And Spenser copied his master Chaucer. The world is a continued Allegory and a dark Conceit.

VANNBRUGGHE. And what is your Allegory, sir?

DYER. (*Somewhat drunken now*) I build in Hieroglyph and in Shadow, like my Ancients.

VANNBRUGGHE. (*Interrupting*) So you speak of your Churches at last!

DYER. No! But yes, yes, I do, I do. For just as in the Narration of Fables we may see strange Shapes and Passages which lead to unseen Doors, so my Churches are the Vesture of other active Powers. (*He warms to his theme as the Brandy warms him*) I wish my Buildings to be filled with Secresy, and such Hieroglyphs as conceal from the Vulgar the Mysteries of Religion. These occult ways of Proceeding were treated of by the Abbot Trithemius in his very learned and

[180]

ingenious Discourse de Cryptographia . . . (*He breaks off here sudden-*
ly and nervously)

VANNBRUGGHE. Do not be abashed, Mr Dyer.

DYER. (*In a lower tone*) But this Art, like that of Painting upon Glass, is
but little practiced now and is in great measure lost. Our Colours are
not so Rich.

VANNBRUGGHE. But they are rich enough else where.

DYER. How so?

VANNBRUGGHE. In the Elaboratory, or so I am told, they use Salts to
turn blew into red, and red into Green.

DYER. I see you have not understood this Discourse.

Both men growing uneasy, they turn to look at the Company; but the
Hour is past Midnight, and the Tavern empty except for the Boy cleaning
the Tables.

VANNBRUGGHE. I am tired now: I must find a Chair to take me home.

He comes forward, as Nicholas Dyer sleeps uneasily in his Cups, and
addresses the Audience with a

SONG

What foolish Frenzy does this Man possess
To cling to Ancients and expect Success?
To bring old Customs on the modern Stage
When nought but Sense and Reason please this Age?

Goodnight, Mr Dyer.

He makes a low Bow to him, and exits. Dyer wakes suddenly and stares
wildly around. Then he stands up unsteadily and delivers to the Audience
another

SONG

And yet who was that miserable Creature
Who trusts to Sense and coppies Nature?
What Warmth can his dull Reasons still inspire
When in Darkness only can be seen the Fire?

He exits.

BOY. (*Calling out after him*) What, no Epilogue?

No, and there will be none, for this Play is follow'd by a Masquerade. When I return'd to my Lodgings, much incens'd at the high
talk of Vannbrugghe, I tyed an Handkerchief about my Head, tore a
woollen Cap in many places, as likewise my Coat and Stockings, and
looked exactly what I design'd to represent: a Beggar-Fellow, and one
who might merit the World's just Scorn. Then I slipped out of my
Closet at Two a clock, when all the Household was abed, proposing to

make my way through the Streets without a Lanthorn. As I passed the Bed-chamber of Mrs Best I heard her call out, Lord what Noise is that? And then a Man (so, *says I* to myself, she has found fresh Meat) replied, Perhaps the Dog or Catte. I was instantly in the Entry and came out at the Street-door without any other Disturbance. And as I walk'd the Street the fearful Lightness in my Head, which so afflicted me, passed away and in these Beggar robes I was once more fastened by the Earth: in that manner, all my Fears and anxious Perplexities left me.

At Three in the Morning, with the Moon on my left Hand, I came to an old House by Tottenham Fields and here I sank into a corner with my Chin upon my Breast: another Beggar came but he did not like my Looks and was soon gone. Then I rous'd my self and walked into the Pasture by Montagu House, close behind my new Church at Blooms-bury. It was a silent Night but that the Wind made a low Sound like a Woman sighing; I laid my self down upon the grass curled like an Embrio and was recalling Days far gone when I heard a Whistling borne to me by the Wind. I rais'd my self upon my Knees, crouch'd ready to Spring, and then I saw a young Fellow crossing the Pasture towards me: he was as like to have walked straight to the Bloomsbury Church, in which Path I would assist him. I stood upright and went to him with a Smile: How do you do my little Honey, *says I*, How do you do my Sweetheart?

At that he was much affrighted and said, For God's sake who are you?

I am your pretty Maid, your merry Wren. And will you show me the Church yonder so that we may hug in its Shaddowe?

I see no Church, *says he*. But these were desperate Words, for he was tied like a dead Bird to a Tree. And it was some time after when I returned to my Lodgings, singing old Songs in the silent Feelds.

On the fifth Day after I did see an Advertisement for that pritty young Fellow: Run away on Friday last from his Master, Mr Walsall, in Queen's Square, a Boy about 12 Years of Age, *Thomas Robinson*; he had on dark grey Cloaths all of a sort, the Sleeves of his Coat faced with Black, a brown Peruke, a red Mark on one of his Hands. Whosoever brings him to Mr Walsall's aforesaid, or at the Red Gates in Grape Court, shall have £5 Reward and no questions ask'd. This is well put; ask no Questions and you shall hear no Lies, Mr Walsall, and I shall tell you this also without a Recompense: your Boy has more Marks now.

And so I busied my self about the Churches of Bloomsbury and Greenwich with a lighter Heart, and this in spite of the Fact that Walter had not return'd to the Office and, it was said, had grown so heavy with Hypochondriacall Melancholie that he was like to sink into the

Ground. It was some Days following that I made a Visit to him in his Lodgings in Crooked Lane, on the east side of St Michael's Lane, where a nasty slut his Landlady whisper'd to me as I enter'd through the Door: He is sick of the Feaver and we despair of him, sir, (at this she clinched her Hands as if there were Silver in them) and he speaks mighty strange and is sometimes crying or roaring like a little Boy that has been whipped. What shall we do, sir?

Then she led me to his mean Chamber which stank of Sweat and Piss like the Hovel of a Car-man; when Walter saw me he tried to rise from his Bed but I put my Hands upon him: No, no, *I whisper'd*, stay, stay, Walter. Then he showed Signes of great Terrour which perplexed me: Do you know me? *I asked* him.

Know you? Yes, very well.

How do you do, then?

Very bad, master. I care not much indeed what becomes of me. Here he stopt and fetched a Sigh.

I tried to cheer him: And then, Walter, what then? You cannot Sigh for ever, and what will you do with your self then?

I don't know, not I; hang myself, I think. I don't know anything I can do better.

Tell me, Walter, what is the Matter? Is it such a Secret that you dare not tell it? I hope you have not committed Murther.

But he did not Laugh as I had hoped: I am not sure, *he replied*, and now it is no such great matter neither.

No great Matter, and yet you talk of hanging your self! I made a Stop here and, taking my Eyes from his Face which was wonderfully Pale, I saw fastened with Pins to the Wall divers Planns and Draughts of my London Churches; and this touch'd my Heart for the poor Boy, silent as he might be in the Office, showed his Devotion here. And now, as he lay Sick among my Images, he raised his Head from the Pillow: I thought, *said he* at last, that you might leave your Post and forget me.

Why so, Walter, when I can never cancell my Obligation to you for your Labours? You are my right Hand.

No, no, I wished you to leave: I wished to be free from your Service.

You are filled with disturbing Thoughts and melancholly Vapours, Walter. You must lie now and rest.

But then he raised his Head a little higher still: How far is the Pillar at Bloomsbury advanc'd, *he said*, let it not stand upon the cold Ground but lift it above the Tower! And have you finished the Moddell of Greenwich Church? At that he took Pen and Ink, and wrote down a great many things upon his Paper, and made Lines with a short brass Rule, but I understood nothing of them.

Let them alone, *I said*, you are too Sick, too Sick.

Then he glared at me: You saw the Lines I wrote before?

[183]

I saw some Musty Stuff in Anagram placed in the Box beneeth your Chair, *I replied*, but it was of no account.

Walter grew yet more agitated: I assure you, there was no Anagram. I speak of the Letters I left for you.

This is not clear to me, Walter.

I wish'd to entice you to leave the Office for I was so much at your Mercy there, *said he* staring at me wildly, but I never wish'd to cause you such Agonie. I was in a Box and could not creep out of it: I wish'd to be free but instead I have bound my self.

Those letters were the work of the villain Hayes, *I replied* (without thinking of what I said), and they were not of your Doing.

But then he took from beneath his Pillow a seal'd Letter, conveyed it to me, and as our Eyes met he sank back affrighted. I will tell you a Mystery, *says he*, I followed you and then I lost you. That night I dream'd I killed Mr Hayes and then on the next Day I found his Corse. Was there Truth in this Dreame? And what must I do?

The nasty Slut appear'd in the Room againe: He is always disturbed so, *said she*, since he discovered the Body. And his wild Talk is filled with you and Mr Hayes.

The Fever has grown so considerable, *I told her*, that you must tie him firmly to the Bed. We must make Time his Cure.

Walter lay groaning, and I contemplated his Face for the last time before I turned my Back on him and went on my own Way. This visit had given me News indeed, and as I climbed down the narrow Stairs I unsealed the Letter which he had left with me: at once I saw it to be one of those which had threatened me and which I had layed to Mr Hayes. And so my own Assistant had watch'd me and plotted against me: it was he, he alone, who wished to be rid of me. It was he who laid deep Planns for me to be gone. And who knows what else he might now have committed to Paper in his Delirium? I was uncertain which way the next Winde might toss me, and as I walked back to my Lodgings I watched as those who travel in suspected Places.

I spoke nothing of my Visit to Walter when I came into the Office on the next morning, for I had too private a Sense and was too close in my Manner of speaking to give them a Rod (as they say) to beat me with. But they suspected me of I know not what, and the absence of Walter was cried up as a Stroke against me: they whispered against me so as not to be over-heard, but I needed no Trumpet-tongued Devils to understand all their Plots and Intrigues. They avoided me as if my Breath were Contagious, or a Plague-sore running upon me. And then three days following this, Sir Christopher asked to see me: he did not tell me what the Purpose was and, tho' I imagined my self to be Undone, I did not ask Questions for fear of giving him Suspicion. I went into his Chamber trembling, but he did not so much as Hint at

[184]

Walter but spoke of Mr Vannbrugghe his Projects in a most familiar Manner.

I was easy for a while but then the Purpose behind his Discourse became most plain when, in the next Week, I received a very flaming Injury which was so loaded with Aggravations that I cou'd scarce get over it. For I read this in the Gazette: *His Majesty has been pleased to appoint Sir John Vannbrugghe to be Comptroller of His Majesty's Works in England.* One remarkable Passage I had like to forgot: the new King had made Vannbrugghe a Knight, but that was as nothing beside this new Case. What are we coming to, and what is to be expected, when those like this Reptile Knight are advanc'd before me? Yet I am held in such Despight that I cannot over-reach him, and so I must burn. It is the same the World over: Persons that have nothing to recommend them but the Marks of Pride and a high Value for them-selves have gained Esteem; being supposed to have some Merit only for pretending it, the Cox-comb struts like a Crow in the Gutter while the others laugh at me behind their Hands. With the Queen dead, Sir Chris. shall lose all Favour with those now in Power and what Hope for me then? They wish to turn me out and thus destroy me, and there is a known Maxim for this purpose: Throw Dirt and if it does not stick throw Dirt continually and some will stick. So I must stay out of their Way: suspicious and jealous Men have good Eyes, and they will now be fasten'd on me.

Such Thoughts were heavy upon me when I enlarged upon my new Work to the Commission thus: We desire the Honble. Board to know that the Walls of the *Bloomsbury Church* are complete and all is prepar'd for the Plaisterers; it will be proper that they begin the Ceilings and Walls during the best of the Winter, that the Work be thoroughly dry before any Frost take it. The Church is bounded by Russell Street to the North, Queen Street to the West, and to the South-east Blooms-bury Market; this area being very populous in the months of Summer, the Fields being close by, what Preparations are to be made for outside Doors so that the Church may be shut from the Rabble? The West Tower is advanc'd about 25 or 28 Feet above the Roof of the Church, and I will place upon that my Historical Pillar which will be of square Form and built with rough Stone. (And this I do not add: on the Apex of this Shaft will be placed the seven-edged Starre which is the Eye of God. The Emperour Constantine set up a Pillar at Rome as big as this, in one Stone, and placed the Sunne on the Sumit of it. But that *parhelion* or false Sunne was forced to leave Shineing: my Fabrick will last 1000 yeares, and the Starre will not be extinguish'd.) I also humbly offer to the Commissioners the following account of the present state of the *Church of Greenwich*, viz. the Stonework on the South side and part of the East and West End is advanc'd about four feet above the

[185]

level of last year's Work, and the Masons have a good Quantity of Stone wrought to carry on the side next the Street. (And this I keep conceal'd: Dr Flamsteed, the Astronomer Royal and a man of snivelling covetous Temper, predicts a total Eclipse of the Sunne on the date 22 April 1715: at that dark Time, when the Birds flock to the Trees and the People carry Candles in their Houses, will I lay the last Stone secretly and make the Sacrifice due.) Further, I have been ordered by the Honble. Board to prepare and lay before the Commissioners a particular Estimate of the charge in building the *Church of Little St Hugh* in *Black Step Lane*. I have examined the Prices proposed and find them the same with the Churches of Limehouse and Wapping. The parts of Land shaded with a faint Brown are granted already, and the parcels of Land in private Hands are shaded Yellow. The vacant Ground in the Front is worth 3 pounds per annum and at 20 years purchase of 60 pounds; the Buildings backwards are let at 72 pounds per annum at six years purchase and worth 432 Pounds, *viz.* the Tobacconist, the Tallow Chandler, the Pewterers and the Weavers. These are washed with Blew. All of which is humbly submitted, *N. Dyer.*

And across these mean Dwellings of Black Step Lane, where as a Boy I dwell'd for a while, the Shaddowe of my last Church will fall: what the Mobb has torn down I will build again in Splendour. And thus will I compleet the Figure: Spittle-Fields, Wapping and Limehouse have made the Triangle; Bloomsbury and St Mary Woolnoth have next created the major Pentacle-starre; and, with Greenwich, all these will form the Sextuple abode of Baal-Berith or the Lord of the Covenant. Then, with the church of Little St Hugh, the Septilateral Figure will rise about Black Step Lane and, in this Pattern, every Straight line is enrich'd with a point at Infinity and every Plane with a line at Infinity. Let him that has Understanding count the Number: the seven Churches are built in conjunction with the seven Planets in the lower Orbs of Heaven, the seven Circles of the Heavens, the seven Starres in Ursa Minor and the seven Starres in the Pleiades. Little St Hugh was flung in the Pitte with the seven Marks upon his Hands, Feet, Sides and Breast which thus exhibit the seven Demons – Beydelus, Metucgayn, Adulec, Demeymes, Gadix, Uquizuz and Sol. I have built an everlasting Order, which I may run through laughing: no one can catch me now.

10

AND HAWKSMOOR laughed at this. 'You can see things in whatever order you want, Walter, and we'll still catch him. He's cunning, though.' Then he pointed at his own head. 'He's very cunning.'

'Time will tell, sir.'

'Time will not tell. Time never tells.' Once more he raised his arm involuntarily, as if in greeting. 'So let's start again. Where were the bodies found?'

'They were found at St Alfege's, Greenwich, and at St George's, Bloomsbury.'

Hawksmoor noticed that the sky had cleared quite suddenly, going from grey to blue like an eye which had suddenly opened. 'And what was the order again?'

'One after another, within a few hours.'

'The report said that it could have been minutes.'

'Minutes is impossible, sir.'

'No, we can't deal in minutes.' And yet what might happen in a minute, when his back was turned? He looked down at the pattern of dust on the carpet and, as he did so, he heard the noises within his head like the sounds of a crowd roaring in the distance. When he looked up, Walter was talking again.

'What I can – well I can't – I mean, we have nothing positive off the paperwork.' And they both looked at the documents scattered across Hawksmoor's desk. 'I can't believe,' Walter continued, 'I can't believe it.' And he picked up the forensic report on the two most recent murders. Both victims had been strangled with a ligature which had not been tied – there was no mark of a knot, at least – but had been held tight for at least fifteen to twenty seconds at an unusually high level in the neck. The ligature was evidently a folded hard cloth of some kind, set in four distinct lines across the front of the neck. The marks extended around the sides, especially the right, but faded at the back, showing that both victims had been strangled from behind on the left. In spite of the closest possible examination of the cuticle, the pathologist was unable to detect any weave or pattern that would reflect the actual structure of the ligature. Exhaustive forensic tests had also failed to identify any prints, marks or stains which might be connected with the perpetrator of these actions.

Two days before Hawksmoor had crossed the Thames in a police launch to Greenwich, and as he came up to the dock he leaned forward over the side and allowed his index finger to trail in the oily water. He walked from the harbour and, catching sight of a church tower, turned down a small alley which seemed to lead in that direction. Almost at once he found himself surrounded by small shops in which there was very little light: they were of an old design, leaning forward over the pavement, and in his confusion he hurried down another lane only to stop short when the stone wall of the church apparently blocked off the end; but this was an illusion since a child then walked across it, singing. And at last Hawksmoor emerged into the street, just in time to see the church rising above him. He calmed himself by reading the gold script painted upon a board by the portico: 'This church was built on the traditional site of the martyrdom of Alfege. It was rebuilt by . . .'. His eyes wandered down the elaborate scroll, but such things bored him and he was distracted by a flight of birds returning to the branches of a single tree, each bird distinct against the winter sky.

He walked around the side of the church where a group of police officers waited for him – from the way they stood, self-consciously talking in low voices, Hawksmoor knew that the body was behind them on the grass. He walked over and, in those first moments when he was staring down at it, he wondered how he would look to the strangers who encircled his own corpse; and would the breath have left his body like a mist, or like the air evacuated from a paper bag which a child blows up and then explodes? Then he returned to the others: 'What time was he found?'

'At six o'clock this morning, sir, when it was still dark.'

'Do we know –'

'He might have fallen from the tower, sir. But nobody knows.'

Hawksmoor looked up at the spire of St Alfege's and, when he blotted out the sun with his right hand, he noticed the white dome of the Observatory which was half concealed by the dark stone of the church. And he remembered that there was something here which he had heard of many years before, and which he had always wanted to see. Eventually he was able to break free from the others, muttering his excuses, and when he came to the foot of the hill he began to run, bounding over the short grass until he reached the summit. There was a guard by the iron gate in front of the Observatory and Hawksmoor stopped in front of him, out of breath. 'Where,' he said, 'where is the zero meridian?'

[188]

'The meridian?' The old man pointed to the other side of the summit. 'It's over there.'

But when Hawksmoor came to that place, he found nothing. 'Where is the meridian?' he asked again, and he was directed a little way down the hill. He looked around, and saw only dirt and stones. 'It's over there!' someone else called out. 'No, over there!' was the cry from another. And Hawksmoor was bewildered for, no matter how he turned and turned about, he could not see it.

Walter had put down the forensic report and was grinning at him. 'And so we're stuck,' he said. And then he added: 'As sure as eggs is eggs'.

Hawksmoor smoothed the pages of the report which had been creased by Walter. 'Where does that expression come from?'

'It doesn't come from anywhere, sir, not as far as I know. I mean, everyone says it.'

Hawksmoor paused for a moment, wondering what everyone said about him. 'What was it you were asking me just now?'

Walter no longer tried to conceal his impatience: 'I was asking basically, sir, well, where do we go from here?'

'We go on. Where else should we go? We can't turn back. No one can turn back.' He had heard the annoyance in Walter's voice, and now he tried to console him. 'He's at my fingertips – don't worry, I can reach him. I feel it.' And after Walter had left him, he drummed his fingers on the desk as he contemplated new aspects of this problem: at the same time as the body of the child had been found in the grounds of St Alfege's, another body had been discovered propped against the back wall of St George's, Bloomsbury, where it runs alongside Little Russell Street. Hawksmoor had visited that spot also, and to those officers already working there he had seemed almost indifferent; it was not indifference, however, but agony. The pattern, as Hawksmoor saw it, was growing larger; and, as it expanded, it seemed about to include him and his unsuccessful investigations.

It was dark now, and the light from the buildings beyond his window shone on his face as he gave a great yawn. He left the office quietly, made his way out of the yard, and as he walked through the clear night to St George's, Bloomsbury, the cold December air turned his breath into clouds of moisture which rose above his head. He paused at the corner of Russell Street and New Oxford Street as a vagrant, muttering 'Jesus fucking Christ! Jesus fucking Christ!', glared at him; and in alarm he walked quickly up to the church, opening the iron gate which led to the small courtyard beside it. He stood beneath the white tower, and looked up at it with that mournful expression which his face always carried in repose: for one moment he thought of climbing up its cracked and broken stone, and then from its summit screaming down at the silent city as a child might scream at a chained animal. But his sudden anger was destroyed by a noise quite close to him. He remained still; a wooden door to his right seemed to be moving in the wind and, as he peered at it, he saw the sign Crypt Entrance written above the portal. The wind continued to blow the door gently backward and forward: to prevent it from opening too suddenly upon him, he hurried towards it and held it closed with his palm. But the wood felt unnaturally warm, and he snatched his hand away. The door opened slightly once more, and Hawksmoor decided to move it towards him with the tips of his fingers, very softly and very slowly so that it was only gradually he heard a faint but sustained laughter coming from within.

When he had opened the door to a sufficient width he slid through its entrance, holding his breath as he did so although the odours of wood and old stone were already forming a metallic taste in the back of his throat. The passage of the crypt was warm, and in his anxious state he imagined a host of people pressing around him – not touching him but close enough to forbid him movement. He walked forward slowly, since his eyes were not yet accustomed to the darkness, but he paused when he thought he heard scuffling noises somewhere in front of him. He did not cry out, but he lowered himself to the ground and put his hands across his face. The faint sounds had diminished, and now he could hear a voice murmuring, 'Oh yes, oh yes, oh yes, oh yes'. Hawksmoor stood up at once and, poised for flight, he bent his body away from the direction of that voice and its whispered words. Then there was silence, and Hawksmoor knew that his presence had been sensed; he heard the sound of something being struck, and the light at the end of the passage made him jerk back his head in astonishment for in that instant he saw a young man, with his trousers draped around his ankles, holding onto a girl who was leaning against the stone wall. 'Fuck off!' the young man screamed, 'fuck off, you old sod!'

And Hawksmoor laughed in relief: 'I'm sorry,' he called out to the couple, as the match flickered out and they once more vanished into the darkness, 'I'm sorry!' When he got out of the passage, he leaned against the wall of the church, fighting for breath; once more he could hear the sound of laughter but, when he looked around, he saw only the rubbish of the city being blown against the church steps.

Slowly he walked back to Grape Street, his head bowed against the wind; when he reached the door, he looked up at Mrs West's window and saw two shadows thrown by the firelight upon the ceiling. So she has found a man at last, was his thought as he entered the passageway; it was dark here but at once he saw a small package, addressed to him, which seemed to have been tossed over the threshold. It was wrapped in coarse brown paper: he took it in both hands, held it out in front of him, and climbed the stairs to his own flat. Then, still in his overcoat, he sat down in his bare front room and tore open the parcel greedily: there was a small book within it, with a shiny white cover which was slightly sticky to the touch as if it had recently been coated in wax or resin. As soon as he opened it he saw the same drawing: the man was kneeling and holding something like a spy glass against his right eye. On other pages there were verses, sketches in the form of a cross and then on separate sheets certain phrases inscribed in brown ink – 'The Fortitude of the Stars', 'The Power In Images', 'The Seven Wounds'; towards the end Hawksmoor read, 'O Misery, They Shall Die' and in his horror he dropped the white book upon the floor, where it lay as the darkness of the night changed to the grey of the winter dawn. At which time he was thinking of the man who had drawn the kneeling figure beside St Mary Woolnoth; the tramp's shape was just above Hawksmoor's own as he stretched wide-eyed upon his bed, as if both of them were stone effigies of the dead lying above each other in an empty church.

*

'I'm still interested in that tramp,' he said as soon as Walter had entered the room.

'Which one was that, sir?'

'The tramp by the church. The one who made the drawing.' He turned away from Walter to hide his eagerness. 'Do you still have the letter?' And after a brief search among the files arranged neatly on Hawksmoor's desk, it was found. It seemed so flimsy, just a sheet torn from a memorandum pad with the words 'Don't Forget' printed at its top, and at that moment Hawksmoor made a simple connection: it was as if he had climbed higher and, seeing much further into the distance, had lost his fear. 'Where,' he asked, 'is the nearest doss-house to that church?'

'The nearest one to the City is in the Commercial Road, it's that old building –'

'The one between Limehouse and Wapping?'

As they drove across London to the Commercial Road, Hawksmoor felt quite calm and allowed his fingers lightly to touch the letter placed in the inside pocket of his jacket. But as soon as they arrived he left the car hurriedly and dashed up the steps of a grimy brick building: Walter looked at him running ahead, beneath the grey London sky, and pitied him. Following Hawksmoor, he opened the wooden doors of the hostel, saw the faded green paint of its interior and the linoleum floors stained with grease or dirt, smelt the mixture of disinfectant and stale food, heard the faint calls and sounds from within the building.

[191]

And by this time Hawksmoor was knocking on a glass partition, behind which sat an elderly man eating a sandwich: 'Excuse me,' he was saying, 'Excuse me' as the man slowly put down his food and, apparently with reluctance, slid back the glass partition and murmured 'Oh yes?'

'You work here, I take it?'

'What does it look like to you?'

Hawksmoor cleared his throat. 'I am a police officer.' He handed him the letter. 'Do you recognise this piece of paper?'

The man pretended to study it. 'Yes, I've seen this kind of paper. The staff use it. Don't ask me why.' He took out of a drawer a memorandum pad with the same words printed across it. 'What can you forget in a place like this?'

'And do you recognise the handwriting?' Walter noticed that Hawksmoor had become very still.

'Well, it's not mine.'

'I know it's not yours. But do you recognise it?'

'Not as far as I know.'

And Walter saw Hawksmoor nod, as if this was exactly what he had expected. 'Tell me this, then. Have you come across a tramp called the Architect, or anything like that?'

He blinked and put his finger in the air. 'We have the Preacher, the Flying Dutchman, the Pilgrim. But I don't know of any Architect. He'll be a new one on me.'

Hawksmoor stared at him. 'Do you mind if we have a look around?'

'Be my guest.' His eyes briefly met those of Hawksmoor. 'You'll find just two of them there. They're supposed to be sick.'

Walter followed Hawksmoor down a corridor and into a large room which contained some formica tables and metal chairs: a large television set, placed upon a high shelf, had been turned on and the sounds of a children's programme chimed as emptily as an ice-cream van in a deserted street. Hawksmoor glanced up at it before walking through into another room where a number of mattresses, wrapped in plastic, had been arranged in two rows. On one of them a tramp lay upon his stomach, while a second man was crouched in a corner smoking. 'Hello,' Walter called out, 'And what do they call you, then?' Neither of the men looked up. 'We are police officers. Do you know what I mean?' And then, in the silence, Walter added loudly: 'They're not very friendly, sir, are they?'

The tramp in the corner turned his head: 'I know what you mean. I know full well what you mean.'

Hawksmoor stepped up to him, without coming too close: 'Oh do you? And I suppose you know someone called the Architect?'

There was a pause. 'I don't know anyone by that name. No one at all by that name.' He wrapped his arms about his body as he crouched there: 'You don't enquire about people. You don't ask questions'. It was not clear whether he was addressing these remarks to himself, or to Hawksmoor who was now surveying the dilapidated room.

'The Architect!' The tramp on the bed had propped himself on one elbow and was calling out to them. 'The Architect! God bless us all and every one!'

Hawksmoor moved up to the end of the bed, and stood with his hands clasped as if in prayer. 'Do you know him?'

'Do I know him? Do I know him? Yes, I know him.'

'And do you know his name? I mean, his real name.'

'His name is Legion.' When the tramp laughed it was obvious to Hawksmoor that he was lying on the bed because he was drunk, perhaps still drunk from the night before.

'And where can I find him?'

'Do you have a little cigarette on you, officer?'

'I don't have one now, but I will give you some later. Where did you say I could find him?'

'I don't find him. He finds me. Now you see him and now you don't.'

Everyone remained silent and, as Hawksmoor sat down on the side of this bed, he heard the noise of a plane travelling somewhere overhead. 'And when did you see him last?'

'I saw him in Hell. He was roasting nicely.'

'No, you weren't in Hell were you? Tell me again.'

Then the man's mood changed as he curled up on the bed and faced the wall. 'I was with him,' he said and the whole sad weight of the drink seemed to hit him so that he could barely speak.

Hawksmoor gently touched his filthy overcoat. 'You were with him, were you? You look like a man who could deal a powerful blow.'

'Hop it. Fuck it. I'm saying no more.'

Walter came up to stand beside him as Hawksmoor whispered, 'Now don't be frightened. I'm not going to frighten anybody.' There was a sound of weeping in the corridor.

'I'm not frightened. I've done nothing.' Then he pretended to sleep, or perhaps did sleep; Hawksmoor pointed to the tramp's arm which lay stretched out, and Walter gave it a jerk so that the man rolled off his bed.

'You're wanted,' Hawksmoor told him, loudly now, as Walter dragged him to his feet. 'I'm not arresting you. I'm asking you nicely to come with me.' The tramp stared at him. 'There will be something in it for you, you'll see. We're just taking you for a little ride.'

They dragged him outside, passing the receptionist who kept on chewing his sandwich as he watched them, and as they came out into the air the tramp stared across at the church of St Anne's, Limehouse, and then looked up at its tower which loomed over the three of them in the dark street. Then he closed his eyes, as if he was about to faint. 'Help him, Walter,' Hawksmoor murmured as they bundled him into the back of their car. But the tramp neither knew nor cared what was happening to him, since there would be other times when he would have no memory of this. And now he was in a small white room, with the same man facing him across a table, while behind a two-way mirror Walter took notes and watched this scene:

HAWKSMOOR. How are you feeling now?

TRAMP. Feeling? Oh not so bad. Not so bad, you know. Do you happen to have a fag on you?

HAWKSMOOR. Not so bad? That is good news. (*He takes off his glasses*) Can I talk to you then?

TRAMP. Yes. Yes, I hope to talk to you soon. Do you have a fag on you? By any chance?

Pause. Hawksmoor lights a cigarette and hands it to him.

HAWKSMOOR. I am having a nice time. Are you? (*Silence*) You were telling me about the Architect? Am I right in thinking that?

TRAMP. (*Genuinely puzzled*) Yes, that is possibly true. I think I was. Yes.

HAWKSMOOR. Yes?

TRAMP. (*Nervously*) Yes, I said that. Yes.

HAWKSMOOR. And so you know him? Am I right to say that you know him?

TRAMP. I think I do. You can say that. I think I do.

HAWKSMOOR. Can you give me his name at all?

TRAMP. Oh, I wouldn't know about that. Not his name.

HAWKSMOOR. But you saw him?

Silence.

TRAMP. When?

HAWKSMOOR. I'm asking you the very same question. When did you see him?

TRAMP. I saw him that night.

HAWKSMOOR. (*Eagerly*) What night?

TRAMP. That night.

Silence.

HAWKSMOOR. Well, what time was it?

TRAMP. Oh good God, now you're asking me something.

HAWKSMOOR. (*Softly*) Was it very dark?

TRAMP. Pitch black.

HAWKSMOOR. I'm not going to hurt you. I would like you to remember.

TRAMP. Next thing there was police and so forth. I won't say I was genuinely sober. Next thing the police was in.

HAWKSMOOR. In where?

TRAMP. I've seen you before, haven't I?

HAWKSMOOR. In where?

TRAMP. In that church.

HAWKSMOOR. This is a coincidence, isn't it?

TRAMP. I remember nothing more than that. I'm not joking you. Nothing more than that. (*He is silent for a moment*) What time are you letting me out? (*Pause*) I've had enough of this. (*Silence*) I'm that tired.

HAWKSMOOR. (*Suddenly*) What does he look like?

TRAMP. Oh I don't know. (*Pause*) All that hair. It's wicked, isn't it? Hair like tobacco. And then he draws. Draws the life out of you. I never saw such drawings. (*Silence*) Can I go out now? (*Silence*) Well then I'll go.

   He gets up to leave, looks at Hawksmoor, and then walks out of the door as Walter comes in.

HAWKSMOOR. (*Excitedly*) It was the same man. Doesn't it seem to you to be the same man?

He read the brief jottings which Walter had made in his notebook during the interview and a small fly, attracted by its brightness under the neon, settled on the left-hand page. Hawksmoor noticed its legs waving like filaments bending in a sudden heat, and the shape of its wings cast a shadow upon the whiteness of the paper. Then as he turned the page he killed the insect, and its body smeared across the ink became an emblem of this moment when Hawksmoor had a vision of the tramp dancing around a fire, with the smoke clinging to his clothing and then wrapping him in mist.

'It is the same man,' he said again, 'It must be him.'

Walter anticipated his thoughts now: 'And we must be seen to be taking some action. At last'.

And so they walked to the Incident Room from where a carefully worded press statement was released, suggesting that the police were anxious to interview a certain vagrant in connection with the murders and giving a description of the man in question. And Hawksmoor called out to the various members of the investigating teams, 'I want the hostels checked, and the parks, and the derelict houses. Even the churches . . .' A young uniformed officer, who had a large birth mark splayed across his cheek, came up to him: 'One of the problems, sir, is obviously going to be the fact that there may be a few like him, a few who look like him'. Hawksmoor avoided looking at the scarlet brand: 'I know that, but that's the way it is . . .' And once again his voice trailed off for he knew that, just as he would recognise the murderer, so also would the murderer recognise him.

It was dusk now as he walked down Brick Lane to Christ Church, Spitalfields, passing Monmouth Street and turning down Eagle Street where the east wall of the old church rose among the ruined houses. As he walked forward the street lamps flickered alight, and the shape of the church itself altered in their sudden illumination. Hawksmoor reached the gate through which he could see the abandoned tunnel, now boarded up, and in the neon's reflected light the grass and trees beside the church seemed to glow. He opened the gate, and as he walked down the path he was momentarily startled by a white moth which flew around his shoulders: he lengthened his stride to escape it but it stayed with him until he had turned the corner of the church and saw the main road and the market in front of him. In the gathering darkness he moved towards the small pyramid, placed his hands upon it as if to warm them, but in that instant he felt a wave of disorder – and, with it, the sensation that someone was staring fixedly at him. He turned around quickly but in the sudden movement his glasses fell to the ground; he stepped forward, without thinking, and broke them. 'Now,' he said out loud, 'Now I won't be able to see him.' And, curiously enough, his feeling was one of relief.

Joyfully he turned down Commercial Road towards Whitechapel; there was a fight in a side alley, and one man was kicking another who had already fallen; a blind woman was standing by the side of the road, waiting to be helped across; a young girl was murmuring the words of a popular song. And then he saw on the other side of the street, going in the opposite direction and towards the church, a tall but indistinct figure who seemed to be drawn to the protection of the shop-fronts and the dark walls of brick. The man's clothes were torn and old; his hair was matted into a slab, like tobacco. Hawksmoor crossed the road rapidly and walked a few yards behind the tramp, but in his nervousness he coughed: the tall figure turned and seemed to smile before quickening his pace. Hawksmoor cried out in alarm, 'Wait! Wait for me!' and then ran in pursuit. Both of them were in sight of the church and the still indistinct figure ran across the grass by its side; Hawksmoor followed but as he ran past the pyramid he collided with a small boy who had been standing in its shadow. And as the boy looked up at him Hawksmoor noticed how pale his face seemed. In that instant of inattention the tall figure had run around the corner of the church and, by the time Hawksmoor had turned it, had already disappeared. He ran back to ask the child if he had seen anything of the fleeing man, but the small park was now empty: the grass and trees had ceased to glow and, in the darkness, they seemed to be crumbling back into the earth. If he did not act now the atmosphere of the church-yard would overpower him and he would be lost: he started walking in the direction of Limehouse for, if there was one place a vagrant might think to hide from a pursuer, it was in the abandoned sites and derelict houses near St Anne's.

He hailed a taxi and took it as far as the Limehouse church; as he stepped out the cold wind caught him in the face and for a moment he sought shelter behind an advertisement hoarding on which could be seen a number of computers floating above the city. Eventually he went towards St Anne's, but then veered to the right and crossed a patch of waste land beside it: the wind blew even more strongly here, since it came directly from the river, and it brought to him the scattered shouts and calls of the meths-drinkers who were a few hundred yards away from him. As he walked forward he noticed the sparks rising above a fire, and when he came closer he could see the dark shapes which were apparently dancing around it. They are happy, he thought, for they do not remember; and then he began running towards them. 'You!' he cried, 'You! What are you doing and what do you want here?' But they did not stop their dancing when he came up to them: it seemed that he was being grabbed, as if to enter the ring, but with a shout he pulled himself free. Then they became still and gazed at him when he questioned them. 'Have any of you seen the one called the Architect? He's one of you. Have you seen him?' They were all old ones, dishevelled and weary now that the spell of the dance had passed. They said nothing but stared into the flames and one of them began to moan. Hawksmoor noticed that the head of a toy bear had been thrust onto a pole, and was lying upon the charred ground. He shouted at them impatiently: 'I am a police officer! Put out that fire now!' None of them moved and so Hawksmoor himself walked into the fire and stamped upon it ferociously until there were only ashes and burned sticks remaining. 'Where is he?' he shouted at them again as they began to retreat from him, 'Do any of you know where he is?' But still they made no noise and Hawksmoor, disgusted at himself for behaving in a manner which he had not foreseen, turned away. As he walked back he called out into the air, 'I don't want to see any more fire, do you understand me? No more fire!'

He found the road which leads down to the river and, wrapping his dark coat closely around himself so that he might withstand the wind, he passed an old tramp who was squatting by the roadside and with his fingers digging into the damp earth. Hawksmoor looked at him closely, but he was not the man he sought. The tramp stared back at him as he passed, and continued staring as he walked into the distance: Hawksmoor heard him shouting out something but the sounds of the river were closer to him and he could not distinguish the words. The muddy water raced beneath his feet and the lights of the city had changed the sky to a transient purple, but he was thinking only of the figure fleeing before him in Spitalfields and of the pale face of the boy as it had looked up at him in the shadow of the church.

And he could not escape these images, as the time passed and the disorder spread. The circulation of the suspect's description, followed inevitably by rumour and speculation in the newspapers, had not materially assisted the investigation of the six murders; it had, in fact, only inflamed the passions of those for whom the description of the tramp seemed to act as an emblem of all that was most depraved and evil. On the first day of the 'photo-fit' being released, there were scores of sightings of the man from all over the country, and the number of such sightings did not greatly diminish until public attention had been diverted elsewhere. More unfortunately, however, a number of tramps were abused or assaulted by gangs who used the excuse of 'the child murderer' to express their resentment at harmless wandering men. One group of small children actually killed one such vagrant: he was sleeping drunkenly on a patch of waste ground, and they set him alight. After these events it became accepted that Hawksmoor had committed an 'error of judgment' in releasing such sketchy details of the suspect – and Hawksmoor's position was made all the more precarious by the fact that, after exhaustive searches and inquiries, no trace of the man had been discovered. It seemed that he had just disappeared – that is, as some of the officers involved in the case used to say to each other, if he ever existed in the first place.

But Hawksmoor knew that he existed and, although he had never mentioned to anyone the night of his pursuit, he knew that the murderer was closer to him than ever. There were even occasions when he believed that he was being followed and, as he lay awake one night, he conceived the fantasy that he too should dress as a tramp in order to surprise him – but even as the idea occurred to him he rejected it, trembling. He took long walks in the evening in order to avoid such thoughts, but he found that he was treading the same paths as before. There was a time, for example, when he walked into the park behind St George's-in-the-East and sat upon a bench close to the abandoned museum – it had been upon this bench that he had spoken to the father of the murdered child, and glimpsed the illustrations in the book which the weeping man had held in front of him. And as he stared at the trees beside the church he contemplated the calm of a life which itself resembled a park with no people in it – then he might sit and stare at these trees until he died. But his momentary serenity unnerved him, for it seemed to imply that his life was already over.

Each night he came home from his wanderings and held the white notebook in his hands, first bringing it close to his nose in order to savour the slight odour of wax which still lingered upon its stiff covers. He read again each phrase, and then stared intently at the drawings as if they might yield some clue. But they offered nothing and one night, in his anger, he tore the pages from the book and threw them across the floor. When he arose in panic the next morning, he looked down at the scattered sheets and said out loud, 'What rage is this? What fury? Of what kind?' Then he took the pages, smoothed them with the palm of his hand, and fixed them with pins to the walls. So that now, if he sat looking down upon Grape Street, the letters and images encircled him. And it was while he sat here, scarcely moving, that he was in hell and no one knew it. At such times the future became so clear that it was as if he were remembering it, remembering it in place of the past which he could no longer describe. But there was in any case no future and no past, only the unspeakable misery of his own self.

And so when he sat with Walter in the Red Gates he could scarcely talk, but looked down at his glass as Walter anxiously watched his face. Yet he drank in order to speak freely, for it seemed to him that he had lost his connection to the world and had become much like one of the cardboard figures in a puppet theatre, shaking a little as the hand which held him trembles. But if he could speak, and the voice came not from someone crouched below but from himself . . . 'Do you know,' he murmured and Walter craned forward to hear him. 'Do you know that when murderers kill themselves, they try and make it look like another murder? But do you know how many of them are struck by lightning? A lot. More than you think.' He glanced around furtively. 'You know what we were told years ago, it must be years ago now, that you could see the image of the murderer imprinted on the victim's eyes? If only I could get that close, you see. And I'll tell you something else. There are some people so frightened of being murdered that they die of their own fear. What about that?' Walter felt his legs trembling with the suppressed desire to run, and he got up quickly to order more drinks. When he returned Hawksmoor stared at him. 'I know it, Walter, I can feel it. Do you know, I can go into a house and feel if a murder has taken place there? I can feel it.' And he let out a loud laugh, which for a moment silenced the other conversations in the pub.

A broken glass was being swept from the floor and, as Hawksmoor noticed how each of the shattered pieces shone quite differently in the light, Walter seized his opportunity to speak. 'Do you think we need a break from this case, sir? A real break?'

Hawksmoor was visibly alarmed: 'Who told you to say that?'

[199]

Walter tried to calm him. 'No one told me, but it's been eight months now. You deserve a rest from it.'

'That's a strange word, deserve, isn't it? Do you know what it means?'

'It means to need something, doesn't it?'

'No, it means to be worthy of something. And so I'm worthy of rest.'

Walter noticed how his hand trembled, and Hawksmoor gripped his glass more tightly. 'I don't know what to say to that, sir.' He gazed at Hawksmoor, not without friendliness. 'You'll start to dream about it soon,' he put it to him gently.

'What makes you think I don't dream about it now?' He had spoken too loudly, and once again there was a sudden silence in the room.

Hawksmoor looked down, abashed, and this was the occasion for which Walter had waited. 'It just seems to me, sir, that we're not getting anywhere.'

'Is that how it seems to you?'

'That's how it seems to everyone, sir.' Hawksmoor looked up at him sharply, and in that moment the relationship between the two men was subtly but permanently changed. 'We don't have the facts,' Walter was saying, 'and that's our problem.'

'You know about facts, do you, all these facts we don't have?' Hawksmoor was very grim. 'In your experience, Walter, do any two people see the same thing?'

'No, but –'

'And so it's your job to interpret what they have seen, to interpret the facts. Am I right?'

The conversation puzzled Walter, and he decided to retire from it. 'Yes, sir.'

'And so the facts don't mean much until you have interpreted them?'

'That's right.'

'And where does that interpretation come from? It comes from you and me. And who are we?' Hawksmoor raised his voice. 'Don't you think I worry when everything falls apart in my hands – but it's not the facts I worry about. It's me.' When he stopped, he passed his hands trembling across his face. 'Is it hot in here or is it just me?' He took out a handkerchief to wipe the sweat from his forehead and then, as Walter still said nothing, he added, 'I'm going to find him.'

And then, later, he heard himself saying, 'I told you about that notebook, didn't I?' But he managed to stop himself and, muttering an excuse, went once more to the bar where three women turned and laughed when he began speaking to them. Walter watched the sweating, shambling figure as he winked and said, 'I'll show you something you won't forget. Do you want to see something?' And

[200]

they laughed again: 'What is it?' one of them asked 'Something you've got for us? Something small, I should think'. And they cackled. But they stopped when he took some pictures out of his jacket pocket and held them up to the light in triumph. 'Get them out of here!' the same woman cried in disgust, 'We don't want any of that filth!' Then Hawksmoor himself looked at what he held in his hands, and bowed down as if in prayer when Walter came up to him and saw that he was holding photographs of the murder victims. 'Put them away now, sir,' he murmured, 'I'll take you back.' Hawksmoor stuffed the photographs into his pocket, yawning, and Walter led him home.

*

The ringing of the telephone startled Hawksmoor as he sat at his desk: it was the Assistant Commissioner who wished to see him at once but, as soon as he rose from his chair, he became quite calm. He remained calm as he ascended in the lift to the thirteenth floor and, when he entered a large office, the Assistant Commissioner was staring out of the window at the grey rain: this will be the shape of your damnation, Hawksmoor thought, to look out perpetually and mournfully. But the figure turned round swiftly. 'Forgive me, Nick.'

'Forgive you? Forgive you for what?' There was turmoil in Hawksmoor's face.

'Forgive me for summoning you like this.' Then he sat down, and cleared his throat. 'How's the case going, Nick? How close are you to finding him?' The telephone rang but he ignored it and waited for Hawksmoor to speak. Then he added, in the gathering silence, 'I'm not sure we're getting anywhere, Nick.'

'I'm sure we are. In time, sir.' Hawksmoor stood with his arms straight down by his sides, almost at attention.

'But we're not becoming any wiser. We've got nothing extra have we?' Hawksmoor averted his eyes from the man's gaze and stared out of the window behind him. 'I've got something else for you, Detective Superintendent, not quite in your usual line but –'

'You mean you're taking me off the case?'

'I'm not so much taking you off this case as putting you on another one.'

Hawksmoor took a step backward. 'You're taking me off the case.'

'You've got things out of perspective, Nick. You laid the foundations, and you did a good job, but now I need someone to build the case up stone by stone.'

'But the bodies are buried in the foundations,' Hawksmoor replied, 'generally speaking, that is.'

The Assistant Commissioner lowered his voice slightly: 'There's been some talk about you recently. They say you've been under a lot of strain.'

'And who is *they*?' Whenever he heard that word, he imagined a group of shadows moving from place to place.

'Why don't you take some time off? Before you begin the new case. Why don't you have a good rest?' And he rose, making a point of looking directly at Hawksmoor, who looked back helplessly.

When he returned to his own office Walter was waiting for him: 'How did it go?'

'So you knew.'

'Everyone knew, sir. It was only a matter of time.' And Hawksmoor heard a vast sea roaring around him: he saw quite distinctly a small creature waving its arms in panic as the water swirled around him like storm clouds. 'I tried to help –' Walter began nervously to say.

'I don't want to hear it.'

'But you wouldn't let me. Things had to change, sir.'

'Everything has changed, Walter.' He took the files from his desk. 'And I hand everything on to you. It's all yours now.' Walter stood up as Hawksmoor gave him the files; they were both on opposite sides of the desk, and their fingertips met accidentally as they leaned towards each other.

'Sorry,' said Walter drawing back quickly and apologising for his touch.

'No, it wasn't your fault. It had to happen.'

Hawksmoor sat very still after Walter had left the room, and during the course of the afternoon he tried to look at himself as if he were a stranger, so that he might be able to predict his next step. Time passes, and he looks down at his own hands and wonders if he would recognise them if they lay severed upon a table. Time passes, and he listens to the sound of his own breathing, in its rise and its fall. Time passes, and he takes a coin from his pocket to observe how it has been worn down in its passage from hand to hand. When he closes his eyes at last, he finds himself slipping forwards and wakes at the moment of his fall. But still he goes on falling; and the afternoon changes to evening, and the shadows around Hawksmoor change.

He left the office at last, and went back to Grape Street. He sat in his room and turned on the television: there was a man playing patience in a darkened alcove, and Hawksmoor leaned forward eagerly to scan that darkness, looking beyond the actor and examining the chair, the velvet curtain, the vase of dusty flowers. Then, with the television still on, he walked into the next room, lay down upon his bed, and did not wake up when the morning light lay in a band across his face.

11

THE RAYES of the Morning did not rouse me, and when I woke I scarce knew in what House or Place or Year I found my self. And tho' I resolved to walk out my Wretchednesse I only reached the Corner when I returned exceeding weary: there was a light Rain, also, which frighted me for if a Cold grows inveterate you may reckon it the beginning of a mortal Distemper. So thus uneasy I returned to my Closet, where I fell to thinking on the shape of my new Church which even then rose above the Mire and Stink of this City.

I went to bed at Eight of the Clock but between One and Two, after I had slept but four hours, I came to Vomiting: whether from my Distemper, or from the pannick Fright which comes to me in the Night, I am not certain. I drank a Spoonful or two of Cherry Brandy, which put me to Sleep until Nat Eliot woke me at Seven. But then I fell to Vomiting againe and, as all the while my Urine was as red as Blood, I lay sighing upon my Bed and saying: What will become of me? What will become of me?

Then with much Trembling I writ in my own Hand to the Reptile Knight: Sir John, pray do me the Favour to tell the Board that I did intend to be up at the Yard today, to speak of those matters concerning the Church of Little St Hugh in Black Step Lane, but that being pritty sick I would wish to stay a Day or two longer to hasten my Recovery. Your most humble Servant to command etcetera. I called for Nat to run with the Letter to Whitehall, and he enters all of a hot Sweat: Another man came, *says he*, but I denied him to you. I let no one visit you as you ordered me, and when he says *Is your Master withinne?* I replied Yes, he is in but he is just sat down to Breakfast and can on no account be roused at this time; and then sometimes I tell them you are Sick, so I vary my Tricks with the Wind. I am a true Barricadoe to all who come!

He was scratching all over like a Wherry-man as he spoke: What Company do you keep in your Clothes, sir, *I cried*, that they must needs Bite you?

They are my Friends, *he replied*, since they never leave me.

Then why so melancholy at it? Your Face is as long as my Pencil and not so useful.

They are my only Friends. Then he stops short, growing uneasy at his own Words, and lookd down upon the Floor. And that, I said to my self, is the manner in which I will allways remember you, my boy Nat: looking down in Perplexity after a sudden Pause. But he ceases stirring his Foot in the Dust and asks: What is a hyena, Master?

It is an Animal which laughs and imitates Humane voices.

Good, good, *he said* as he rushed out of the Door with my Letter.

I know well enough why it is that they come to Visit me: they wish to see me in my Sicknesse so that they can triumph over me. Even still they suspect me and in the Office they murmur against me for the late death of Walter; their Suspicions are encreased by my Solitarinesse, yet why should I suffer them to speak to me when I become confused and Tonguetied in their Company? But to leave the Passions and to go on with the Facts: Walter hanged himself on the Door of his Bed Chamber; it was on a Sunday, the week following my Visit to him, between Nine and Ten in the Morning and he was not discovered by the sluttish Mistress of the House until the evening. He had only his Shirt and there he hung until between Seven and Eight at Night when the Coroner, being brought to see him, pronounced that he was not Compos Mentis. I was pritty composed: I told the impannelled Jury that in his Ravings he had confessed to the Murther of Mr Hayes, but that I did not beleev him until this Self-murther. Thus once again did I kill two Birds; I was a good Joyner and worked in Wood and then I became a good Plaisterer and worked with Stucco: the death of Yorick Hayes has been laid to Walter, so putting me out of the Road of eager Inquirers, and Walter has despatch'd himself, so saving me the Labour. I would willingly have transmitted to him in succession all the Secrets of my Art but he watched me, pursewed me, threatened me, betrayed me. And if he is quite undone now, why should I feel Guiltinesse: if a Dog should by chance Bark at me, should I not tread upon its Taile?

At about Eleven at Night, Walter was buried stark Naked in the open Ground: I would have preferred him to be beneeth Little St Hugh, but it is no great Matter. There is a Mist in Humane affairs, a small thin Rain which cannot be perceeved in single Drops of this Man or that Man but which rises around them and obscures them one from another, yet it takes Form in the Fabrick of my new built Church. When I look up from my Bed as if to gaze at my Ceeling, I see its Tower and feel the Wind blowing about my Face; when I touche the Hand or Arm of another, as it may be Nat, I feel its Stone rough upon the Stroak; when I am Hot, in my Mind I enter its Aisles and I am cool againe. I am sensible of the Malice which this Work has drawn upon me, but why should I murmur or repine at these Injuries: let it be Interest, Folly or Malice they act by, they are their own Enemies and not mine for, like Basilisks desirous to infect a Looking-glass, they kill themselves by Repercussion of Vapours. I have compleeted my Business, and I bid the World go whistle as I see before me the unbroken Stone and the pattern of Stone.

I have finished six Designes of my last Church, fastned with Pinns on the Walls of my Closet so that the Images surround me and I am once more at Peece. In the first I have the Detail of the Ground Plot, which is much like a Prologue in a Story; in the second there is all the Plan in a small form, like the disposition of Figures in a Narrative; the third Draught shews the Elevation, which is like the Symbol or Theme of a Narrative, and the fourth displays the Upright of the Front, which is like to the main part of the Story; in the fifth there are designed the many and irregular Doors, Stairways and Passages like so many ambiguous Expressions, Tropes, Dialogues and Metaphoricall speeches; in the sixth there is the Upright of the Portico and the Tower which will strike the Mind with Magnificence, as in the Conclusion of a Book.

There is also a Narrative which is hidden so that none may see it, and in a retired Place have I put the effigy of Friar Bacon who made the brazen Head that spake *Time is*. Nor shall I leave this Place once it is completed: Hermes Trismegistus built a Temple to the Sunne, and he knew how to conceal himself so that none could see him tho' he was still withinne it. This shall now suffice for a present Account, for my own History is a Patern which others may follow in the far Side of Time. And I hugg my Arms around my self and laugh, for as if in a Vision I see some one from the dark Mazes of an unknown Futurity who enters Black Step Lane and discovers what is hidden in Silence and Secresy. I will break off now –

*

And now I break. In the space of these last seven Nights I have had wild frightfull Dreames, and there is a new Smell in my Nose like that of burnt Raggs. I know that some Alteration has come upon me, for I seem to hear Spirits who speak with a Low-sunk Voyce as many Persons have in Colds. Yet they are without any Hoarseness, being very clearly discernable, and they say, *What Wind blew you hither Nick, Nick? Do you know us Nick, Nick?* and when I cry O God Yes they go on, *When are we Nick, Nick?* and the Question becomes a Roaring in my Ears.

I do not fear Death for the Pain of it, being perswaded that I have endur'd as great Pains in this Life as I should find in Death; and yet it may also be that I cannot die. You may scorn this, but there have been

[205]

Wonders just as great: I took my first Walk, about Eleven yesterday morning, and there by Hogg Lane I met with my own Apparition – with Habit, Wigg, and everything as in a Looking-glass. Do I know you? I call'd out, much to the Bewilderment of those who passed by, but the Thing did not answer me and walked quickly away. I was much surprized but I was not affrighted. Then on this very Morning in my own Chamber I saw an Image again before me – a species of such a Body as my own, but in a strange Habit cut like an Under-garment and the Creature had no Wigg. The Back of it was always towards me and as I turned my Head it turned away equally so that I could not see its Face: my Night-gown was dark with Sweat, as if a Shaddowe had passed over it, and I must have cried out some thing for Nat was calling Master! Master! Open the Door and let me in!

Have a little Patience and I will let you in immediately, *I replied* and, keeping my Eyes fixed on the Image which did not move, I went across to the Door.

You will have Mrs Best afflicted if you call so loud, *says Nat* hurrying into the Room.

I nodded towards the Image: I have this morning, Nat, vomited up an abortive Child.

Oh well, *says he* not knowing what it signified, shall I bring you water to wash your Mouth? Mrs Best says –

For God's sake hold your Tongue, can you not see I have some thing with me? And I pointed at the Image, which still sat with its Back to me but which now bent forward and a Sigh rose like Smoak out of its Mouth, like Smoak out of a Lamp. I know not, Nat, *I said*, but it seems to be Real.

And Nat heard or saw something for thereupon he began to look Red and was seiz'd with violent Tremblings: Good God, *he cried out*, let me see nothing! And then the cold Sweat ran from his Face as he stumbled towards the Stairway. But I murmured my own Words as the Image began to fade: *I am ready now for my approaching Change.*

*

I am cut down out of Time and I turn and turn about upon my Bed: what says Mr Andrewes his Almanack for this month, Nat? And he reads to me from *News of the Starres*: in this month Mars is in Scorpio, Master, and if he is not bitten he will continue direct in Motion until the sixth Day. From thence he becomes retrograde, which means backwards –

Leave off your Commentaries, Nat!

– all the month after and is in square to Venus the second Day. Nat blushes at the mention of Venus and then goes on: at present, Master, the Starres do not favour Building and London labours under weighty

Pressures and Difficulties not yet accommodated. I must take this to Mrs Best who has the Lumbago and is still troubled about the Loins –

– Nat, Nat see if there are Prognostications of Plotting and other scurvey Designes.

He pores upon the Pages and then comes to a Stop: Yes, here in the *Starry Messenger* it is said that there are some Spirits at work and Danger at Home. Then he bends his Head again: and, look, here in Poor Robin's *Vox Stellarum* there is a Rhyme full of Meaning. Up he gets with a grave Look and begins to recite, holding the Page before him:

> I saw a church Tower twelve yards deep
> I saw Dust made of Men's teares that weep
> I saw a Stone all in a Flame of Fire
> I saw a Stairway big as the Moon and higher
> I saw the Sunne red even at midnight,
> I saw the Man who saw this dreadful Sight.

What is the answer, Master? I cannot fathom it.

There is no Answer, Nat, for there is no End to this Rhyme.

And then I slept, and now in my long Sicknesse I am lifted above the poor Globe of this time-broken World: the rebels have come as far as Lancaster, a Fire last night in Tower Hill, a Dog howling by Moon-night and now I no longer have Fitts when I drink my Brandy, Hannover's troops are assembling at Warrington, the Clowds beneeth me, the Rebels are cut to peeces at Preston, and I cannot hinder the Cold from passing through all the Cloaths I put on my Bed and my Lord Warrington is killed in this Action as my Hand touches the Sheets and their Voices eccho as I try to hide myself withinne the Rocks in an area foresaken of Men and Nat calls as my Fever mounts and then breaks and as I sweat the Snow falls and the Rebels are come into London as Prisoners and I open my Eyes and now there is Frost Fayre upon the Thames.

And on this Day my Feaver abated: I rose from my Bed calling Nat, Nat where are you? but he had gone I knew not wither, and I was alone. I had been woken by the firm Resolution to visit my new completed Church, so I dressed with all Haste and yet with Care: the cold Winde had left Ice upon the Windows, and I wrapt my self up in my dubble-buttoned Coat tho' it was spotted with Tallow. As I came out into the Street a Chair-man gave a Blow to my Knees with his Pole which sent me cursing back into the Doorway and, Lord, the Coaches and Carts so shook the Ground that it was as like a natural Tremour or Convulsion of the Earth: and how many Dayes and Nights, *thought I*, have I laid in my fiery Feaver? What Time is this? There were some

Prentices rolling along a Foot-ball in the Street beside me but when I called out to them What a Clock is this? they made no Answer, as if I were a man invisible and not to be heard. And yet some Labourers seemed to be returning home with Planks and Ladders, which suggested to me that I had risen at the close of Day, but I knew not. I walked by Leicester Feelds and heard the Mountebank calling *What do you have? What do you have?* I have that, thought I, which your Drops will not cure. *Make way there*, says some Fellow pushing a Wheelbarrow, *will you have your Guts squeezed out?* and I stepped back into a Crowd of common Women with their ragged Handkerchiefs, blew Aprons, and their Faces, like mine own, descended from some unknown Original. I walked down Cranborn Street, where the Cooks stood dripping at their Doors, and then into Porters Street, where the Nuts and Oysters were piled high in Shops that ran upon Wheels. All this shall pass, and all these Things shall fall and crumple into the Dust, but my Churches shall survive. From there I walked into Hogg Lane, where a Rag-seller laid hold of my Arm and asked me, *What do you lack, sir?* I? I lack the World, for I move like a Ghost through it.

The Noises of the City so confused me, and left me so Weak, that I could barely stand but coach'd it quite up into Fenchurch Street where a Cart, overturn'd upon the Road, forced me to alight. Once more I could hear the Cryes around me: *Buy my dish of great Eeles*, one call'd and to its Echoe another took up the Plaint of *Any Kitchin stuff need you, my Maides?* and I murmur'd these to my self as I trod upon the Stones. As I came up into Lime Street the Skie grew dark with the Cold and yet here was an old Woman with a Child on her Back singing *Fine writing Inke! Fine writing Inke!* and I too might have been a Child againe, so familiarly did it sound. Then there rose that Cry which I have heard all my Life, *Have you something to Mend, have you something to Mend?* and I passed thro' Leadenhall Street weeping, for I knew I would never more hear it. I walked down St Mary Axe to London Wall, and my Teares fell upon the Mosse as I bent to touch it; then thro' Bishopsgate and down old Bedlam into Moorfields, and here it seemed to me that I heard the Rejoycing of the Mad who have no thought of Time as I do; then thro' Long Alley where I passed the great Musick Shop where the Crowd at the Door were dancing to the latest Tune, and one little Red-faced Blade beat Time upon the Counter as I went on.

And then I turned into that part called the Great Feeld. Some children in Blew jackets and Kite-Lanthorned Caps ran past me: *You will be dead before I return* was my Thought as I stared into the Entry of Black Step Lane. With an even Pace I walked forward and at last my Church was rising above me: like the Noise of Thunder it struck even my own Spirit with an air of Greatnesse beyond any thing I had seen before. A man in fur Cap and grey Stockings passed me and looked back in Astonishment, so rapt was I in the sight of the vast Stone; and all the Cryes died away as I mounted the Steps and approached the Porch of Little St Hugh. The Church was above me now and, tho' I was plunged into Shaddowe, I did not move but waited until my Eyes had cleared a little. Then I opened the Door and crossed the Threshold. I walked forward saying, *From my first Years Thy Horrours have I endured with a troubled Mind*, and I stood in the Aisle looking upwards till I could look on more: I had run to the end of my Time and I was at Peace. I knelt down in front of the Light, and my Shaddowe stretched over the World.

12

THE SHADOW moved slowly over his face until his mouth and eyes were obscured: only his forehead still caught the sun's rays, and they illuminated the beads of sweat that had accumulated there before he woke. Even in sleep he knew that he was sick, and he had dreamed that the blood poured from him like coin; he was woken by the sound of an argument in the street below and, as he knelt upright with his hands over his ears, he considered the possibility that he had gone mad. 'But how could I be mad yet?' he said, and smiled at the sound of his own voice just before he heard three knocks upon the door. He dropped his hands and waited, hardly breathing, and it was only when he heard three further knocks that he got up from his bed, walked slowly into the hallway and called out, 'Who's there?'

'It's only me, Mr Hawksmoor!'

He opened the door on Mrs West, averting his eyes as he listened to her: 'I thought I heard you call, Mr Hawksmoor. Did you call?' He said nothing and she took a step forward: 'There was a man came for you last night. I was just putting out the bottles, not that I can hardly bend, and he was ringing and ringing so I said you was out. Was I right? And then I heard you call just now and I thought, you never know do you? So I came up.' And all the while she examined his face with open curiosity. 'I thought there might be a reason, Mr Hawksmoor.'

He smiled, still saying nothing, and was about to close the door upon her when he remembered: 'Oh, Mrs West, I'm about to go away –'

'You need a good rest do you?'

He looked at her with suspicion. 'That's right. I deserve a rest. So if anyone comes will you tell them?'

'I'll tell them.' Her hands were clenched, into fists.

Hawksmoor watched her descend the stairs, leaning heavily against the banister as she did so, and only when she had turned out of sight did he close the door. He walked back into the bedroom and, when he looked down at his arms, he saw long furrows where he had scratched himself in his sleep: and in that moment he was consumed by his hatred for those he worked with. They had not wanted him to succeed, they had tricked him, they had betrayed him, and now they had triumphed over him. He could not breathe and in alarm he crossed over to the window and opened it: it was a cold December day and, as he leaned out, he could feel the heat leaving his body like an exhalation until he became calm again. From this height, the movements of those in the street seemed to him to be marked by a peculiar fatality, as though they were being drawn by a thread which they would never see; and as he stared down at their faces he wondered what a face was, and from what original it had sprung.

It was time now to join them. He crept down the hallway, pausing only to put on his coat and shoes before walking slowly down the stairs and into the street. A light rain was falling, and he had just reached the corner when he glanced up at the clouds and suddenly decided to turn back; then, as he passed the Red Gates, he noticed his own reflection in the frosted window, beneath a sign for Beers and Spirits. The reflection turned to stare at him before walking on: Hawksmoor passed his hand across his face and then called out, 'Do I know you?' and several passers-by stopped in astonishment as he ran out into the road crying. 'Do I? Do I?' No answer came and, as he tried to follow the retreating figure, the crowds of the city hampered his progress and closed him in. Eventually he retraced his steps to Grape Street: he was so tired now that he no longer cared who might be watching or waiting for him on his return. He lay down upon his bed with his hand covering his eyes, but the sounds of traffic came through the open window and he could not sleep. Then his eyes opened: and that's another thing, he thought, why are churches built in that shape? And he repeated the word – churches, churches, churches, churches, churches – until it meant nothing.

*

'Cooee! Cooee!' The voice could have come from somewhere within the room, and on first waking he did not know what he had heard. 'Mr Hawksmoor!'

He jumped out of bed shouting, 'What is it? What's happened?' and then crouched beside the bedroom door, putting his weight against it in case Mrs West should try to enter.

'Your front door was open and I didn't know did I? I thought you was going away . . .'. And then after a pause she asked him, 'Are you decent?'

She was still just outside his door, and he wanted to pound upon it in his fury. 'Just a minute!' he shouted and he was surprised to find that he was still wearing his coat and shoes. Where had he been as he slept? He opened the door, and hurried past her into the bathroom where he ran cold water from the tap; he was about to splash it over his face, but instead he watched the surface of the rushing water. 'I *am* going away,' he called out to her, 'Eventually.'

'Where will you go?'

'Oh I don't know,' he muttered, 'Where does anyone go?' And he heard her moving about the flat. He came out of the bathroom quietly, to find her peering at the pages of the white notebook which he had pinned against the walls of his front room. He noticed that her hair was still lustrous and was about to stroke it when he realised that she had to move her whole body as she turned from one drawing to the next: 'What happened to your neck?' He tried to conceal his disgust.

'Oh that's nothing. That's my arthritis. I'm used to it.' She continued to look at the drawings, with the verses and phrases beneath them. 'What are you doing here then? Are these yours?'

'Mine? No, they're not mine.' He tried to laugh. 'They're just a story I'm working on. I don't know the ending as yet.'

'I like a nice ending.'

'That's the same as saying, you like a nice death.'

She was puzzled at this and simply murmured, 'Oh yes?' as she turned to go.

'But what do you really see in them, Mrs West?' He blocked her passage to the door. 'Do you see anything strange in them?' He was genuinely interested in her reply.

'Good God, don't ask me. I see nothing.'

She seemed disturbed. 'Well, don't take it to heart,' he said, 'I was only asking.'

At the word 'heart' she trembled and the weight of the years was released from her momentarily. 'What sign are you, Mr Hawksmoor?'

'Sign? I know nothing about signs.'

'You know, signs. Star signs. I bet you're a Pisces, like me. Secretive. Am I right?' He did not answer her but looked once again at the drawings. 'They say we're going to have a good year, when Venus gets into our quarter.'

He blushed. 'I wouldn't know about that now, would I?'

She sighed and prepared once more to leave him. 'Well have a nice time, Mr Hawksmoor.' Then she winked at him. 'Once you know where you're going, that is.'

*

He traced his name in the dust along the window-sill and then erased it. He turned on the radio but he could hear the voices whispering, 'What wind blew you here? What wind blew you here?' As he sat in the middle of the room sometimes he could see moving shapes, just out of the corner of his eye, but they were as indistinct as shadows on water and when he turned his head to look at them they were gone. And as dusk fell he recited one of the verses inscribed in the white notebook:

> I saw a door which opened on a fire
> I saw a pit which rose up even higher
> I saw a child who danced round and round
> I saw a house which stood beneath the ground
> I saw a man who is not, nor ever could he be,
> Hold up your hand and look, for you are he.

And as Hawksmoor's voice reverberated around the room, some coins fell off the mantelpiece. There were more verses beneath these but, since the poem seemed to go on for ever, he lost interest. And he switched on the television set, craning forward eagerly when he saw the image of a man with his back turned towards him. He turned up the contrast, and then the brightness, but the image became no more distinct. And Hawksmoor stared at the screen, as time passed.

Now a morning service was being transmitted, and he knew that it was a Sunday. The priest was raised above his congregation: 'So you may say how complicated and perilous modern life is, and how dark the future seems, and how distant our ancestors. But I will tell you this, my good friends, that each age has found itself to be dark and perilous, and each age has feared for its future, and each age has lost its forefathers. And so they have turned to God, thinking to themselves, if there are shadows there must also be light! And beyond the years, my friends, there is an eternity which we may see with the help of God's grace. And what is so wonderful is that this eternity intersects with time, just as in this church –' Hawksmoor's attention wandered to a fly which was trying to find a way out of the closed window, and when he looked at his television again the priest had moved on – 'when a mother glances at a child with love, the light from her eyes soothes and nourishes the infant; the voices we raise in this church can also be instruments of light, banishing shadow; you must learn to see this light, my friends, and you must move forward towards it for this light is a reflection of the Light of God.'

Hawksmoor seemed to recognise the interior of the church as an image of the hushed congregation appeared on the screen; and then the exterior of the church was shown as the camera moved downwards from the bell tower to the steps, lingering on the sign beyond the porch which read 'Christ Church, Spitalfields. Erected by Nicholas Dyer, 1713'. And the time before had been a dream for he knew now: he was looking down at the body in front of St Mary Woolnoth and once again noticing the sign which read, 'Founded in the Saxon Age and Last Rebuilt by Nicholas Dyer, 1714'. There had been such a name upon the board by the Greenwich church, and he recognised what a symmetry this was.

He allowed the knowledge of the pattern to enclose him, as the picture on the television screen began to revolve very quickly and then to break up into a number of different images. Where before the churches had been for him a source of anxiety and of rage, now he contemplated each one in turn with a beneficent wonder as he saw how mightily they had done their work: the great stones of Christ Church, the blackened walls of St Anne's, the twin towers of St George's-in-the-East, the silence of St Mary Woolnoth, the unbroken façade of St Alfege's, the white pillar of St George's Bloomsbury, all now took on a larger life as Hawksmoor contemplated them and the crimes which had been committed in their name. And yet he sensed that the pattern was incomplete, and it was for this that he waited almost joyfully.

It had grown colder when he left the house the next morning, and the frost obscured the windows of the public library when he took down the encyclopaedia and turned to the entry for DYER Nicholas. And this is what he read: '1654 – c. 1715. English architect; was the most important pupil of Sir Christopher Wren, and a colleague both of Wren and Sir John Vannbrugghe in the Office of Works at Scotland Yard. Dyer was born in London in 1654; although his parentage is obscure, it seems that he was first apprenticed as a mason before becoming Wren's personal clerk; he later held several official posts under Wren including that of surveyor at St Paul's. His most important independent work was completed as a result of his becoming the principal architect to the 1711 Commission for New London Churches; his was the only work to be completed for that Commission, and Dyer was able to realise seven of his own designs: Christ Church Spitalfields, St George's-in-the-East Wapping, St Anne's Limehouse, St Alfege's in Greenwich, St Mary Woolnoth in Lombard Street, St George's Bloomsbury and, finest of all, the church of Little St Hugh beside Moorfields. These edifices show most clearly his ability to handle large abstract shapes and his sensitive (almost romantic) lines of mass and shadow. But he seems to have had no pupils or disciples in his lifetime, and changes in architectural taste meant that his work has had little influence and few admirers. He died in London in the winter of 1715, it is thought of the gout, although the records of his death and burial have been lost.' Hawksmoor stared at the page, trying to imagine the past which these words represented, but he saw nothing in front of him except darkness.

The streets were already filled with people when he left the library and returned to Grape Street. Despite the intense cold he was sweating as he took down the pages from the white notebook, placed them carefully in order, and then with a gesture of impatience stuffed them in his pocket. He tried to concentrate on what he should do next, but his mind wavered and fell away into the shadows of the unseen church of Little St Hugh. He had come to the end by chance, not knowing that it was the end, and this unanticipated and uncertain climax might yet rob him of his triumph: his will was emptied, replaced by the shape of moving things as he sat in his dark coat and watched the sun rolling across the roof-tops. Then he shook his head and stood up with an urgency which suggested that he wished to forestall, at least, another death. But as soon as he stepped into the street he felt afraid; someone knocked against him and he might have turned back at this moment, if the bus which travelled between Bloomsbury and Fenchurch Street had not arrived and if Hawksmoor had not entered it without thought. He sat huddled in his seat while in front of him an infant lay asleep with its chin upon its breast: and that, Hawksmoor thought, is how you will sleep when you are old. His forehead burned; he pressed it against the window and gazed at the mist which rose from the mouths of the people as they hurried through the streets of the city.

He descended at Fenchurch Street, expecting to glimpse the spire of the church somewhere above him, but here were only the burnished towers of office-blocks which gleamed in the winter light. A seller of hot chestnuts stood on the corner of Gracechurch Street, and for a moment Hawksmoor watched the coals of his brazier as they brightened and then dimmed with the passage of the wind down the crowded thoroughfares; he went up to him saying, 'Little St Hugh?' and the man, not pausing in his cries, pointed up Lime Street. And his refrain of *Hot chestnuts! Hot chestnuts!* was taken up by another calling *Woe! Woe!* and then by a third who cried out *Paper! Paper!* These were the calls he had known all his life and Hawksmoor grew melancholy as he walked up Lime Street into St Mary Axe. He passed a record shop from which came the loud sounds of a popular song, and when he glanced inside he saw a young man at the counter beating time with his finger. But as he watched him he missed his footing on the pavement, and jumped back as a car swerved to avoid him. 'What time is it?' he asked an old woman who walked beside him, but she stared through him as if he had become invisible. He continued down Bishopsgate, carried by the movement of the crowd, and asked a stall-holder for the direction of the church: 'Follow the wall,' the man said and turned slowly to point down Wormwood Street, 'Follow the wall'. And as he came close to London Wall he sensed a smell like that of mown grass or cut flowers, so unusual a scent for the middle of winter that it must have sprung from the moss sprinkled upon the old stones. And from London Wall he passed into Moorfields where in the middle of the road a mad woman cried out, her words lost in the roar of the traffic. And as the pavement shook beneath his feet he hurried down Long Alley: some children in blue caps and blazers passed him laughing, and their motion turned him round so that now he saw ahead of him Black Step Lane. So still did he stand that a young man in a fur cap passed him and then looked back in astonishment, as Hawksmoor now walked towards Little St Hugh.

It stood at the back of a deserted square; weeds and long grass had sprung up between the cobblestones inside this square, and the flagstones against the walls of the church were cracked and pitted. When he looked up at the front of Little St Hugh he saw how its large stones were eroded also, and one area had a blackened surface as if the darkness had been painted upon it. There was a circular window above the porch, like an eye, and the reflection of the weak sun glittered upon it as Hawksmoor walked forward. He mounted the steps slowly and then paused in the shadow of a stone effigy which crouched above him. He could hear no noise coming from within. He noticed a rusted metal chain which hung from some old brick; he looked up suddenly and saw a cloud which for a moment possessed the features of a human face. Then he opened the door and crossed the threshold. He paused again within the porch so that his eyes might become accustomed to the gloom and there, above the wooden doors which led to the nave of the church, had been placed the painting of a young boy lying inside a pit; it was covered with dust but he could just make out the inscription beneath it, 'I Have Endured All These Troubles For Thy Sake'. There was a smell of dampness, and Hawksmoor bowed his head before entering the body of the church.

Which seemed to spring to life around him, for the creaking of the doors and the sound of his footsteps upon the stone echoed through the interior. He was in a great square room; above him a plaster ceiling, curved like a shallow dish and lit by circular windows of plain glass; as he stood in the nave, he was surrounded on three sides by galleries which were supported by thick columns of old stone; the altar was covered with a canopy of dark wood, and the rails in front of it were made of iron. Hawksmoor looked for relief from the darkness of wood, stone and metal but he could find none; and the silence of the church had once again descended as he sat down upon a small chair and covered his face. And he allowed it to grow dark.

And his own Image was sitting beside him, pondering deeply and sighing, and when he put out his hand and touched him he shuddered. But do not say that he touched him, say that they touched him. And when they looked at the space between them, they wept. The church trembled as the sun rose and fell, and the half-light was strewn

[216]

across the floor like rushes. They were face to face, and yet they looked past one another at the pattern which they cast upon the stone; for when there was a shape there was a reflection, and when there was a light there was a shadow, and when there was a sound there was an echo, and who could say where one had ended and the other had begun? And when they spoke they spoke with one voice:

and I must have slept, for all these figures greeted me as if they were in a dream. The light behind them effaced their features and I could see only the way they turned their heads, both to left and to right. The dust covered their feet and I could see only the direction of their dance, both backwards and forwards. And when I went among them, they touched fingers and formed a circle around me; and, as we came closer, all the while we moved further apart. Their words were my own but not my own, and I found myself on a winding path of smooth stones. And when I looked back, they were watching one another silently.

And then in my dream I looked down at myself and saw in what rags I stood; and I am a child again, begging on the threshold of eternity.

Acknowledgments

Any relation to real people, either living or dead, is entirely coincidental. I have employed many sources in the preparation of *Hawksmoor*, but this version of history is my own invention. I would like to express my obligation to Iain Sinclair's poem, *Lud Heat*, which first directed my attention to the stranger characteristics of the London churches.